celq

D0672488

THE INVENTION OF FIRE

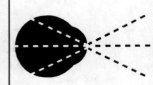

This Large Print Book carries the
Seal of Approval of N.A.V.H.

THE INVENTION OF FIRE

BRUCE HOLSINGER

THORNDIKE PRESS

A part of Gale, Cengage Learning

GALE
CENGAGE Learning·

Farmington Hills, Mich • San Francisco • New York • Waterville, Maine
Meriden, Conn • Mason, Ohio • Chicago

GALE
CENGAGE Learning®

LIBRARY OF CONGRESS CATALOGING-IN-PUBLICATION DATA

Holsinger, Bruce W.
  The invention of fire / Bruce Holsinger. — Large print edition.
    pages cm. — (Thorndike Press large print historical fiction)
    ISBN 978-1-4104-8000-2 (hardback) — ISBN 1-4104-8000-3 (hardcover)
  1. Chaucer, Geoffrey, –1400—Fiction. 2. Gower, John, 1325?–1408—Fiction.
3. Large type books. 4. London (England)—History—To 1500—Fiction.
5. Murder—Investigation—Fiction. I. Title.
PS3608.O49435658I58 2015
813'.6—dc23   2015009328

Published in 2015 by arrangement with William Morrow, an imprint of HarperCollins Publishers

Printed in Mexico
1 2 3 4 5 6 7 19 18 17 16 15

For Betsy and Bob

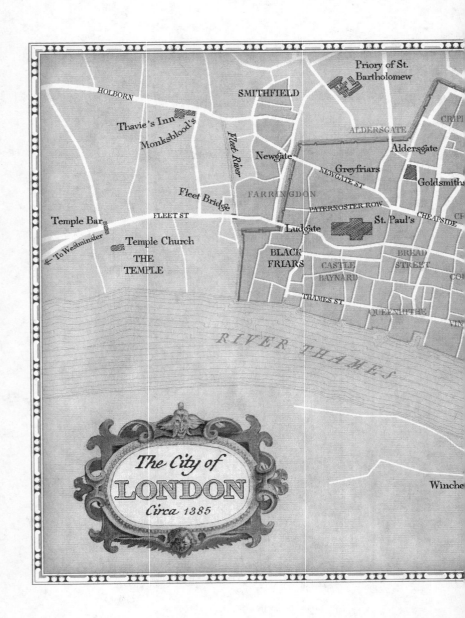

HOLBORN

SMITHFIELD

Priory of St.
Bartholomew

CRIP

Thavie's Inn

Monksblood's

ALDERSGATE

Aldersgate

Newgate

Greyfriars

Goldsmiths

Fleet River

NEWGATE ST

FARRINGDON

PATERNOSTER ROW

CHEAPSIDE

Fleet Bridge

CH

Temple Bar

FLEET ST

Ludgate

St. Paul's

To Westminster

Temple Church

THE
TEMPLE

BLACK
FRIARS

CASTLE
BAYNARD

BREAD
STREET

CO

THAMES ST

QUEENHITHE

VIN

RIVER THAMES

Winche

The City of
LONDON
Circa 1385

The Moorfields

Spitalfields

Cripplegate

Postern

Priory of St. Mary
of Bethlem

LEGATE

BASSISHAW

The Guildhall

COLEMAN
STREET

Hall

Bishopsgate

BISHOPSGATE

PORTSOKEN

BROAD
STREET

Grocers' Hall

CHEAPSIDE

BROAD ST

Merchant
Taylors' Hall

St. Pancras

CORNHULL ST

CORNHULL

LIME
STREET

ALDGATE ST

ALDGATE

Aldgate

LOMBARD ST

WALBROOK

DWAINE

GRACECHURCH ST

LANGBOURN

FENCHURCH ST

Skinners' Hall

CANDLEWICK

DOWGATE

BRIDGE

BRIDGE ST

BILLINGSGATE

TOWER

TOWER ST

Fishmongers' Hall

London Bridge

Customhouse

Tower
of
London

ROSE ALLEY

Priory of St. Mary Overey

ter Palace

THE HIGH ST

CUTTER LN

SOUTHWARK

The Tabard

Map copyright © 2012 Springer Cartographics LLC

A NOTE TO THE READER

The word *handgun* enters the English language in the final decades of the fourteenth century. The compound noun first appears in an inventory record from the Tower of London, occurring at the end of the phrase *"iiii canones parue de cupro vocate handgonnes"* ("four small copper cannon, called *handgonnes*"). These medieval *handgonnes* were metal tubes packed with gunpowder and fired with a burning coal or cord, a far cry from the sophisticated pistols and rifles found in modern arsenals. Yet across Europe, these decades witnessed unprecedented innovation and experimentation in the development of small arms, as gunpowder weapons grew increasingly portable, efficient, and thus terrifying. The emerging use of *handgonnes* on the battlefields of Europe, as well as their appearance in civilian contexts, marked a crucial technological shift in the development of weap-

9

onry — as well as a subtle but profound transformation in the long history of human atrocity.

And in the autumn of that year, in the village of Desurennes, a company came from the woods with small guns of iron borne in their hands, and laid great waste to the market, to the wares and those who sold them along the walls, and in the eyes of God made wondrous calamity with fire and shot.

— LE TROISIÈME CHRONIQUE DE CALAIS, ENTRY FOR YEAR 1386

PROLOGUE

The water seeped past, groping for the dead.

It was early on an Ember Saturday, and low down along the deepest channel in London, Alan Pike braced for a fall. He sucked a shallow breath as beside him his son moved through the devilish swill. The boy's arms were thin as sticks but lifted his full spade with a ready effort, even a kind of cheer. Good worker, young Tom, a half knob shy of fourteen, reliable, strong, uncomplaining, despite all a gongfarmer had to moan about — quite a heavy lot, helping the city streams breathe easy. Tom filled another bucket and hefted it to one of the older boys to haul above for the dung-cart. From there it would be wheeled outside the walls, likely to feed some bishop's roses.

Night soil, the mayor's men primly called it, though it had commoner names. Dung and gong, fex and flux, turd and purge and shit. Alan Pike and his crew, they called it hard work and wages.

Dark work, mostly, as London didn't like its underbelly ripped open to the sun, so here he was with his fellows, a full four hours after the curfew bell, working in the calm quiet a few leaps down from the loudest, busiest crossing in London. The junction of Broad Street, Cornhill and the Poultry, the stocks market, and everything else. The brassy navel of the city by day; a squalid gut in the night.

Alan squinted through the pitch, peering past his son down the jagged line of buildings spanning this length of the Walbrook. Twenty privies, by his estimate, most attached to private houses and tenements hulked up over the open stream, but two of the highest seats had been built to the common good for use by all. The Long Dropper, this great institution was called, and a farthing a squeeze the custom, the coins collected by a lame beggar enjoying the city's modest gesture of charity toward its most wretched.

At night, though, no one was posted at the hanging doors up top. The parish was at a hush. The only sounds to be heard were the shallow breathing of his son, a faint snore from one of the houses above, the scurryings and chewings of the brook rats all round.

"Any closer, Father?" Tom, always respectful even when tired out, though Alan could tell he was ready to leave off. It had already been a long night.

"Let us have a look," said Alan, lengthening his back, hearing a happy pop. He legged it through the muck and mud to the middle of the stream. Earlier they had rigged up a row of lanterns at either end of the stretch to light the crew's work, show them what they were meddling with. In the past hour the stream had loosened up fairly well at the north end, but the water was still damming farther in, and as he squatted and peered through the stink he had to shift both ways to spy the three orbs of pale light at the far end of the clogged channel.

He shook his head, sucked a lip.

A major blockage, this one.

Something big. Something stuck. The Walbrook's moderate flow should have pushed most anything down to the Thames. Not this lot, whatever it was. A pile of rotten lumber, could be. Or a horse, lamed on the street and shoved over the bank to struggle and drown, like that old mare they'd roped out of the Fleet Ditch last month. Whatever this bulk turned out to be, the Guildhall would hear about it, that was certain.

Alan turned to his crew. "Fetch me one of those lanterns there." The young man behind Tom repeated the command to another fellow closer to the lamp string, who trudged back and removed one of the oil lamps dangling from the line. When Alan had it in his grip he held the light before him, up and to the side, and moved ahead.

One step, another. This section of the stream was almost impassable. Up to his hips now. The thick, nearly immovable sludge clung to his legs like a dozen rutting dogs. He had to will his body to move forward, every step a victory.

He was taking a risk, he knew that, and for what?

A gongfarmer's pay was good enough, sure and certain, but one false step and he could be sucked right under, or release a pocket of devil's air that would ignite and turn him into one of these lanterns, sizzling hair and all. Alan knew more than a few gongers who'd fallen to their deaths or close to it in these narrow depths. Why, just upstream from here, old Purvis crashed through the seat of a public latrine like the one over Alan's head right now, poor gonger was rat food by the time they found him, a chewed mess of —

Then he saw it. A hand, pale and alone in the lamplight, streaked with brown and standing out against the solid mound of dung behind it.

"By Judas!" Alan Pike swore, and would have fallen backwards had the thick flow not braced him.

"Father?" Tom's worried voice came from behind.

Alan looked again. The hand was not severed, as he'd first feared. No, the hand was attached to an arm, and the arm was attached to another arm, looked like, and that arm, why, that arm was sprouting from a leg — no no no, from a head, but that was impossible, so then what in —

It bloomed in Alan Pike then, just what he was seeing. This was no pile of gong blocking the Walbrook, nor no horse neither. Why, this was —

"Father, what is it then?"

Tom, beside him now, peering ahead with that boy's curiosity he had about most everything in the world. Alan heaved an arm, wanting to cover his son's eyes against the devilish sight, but Tom pushed it aside and grasped the lamp and Alan let it go, a slow, reluctant loosing as the oily handle slipped from his grasp and then he felt Tom's smaller, smoother hand against his

17

own. Slick clasp of love, last touch of innocence.

They stared together, father and son, at this mound of ruined men. No words could come.

PART I

CHAPTER 1

What use is a blind man in the face of the world's calamities? Turn to Scripture and you will quickly learn that the blind are Pharisees and fools, sorcerers and unbelievers. The Syrian army blinded at the behest of Elijah (2 Kings 16). The blind and the lame banished from David's house (2 Samuel 5). Horses smitten with blindness (Zachariah 12). More often the blind are mere figures of speech, emblems of ignorance and lack of faith. The blind leading the blind (Matthew 15:14). The eyes of the blind, opened through the grace of the Lord (Psalm 146:8). The hand of the Lord rests upon thee, and thou shalt be blinded (Acts 13:11). Our proverbs, too, reek with the faults of the blind. Blind as a mole. Oh, how blind are the counsels of the wicked! Man is ever blind to his own faults, but fox-quick at perceiving those of others.

Blind blinded blinding blindness blind.

What did the men who wrote such things know of blindness? What can I know? For I am not blind, not just yet, though I am well on my way. If the final dark of unsight is a dungeon in a dale I am halfway down the hill, my steps toward that lasting shadow lengthening with each passing week even as my soul shrinks against that fuller affliction to come.

Yet this creeping blindness itself is not the worst of it. Far worse is the swelling of desire. As my sight wanes, my lust for the visible world surges, a boiling pot just before the water is cast to the dirt. Dusted arcs of sunlight in the vaults of St. Paul's, crimson slick of a spring lamb's offal puddled on the wharf, fine-etched ivory of a young nun's face, prickle of stars splayed on the night. Color, form, symmetry, beauty, radiance, *glow.* All fading now, like the half-remembered faces of the departed: my sisters, my children, my well-beloved wife. All soon enough gone, this sweet sweet world of sight.

There are some small compensations. Sin is to human nature what blindness is to the eye, the blessed St. Augustine writes, and as the light dims, as crisp lines blur, I find I am discovering a renewed fondness for the weighty sensuality of sin and its vehicles.

The caterpillar fuzz of parchment on the thumb. A thin knife slipped beneath the wax. The gentle *pip* of a broken seal. A man's secrets opened to my nose, whole worlds of sin spread out like so many blooming flowers in a field, scent so heavy you can chew it. I have a sweet tooth for vice, and it sharpens with age.

No pity for me, then. Save your compassion and your prayers for the starving, the maimed, the murdered. They need them far more than I do, and in the weeks that concern me here pity was in especially short supply. It was instead malevolence that overflowed the city's casks that autumn, treachery that stalked laborer and lord alike up the alleys, along the walls, through the selds of Cheapside and the churchyards of Cornhill. And if the blind must founder in the face of monstrosity, perhaps a man clinging to his last glimpses of the visible world may prove its most discerning foe.

Sitting before me that September morning was my dead wife's father. A mess of a man, skin a waxy pale, his clothing as unkempt as his accounting. Ambrose Birch: a weeping miser, and a waste of fine teeth.

"For — for her sake, John." He thumbed his moistening eyes and looked up into the timbers, darkened with years of smoke from an unruly hearth. My reading room, a low, close space lit only by a narrow slip of light from a glazed window onto the priory yard.

"Her sake," I said. His daughter dead for nearly two years, and still the dull pieties. I stared through him, this cruelest of fathers, cruel in ways even I had never learned, despite all that Sarah once told me. Sarah, a soul always ready to give more than necessary. She had absolved him long before her death, and wished me to do the same.

Something I had noticed previously but never put into words was that peculiar way Birch had with his chin, rather a large one considering his smallness of face. When he said my name his chin bobbed, always twice, and his voice lowered and rasped, as if throwing out each *John* while a hoof pressed his throat.

"How did you get it?" Birch whispered. "I cannot — who sold it to you, John?"

His fortune and reputation hanging by this thread on my desk, and he is curious about a sale.

"That should be your last concern, Ambrose," I gently told him. "The prickly question is, who will John Gower sell it to?"

"How *dare* you threaten me, you milk-blood coward!" His lips quivered, the upper one raised in a weak snarl. "Here you sit in your little hole, bent over your inky creations, your twisted mind working itself in knots to spit out more of this — what?" He turned to look at the orderly rows and stacks of quires and books around the room, many of them lined with my own verse. Back at me.

"She pitied you, John."

I scoffed.

"Ah, but it's true," he said, warming to it. "She talked about it with her mother. What a burden it was getting to be, your trade in threats and little scandals. How it pushed away your friends and relations, reduced everything to the latest gossip or bribe. How sad it was to see you waste your life, your mind, your spirit." He paused, then, with meaning, "Your eyes."

I flinched, blinked against the blur.

"Just as I thought. You believe a husband's growing blindness can be hidden from a wife, a wife as perceptive as our late Sarah? And do you think for a moment, John, that your position will not weaken once news of this affliction gets out? Imagine a blind man trying to peddle secrets at the Guildhall or Westminster. They'll all be slipping you snipped nobles, laughing in your face, cheering behind your back. The mighty John

Gower, lord of extraction, brought down by the most just act of God imaginable. A spy who cannot see, a writer who cannot read."

I lifted a corner of the document. "I have no difficulty reading this, Birch."

With a scowl he said, "For now, perhaps. For now. But in future you would be advised to remember that I have as much information on you as you have on me. Of course, I am a temperate man." He jerked at his coat, remembering why he was there. "Given the — the more *immediate* matter before us, I suppose there is room for a negotiation. But don't expect to come back to me with additional demands, John. A man can last only so long doing what you do."

We settled on three pounds. A minor fortune to Ambrose Birch, if a mouse's meal to his son-in-law. The money, of course, was beside the point. It was the information that bore the value. Each new fragment of knowledge a seed, to be sown in London's verdant soil and spring yet another flower for my use.

I gave him the usual warnings. *I've made arrangements with a clerk across the river . . . In the event of my passing . . . And should there be another incident . . .* Birch, still ignorant, left the house through the priory yard, the clever forgery he had just purchased curled in his moistened palm.

Will Cooper, my servant, bobbed in the doorway. Kind faced, impossibly thin but well jowled, with the crinkled eyes of the aging man he was. "Master Gower?"

"Yes, Will?"

"Boy for you, sir. From the Guildhall."

Behind him stood a liveried page from the mayor's retinue. I gestured him in. "Speak," I said.

"I come from Master Ralph Strode, good sir," the boy said stiffly. "Master Strode kindly requests the presence of Master John Gower at Master John Gower's earliest."

"The Guildhall, then?" Ralph Strode had recently stepped down from his longtime position as the city's common serjeant, though the mayor had arranged an annuity to retain him for less formal duties.

"Nay, sir. St. Bart's Smithfield."

"St. Bart's?" I frowned at him, already dreading it. "Why would Ralph want me to meet him in Smithfield?" Located outside the walls, the hospital at St. Bartholomew tended to the poorest of the city's souls, its precincts a stew of livestock markets and old slaughterbarns, many of them abandoned since the pestilence. Not the sort of place to which Strode would normally summon a friend.

"Don't know, sir," said the boy with a little shrug. "Myself, I came across from Basinghall Street, as Master Strode was leaving for St. Bart's."

"Very well." I dismissed him with a coin. Will gave me an inquisitive look as the boy left. My turn to shrug.

I had eaten little that morning so stood in the kitchen as Bet Cooper, Will's wife, young and plump to his old and lean, bustled about preparing me a plate of greens with cut lamb. A few swallows of cider and my stomach was content. At Winchester's wharf I boarded a wherry for the London bankside below Ludgate at the mouth of the Fleet. A moderate walk from the quay took me across Fleet Street, then up along the ditch to the hospital.

St. Bartholomew's, though an Augustinian house like St. Mary Overey, rarely merited a visit given the unpleasant location, easily avoidable on a ride from the city walls to Westminster. The hospital precinct comprised three buildings, a lesser chapel and greater church as well as the hospital itself, branched from the chapel along a low cloister. An approach from the south brought visitors to the lesser church first, which I reached as the St. Bart's bell tolled for Sext. I circled around the south porch toward the hospital gates, where the porter shared his suspicions about my business. They were softened with a few groats.

The churchyard, rutted and pocked, made a skewed shape of drying mud, tufted grass, and leaning stone, all centered on the larger church within the hospital grounds. Not a single shrub or tree interrupted the morbid rubble. Shallow burials were always a problem at St. Bart's. Carrion birds hooking along, small demons feeding on the dead. Though the air was dry, the soil was moist and the earth churned underfoot, alive with the small gluttonies of worms.

Three men stood along the south wall gazing down into a wide trench. Ralph Strode, the largest and widest, raised his head and turned to me as I walked across, his prominent jowls swaying beneath a nose broken years before in an Oxford brawl and never entirely healed. His eyes, somber and heavy, were colored a deep amber pouched within folds of rheumy skin.

"Gower," he said.

I opened my mouth to speak, closed it against a gathering stench, and then I saw the dead. A line of corpses, arrayed in the trench like fish on an earl's platter. All were men, all were stripped bare, only loose braies or rags wrapping their middles. Their

skin was flecked with what looked like mud
but smelled like shit, and gouged with
wounds large and small. At least five of
them bore circular marks around their necks
in a dull red; from hanging, I guessed. My
eyes moved slowly over the bodies as I
counted. Eight, twelve — sixteen of them,
their rough shrouds still open, waiting for a
last blessing and sprinkle from a priest.

"Who are they?" I asked Strode.

The silence lengthened. I stood there, the
rot mingling with the heavy buzz of feeding
flies. Finally I looked up.

"We don't know." Strode watched for my
reaction.

"You don't *know*?"

"Not a soul on the inquest jury recognized
a one of them."

"How can sixteen men die without being
known, whether by name or occupation?"

"Or rank, or ward, or parish," said Strode.
He raised his big hands, spread his arms.
"We simply don't know."

"Where were they found?"

"In the Walbrook, down from the stocks
at Cornhill. Beneath that public privy
there."

"The Long Dropper," I said. Board seats,
half a door, a deep and teeming ditch. "And
the first finders?"

"A gongfarmer and his son. Their crew were clearing out the privy ditches. Two nights ago this was, and the bodies were carted here this morning by the coroner's men. Before first light, naturally."

My gaze went back to the bodies. "An accident of some kind? Perhaps a bridge collapse? But surely I would have heard about such a thing."

"Nothing passes you by, does it, Gower?"

Strode's tone was needlessly sharp, and when I looked over at him I could see the strain these deaths were placing on the man. He blew out a heavy sigh. "It was murder, John. Murder en masse. These men met violent deaths somewhere, then they were disposed of in a privy ditch. I have never seen the like."

"The coroner?"

"The inquest got us nowhere. Sixteen men, dead of a death other than their natural deaths, but no one can say of what sort. They certainly weren't slashed or beaten."

"Nor hung by the neck," said the older of the two men standing behind us.

Strode turned quickly, as if noticing the pair for the first time, then signaled the man forward. "This is Thomas Baker and his apprentice," he said. "Baker here is a master surgeon, trained in Bologna in all matter of medical arts, though now lending his services to the hospital here at St. Bart's. I have asked him to inspect the bodies of these poor men, see what we can learn."

"Learn about what?" I said.

"What killed them."

Strode's words hung in the air as I looked over Baker and the boy beside him. Though short and thin the surgeon stood straight, a wiry length of a man, hardened from the road and the demands of his craft. His apprentice was behind him, still and obedient.

"Surely you're not thinking of the Italian way," I said to Strode.

His jowls shook. "Even in this circumstance the bishop won't hear of dissection. You know Braybrooke. His cant is all can't. Were these sixteen corpses sixteen *hundred* we'd get no dispensation from the bishop of London. Far be it from the church to sanction free inquiry, *curiositas,* genuine knowledge." A familiar treatise from Ralph Strode, a former schoolman at Oxford, and I would have smiled had the circumstances not been so grim. He looked at Baker. "Our surgeon here is more enlightened. One of these *moderni,* with ten brains' worth of new ideas about medicine, astronomy, even music, I'll be bound."

"What makes you believe these men weren't hung?" I asked the surgeon. "Those red circles around some of their necks? I would think the solution is apparent."

Baker shook his head, unaffected by my confidence. "Those are rope burns, Master Gower, or so I believe, though inflicted after death, not before."

"How can you be sure?"

From a pouch at his side Baker removed a brick-sized bundle bound tightly in brushed leather. Unwrapping the suede, he took out a book that he opened to reveal page upon page of intricate drawings of the human form. Arms, legs, fingers, heads, whole torsos, the private parts of man and woman alike, with no regard for decency or discretion. Brains, breasts, organs, a twisted testicle, the interior of a bisected anus. The frankness and detail of the drawings stunned me, as I had never before seen such intimate renderings of the corporeal man.

Baker found the page he was looking for. Strode and I leaned in, rapt despite ourselves by the colorful intricacies of skin and gut.

"The cheeks of a hanged man will go blue, you see." His finger traced delicately over the page, showing us the heads of four noosed corpses, the necks elongated and

33

twisted at unlikely angles, eyes bulging, tongues and lips contorted into hideous grins, skin purpled into the shades of exotic birds. "I have seen this effect myself, many times. The blood rushes from the head, the veins burst, the aspect darkens. Leave them hanging long enough and they start to look like Ethiops, at least from the neck up. And there is more."

He squatted over the pit, gesturing for us to join him. In his right hand Baker bore a narrow stick, which he used to pry open the left eye of the nearest victim. "Do you see?"

I looked at the man's eyeball. "What is it I am to see?" I said.

"The iris is white," said Baker, reaching for the next man's eyelid, this time with a tender finger. "As is this one. And this." He moved along the trench, pausing at each of the ring-necked victims to make sure we saw the whites of their eyes. "Yet the eyes of a hanged man go red with blood. See here." He fumbled with his book to show us another series of paintings a few pages on. Bulbous eyes spidered with red veins, like rivers and roads on a map of the world.

I glanced at Strode, unsure what to think of this man's boldness with the ways of death.

"In Bologna the tradition is more — more

practical than our own," said the physician, noting our unease. "They slice, they cut, they boil and prove and test. They observe and they experiment, and they admit when they are wrong. Such has it been for many years, good gentles, since the time of Barbarossa. If you gentlemen are in any way interested in this line of inquiry I recommend the *Anatomia* of Mondino de' Liuzzi, a surgical master at Bologna some years ago who was an adept of the blade, a man thoroughly committed to dissection and —"

"Not hanged, then," I said, less impressed by the man's eloquence than convinced by the soundness of his evidence. "So how, in your learned view, were these men killed?"

He smiled modestly, raised the second finger on his right hand, and reached for the chest of the nearest corpse. His fingertip found an indentation to the left of the victim's heart, a mark I hadn't noticed before. He gently pressed down, and soon his finger was buried up to the first knuckle.

"Stabbed?" guessed Strode, probing with a stick at a larger, more ragged wound on the second man's chest.

"Run through with a short sword, I'd wager," I said, walking down the row of corpses and pausing at each one. All had holes at various places on their bodies: some in the chest, others in the stomach or neck, some of them a bit sloughy but not unusually ragged, though one poor fellow was missing half his face. Fragments of wood were lodged above his lips, like the splinters of a broken board.

"Not a blade, I think," said Baker, his voice hollow and low. "These wounds are quite peculiar. Only once before have I seen anything like them." He looked up at Strode. "With your permission, Master Strode?"

Strode, after glancing back toward the church, gave him a swift nod. Baker moved to a position over the first corpse and flipped the man onto his front, exposing a narrow back thick with churchyard dirt. His apprentice handed him a skin of ale, which Baker used to wet a cloth pulled from his pocket. He washed the corpse's back, smoothed his hand over the bare skin.

"As I suspected," said Baker. "This one stayed inside, you see."

"What stayed inside?" I said. "A bolt, perhaps, from a crossbow?"

Baker returned the corpse to its original position and held out a hand to his apprentice, who gave him what looked like a filleting knife of the sort you might see deployed by lines of fishermen casting off the Southwark bankside. With a series of expert movements, Baker sliced across the flesh surrounding the hole, widening it until the blade had penetrated several inches into the man's innards.

Another raised hand. The apprentice took the knife and replaced it with a pair of tongs. Baker inserted them into the hole, widening the wound, harder work than it looked. An unpleasant suck of air, the clammy song of flesh giving way to the surgical tool, and my own guts heaved, but soon enough the tongs emerged clasping a spherical object about the diameter of a half noble. The apprentice took the tongs, then, at Baker's direction, poured a short stream of ale over the ball. Baker put it between his front teeth and winced.

"Not lead. Iron, dripped from a bloom into a mold. The Florentines have been casting iron balls like these for many years." He tossed the ball up to Strode, who caught it, inspected it for a moment, and handed it to me. I marveled at the weight of the little thing: the size of a hazelnut, but as heavy as a lady's girdle book. I had never seen anything quite like it, though I had a suspicion as to its nature and use. I handed it back to Baker.

Strode was signaling for the gravedigger,

who left the churchyard to summon a priest.

"And the others?" I asked Baker.

"At least one was killed with an arrow, that one there." He gestured to the third body along the line. "Half the shaft's still in his neck. As for the rest, I am fairly confident in my suspicions, though I would have to perform a similar inspection on all these corpses to be sure." He came to his full height and used more of the ale to cleanse his hands. "I assume that will not be possible, Master Strode?"

Strode pushed out a wet lip. "Perhaps if the bishop of London were abroad. Unfortunately Braybrooke's lurking about Fulham, with no visitations in his immediate future."

"Very well," said Baker, and he watched with visible regret as a chantry priest arrived and started to mumble a cursory burial rite. The four of us made for the near chapel, keeping our voices low as Baker went over a few more observations gathered in the short window of time he had been at the grave. Some rat bites on the corpses but not many, and no great rot, suggesting the bodies had been in the sewer channel for no more than a day or two. I asked him about the wood splinters I had seen above the one man's mouth.

"Shield fragments, I would say," said Baker. "Carried there by the ball, and lodged in the skin around the point of penetration." We both knew, in that moment, what he was about to tell us, though neither of us could quite believe it. "These men have been shot, good masters, of that I am certain. Though not with an arrow, nor with a bolt."

The surgeon turned fully to us, his face somber. "These men were killed with hand cannon. Handgonnes, fired with powder, and delivering small iron shot."

Handgonnes. A word new to me in that moment, though one that would shape and fill the weeks to come. I looked out over the graves pocking the St. Bart's churchyard, their inhabitants victims of pestilence, accident, hunger, and crime, yet despite their numberless fates it seemed that man was ever inventing new ways to die.

"Why am I here, Ralph?"

"Because you are you." Strode raised a tired smile, his face flush with the effort of our short but muddy trudge back to the hospital chapel, where he had left his horse. Over the last few months he had been walking with a bad limp, and now tended to go about the city streets mounted rather than on foot, like some grand knight. No injury that I knew of, merely the afflictions of age. I worried for him.

He adjusted the girth, tugged at the bridle. "And you know what you know, John. If you don't know it, you know how to buy it or wheedle it or connive it. Brembre is smashing body and bone at the Guildhall. I have never seen him angrier. He considers it an insult to his own person that someone should do such a thing within the walls, leave so many corpses to stew and rot."

Nicholas Brembre, grocer and tyrant, perhaps the most powerful mayor in London's history. "And namelessly so," I said.

"The misery of it." Strode wagged his head. "There must be a dozen men in this city who know the names of those poor fellows eating St. Bart's dirt right now. Yet we've heard not a whisper from around the wards and parishes in the last two days. Aldermen, beadles, constables, night walkers: everyone has been pulled in or cornered, but no one claims to have seen or heard a thing, and no men reported missing. As if London itself has gone blind and dumb."

"No witnesses, then?"

He hesitated. "Perhaps one."

I waited.

"You know our Peter Norris."

I smiled, not fondly. "I do." Norris, formerly a wealthy mercer and a beadle of Portsoken Ward, had lost his fortune after a shipwreck off Dover, and now lived as a vagrant debtor of the city, moving from barn to yard, in and out of gates and gaols. We had crossed knives any number of times, never with good results.

"He claims to know of a witness," said Strode. "Someone who beheld the dumping of the corpses at the Long Dropper. He tried to trade on it from the stocks in order to shorten his sentence, though Brembre has refused to indulge his fantasy, as he called it."

"Who is the witness?"

"Norris would not say, not once he learned the mayor's mind. Perhaps you might convince him to talk. At the moment he's dangling in the pillory before Ludgate, and will be for the next few days."

"I'll speak with him tomorrow," I said.

"Very good."

"And what of the crown?" I was thinking of the guns. Weapons of war, not civic policing. To my knowledge the only place in or near London that possessed such devices as culverins and cannon was the Tower itself.

Strode's brows drew down. He led his

41

horse to the lowest stair, preparing to mount. "The sheriffs have made inquiries to the lord chancellor, though thus far his men have flicked us away, claiming lack of jurisdiction. A London privy, London dung, a London burial, a London problem. No concern of the court, they claim, and the only word I've had from that quarter is from Edmund Rune, the chancellor's counselor, who suggested we look into this as discreetly as possible — in fact it was he who suggested bringing you into the matter, John. With all the trouble the earl is facing at Parliament-time I can't think he would want another calamity to wrestle with."

Though he might prove helpful, I thought. Michael de la Pole, lord chancellor of the realm, had recently been created Earl of Suffolk, elevating him to that small circle of upper nobles around King Richard. Yet the chancellor was swimming against a strong tide of discontent from the commons, with Parliament scheduled to gather in just one week's time. De la Pole owed me a large favor, and despite his current difficulties I could not help but wonder what he might be holding on this affair. The unceasing tension between city and crown, the Guildhall and Westminster, rarely erupted into open conflict, more often simmering just beneath the urban surface, stirred by all those professional relations and bureaucratic niceties that bind London to its royal suburb up the river.

Yet such conflicts are indispensable to my peculiar vocation. Nicholas Brembre was a difficult man, by all accounts, though I had never discovered anything on him, and John Gower is not one to enjoy ignorance. If I could nudge the chancellor the right way, then use what he gave me to do a favor to the mayor in turn, I would be in a position to gather ever more flowers from the Guildhall garden in the coming months.

I put a hand on Ralph Strode's wide back and helped him mount. He regarded me, his large nostrils flaring with his still-labored breaths. "You will help, then?"

A slight bow to Strode and his horse. "Tell the lord mayor he may consider John Gower at his service."

He sucked in a cheek. "That I cannot do." He glanced about, then hunched down slightly in his saddle, lowering his voice. "Here is the difficult thing, John. The mayor has been stirred violently by this atrocity, yet despite his anger he seems reluctant to pursue the matter, for reasons I cannot discern. He's bribed off the coroner, discouraged the sheriffs from looking into things, and threatens anyone who mentions it. It was he who ordered me to oversee this quick burial, with quicker rites, and no consideration for the relations of the deceased, whoever they might be. Nor will he hear Norris out about his witness."

Here Strode paused to look over his shoulder. Then, softly, "There are whispers he may have had evidence destroyed."

"What sort of evidence?"

"Who can say? The point is that Brembre has decided this will all be quashed, and no one has the stomach to gainsay him."

"What about the sheriffs and aldermen? Surely they would wish for an open inquiry."

He grimaced. "They are as geldings and maidens, when what's needed is a champion wielding a silent and invisible sword." Strode looked back toward the churchyard and the murmuring priest, then straightened himself. "That is why I have come to you. For your cunning ways with coin, your affinity with the rats, the devious beauty of your craft. And for your devotion to the right way, much as you like to hide your benevolent flame under a bushel of deceit. This atrocity has thrown you as much as it has thrown me, John. I can see it in your eyes."

I looked away, a sting in those weakening

eyes. A friend is a second self, Cicero tells us, and knows us more intimately than we know ourselves.

"The mayor cannot learn you are probing this out for us, or it will be my broken nose fed to the pigs."

"I understand, Ralph," I said, looking appropriately solemn, yet secretly delighted to learn of the mayor's peculiar vacillations. A new bud of knowledge on a lengthening stem. "My lips shall be as the privy seal itself."

"Good then." With a brisk nod, Strode pulled a rein and made for Aldersgate. I followed him at a growing distance, watching his broad back shift over the animal's deliberate gait until man and beast alike faded into the walls, blurring with the stone.

CHAPTER 2

The Gates of London are so many mouths
of hell, Chaucer once observed, swallowing
the sinful by the dozen, commingling them
in the rich urban gruel of waste, crime, lust,
and vice that flows down every lane. Yet
each gate possesses a character and history
uniquely its own: its own guards, residents,
and prisoners, its own parish obligations,
the particular customs and rituals that
define every entrance to the inner wards as
a small world unto itself. To know the gates
of London is to know the truest pathways
to the city's soul.

In those middle years of King Richard's
reign the city gates were all connected by a
series of towers, sentry walks, and repair
scaffolds that together traced a wandering
crescent around the lofty stone walls and
provided the most efficient means of getting
from gate to gate. You couldn't stroll along
the inner wall down below given all the

clearing and destruction, while skirting the outer circumference would land you in waste ditches and subject you to the streams of refuse and trash — some foul, some quite dangerous — hurled from above.

On that windy day following the examination in the St. Bart's churchyard I had determined to visit every gate in turn, worming beaks with coins as I went. If sixteen men could die in London, and not one of them be known to Ralph Strode, to the mayor and his men, to the king's coroner and his, nor even to one of the dozen freemen of the city gathered for the inquest, they must have come from outside the walls. London is a large place, though not exceedingly large, and to conceive of so many Londoners unrecognized and unsought by loved ones seemed an impossibility. Somewhere along the walls was a guard or a warden who had seen something, or knew someone who had.

My day would begin at Aldgate, where the walls separated the parish of St. Katharine Cree from St. Botolph-without, and end at Ludgate, where Peter Norris slumped in the pillory, claiming knowledge of a witness. I left Southwark early in the day to cross the bridge, angling from the bankside up to Aldgate Street, which I took to the edge of town. A stiff September wind burned at my eyes, creating especially fierce gusts along the broadening way before the gate, where thousands of colorful shapes whorled in a circling gale. A dozen children jumped about beneath them. The dancing shapes were cloth, I realized as I reached out to pluck one from the air. A sack of fabric scraps, spilled before some tailor's shop and now dancing with the winds. Then a stiffer gust, and the spiral of color was gone as quickly as it had arisen, the children chasing the shapes away to the west. Another beautiful, meaningless thing I would never see again.

Unlike the high and ugly bulk of Aldgate, which loomed above me now, a begrimed surface of stone and stupidity that seemed to attract more featherbrained schemes for enlargement and improvement than its brothers. As a result Aldgate had suffered its share of minor collapses over the years, as the collective folly of builders and masons led to ever more perilous attempts to re-shape the fabric. A broad length of sailcloth hung down to cover a pitted scar in the stonework on the north tower, while above, a crane arm jutted awkwardly from a high opening, its intent to pulley stones to the upper reaches, though it looked to have gone unused for months.

Halfway up, where one set of stairs forked to the gate's north tower, the other to a set of apartments in the south, I had to pause, scarcely believing my ears.

"Sell this one — no, *this* one, and leave the others for Philippa to barter away. She's hardly in a position to object. Perhaps her slutting sister can help her."

A familiar voice, though tightened with uncommon anger. Reversing direction, I climbed up the right stair and made my way along the groaning walkway to an unassuming door, the main entrance to the series of rooms making up the small apartment atop the gate. For twelve years the house in the south tower had been the home of Geoffrey Chaucer, my oldest friend, though I thought he had left London some weeks before.

The door stood open, wedged with a chipped brick, and in the front chamber Chaucer was stooped over, tussling with an array of silver trinkets and goblets spilling out of a wood box. Crates, a stack of trunks, rolls of twine: the modest house was in a tremendous disarray, made all the more dire by the continual gusts blowing in from the door and scattering dust and invading leaves about the rooms. Despite the piles of belongings the place felt empty and bare, the only light coming from narrow slits low along the walls.

I stepped inside, further darkening the place. Chaucer turned. His scowl softened at the sight of me. A sad smile, and he tilted his head. *"Mon ami,"* he said, coming to his full height. We embraced in the middle of the low space, surrounded by the detritus of his Aldgate life. Two servants brought in pieces of furniture from the back room, set them on the floor, returned for a next load.

We held each other at arm's length. I searched his eyes. "You're in London." A statement, also a question.

"I am not in London, nor anywhere near the place." He went to the door, peered out. He turned back to me. "At least as far as Philippa is concerned. If you see her you never saw me, yes?"

"Fine, fine," I said, amused, though also a bit melancholy about Chaucer's continuing estrangement from a woman I admired so deeply. "You're packing up then?"

"I must surrender the apartment and Aldgate altogether." He said it with a careless air that I could tell was put on. "You haven't heard? The common council wants me out. It seems that Richard Forster will take up residence here in a few weeks. Everything must go, to be sold or carted out to Greenwich." A village several miles from the city, and site of Chaucer's new residence while performing his duties as justice of the peace in Kent. "Books, plate, books, furniture, books — oh, and also the books."

Chaucer's small apartment above Aldgate had once been stuffed with volumes. The four locked trunks along the far wall must have held dozens of manuscripts between them. It struck me how many times I had visited the Aldgate house over the years, for poetical exchanges reaching into the night.

He invited me to sit. I declined, with a hint at the day's business.

"An errand for Strode, then?" he said, wanting to know more, though unwilling to ask directly.

"A fool's errand, I would call it. Aldgate seemed as good a place as any to begin." I gave him the bones of it, as the discovery of corpses in the privy was being bandied through the streets already. I kept quiet about the victims' peculiar means of death, nor did I hint at the mayor's apparent attempt to scuttle an inquiry. Chaucer had worked under Brembre in the customs office for several years, and the two remained close. "So today I troll the gates," I said, "hoping to scare up anything I can find about these men."

His reaction was muted. "A dozen a day die in this city. Women, the elderly, children. Mass graves surround us on every side. What makes these unnamed men worthy of your time, John?"

The question surprised me. "Sixteen at once, thrown in the Walbrook? Curiosity, I suppose. And a fair measure of fear. No mayor wants to give death free rein in his city. The crown will use any excuse to tighten its choke hold on London. This is just the sort of thing to attract the worst kind of scrutiny from the king's men."

"Now you sound like Strode himself," said Chaucer with his curling smile.

"The freer the city, the looser its purse."

Chaucer moved to an east-facing window and glanced at the turret clock on St. Botolph. "I'm due at Westminster shortly, you know, otherwise I would accompany you. I would welcome a break from all this." He looked around, gesturing to his crates and trunks. "But let me hail Bagnall up."

"Who?"

Chaucer walked to his door. "Matthew Bagnall," he said over his shoulder. "The warden of the gate. A man who knows more about the doings in and around Aldgate than all our ward-rats put together. I'll get him up here." He stepped out to the rickety landing and called down to the foregate yard. "You there! Is Bagnall about?"

A faint reply floated up from street level.

"Well, send him up, will you? Master Chaucer has a question for him!"

He turned back and flattened himself against the wall. The servants slid around us bearing a large chest between them, which jostled and bumped along the railings as they descended the street-side stairs. When they were gone he looked at me, gestured at his eyes.

"The same?"

"No worse, at least," I lied, blinking away a spot. "Some days I scarcely notice, others . . ."

"Ah," he said, his hands clasped. He tilted his head. "You know, John, there may be remedies other than resignation and despair."

I said nothing.

"There is a medical man newly in town, a great surgeon-physician. He is an Englishman, but trained in Bologna."

"Thomas Baker."

"You know him?"

"We've recently met," I said, recalling the man's fingers digging in a corpse. "He seems bright enough."

"More than bright," said Chaucer. "He

was in my company on the return from Italy last year, and I got to know him quite well. Familiar with all the new techniques, unafraid to wield the knife when it's needed. He is lodging in Cornhill for now, above the shop of a grocer named Lawler. Do you know the place?"

"I do."

"I suggest you make an appointment to see him." Then, less formally, his voice lowered, "Surely it's worth a visit, John, even if nothing comes of it. You have only two eyes. You'll never get a third no matter whom you extort."

Matthew Bagnall arrived at the door. Squat, thick necked, official, looking eager to get back to the gatehouse. Chaucer offered him drink. Bagnall declined, nor would he seat himself.

"Mustn't stay up here above my men for too long, Master Chaucer," Bagnall said, as if Chaucer's house rested on an eagle's aerie or some grand mountaintop in the Alps. He wore a cap that fitted tightly over a low forehead, covering what looked like a permanent frown.

Chaucer explained why I was there, then nodded at me to begin.

"Fair thanks, Bagnall, for the trudge up the stairs." I handed him a few pennies.

54

He took the coins silently, glancing at them before slipping them into a pouch at his side.

"The Guildhall is seeking information on a company recently arrived in London, and now deceased."

His eyes widened slightly.

"Violently deceased," I said.

"Killed, you mean."

"It appears so. They were a group of men, a large group. Not freemen of the city. Outsiders of some kind."

"Frenchmen or Flemings, then?"

"I think not," I said, recalling the stolid, rural look of the bodies, their rough hands, the dirt caked in their nails. "These were Englishmen, or I'm a bishop."

"Not soldiers — cavalrymen, say?"

I thought of those iron balls lodged in the victims' chests. The gun wounds could have been inflicted in a battle, some factional conflict on the highway. Yet the fact that the men had been killed with bullets argued against the mess and melee of actual combat. "They might have been conscripts, I suppose, but recent ones if so. These men worked with their hands. Plowmen, some of them, used to harrowing and manuring their fields."

"Dead when they got here, or killed within

the walls?"

"You ask sound questions, Bagnall. I don't know."

He considered me, hand at his thick chin. "You're looking after that mess up at the Long Dropper."

I allowed my silence to answer him.

"Gongfarmers're all jawing about it, the rakers and sweepers as well," he went on, loosening up. "It's the gab of London. Fifty men, thrown in the sewers to drown and rot."

"An exaggeration," I said breezily. "Sixteen victims, all happily dead before they were tossed in the privy."

"That may be," he said, his black look making me regret my light and careless tone. "Yet treated no better than shit from a friar's arse. Denied the ground, and a Mass, and a proper burial. Whoever's done it had best keep his murdering nose free of Aldgate, or he's in for a rough time of it from the guard, that's certain."

"To be clear, Bagnall, you know nothing about these men?"

"Aldgate hasn't heard a whisper about this matter, Master Gower." He tugged at his cap. "I'll own we're a busy gate, what with all the Colchester traffic, marches out to Mile End. But a company of sixteen, riding

56

or walking in from outside? Even the sleepi-
est of my men would take notice, and a pile
of corpses would fare no better. Wherever
those poor carls came in, they didn't come
in through Aldgate, nor the Tower postern,
or I would have heard about it." The postern
was a small entrance along the wall north of
the Tower. Not a full-fledged gate but a
heavy door, though just as carefully
watched.

Bagnall left us with a curt nod. Chaucer
stared after him as the old stairs protested
his descent with a groan of loose nails.
"Blunt man. Always has been."

"Bluntness has its place," I said. "Though
I'll need such frankness from more than
your gateman if I'm to learn who these poor
fellows were, and where they came from."

Chaucer pressed my arm as he walked me
to his Aldgate door for the last time. "I shall
be back for Parliament soon. You will be in
town?"

"Do I ever leave?"

"You've not come out to Greenwich yet,
John. I have plenty of room for visitors —
more than I ever had in this place." He
looked around, his bright eyes mellowed
with regret at leaving a city so much a part
of his blood. Like his father, a London
vintner, Chaucer had been born and would

surely die within these walls, which he had always regarded as a sort of outer skin. I thought of him strolling through the countryside, waking to roosters instead of bells, attending Mass at the tiny church in Greenwich rather than at the urban parish that had been his devotional home for so many years.

He caught my sad smile, and at the door he turned his full attention on me. Ours was a unique friendship, its complexity never more deeply felt than at those moments of farewell, all too frequent in recent years.

"Be careful with yourself, John, and mind your back." His palm was on my wrist. "Whoever threw those bodies in the Walbrook knew they would be found." He looked out along the rooftops of the inner ward. His grip tightened. "And didn't much care."

From the narrow passage before Chaucer's house I walked north through the boundaries of the parish of St. Botolph, lingering at each tower to dispense coins and questions. From that height London appeared almost tranquil, cleaner and somehow nobler than the square mile of squalor and moral compromise sprawled between these walls. The city's roofs formed a grand patchwork of ambition and decay, the spans of greater halls and the thrusting heights of new towers set within the humbler timbers of tenements and lower shopfronts. Even the smoke rising from smithies and ovens possessed a humble majesty, grey tendrils striving for the sky, vaporous strands of the city's hopes.

Yet London was hardly at peace. Masons were at work at every turn, fortifying the wall and heightening it in certain places deemed particularly vulnerable to engine or incursion. It was known that a great navy had been assembling at Sluys since midsummer, ready to seek vengeance for years of English brutality in France and Burgundy. With the Duke of Lancaster in Castile seeking a crown and much of the upper nobility increasingly belligerent toward the king, a mood of lowering doom had settled over the realm of late, as the nation braced itself for invasion from the sea.

The feeling sharpened as I neared Bishopsgate and the armories. Somewhere below three smiths worked in tandem, the varied weights of their hammers entwined in a clanging motet, turning out breastplates, helmets, hauberks, the mundane machinery of war. I spoke for a while to the tollkeeper, whose wife I had bought out of a city gaol the previous summer, though learned no more than I had from Bagnall.

Now Cripplegate. On the second level above the gatehouse there was a small hermitage, filthy from the habits of its longtime occupant though an unavoidable stop given my needs. The low and nearly secret door, reached by squeezing around one of the guard towers from the lower walkway, was closed against the wind. A smudged face could be seen through the rectangular gap in the bricks that served as the chamber's sole window aside from a narrow squint low on the far side. The hermit's eyes were closed above his massive beard, a swath of matted filth that covered nearly every inch of a face thinned by years of self-denial and hunger. The stench from the hole was a rich stew of man, dung, and time.

I squatted and peered in. "Good day to you, Piers."

With a start the hermit opened his eyes, then gapped his mouth in a dark and toothless smile. He kept his door closed but scooted his ragged frame toward the window, jutting his nose and lips into the aperture. "Why, John Gower himself, the Saint of Shrouded Song! You have — oh —

spices in your pouch for Piers, do you, or
— oh — a heady lass?"

Piers Goodman, though thin of brain, was
one of the city's more useful hermits, with
sharp eyes and good ears, unafraid to stick
his head out of his hole and sell what he
knew, which tended to be a great deal. The
Hermit of St. Giles-along-the-Wall-by-
Cripplegate was the rather pompous title he
had chosen for himself long ago, and for
years its grandeur fit him. Nobles from the
king's household, bureaucrats from the
Guildhall and Chancery, mercers and aldermen: all sought his counsel on matters large
and small, climbing up to the old storeroom
he had claimed as his hermitage, offering
thanks, charity, and spilled secrets to a man
as discreet as he was pious — or so it appeared to most of those who consulted him.
In reality the hermit leaked like an old wine
cask, sharing the private lives of others for
trifles: coins, fruits and pies, the occasional
whore. In recent years the cask would often
run dry, though with Piers Goodman you
seldom knew what you might get.

It took a while to lead him around to the
subject of the day, but when I finally did, he
was as usual quite forthcoming. "Strangers,
you say? Company of men? Oh, we've had
our share of strangers we have, and compa-

nies — why, just Saturday or was it Tuesday a little brace of — oh — Welshmembers it was. Whole flock of Welshmembers, herded through Cripplegate quick as you please. Piers saw them he did, looking down through his slitty slit, and Gil Cheddar told him all about it. Big trouble for the mayor, says Gil Cheddar, those Welshmembers. And had a carter of Langbourn Ward up here — oh — last week? Weeping mess he was, too, with a sad sad sad sad story to tell about his cart and his cartloads. What's in his cart and cartloads, Gower, hmm, what's in his cart and all his cartloads? Not faggots, mind, not beefs, mind, not Lancelot, mind, but —"

"Stop there, Piers. A company of Welshmen, you say?"

"Aye, Welshmembers they were, and right through the gate they went, says Gil Cheddar, who brings Piers his supper and his —"

"You said this Gil Cheddar told you about them?"

"Aye he did, told me all that business. Not ale, mind, not —"

"And who is Gil Cheddar?"

"An acolyte of St. Giles Cripplegate is Gil Cheddar, and the sweetest face you'll ever see on him. Gil Cheddar brings his old hermit his suppers he does — not every day, but some days his suppers he does. Breads, fishes, cheeses, a dipper of ale for Piers and I'll thank you for a piece of silver, and now a song for you, Gower? A song of hermits pricking bold, aye, that is what Piers'll seemly sing." And he intoned it in his nose: *"I loved and lost and lost again, my beard hath grown so grey. When God above doth ease my pain, my cock shall rise to play . . ."*

I pushed a coin through the window and left him to his melody. Back on the walkway I had a decision to make: proceed along the wall through the remaining gates or descend to the outer part of the ward and try to find Gil Cheddar. It was not a feast, and as an acolyte, Cheddar would likely not appear at St. Giles until later in the day. I would return in several hours.

Soon after Cripplegate the wall bent southward, angling past the peculiar roof of St. Olave's and the five towers placed like sentries above this misshapen corner of the city. I learned nothing at Aldersgate nor at Newgate, where I had extensive connections among the guard, though I did gather a few nuggets about unrelated matters for later use. On leaving Newgate I got a warning from one of the guards to watch my step farther on. As I soon discovered, the walkway had collapsed perhaps forty feet short of Ludgate, beams leaning askance from the wall, planks dangling creakily in the wind. A heavy scaffold had crushed an abandoned shack beneath, leaving a sprawl of broken timber that looked too rotten for salvage.

I retraced my steps to the stairs before Newgate and descended into the narrow ways of St. Martin, the small parish spread between St. Paul's and the wall. My whole day had been spent floating above London, with scarcely a thought for the eternal squalor below, though descending now to the close streets I knew so well came almost as a relief, despite the fatigue of a long and trying day. I walked nearly to the cathedral before turning to approach Ludgate from the east, angling around the gateyard to avoid repair work on the conduit ditch, which looked to have sprung a leak. At the corner of the yard I bought three bird pies and a dipper of ale.

From the pillory holes in the yard dangled the hands of Peter Norris, a parchment collar affixed to his neck, his uncovered hair lifting morosely with each gust of wind. He must have been in place for hours already, as the area was free of hasslers. A boy of about eleven sat at the foot of the stocks, faking a cough.

Norris's eyes were to the ground as I approached. His unshaven neck rasped against the parchment collar, inscribed in high, dark letters with his crime: *I, Peter Norris, stole pigeons.* His was quite a fall, for Norris had been a powerful man in former days, a wealthy mercer with nearly exclusive command of the city's silk trade with France, though that was before he would be brought low by his own poor decisions.

"Norris," I said, handing two pies to the boy and holding one out to his father's mouth.

As the boy started to eat Norris made an effort to turn his head, angling his gaze up to meet my own.

"Spit that out, Jack!" Norris commanded weakly when he saw me. The boy stopped chewing, his eyes gone wide. "John Gower here's like to poison you dead, without a thought for your boy's soul."

I sniffed. "Not today, Norris."

I glanced at his son. The boy, twig thin, wore a woolen cap, his golden hair stuffed beneath the narrow brim. The cap had ridden up slightly, exposing ugly stumps where his outer ears had once been. A cutpurse, then, caught knifing and sliced for his crime. He took a few coins from my hand and wandered off toward the gate, both pies already gone.

Norris looked after his son as long as he could, neck straining against the skin-slicked wood. "That boy, he's a loyal one, he is. He's got as much rot thrown in the face this week as his father, with no fuss about it, and sits here with me all through the day. 'The Earl of Earless,' they taunt him on account of his stubs. Worse things, too." He shook his head.

"Can he hear it all?" I asked, curious about the boy's affliction, thinking of my own.

"Oh, young Jack hears what he wants to hear, as all boys do." He laughed fondly.

Norris, I realized as I followed the boy's progress, had a perfect angle on the traffic into the city from Ludgate. Beyond the imposing façade lay the legal precincts and the royal capital. An important city entrance, bringing visitors and goods from Temple Bar, the inns, and finally Westminster a good walk up the Strand.

"How long have you been at the pillory, Norris?" I held the cup for him.

He took a slow sip of ale, smacked his lips. "Since the dawn bell," he murmured. Another sip. "But an hour and a bite and I'm free, for all that's worth."

"This is the last day of your sentence?"

"Aye."

"And the rest of it?"

"Ten hours in a day right through a week, as was my sentence at the Guildhall, and all for a festering brace of pigeons swiped and sold to a pieman! Constable wouldn't have taken me in at all, if an alderman's daughter hadn't happened to stomach one and empty her guts." He looked out at one hand, then the other. "Give me Jesu's cross over the pillory. A man's not meant to stand bent this long."

He was right about that. Though the punished generally stood at the stocks for no more than an hour at a time, the longer sentences could lead to permanent disfigurement. Pillory back, its sufferers easily identifiable by their crooked spines and frequent grunts of pain as they hobbled through the streets.

After a few pitying murmurs I began gently, asking Norris whether he had noticed any unusual activity at the gate in recent days, particularly involving a large company of men.

"Not Londoners, but a company from outside the city," I said. "Sixteen of them. All dead now, thrown in the privy ditch beneath the Long Dropper. They were walked in some time in the last week — or carried, I suppose. Does anything come to mind?"

Norris thought for a moment, then looked up and surprised me. "Welshmen, I'll be bound," he said.

I felt a satisfied warmth. "What do you know of Welshmen, Norris?"

"The first day of my sentence. A Wednesday it was," he said. "Caught a little glimpse of them skirting along the yard, just there." He nodded toward the mouth of Bower Row. "Only reason I remember it is, those Welsh carls gave us a nice respite."

"How is that?"

"My first day in the stocks. Seemed half of London was out hurling eggs, cabbages, dungstraw at me and my boy, anything they could lift. But then those strangers come by, and all at once every man of them leaves off and starts tossing his rot at the poor Welshers instead." He laughed weakly. "Should have heard them, Gower, our good freemen. 'Savages!' 'Sodomites!' 'Child burners!' 'Leap off the walls, you filthy Welshers!' Those sorts of roses, is what they shouted. And so it went until the strangers were beyond the bar."

"What were they doing at Ludgate?"

"Wouldn't know. Couldn't hear a thing of them."

68

Young Jack had returned and took his place to the right of his father's protruding head and hands. He had purchased himself an oat-loaf and nibbled at it slowly.

"You didn't see who was leading them through?" I asked.

He sniffed and spat. "What I've seen a lot of is my feet, and little Jack's fair nose. Hard to look at Welshmen when your face is forced to the ground."

He bent his straitened neck upward into an awkward angle, grunted from the effort and relaxed, his frame sagging with the work. I wetted his lips again, then held the last pie below his mouth. He took a small nibble, a larger bite.

"Tell me about your witness."

His jaw stopped, his eyes shifting to the side, away from me. "Ah. No act of charity, these pies and ale?"

"You know me better than that, Norris. Who is it? What did he see?"

A heavy gust spiraled a pile of leaves into the air above the pillory platform. "Why should I tell you? You'll go and sell what I say to the Guildhall, and then where will Peter Norris be?"

I shook my head. "The Guildhall is not disposed to believe anything you say. No buyers there, as you well know."

69

His eyes closed. He sighed. "Perhaps. Though I shall bide my time, Gower. My witness is quite convincing, and my sentence ends at the next bell. The right moment will come, I trust."

Was he lying, or simply a fool? Either way I could get nothing more out of the man despite my offer of considerable coin. I turned to leave him, and his earless son gave me a hateful and piercing look, as if my hand had been one of the many hurling filth at the boy and his father. I walked away and toward the gate.

The guards and tollkeeper at Ludgate were forthcoming but unhelpful, none of them recalling the Welsh company, though promising to ask about. It was now past four. I hesitated just outside the walls, knowing I should walk back up through Cripplegate to see Gil Cheddar, the acolyte at St. Giles. Yet the occasional gaps in my vision had returned, as they often did with the fatigue of a long day and a late afternoon. The wind had moistened somewhat, too, and a distant rumble of thunder threatened a city storm. I would visit St. Giles the following morning, I resolved, and call on Cheddar then. It was one of several mistakes I made that day along the walls of London,

70

hearing only what I wanted to hear, deaf to what mattered most.

CHAPTER 3

Like pouring out the sun. A lethal river of metal flowed from the cauldron, killing the thickness with a long hiss, filling the space between the clay molds. A heavy steam rose from the melting wax. Stephen Marsh, his gloved hands gripping the cauldron's edge and an apprentice at each side for balance, tipped the last of the molten alloy into the small hole at the top of the mantle. Iron bars, tin ingots, a touch each of copper and lead, all melted together and skimmed for impurities before the pour. Soon enough the liquid bronze would cool into a bell duly stamped with the lozenge of Stone's foundry. Then trim, sound, file, and polish until the instrument achieved its final shape and tone, made fit for a high tower across the river.

Like pouring out the sun. For that was how his master Robert Stone always liked to describe it, this mysterious shaping of earth's metal into God's music. Pouring out the sun — until the sun withered and killed him.

With the cauldron locked and pinned, Stephen wiped his brow and dismissed the two apprentices. He looked over toward the door to the yard, where the sour-faced priest stood with crossed arms, watching the founders at work.

"Two bells formed like this one, Father," Stephen said, removing his gloves as he walked toward the foundry's newest customer. The parson of St. Paulinus Crayford, a parish to the southeast of London, here at the beck of the churchwardens about a commission for the new belfry. "The first tuned at *ut,* the second at *re.* I sound them myself after the molding, and I have the ear of Pythagoras, so you needn't worry about a symphonious match. If our bells are not well sounding and of good accord for a year and a day, why, we'll cart them back here to the city, melt them down from waist to mouth, and cart the new ones to you out at Crayford. All at Stone's own expense, and all inside a month."

The parson looked skeptical. "And reinstall them in the belfry?"

"Aye, and reinstall them in the belfry, hiring it out to the carpenters ourselves," said

Stephen. He removed his apron, a heavy length of boiled leather, and hung it on its posthook. "I poured side by side for five years with the master, bless his memory, and now am chief founder and smith retained at the widow's will and pleasure. Your wardens shall be satisfied, I promise you that."

The parson asked a few more questions, then Stephen took him up front to the display room to settle sums. An advance of two pounds on six and thirteen, with the balance due upon delivery to Crayford, where the bells would arrive before the kalends of —

"And installation," said the parson, raising his chin, clearly fashioning himself a shrewd businessman.

Stephen nodded briskly. "And installation, Father, with clapper and carpentry entire. Cleanup as well, and Stone's will be pleased to throw in a cask of strong ale for the company." The parson's eyes twinkled at this. Stephen had seen it before, the way that last, trivial detail worked on the pastoral mind. *How pleased my flock will be with their good parson, for getting them an extra day's work and a free drunk in the bargain!*

The note was signed, the deal waxed, sealed with Stone's lozenge stamp. Stephen was watching the parson leave the shop, preening over his bit of successfully transacted London business, when Hawisia Stone came in from the house passage. She stood there in her frozen widow's way, her mouth a flat line on the hard rock of her face. She had thick, muscular hands for a woman her age, which was a year shy of thirty, or so Stephen thought, and her swollen middle mounded out obscenely beneath her bulky blacks. No confinement for Hawisia Stone, no feminine modesty for this steely widow, convention be damned.

"Mistress Stone," he said, and never knew what to say next. How does the good widow fare this day, Mistress Stone? What thousand tasks do you wish me to perform in the smithy today, Mistress Stone? And what new curses have you called down upon your servant's murderous blood, Mistress Stone?

"The parson's to buy, then?" she rasped.

"He will," said Stephen. He nodded at the note and coin on the board counter. "A solid commission."

"Fine." She went to the ledger and tucked the note into the book's back lining. The coin went in her purse.

He stood there, acting the thrashed whelp, Hawisia the grey bitch of the place. In the months since Robert's death he had become

75

newly familiar with her little noises, all those telling grunts he'd once been happy to ignore. Disapproving murmurs, low growls of contempt, long-suffering sighs in place of words withheld.

"You've work to do?" she asked him without looking up from the ledger.

"Aye."

"Go then."

Stephen backed and turned, slinking through the door to the foundry yard. He kicked a bucket, scaring off a yard dog, his gut clutched with all that might have been, and all that might still be.

Only six months ago Stephen had been looking ahead to a full and verdant future. Robert Stone was on the verge of making him partner in the foundry and smithy, giving him his daughter's hand to bind it all tight as you could like. Stephen's master had worried often about losing him to a house of his own, where he could keep a greater share of his made coin. Why, if we lose our Stephen, he'd say to his wife, half our men're like to go with him to start up a rival shop. We need him here, Hawisia, with all his cunning and craft. She had agreed.

For Stone's was a sprawling operation: a foundry, a smithy, an ironmonger all in one, and though Robert Stone had been its rightful master, it was Stephen Marsh at the art-ful center of this world of metal, bending, twisting, tapping, his adept hands shaping bronze and lead with the delicacy of a king's silversmith, finding ways to swirl the hard-est irons into the most intricate forms and configurations. "There is surely something of the devil in you, Stephen Marsh," Robert Stone would say, always with a smile, and Stephen would smile with him, even as he inwardly spurned such talk of demons. His skill was inborn, a thing of kind wit, the work of Lady Nature at her forge, as much a part of him as his very tongue; the devil had naught to do with it.

By his nineteenth year Stephen Marsh had won a reputation as the fellow to see for the subtlest metalwork to be had between Bish-opsgate and the river. Magnates' men would come to Stone's to commission new armo-rial bearings for a bishop's door, or to repair the hinges on an earl's ewer, and Stephen would take up every job with a swiftness to match his skill. With the coming arrange-ment Stephen could keep his mind on his craft without a care for the management or upkeep of the shop, leaving these to Robert, who was more skilled at such things as recording accounts and filling supplies, or maintaining good relations with the guilds and the parish. God's grace, the curate would say, grazing in the fields of our hearts.

Then he dies, and everything changes. Hawisia Stone inherits the foundry and cruelly weds Robert's daughter off to a vintner's son, while Stephen is bound with ten full years of servitude to Stone's, and all for an errant cauldron. A large job, a rushed pour, Robert's arm aflame like a torch as he holds it aloft and screams those terrible screams.

Now Stephen was bound to the place like a wheel to a mill, his labor and his hand the due property of Hawisia Stone. Ten more years of service to the widow and her shop: such was the sentence of the wardmoot after the incident, the result of Robert's exhaustion and Stephen's impatience — though was it simply haste? Or something malign, a demon's breath on his hand, tipping the cauldron too early, bringing a death some dark part of him desired, despite everything his master promised him?

For it often seemed that Robert Stone still haunted the foundry, as if part of his soul inhered in each cast, his deep voice moaning from the hollows of every founded bell, calling out Stephen's blame, a worm feeding at his conscience.

"Fill the cooling troughs, and quick," he

ordered an apprentice. The boy scurried off, two buckets yoked over his narrow shoulders.

Stephen went to the central forge, slipped on an apron, stomped the bellows, took up a steel bar. These days he found his sole consolation in his craft, the strength and spirit of the metals. If his fortunes wheeled from high to low, these things of the earth would remain ever the same, constant and receptive in their beautiful predictability. Good Sussex iron, smelted in the furnaces of the Weald. The dearer Spanish ore, purer and more responsive to hammer and heat. Cornish tin and Welsh copper, the prices argued back and forth with the crown's stannaries. Lead from the Mendip Hills. All of it ripped and drowned and raped from the bowels of the world, and now stacked here, some of it dull, some of it bright, all of it solid and silent, ready to do the bidding of his hands. He grasped his hammer and tongs, and soon enough was lost in the burning engine of his craft.

Later, as dusk closed around the streets of Aldgate Ward, Stephen wandered up through the parish of St. Katharine Cree to the Slit Pig, an undercroft ale-hole against the walls and the evening haunt of London's best metalmen. Low-ceilinged and poorly lit, heavy with hearth-smoke and the breaths of tired men, and soon Stephen Marsh was in the loud thick of it, taking strong beer with his fellows at the central board, slapping backs, trading lies. Every man could sense the approach of the curfew bell, like a pious curate chasing whores from the stews, and all did their best to drink their fill before it sounded. The cask boys were kept busy.

The talk of the evening was guns. Several of the city's founders and smiths were boasting of their lucrative new commissions, having recently been recruited to assist the king's works in the manufacture of artillery. Cannon, culverins, ribalds and bombards: a mass of powder-fired heavy arms, much of it hammer-welded and smithed, some founded from bronze, all of it for the defense of the Tower and the city when the French invasion came — quite soon, if the talk was to be believed.

Stephen listened to their exchange with a mounting scorn and an itching envy. At one point, as the talk ebbed, he said, "A gun is but a bell turned on its side and poorly sounded." Two dozen eyes now on him. "Why, at Stone's we could fashion twenty, thirty cannon in the coming months," he went on. "And with a quality of craft and precision you will be hard-pressed to find at the Tower." A boast but a true one. He was pleased to see some nods, along with a few scowls.

"Could you now?" said one of the scowlers. Tom Hales, the aged master of a venerable smithy well across town off Ironmongers Lane.

"That's right, Hales. Power, precision, speed. You'd be hard-pressed to find a better gun than a Stone's gun."

"All three of them," Hales scoffed.

"Give me a large enough commission and I shall line the walls of London."

"If the good widow allows it," said Hales.

A few rough laughs, a low whistle. This was another of his mistress's small cruelties. While Robert had taken several gun commissions before his death, Hawisia soon curtailed any of Stephen's ambitions in that direction. Together Robert and Stephen had poured just five large bombards, designed to fire the heavy bolts favored by the Tower. Though they were adequate devices, Robert's death had prevented Stephen from making further assays into the fashioning of guns.

"That may be," Stephen went on, undaunted. He was too respected in the trades to be cowed by an old hammer man. "Yet at Stone's I could bronze out a bombard to shoot twice as fast and thrice as long as any in the Duke of Burgundy's army, or the devil take my body and bread!"

More laughs, some cruel, though soon enough the talk moved on to other subjects — the new scarcity of tin, the demands of young wives — and as the men settled back into their ales, Stephen's gaze wandered over to the far end of the undercroft.

In the south corner a man stood alone, looking straight at Stephen over the mingled crowd. Not a tall man but broad of shoulder, confident in his demeanor despite his solitude within the crowded space. He wore a short courtepy of dusky green, a hat fringed in black over dark hair falling in loose ringlets around a neatly trimmed beard and a thick neck. Stephen didn't know the fellow, the Slit Pig tending to draw only men in the trades, and he thought little of the stranger's presence until he came down from a piss to find the man waiting for him by the tavern door.

"*Depardieux,* my good brother," said the man with a pleasant enough smile.

"And fair evening to you." Stephen looked carefully at the stranger's face. "We have met?"

He shook his head, the ringlets bouncing at his neck. "I am unknown in this parish and your own, though I should like to make your acquaintance very much, Stephen Marsh. Have you a span to spare? Your next jar will be mine to coin." He jangled a purse.

They found a place away from the benches, where a high stew table stood against the wall flanked by five empty casks ready for hauling up the cellar stairs to the street above.

"What are you called?" Stephen asked when they had settled.

"I am called many things," said the man with a faint smile. "Though you may call me William."

"And why have you come for me here?"

"I am come for your skills, Stephen. Your metaling, a subject of great renown."

Stephen dipped his head to acknowledge the compliment. Nothing odd about a man coming around to sniff out his art, though it didn't ordinarily happen in a tavern. "Very well. And what is your business?"

"My business." He took a long, slow draft of his ale, narrowed his eyes. "My business is guns."

Stephen frowned. "What of them?"

"Just now you were speaking to your fellows over there about your bronzecraft." He

83

nodded toward the board. "About Burgundy's bombards."

"Aye," said Stephen. He stole a look over to the benches. One of the apprentices from Stone's, almost old enough to be counted a guildsman and get his key, caught him looking and gave him a friendly nod before turning back to the cheer. "The Duke of Burgundy's said to have the cleverest cannon this side of Jerusalem. Bombards, culverins, your ribalds and *pots-de-fer.*" He sipped, then shrugged. "I was merely jawing."

"And you believe you could surpass Burgundy's guns or — how did you speak your oath — 'the devil take my body and bread'?"

"Well now, as to that —" He grimaced. "I've never put my hands on 'em. But the Tower's bombards are unsound, I will tell you truly, cast in haste and unworthy of war. I have seen them tested along the Thames, watched more than a few of them crack with the powder and shot. A weak alloy, a bad pour. Stone's could do better, is all I meant to say."

"A bad pour," the man mused. "Something you would know all about, aye? And how is the widow Stone faring, Marsh?"

"Well now," Stephen snarled. He reared back and stood. "Who are you, to enter this

84

parish and bring such knifing words with you?"

The man's eyes had gone cold, metallic. He remained seated and still. "I am William Snell, chief armorer to His Royal Highness the king."

Stephen felt the blood rush from his head. William Snell, a name whispered with equal reverence and fear among the founders and smiths of London. A fierce, demanding master, with countless arms at his beck and command, charged with the very life of London in the event of war — and Stephen had just insulted his guns.

"A fair welcome to our humble alehouse, Master Snell," said Stephen weakly. He retook his seat.

Snell considered him for a while. Then he leaned forward, his voice lowering as the tavern din reached a peak. "Here is why I have come, Marsh." He pushed a chunk of wood and metal across the board, then emptied his jar in one long swallow. Stephen hefted the object. It was heavy in his hand, a darkened length of iron between fixed bands, a stubbed tube sawed from a longer rod. The wooden piece resembled a barrel stave, though it was the length of a forearm rather than the height of a boy. Stephen brought the object to his nose, catching the distinctive whiff of sulfur. He stroked the wrought metal, then turned the object over in his palm.

He set it back on the stew table. "What is this?"

"A chamber, stock, and firing hole, hacked from one of our small guns," said Snell, leaving the thing in front of Marsh. "It's an ugly thing, inefficient and clumsy. I would like you to design and fashion a better one, with more reliable results. These keep misfiring, or worse, exploding on my men."

Stephen looked down at the piece and ran his finger along the seam. "A better hammer weld would improve it, I'd think. Hot work, but not complicated."

"We need these devices to be lightweight and made to survive a dozen rounds at the least," said Snell. "Uniform in their shape, so they can be moved down a line from hand to hand. Cast of bronze, perhaps. Strength, yes, but also flexibility."

Stephen thought about it. "Why not keep this in the Tower? You have your own metalers over there. Michael Colle, Herman Newport. I've trained some of those fellows myself, apprenticed with them before I got my guild key." Along with its outside commissions, the royal armory had long employed its own smiths and founders and farriers, lines of men whose days were given over to the forging and pounding of guns and shot, boltheads and engines of war, infantry plate and helms and horses' shoes.

Snell lifted, then dropped the awkward lump of metal and wood. It hit the scarred surface of the table with a dull *thud* and took a half roll. "This is a special job, Marsh. A *particular* job, you see. I am concerned about the privity of the armory. I want to have this done outside, and discreetly, so as not to arouse suspicions."

"Whose suspicions?"

"None of your concern."

"With respect, Master Snell, I am not a fool," Stephen said, leaning in. "You are asking me to risk my position at the foundry, my guild key, my livelihood. I would have to make these devices right beneath the widow's nose, yet behind her back." He thought of Hawisia, the glimmer of suspicion in her eyes whenever she looked at him. "Stone's is her foundry, the whole of it. Every hammer, every awl and anvil, every ingot of tin, every barrel of wax, every mound of clay. I cannot risk my position there, nor earn more of her fury than I have these four months since the master's death."

"Your devotion to the widow is admirable," said Snell with a mocked sincerity.

"Yet there are higher purposes than loyalty to a craft. There is your nation to think of, and your king. We are after something new at the Tower, Marsh. Something . . ." The armorer's eyes narrowed as his tongue sought out the hard spots on his upper lip. "Something more *efficient.* A maximum of delivery with a minimum of effort. Do you see?"

Stephen frowned. "Larger guns, then?"

Snell's nose twitched, and a corner of his mouth turned up. "It's smaller guns we are after. Smaller, quicker to load, more portable, more —" He squinted, as if looking across a great distance. "More deadly. And thus more efficient."

"Efficient?"

"Efficient," said Snell with a tight smile. "It's the common word of the season at the Tower and among the king's *familia,* from top to bottom. After what happened in Edinburgh last year, who could wonder that the king's army is looking for better ways to fight and happier machines of war? We chased the Scots from town to town and pile to pile but they wouldn't engage, nor was our army swift enough to split up and catch them, what with all the equipment and baggage in tow. So now here we are, looking our own invasion in the nose, and the talk is all of effectiveness of operation. Do more killing, we tell the cavalry and infantry alike, but with fewer men, fewer arrows, fewer bolts. More slaughter, we tell them, but with less treasure, less shot, less powder."

"And less gun," Stephen mused.

"And less gun," said Snell, his voice lowering to a gritty whisper. "Now you are seeing it, as I rightly knew you would. You are a man of solutions, Marsh. If we can find the right alchemist with his tinctures or the right priest with his sacraments, why, we should be able to shrink a gun to the size of a ram's cock. I am not concerned with the look of these weapons, you understand. They needn't be beautiful things, like your hinges and such. Deadly efficiency is what we are after here."

Stephen stared at the wall behind Snell, and a procession of guns marched across his inner sight, great cannon leading the small, the *pots-de-fer* before the bombards before the ribalds before the culverins, throwing their balls and bolts to every side. *Less gun.* A stirring goal; an attainable one. He knew little of gunpowder and shot aside from the pieces he'd seen wheeled to the gates and stationed beneath a few sentry towers along the walls, and his sole work on artillery was represented in the few large guns founded for the Tower before the passing of Master Stone.

Yet Stephen could already imagine ways that might be discovered to render such devices more efficient, to constrict their girths, lessen their lengths, improve their firing, and now that the notion had entered his mind he yearned to get his hands on one of them and apply his own skills to the problem, to gauge for himself the intricate balances of weight and mass, force and propulsion guiding these wondrous instruments slowly multiplying across the battlefields of the world.

Stephen sat up straighter, feeling a need to impress the armorer. "Efficiency and beauty are hardly natural enemies," he said, "and weight can be compensated for by other means."

Snell raised his heavy brow. "Go on."

"A simple solution to an unknown problem. A gun is no different from a hinge. The sorts of things I found and smith and repair at Stone's — hinges, buckles, coffers, gates, bells, to say nothing of clocks and the like — they are the fittingest prologue one could imagine to the new guns your men are smelting and forging behind those walls. And no one in London melts and bends and tinkers as I do, or the devil take my —"

"Body and bread," Snell completed the thought. "You make quite free with such oaths, Marsh. Are they sincere? Is this your earnest will, to know the privity of the armory?"

Stephen took a large mouthful of ale and drew a sleeve across his lips. "Let me at your guns, Master Snell. Let me understand the tooling and mechanics of it all. By God's bones you won't be sorry."

Snell studied him, fingers playing at his beard. "I hope not, Marsh. For your sake, and the sake of your craftsman's soul."

"Aye," said Stephen confidently, and Snell seemed to coil up on himself as he reached for his jar. Stephen shivered, despite the tavern's warmth.

"You will come to the Tower in the coming days, then," said the armorer. "Give your name at the east barbican. One of my men will fetch you down to the yard."

"Very well, Master Snell," said Stephen, working to hide his pleasure, an anticipation something like lust. It was a too easy thing, in that flush of ale and ambition, to excuse the minor swell of vanity that had held him there talking to the king's armorer, despite the sentence that kept him so tightly bound to Stone's. For if Stephen's heart lingered always at the foundry and forge, his pride looked now to the Tower, and the machines of a coming war.

Snell slipped out the cellar door as the taverner rang the closing bell. Stephen stood and mingled with the crowd of men staggering out to the lane. He crossed back over Aldgate Street as the first stroke of curfew rang from St. Martin-le-Grand, and as he entered his own parish along Bellyeter Lane his pace quickened with his craftsman's pulse, all his mind on the making of guns.

CHAPTER 4

"I should feel worse," Hawisia Stone said.

"And you don't?" Rose Lipton, midwife of Fenchurch Street, tapped at the sides of Hawisia's belly, then bent to put an ear to her tightened skin.

"The babe is less after prodding my bile this time. Haven't coughed up a caudle in weeks."

"Nor would you, not at this stage," said Rose with a sniff. "You're not longer than six weeks from birth, mistress. Now it's all sore muscles and devil's air, isn't it?"

"Aye, it is," said Hawisia ruefully.

"And will only worsen these last weeks."

Rose adjusted the poultice, an evil-smelling mixture of jasmine, roots, dung, and St. Loy knew what else, all gathered in a sack at the top of Hawisia's bare belly, right below her breasts. Hawisia suspected the midwife reused her herbs and roots for her concoctions, though didn't want to say anything for fear of putting the woman off. It was hard enough keeping Rose Lipton happy and working as she should be. Often as not it felt as if Hawisia were the one hired to serve Rose rather than the reverse, despite the good coin the midwife took away after each visit.

Rose prodded some more, pressed her palms and fingers deeper into Hawisia's heavy mound. At one point the midwife's hands froze. She frowned.

"What is it?" said Hawisia.

"Thing's not turned round as it should be," said Rose as her hands resumed their wanderings. She clucked twice. "Don't like it when they get footstrong."

"What does it mean?"

"Nothing good, my dear," said the midwife, with one of her dark looks. It changed to a smile and she patted Hawisia's wrist. "Should straighten itself out in time, though, with the right charms. Let me see what we have here."

She dug through her bag and came up with a much-thumbed little book. Hawisia had seen it before, heard its bootless charms wheeze out through Rose Lipton's wide lips. "Have you straightened your husband's girdle, as I asked?"

"Just there," said Hawisia, pointing to the

delicate metal chain dangling from a bed-post. Wrought pewter, a gift from Robert on their wedding day, though crafted by Stephen Marsh, his chief apprentice then. Rose lifted it from the post and draped it across Hawisia's waist.

"It is a husband's charm, you know. Shame Robert's not here to sing it himself. I'll lip it out for you, though," she said help-fully.

"I thank you for it," said Hawisia, tighten-ing her jaw.

Rose fixed the clasp before Hawisia's nether way. Hawisia could do nothing but lie there, propped up on her bed, as Rose recited the familiar words by rote. "I bound, as so shall I also unloose. I bound, as so shall I also unloose. I bound . . ." The midwife murmured the girdle charm ten times, not reading from the book, simply thumbing the page containing the words and the rubrics for their use.

When Rose had finished she tucked the book away, followed it with the poultice, and helped Hawisia dress and sit up on the edge of her bed.

Hawisia, unable to stop herself, asked, "All seems well, then, aside from the babe's position?"

Rose waggled a hand, shot out her lower

lip. "You are well past where you've got to before, Hawisia, I'll give you that," she said, but then shook her head. "Yet that means little when it comes to the birthing. How many is it you've lost to the flux since Robert Stone took you to wife? Two is it, or three?"

"Four," said Hawisia, remembering them all. The first three gone in rushes of blood that could have been her menses if she hadn't known better and cramped so badly. The last one was stillborn early, an unchristened lump pushed out into a world it would never see or know.

"And Eleanor, she gave him two, aye? Sweet one, that Eleanor."

"Two. Yes," said Hawisia flatly. "Both girls." Eleanor Stone, Robert's first wife, had been dead these eight years. The daughters were departed from the foundry as well, one recently married off to a wine merchant of Cripplegate Ward, the other gone to fever in her childhood. Robert would often speak of his late wife with a certain longing skidding through his voice, and though he never said so, she could feel the contrast between his wives working on his desires.

Eleanor, fertile and fecund. Hawisia, barren and fruitless. Robert, wanting a son.

"So your evil fortune weren't from his

96

seed, then, was it?" said Rose with her brow raised, an inquisitive tilt to her head.

"I suppose not," Hawisia said.

"Good then." She nodded. "But don't give in to despair, Mistress Stone. For the babe's quick in there now, I can feel him shifting about, and who can say? Could be that Lady Fortune will turn the thing out alive." She wagged a finger. "Though don't let your hope spring too fresh, Hawisia. Not with your luck."

No fear of that, Hawisia thought, feeling her hopes pushed and pulled by the midwife's shifting wisdom.

"Dead birth can be a fearful thing though, can't it?" said Rose. "I well recall it with my third. John, it was." She sat back plumply on her stool and folded her arms. "We thought he was a choked one, too, all grey in the skin, not a twitch from his toes to his nose. But my old gossip Grace, she thwacked the little thing on the arse she did, and out comes his screamin' breath, loud and full as you'd like!" She laughed merrily at the memory, which Hawisia had now heard at least ten times.

Rose packed her remaining things, then pushed the stool back beneath the bed and smoothed her dress as Hawisia shoved herself to standing. "So you see, Hawisia, y'must trust in the grace of God to sort wheat from chaff. Some of us be fecund, bursting with bairns, like my eight. Others are chosen to be virgins in a house a nuns. Others to be barren, such as yourself. But better to be barren than rotting off in a grave, aye?"

Hawisia walked the midwife down the outer stairs and through the house door to the showroom. Stephen Marsh was there, watching the shop in Hawisia's absence.

"Why, good morn to you, Stephen Marsh," said Rose, beaming widely at him.

Stephen gave the midwife a nod. "Mistress Lipton. And Mistress Stone." He showed one of his too easy smiles, brushed away a dangling lock from his brow, and pondered them with those wide-spaced eyes, a soft doey brown. In the parish there were wives and widows alike who giggled and gossiped on those eyes. Not Hawisia. She sniffed and turned away.

Rose, though, paused in the doorway like a mud-stuck log. "How is the work, Stephen? Bells shining bright this autumn?"

"As bright as ever, Mistress Lipton," he said. They spoke for a few minutes of newborn infants in the ward, and of Rose's two unbetrothed daughters, fresh as new buds on an elm, each as lovely as a daisy, the midwife claimed.

Hawisia could sense Stephen's awkwardness. She watched his eye shift toward the rear of the shop and the foundry yard. Stephen hated being trapped up front, she knew, just a hundred feet from his natural home amid the forge and metals, yet in his mind a sea's width away. He was like a penned bear up here, never truly content unless he was at his work — and Hawisia wanted him at his work. For with Robert's sudden passing Stephen Marsh's needful craft was all that stood between pounds and penury for the foundry.

How different it had been while her husband lived, when what she desired most keenly was prestige and the awed respect of the guild wives. If she could not have children of her own she would have the richest, finest foundry and smithy in the city of London, and it was up to Robert and his workers to make it so. More commissions, more customers, an ever-growing share of the city's metaling trades.

And it was this nagging want, this thoughtless avarice that killed Robert Stone, despite Stephen Marsh's hand in the accident. This she knew, and felt the weight of it every day, though it was easier in her mind to blame Stephen — and have him blame himself.

Now all she wanted was to survive the birth of this only child, with enough coin for their bread and this roof. Her ambition had diminished with her future.

"Allow me to walk you through to Fenchurch Street, Mistress Lipton," Stephen was saying. Rose, delighted, took his arm, and together they left the shop.

Hawisia went to the door and watched them walk down Bellyeter Lane and past the Fullers' Hall, Rose chatting gaily, her free hand flying wildly back and forth before her loud and prattling mouth, Stephen nodding, *yes*sing, feigning a youthful interest in the midwife's wisdom and wit.

Hawisia closed the street door, flattened her back against it, felt the rough board against her palms. Grey and old already, even with a babe stewing in her belly. She wondered how it would be, to reside in that world of green life and vitality it seemed everyone inhabited but she.

CHAPTER 5

London's most shadowed church sat nestled against the northernmost span of the wall, which rose behind it to block the morning sun and cast that corner of the parish in an eternal dusk. In those months the outer ward, like the other neighborhoods ringing the city beyond the walls, lived in a state of violent transition, as tenement holders and shopkeepers fought back the royal army with bribes, pleas, and threats, all desperate to hold on to their small scraps of ground in the face of the great events unfolding around them.

For it was the soldiers' mission to clear buildings, trees, and brush from the city's outer circumference, a mission they took quite seriously. With the combined might of France and Burgundy massing in Flanders, the walls of London would need defending when the invasion came. It wouldn't do to leave the enemy a high tree that might be felled, a shop that might be torched, a ready supply of natural engines and dry fuel to be used against the city and its people. So, just over the ditch, for fifty feet in every direction, the army's laborers were beginning to pull down houses old and new, taking axes to the few larger trees that still stood in those precincts.

For all my lifetime the walls had been embraced by clusters of narrow streets and alleys, animal pens, shops and stalls and an occasional smithy, yet now these wide areas in the outer wards would be opened to the Moorfields, and the orchards and grazing grounds beyond. A great denuding, and it had already transformed this part of Cripplegate-without from a teeming precinct of city life into an ugly and mud-churned plain.

The destruction was also stoking an always simmering conflict between city and crown. The aldermen were seething as they watched whole neighborhoods disappear, complaining to the mayor in the overblown terms favored by their superior sect.

A royal trampling of the outer wards!

Gross violations of ancient rights!

The commons kicked about like river rats!

St. Giles, despite its close proximity to the walls, remained, though the old rectory between the sanctuary and the Cripplegate guardhouse had recently been sacrificed to the cause. Some of its rubble filled three handcarts pulled by a trio of sullen workers, pressed into service by the two infantrymen standing to the side. None of the five men acknowledged my presence as I walked past them and up the porch stairs.

A small group of petitioners waited on the porch; then the church's dark and cold interior prickled my limbs. As my eyes searched weakly through the gloom I heard the distinctive voice of the longtime parson. He stood within one of the shallow side chapels, arguing with another man over some aspect of the parish rents.

"Nor has he yet made good on the summer's leasing," said the priest.

"That old hole in Farringdon," said the other.

"Yes."

"Two shill four, as I remember."

"Press him for it, will you?"

"Aye, Father."

"Harder this time. I cannot have a tenant sucking the parish teats without paying for his milk like all our other lambs."

"Aye, Father."

"Be off, then."

The two separated, the other man passing

me on his way to the west doors, the priest making for the altar end of the nave. He spoke again as he disappeared through the chancel screen, calling out instructions to several parish underlings, all of whom answered with a respectful tone of assent. As I neared the low middle door he spoke more pointedly to one of his charges.

"That pile of ash, Gil?"

"Yes, Father, I removed it. As you asked." A higher voice. Young, a touch sullen, as if its owner were being inconvenienced by the parson.

"Very well. Finish up with that polish, then, and you may go."

"Yes, Father. As you please." Almost insolent, as I heard it. I wondered that the parson let one of his charges speak to him in such a way.

The candles on the near side of the chancel beam flickered as I passed. I waited, fumbling with an unlit wick, until the echo of the priest's footsteps receded and the vestry door opened and closed. I looked around and through the screen. Before the low altar two masons worked on the floor, which in that portion of the church had, over the years, decayed into an uneven surface of old planks and broken stones that the men were busily replacing.

I looked through the crossing toward the south door. The sullen voice I had heard belonged to the youth squatting by the door to the sacristy, working a rag over a sacring bell at a low table. He wore the high-cut robes of an acolyte, the plain jet of a young man in minor orders. I approached him quietly, stood at his back.

"Gil Cheddar?"

The hand holding the rag flinched. The acolyte sat back in surprise, losing his squat and half sprawling onto the church's stone floor. With an embarrassed flutter of limbs and robes he came to his feet, his chin and jaw raised at me. "Gil Cheddar indeed. Who's asking?"

"John Gower," I said, unmoved by his tone. His uncovered hair, coal black, swept back from a brow as close to pure white as living skin can be. Early whiskers grew along his cheeks and chin in seemingly random patches, and his narrow shoulders topped a gaunt frame of medium height and slight build. "What does the good parson of St. Giles have you about today, Gil?" I asked him.

There is something in my voice that I have never comprehended, a quality of silken acuity that seems to work its peculiar charm even on those hearing it for the first time.

Chaucer once compared it to a flat of sacrament bread. If unleavened bread could talk, he said, it would talk like John Gower, with no airy lift or taste of yeast to distract from the flat purity of the grain. A weak figure, though I have witnessed the effect of my own voice often enough to lend some credence to the image. There is no levity in it, no room for compromise.

At his own first nibble of this voice, Gil Cheddar answered my question with no trace of the arrogance he had just shown his parish master. "Cleaning tasks, sire, between the day services. Polishing and the like."

"I see. And you are now finished for the day?"

"Nearly so. I'm to finish the burnish on this bell here, then it's my lot to stow the sacristy items back in the cabinet, get it all locked up securely, with the key returned to Father. Then it's —" He stopped himself, looking puzzled by the extent of what he had divulged. His narrow lips found what must have been a familiar frown. "You are here to speak with me? Or is it the parson you wish to see?"

"Oh, I am here for you, Gil, and only you."

He shifted his weight. "Whatever for?"

"As I understand it you spoke rather freely to a hermit in recent days."

106

"A hermit, sire?"

"A hermit of our mutual acquaintance." My head tipped back toward the walls. "A fellow who lives out there, above Cripplegate."

He took a half step away, his mouth fixed in a line. I followed his gaze as he looked up and out across the top of the screen. From where we stood you could see nothing of the walls or the upper reaches of Cripplegate, though Cheddar seemed to be peering through the layers of wood and stone to that low window where he had spoken to Piers Goodman.

"I would very much like to learn about your conversation with our unkempt friend, Gil." I had moved my hand to the purse at my waist. I lifted a coat flap and showed it, though the sight seemed to terrify more than please him. The acolyte glanced toward the vestry, took in the stances of the workers by the altar, assessing the dangers of speaking to this intruder.

"Not here," he said quietly. "The coops, outside Guildhall Yard?"

"I know them," I said. A line of chicken houses along Basinghall Street, a short walk down from Cripplegate.

"I should not be long," he said. "Give me the quarter part of an hour."

The vestry door groaned open, the parson returning to the nave to call out an instruction to an unseen subordinate. Hunching slightly, I took a few sidelong steps and ducked through the screen door, then hurried down the aisle and back out onto the porch. The sun had made no further effort to crest the walls, only brushing my face once I entered through Cripplegate and turned left past Brewers' Hall, nestled just east of the inner gatehouse. I crossed Guildhall Yard and entered Basinghall Street, a narrow, snakelike thoroughfare extending south from the wall to Cheapside, and always bustling with hucksters selling everything from unskinned coneys to silver plate.

There was city business being transacted out here as well, mayor's men taking small coin, dispensing false promises in exchange, and above it all rose the shouts of the criers in a sonorous dance of service and enticement.

"Buy any ink, will ye buy any ink? Buy any very fine writing ink, will ye buy any ink and pens?"

"Any rats or mice to kill? Have ye any rats or mice to kill in your homes and stables, good London? Rob the Ratsbane, at your service!"

"White radishes, lettuces, more radishes, two bunches a farthing!"

"Have ye a sore tooth, an aching gum, an abscess or a bleeder? For know that I am Kindheart the Tooth-Drawer, my good people, with gentle pincers in my hand and opium in my purse."

The criers rattled on, their pitches rising to an impossible volume as I passed down the street.

Then, from the top of the way, the din of a herald's bell, sharp brassy clangs cutting through the street noise. The sound abated as a tall young man in the royal livery stepped up on a half barrel, looking down at the commons and asking for our silence and attention.

He was a palace man, recognizable as one of the showy types increasingly favored by King Richard in those years. A rich coat buttoned tightly at his neck, a fur-trimmed cape chiseled with decorative slits, long legs in particolored hose, three ostrich feathers stemming ostentatiously from his hat. He spread his arms, shook his feathers like a plumed bird, then brought his hands to his mouth, cupping the rhythm of his cries.

"And now for a taste of foul crime, my good gentles and commons! Now shall I shout of brigands and killers, slayers and thieves! A poacher of pigeons, a smith turned to pilfer!

109

The most lawless of ladies at large in our land!"

He had our attention. Several outliers moved closer to the crier's perch, crowding in and looking up at the man's raised and thinly bearded chin as he went on.

"Now give me your ears and your good hearing, people of London! Know all present that Robert Faulk, cook of Kent and poacher of His Highness the king's forests, along with Margery Peveril, gentlewoman of Dartford and murderess of her husband, having jointly slain a sheriff's turnkey and escaped from the sheriff's gaol at the manor of Portbridge, do now flee, together or alone, through country and city, their destination unknown, with great bounty from King Richard to any man who would aid in their apprehension and seizure, singly or together."

There were scattered exclamations, a fair amount of murmuring at the notion of a murderess at large. The crier repeated the announcement, added a brief description, then went on to shout a series of royal proclamations. The crowd loosened, the hubbub returned. Soon enough the royal servant's drones were drowned beneath the renewed barks of the hucksters and their hired mouths.

"Oysters! Oysters! Oysters! Get your oysters here, and your eels!"

"Grind your knives or your shears? The sharpest blades in London ground here, my good gentles!"

"There is Paris, there is Paris in this thread, the finest in the land!"

The poulterers' coops stood along the western span of the street, forming a low, loud wall of fowl that lent an air of barnyard looseness to this city lane. The old ordinances had tried to restrict the poulterers to the wall by All Hallows, though recent mayors had proved more lenient. Hens pushed their feathers and beaks through the slats in a ceaseless hunt for grains, while a rooster strutted proudly along the perimeter. The constant murmur made a happy cover for conversations both ill intentioned and benign.

I gathered a handful of kernels from between the pavers and was pushing them through the slats of the nearest coop when I felt a hand at my shoulder. I turned into the thick-lidded eyes of Adam Pinkhurst, a scribe for the new common serjeant at the Guildhall. As always I was distracted by the pied spectacle of his face, a patchwork of burned and healthy skin patterned like some elaborate Moorish cloth, as if he had got in

111

the way of one of an alchemist's acid flasks.

"John Gower," he said, the cleft in his chin deepening as he spoke, his gaze direct and confident, regarding me as an equal. Pinkhurst's stature among the Guildhall clerks had grown somewhat over the last few years since Chaucer had designated him as his favored copyist, commissioning three manuscripts of his poem on Troilus. I had never employed his services for my poetry, preferring to hire a dedicated bookman along Paternoster Row rather than a city scrivener like Pinkhurst. The Guildhall scribes were notorious for passing around unauthorized copies of their clients' work, and I had no desire to see my making treated like so much fodder for the common gut. Though Pinkhurst, by near-universal acclaim, was trustworthy and discreet, I knew him as a forger of remarkable skill.

"Pinkhurst," I said as we clasped hands, his ink-stained but smooth. "What brings you out of your cage?"

He grimaced. "I drew the short lot today, so I go in search of pies for our chamber of scribblers. Pork, chicken, liver, dog, friar — makes no difference, so long as they're not rancid. Six pies, then I'm back to inking, sadly enough, and on such a delightful day."

"It is that," I agreed, appreciating the man's wit. It was no surprise he was Chaucer's favorite; Geoffrey had told me that Pinkhurst had more than once suggested alternative rhymes and phrases in the margins of his rough copies, just the sort of revisions and improvements to which Chaucer so often subjected my own verse — yet only rarely accepted from me in turn.

He saw the kernels in my hand. "And you? Are you considering renting yourself a chicken coop, relocating from Southwark to Basinghall Street?"

"Hardly," I said. "My residence is as far from the Guildhall as it can be. No city politics for me."

"You are a wise man," he laughed, then, in a lower voice fragrant with a noontime cider, "Brembre cannot depart these precincts soon enough, I tell you. The man is a tyrant, some new Nero laying waste to the city. Even Exton will be a better pick, despite his current lodging in Brembre's purse. How the fair Idonia stands for such mistreatment I will never know."

Nicholas Exton, newly elected mayor, would be inaugurated at the end of October. Chaucer had told me of Pinkhurst's besotted admiration for Idonia, the current mayor's wife. While I already knew of his

113

contempt for Brembre, I wouldn't have expected him to risk such incautious vitriol in front of me.

"We shall hope that Exton brings a new golden age to the Guildhall, then," I said.

Pinkhurst shifted on his feet. He had spoken rather too loosely, and seemed to know it. "Well." He nodded. "You will excuse me, Gower. A pie seeker's quest is not to be taken lightly."

"No indeed," I said, and watched him spin on his heel, then disappear in the crowd bunched near the corner of Cat Street.

Only a few moments passed before I saw Gil Cheddar approaching from the opposite direction. The acolyte had shed his robes and now looked like any respectable young man taking the air on a London afternoon, though his eyes widened when he saw me standing by the coops. As he approached he shot worried glances up and down Basinghall Street.

"Here?" I asked him.

A nervous sulk. "Ask your questions, Master Gower."

"Fine then. I understand you spoke to our good hermit."

"Aye."

"You spoke to him about a company entering the city, yes?"

114

"Aye."

"A company of Welshmen."

"Aye."

"Through Cripplegate."

"Aye."

"And when did you see these men, Cheddar?"

He thought about it. "More than ten days ago it would have been. A Thursday, of that I am certain. It was Holyrood Day."

Five days before Peter Norris had seen the Welshmen circling the gateyard.

"I was sent by the parson to help with the night service. Was after cleaning up from that and dodging home when I saw them."

"What were they doing?"

"Walking through the lodge doors at Cripplegate, and well after curfew bell, too. Can't say I wasn't surprised, such a large group of them." The outer wall of the Cripplegate lodge was served by two doors for use after the shutting of the gates each night. Any company of outsiders entering the city that late would not fail to attract notice, and demands for bribes.

"Surely someone must have bought them in."

"Aye."

Silence.

"And who might that have been?" My

purse came out. He saw it. He twisted on a toe, scratching his reluctance in the dirt. He glanced in both directions and blew out a breath.

"Father's who it was. Left after the service and met them up the street without the walls, below the Moorfields. The parson led them to the gate himself, hustling them along. I was standing on the St. Giles west porch. Had a knot in my breech tie, was trying to untangle it. I saw him leave by the vestry door, go up toward the Moorfields, then he was back quick as you please, hurrying them for the gate, like he was a sheeper herding ewes."

Robert Langdon, the parson of St. Giles Cripplegate, a respected clergyman, buying entrance to the city for a crew of Welshmen. How extraordinarily odd. Purchasing their deaths, too? But whatever for?

"What can you tell me, Will, about Father Robert's motivation? Did you learn the origin of his entanglement with these Welshmen?"

"Aye," he said with a slight smile. "There was another man with them. Not a Welshman but a Londoner, I'd warrant, hanging back with Father." His reluctance was now gone, as if he'd been waiting for the chance to spill. "They were standing just nigh the

116

ditch. The first of the Welshmen were passing through the lodge. The other fellow, he was getting directions from Father."

"Directions to where?"

"To a tenement house off Thames Street, Queenhithe Ward. To a house in the parish rents of St. Giles. I know it, as I ran an errand there for the curate only last month."

"Could you take me to it?"

"Aye, but —"

"Now."

We passed down Ironmongers Lane and over Cheapside, soon reaching Thames Street and the quayside, where Cheddar turned east into Queenhithe Ward. This low way hard by the river smelled eternally of fish, which were cleaned right on the quays, strings of filth laid bare to the sun and washed away only at the end of the day, with the fresh catch hauled off by the fishmongers for sale in the markets. We paused at one point to allow a dungboat to take a load from three waiting carts. The gongfarmers shoveled the slop on board as a water bailiff watched primly from his skiff thirty feet off the quay, eager for a violation and a bribe.

Once the carts had cleared the quay we made our way another hundred feet. Cheddar angled up a crooked street leading north from the bank. He stopped in front of a house towering high over the narrow way. Few windows interrupted the flat surface of the outer wall, which was traversed by diagonal timbers cracked in several places. The door, opened to the street and splintered along one side, hung loosely from leather hinges. It gave onto a low front room, empty but for an octagonal standing table shoved against the far wall. The rushes, rotted and broken, covered only a portion of the splintered floor. The back room was in no better shape, nor was the kitchen, a sunken space shared with the two upper floors. Here several of the larger hearthstones had been removed. Two dented pans hung off hooks on the east wall, the whole of which leaned slightly forward, threatening to collapse inward.

The rear of the building shared a rectangular courtyard with four similar tenements, though the structure seemed in much worse shape than the others. An uncovered staircase climbed up the house's back face. I took the steps gingerly, testing the next before leaving the last. The top two floors resembled the first in their condition, though unlike the lower part of the house, these stories showed evidence of recent habitation: sleeping pallets, several torn or soiled garments, a clay jug and a piss pot, a molded hunk of bread.

Sixteen Welshmen, sharing two floors. Not unthinkable in this section of the city, where the tenements clustered densely above and below Thames Street.

Cheddar's attention was directed out the sole window onto the narrower lane. "Where are they now, do you suppose?" I asked him.

He shook his head. "It's what I was trying to tell you, before you rushed us down here." His palms faced outward, putting his silence on me. "Father Robert said it to the other man. I heard it plain from the porch. 'Four days,' he said. 'Four days they can stay, then they must be moved. After that they are the Guildhall's problem.' Been more than four days, sure, and no one the wiser. As to where they are now? Couldn't say. Nor, I suspect, could Father Robert."

Though I could, or so I believed. The Welshmen brought into the city by the parson of St. Giles were now feeding the worms of St. Bart's, after an ugly sacrifice of their corpses at the shrine of St. Dung. A terrible end to sixteen unknown lives.

There was one part of Cheddar's story that lodged in my throat like a half-swallowed bone.

The Guildhall's problem.

Yet it was the Guildhall, in the person of

119

Ralph Strode, that had set me off on this strange pursuit in the first place, despite the mayor's reluctance to have the matter plumbed. I did not think for a moment that my friend was involved in the deaths of these men. Yet to imagine the mayor, or perhaps an alderman or two, concealing or even sanctioning these foul murders, then keeping the information from Strode — and Welshmen? England was not at war with Wales, any more than London was at war with York.

A city divided against itself, a realm churning with eternal crisis: rich bulges of opportunity for a man who does what I do. Yet London was growing increasingly strange to me, as if our ages and habits, flowing as one for so many years, were slowly parting around a rising isle in the stream. Looking back on that autumn, I liken my own sense of things to the steadily deteriorating condition of my eyes. On a bad day, when I looked at a line of trees, I would perceive it as a fluctuating plane, wobbling blurs of light and dark. If in the light I saw the promise of knowledge and resolution, the dark yielded a flat nothingness, or a foreign and shapeless world.

CHAPTER 6

"Mar— Elizabeth? Now, Elizabeth?"

The woman sighed. She could almost smell his dread, hear it in his tentative voice. Fear repulsed her. "Yes, Antony. Now."

The false name came easily to her, and it seemed to give him some measure of confidence. He stood slowly, brushed at his too-tight doublet with those giant hands, and went to see the keeper in the front room. She heard the soft *tink* of coins, a satisfied "Very well, good sir," from the keeper's wife, then he reappeared in the low doorway.

She looked at his feet. *Stop shuffling,* said her frown. He lifted them, straightened that laborer's spine. She gave him an approving smile as he sat.

"And the horses?" she said, tightening her plait and tucking it back in place beneath her hood. A strand still teased her cheek. She pushed it to and caught him watching her. She felt herself blush.

He nodded stiffly, oblivious to her discomfort, his own neck reddened from the restriction of the high collar. "A few moments. 'Nother company's just arrived, so stablers're quite busy at the moment."

She stifled another sigh. Much work to accomplish here, though the long journey north to Durham would give them plenteous time. St. Cuthbert's bones were hardly planning to get up and walk away.

She coughed into a balled hand. The back chamber was stuffy, close, full of smoke. Gentlefolks' room, the keeper proudly called it, though she had stolen more than one envious look at the airy common hall up front, where a dozen or so lower travelers in their company, man and woman alike, relaxed and drank from the inn's stock of dark, river-cooled ale. She sipped at warm wine, washing down the pigeon pies and greens, wondering if she would ever truly satisfy her hunger after such long privation. She closed her eyes, felt herself shudder in the stiff chair, let the images take her for a moment, as they daily would do. The filth, the fire, the smoke and death. A clearing in the woods, the strange crack of the guns.

When she looked up she saw him staring down at his food. She was happy to see him eating slowly, as she had instructed, but as she watched his bearded jaw work at the supper, other considerations afflicted her. Where would their next meal come from? Should they stay the night here, with this new company of pilgrims, or push on along toward the next town, trusting their luck to find another inn before nightfall? On this main road, just three days north of London, there should be many choices. Yet not any inn would do, not for a couple in their situation. They — *she* — had to choose carefully, with a mind to appearances. *The appearance of appearances.*

She was preparing to push her chair out and find the privy when a clamor sounded from out front. Calls from the yardboys, loud neighs from a struggling horse. Another few shouts, then the inn's street door slammed open. Their view from the back was blocked by a half wall, but they could hear men's businesslike voices from up front.

She grasped his arm, fixed him with a stare. Was it over already? "Steady now, Antony."

"Aye," he said, barely a whisper. He placed a hand on hers. She didn't flinch at his touch, as she had at first. *I am your wife,* she silently assured him, and herself.

The alewife appeared in the doorway. "A

nuncius, from down Westminster," she said, a finger aside her nose. She bent slightly toward them. "They pull in here, smelling like a wet dog, demanding our best, but then they're always off eft soon. We'll have him off your ear quicker'n a pig eats a corn."

Her shoulders tightened as the alewife left, and her gut flipped. A royal messenger. Westminster, London, soldiers, and she saw it all again, heard and smelled the death.

In the front room the nuncius exchanged low words with the keeper, who sounded concerned, though about what she could not discern. She heard the muffled slap of a purse changing hands. The keeper approached their table, his face showing distaste.

"With your pardon, mistress, and yours, gentle sir, this king's man would like a word," he said. He ducked out, visibly relieved his part of the business was done. The messenger replaced him in the doorway. A short, hard man, his skin swarthy with the sun. There was a scar beneath his chin, a thin line of whitened flesh that disappeared into a loose shirt of dun wool, stained and flattened by the narrow saddlebags flung over his shoulders. These were affixed with the badge of King Richard, the white hart on a field of faded blue. His eyes, deep set and impassive, swept past her own as he turned to the man across from her.

Yes, we are done, she thought, her pulse a low throb in her ears. The nuncius started to speak. "Good sir, if you will —"

"What is the meaning of this intrusion?"

"Antony!" she said, pressing his arm, though instantly regretting it. He had done well to question the messenger, to demand an explanation in that gentleman's tone.

The nuncius loomed over their table in the small chamber. "My horse has gone lame," he said flatly. "A mile south of here."

"Oh?" she said, taking on the same superior tone. "And what of it?"

"The gentleman here — his is the best horse in the stable."

"Not the least surprised," said the horse's rider with a proud nod. "Strong fellow, isn't he?"

"I will be commandeering him," said the nuncius, no hesitation or apology in his tone. "I have a full day's ride to the next post, and the need for a swift mount."

She felt her chest loosen. "There are no other horses suitable to your needs?"

He looked aside. "Others suitable? I would think so. But speedy, strong? No, mistress. And I've patents in my pouch that need handing off." He fingered the leather bags yoking his chest and shoulders. "I'll take your horse now."

"If you must." She nodded tightly. "We will be compensated?"

"Aye, and most generously." He opened his palm. On it sat ten — no, twelve nobles. A decent sum for a pressed horse, though the stallion would easily fetch fifteen at one of the larger markets. But she saw no need to quibble, and draw more attention.

She looked across the table. *Take them, Antony.* But he sat there like a lump, his mouth half open, his gaze wide and fixed on the coins. Beneath the table she pressed his foot with her own, then watched as he closed his mouth and gave the nuncius a curt nod. He held out a hand, and the royal messenger let the nobles slip from his palm. *Probably a greater sum than Robert Faulk has ever held,* she mused.

"Will that be all?" she asked the messenger, feeling incautious.

"It will. And the king's thanks." King Richard's messenger turned on his heel, leaving the inn by the yard door.

The keeper reappeared. "Apologies, good gentles." He rubbed his palms. "No choice, really, not when it comes to one of those Westminster riders."

She tried to mask her worry. "You have a

replacement you will sell us?"

"I do indeed, mistress. Fine mare. Chestnut, four years, broke her myself. Name's Nellie."

His eyes had misted, and she could see what the transaction would cost him. Men and their horses. She gave him as kind a look as she could manage. "You have clearly been a good master to her. Nellie will be well taken care of, and you may depend on her safe return upon our own from Durham. We shall purchase you a relic of Cuthbert for your troubles."

The keeper's eyes widened over a spreading grin. He made a silent bow.

Later, as they prepared for sleep, Robert dawdled outside the door while Margery undressed and nestled in the wide bed. When it was his turn she silently watched him in the candlelight. He had removed his low shoes, which stood toes down against the door wall. His doublet lay loosely over a bench, covered by the fine cotte-hardie of dyed wool he had stolen from a drying fence during their flight. He was bare chested now, a silent width in the dim light. He went to his knees. She saw a last flash of his face as he bent to the candle, his lips gathering wind, then ending the flame.

She lay back on the raised pallet. This, a

luxurious breadth of down and heather more fit for a lady's chambers than a country inn, gave softly beneath her spine as she stretched the day's travels away, though her eyes would not close.

He spoke from the floor. "Keeper's not like to see that pretty mare again, or I'm the poxed Duke of Ireland." He grunted, adjusting his lanky frame to the lumps of his travel blanket, his makeshift bed atop the rushes.

She smiled at the low ceiling. "Aye," she said, and nothing more. Soon the rhythm of his breath slowed with the coming of sleep.

It was their sixth night together. She appreciated that he never snored. Not like her dead husband, curse his bones, who'd whistled and wheezed through every pore in his flesh. It wasn't for snoring that Walter Peveril deserved the death he got, though these quiet nights were a blessing in themselves, despite the pressing peril of their flight.

Margery Peveril spoke into the gathering dark, thinking of the north, the stretch of the marches, the man on the floor. "We'll sell the mare in Glasgow," she whispered to the night.

CHAPTER 7

From the great doors the massive hall of Westminster Palace stretched languidly to the east, with partitions of varying heights separating the courts: Chancery, the Exchequer, King's Bench. England had a leaking hulk for a ship of state, defeating the efforts of the palace's small army of servants to maintain and improve its fabric. Despite the hall's condition one could tell at a glance that the opening of that year's Parliament was nearly upon us. Three glazers worked at a few broken windows overhead, limners touched up wall paintings here and there, and a team of masons troweled mortar over gaps and holes in the stone.

The eve of Michaelmas found me in Westminster before the chambers of Michael de la Pole, Earl of Suffolk and the lord chancellor. As Strode had told me at the St. Bart's churchyard on that first morning, the chancellor was resisting all inquiries from the

Guildhall concerning the murders, claiming they were no business of his or of his office. Yet the use of guns made the killings undeniably the business of the crown, a point I intended to press regardless of the chancellor's reluctance.

Edmund Rune, the earl's secretary and chief steward of his sprawling household, stood within the low passage leading to the chancellor's chambers, expecting me. Rune was a new addition to Michael de la Pole's *familia,* his predecessor Edward More having died earlier that year. Where More's reliable and steady manner had mirrored the best qualities of the earl himself, Rune was known as a gossip and a backbiter. The chancellor, it was widely agreed, could have chosen better.

Rune had a protective air about him that morning, his eyes hanging open over a brown beard, his large frame angled toward me as I approached. "Go gently with him, Gower. He's feeling it from all sides these days. None of your coiney cant."

"A peculiar request," I said, and an unnecessary one; I felt nothing but respect and admiration for Michael de la Pole, who had always treated me fairly. Yet for other, more powerful men, old King Edward's most trusted counselor had lately become an object of passionate resentment, even outright contempt, despite the man's long service to the crown. The young king's capricious favors had placed the earl in a precarious position with respect to several of the lords, who would be assembling in Westminster soon for Parliament.

"Surely these rumors of the earl's impeachment are false, Rune," I said. "Lordly gossip, nothing more."

My tone had been light, meant to reassure. The look Rune gave me beneath his brown curls suggested any levity would be out of place. "The coming weeks will be crucial for his lordship. We are doing everything we can to hold off the spite from the Commons and the Lords alike, but I fear we may be too late. All rides on the king."

He led me down the passage to the chancellor's chambers, a set of rooms tucked within the southeastern sprawl of the palace, not far from the Painted Chamber. The chancellor sat not at his study desk but in his receiving room, a low-ceilinged and intimate space long regarded as the hidden heart of Westminster, though its walls were all Yorkshire, washed brightly with rural scenes inspired by the streets and saints of the earl's native shire.

An old man already, Michael de la Pole

seemed to have aged several years since I last saw him a few months before. Eye pockets smudged with fatigue, a neck carelessly shaved, cheeks bowed in above a jaw that had lost its confident jut and now trembled with a creeping palsy that had been coming on over the last two years. Not a broken man, not yet, though I believe he saw his defeat before him, drawn more sharply with each passing day.

"I trust your lordship is well?" I said, feigning ignorance of his distress.

"The wolves are gathering round, Gower," he said brusquely, waving at me to be seated. "You know it as well as I do. So let's slice through the *politique*."

"My lord?"

His look hardened. "What do you want, Gower?"

The abruptness of the question startled me. My voice betrayed it. "You — your lordship may have heard of an incident in the city," I said, with an unfamiliar stammer. "A rather grim discovery."

"In the sewers," said the earl.

"Yes, my lord. Sixteen men, murdered, tossed in the ditch."

"Brembre may have said something about it, yes."

"You've spoken directly to the mayor, then?"

"Just once," he said flatly.

"Did he ask for your assistance?"

"He did, at first, and as I told him, London deaths are London's concern, not Westminster's. I have enough to do keeping the lords at bay this season without meddling in the business of gongfarmers."

"I understand, my lord," I said, recalling Strode's recollection of the mayor's exchange with the earl, whose manner was putting me off at the moment. I knew the chancellor as a man of compassion and good judgment. Surely sixteen unexplained deaths beneath the streets of London should be arousing solicitude, not this show of lordly derision.

"What concerns me, my lord — or rather what concerns the Guildhall, and I am here on the city's behalf — is not simply the murders."

"Oh?"

"What is of most concern is the unknown identity of these men, their nameless anonymity. Particularly the manner of their deaths."

His brow edged up. "And how did they die, Gower?"

I hesitated. "They had been shot, my lord.

133

Though not with arrows or bolts."

Silence.

"With guns, my lord."

"Guns," he said.

"Guns."

"Cannon?" said Rune, leaning in.

I shook my head. "Something smaller, as the corpses were largely intact, drilled through with small shot. Nothing much larger than a child's thumb ball." My fingers brushed my thumb, recalling the heft of that first iron ball removed from one of the bodies, its killing weight.

The earl looked to the side. "Quite interesting."

I waited, then said, "It is that, my lord."

He glanced up at Rune, uneasily this time, then back at me. "Let me repeat my first question, Gower. What do you want?"

Once again I felt taken aback by the chancellor's abrupt and peremptory tone, as if I were being impertinent with the questions I asked him, my presence a nuisance. "An answer, your lordship."

"To what question?"

"Where did the killer or killers of these men procure these guns?"

"Explain yourself."

"The city maintains no such handgonnes, as they are known. Nor are they in the possession of the church, and a hunter would hardly choose such instruments of war to bring down a hart. The only store of light artillery anywhere in or around London — if indeed a store exists at all — must lie within the Tower."

Rune stepped out from behind me. I snapped my mouth shut and looked up at his protective sneer. "What are you implying, Gower? That the lord chancellor of England ordered the execution of sixteen unnamed men and had them thrown down a London privy?"

I showed him my palms, lowered my chin. "Nothing of the sort." I looked back at the earl. "Forgive me if I sound accusatory, my lord."

De la Pole waved a hand.

"I am merely suggesting that the weapons that took these men's lives must have originated from within the royal army. As for who wielded them, and why — those are separate questions, and I am at a loss even to speculate at this point. But the guns strike me as a singular piece of evidence. I should be surprised if they don't lead us to the source of this horrific violence."

"Westminster does not investigate common killings," said Rune. "That is the work of sheriffs, justices, and constables, not chancellors and kings."

"They are hardly common killings, my lord," I said, keeping my eyes on the earl. "Over a dozen men, shot through with iron, left to rot beneath —"

"Rot. Now there's an apt word, eh, Rune?" The chancellor looked at his secretary. "Rotting bodies, rotting rights, rotting laws."

"How have I earned your disfavor, my lord?" I said. "Given all that happened in May of last year, your words to me then . . ." I let my voice trail off, asking for a small favor, and a sharper recollection from the earl.

The moment lengthened until finally the chancellor sighed, drummed his fingers on his desk. His jaw shook slightly. "What you've described, these deaths. A horror, and I will lend you what limited assistance I am able. Yet my authority diminishes by the day. You must be aware of the situation with that young fiend the Duke of Gloucester and the earls. FitzAlan, Beauchamp, even Mowbray is in on this plot. They will rise up to oppose me in the coming Parliament, I'll be bound, and against Oxford as well."

"Though deservedly so, in his case," Rune muttered.

The chancellor laughed gruffly at this dismissal of Robert de Vere, the king's sweet-faced favorite, soon to be created duke if the rumors were true: a title properly reserved for those of royal blood, yet given to this braggart with little thought, and littler wisdom. A further sign of the young king's disregard for tradition and propriety in his royal appointments.

"Is it really all as dire as you suggest, my lord?" I said.

The earl tightened his mouth against the tremors. "Imagine yourself standing in the middle of a field, Gower. A field that has been the ground beneath your feet your whole life. You've tilled it, sown it, harrowed it, harvested it, repeated the cycle dozens, perhaps hundreds of times in your memory. You know every inch of the place. You've dug every furrow, hefted every stone, broken every clod."

His gaze moved to the stone behind me. "Suddenly, without warning, the ground begins to shift. You stumble on unfamiliar rocks, tangle yourself in weeds you thought you had torn out from the root long ago. The soil stirs in places, little patches at first but growing, widening, joining together, and soon the entire field is churning at your feet, surging to your ankles. Then, as you watch, parts of the field begin to fall away. Square feet, square yards, misshapen patches of ground the size of rooms, swallowed by the unforgiving earth. Beneath it all is darkness, a great void, and all that prevents you from pitching into it yourself is the final patch of ground beneath your feet."

He sat silently for a time, statued in his narrow chair. "And now you are powerless to do anything but stand there," he said, "waiting for that last bit of earth to dissolve, and you with it."

The chancellor's bleak vision of his deteriorating position left me rattled. I could scarcely believe it had come to this. For time out of mind Michael de la Pole had been a figure of staunch constancy in the realm, as solid as an oak or the stone cross on Cornhill.

"You are the king's conscience, my lord," I said. "If conscience is defeated, what shall become of the realm?"

He narrowed his aged eyes, all withered shapes and angles. "Conscience, that hidden little worm, mining our souls. King Richard, I am afraid, has lost his worm."

A harsh laugh escaped Rune's throat. I looked up at him as he covered it with a shallow cough. "You'll want an avenue to the Tower, then," Rune said to me.

At last. "Though a twisted alley will be sufficient, my lord, so long as it leads me there by and by."

"There is little enough to lose," said the earl, gesturing for Rune to take a seat next to me. "Edmund, what do you say to our dark friend's entreaty?"

Rune settled himself on the corner of my bench, elbows on his knees, his fingers steepled as he talked through the delicacies of the Tower and its administration. "The place is a labyrinth of competing interests. Lieutenants, captains, treasurers, stewards of the wardrobe, the king's mint, the armorers and their craft, the chief officers of the guard. Even the masons have their own little principality down there. Many pies, many fingers and arses to lick."

"I know what you must be thinking, Gower," said the earl before I could reply. "Shouldn't the king's own chancellor have free rein on Tower Hill?"

"The castle and its appurtenances should be adjuncts of your office, my lord," I said. "As close as your own arm."

"A severed arm, perhaps, and not my own," he mused. "Often it feels as if the Tower is as distant from Westminster as Jerusalem itself, or the seat of the Great Khan."

"There are many good men down there, your lordship," Rune allowed. "Men with larger interests than their own." He turned to me with a smirk. "Though not, perhaps, in the armory."

"Who runs it these days?" I asked. The king's armory, though of central importance to the military machinery of the crown, had rarely provoked my interest, and I had no hold on anyone in the king's wardrobe, under whose jurisdiction the armory fell.

Rune's grey eyes flicked briefly toward the earl. "William Snell. Armorer to the king."

I had encountered the name, though never met the man. "What can you tell me about him?"

"Little enough," the chancellor said slowly, bringing his hands together on his desk. "He is a quite remarkable person, our Snell. An exceptional man, of greatest importance to His Highness. King Richard appointed him at the request of his uncle some years ago, before all the factions started tearing at one another's throats."

"Lancaster?"

"Gloucester. Snell was a man-at-arms in the duke's household, and he's been the king's armorer for going on nine years now." Thomas of Woodstock, Duke of Gloucester, was the youngest of the king's uncles, and one of the most powerful of the lords in the rival faction.

Further questions elicited from Rune and the earl that William Snell was at present charged with the building out and improvement of the king's artillery. "Assembling as many guns as he can down there, more guns than the king's armory has seen in all its history," said Rune. "And not only assembling, but improving, enhancing, inventing, searching for the newest techniques and devices from Burgundy and Milan, the best men to rival their makers. He is also amassing gunpowder sufficient for a year's siege and a great battle to follow. Why, last week I was given a bill for a quantity of saltpetre so immense that I sent my clerk back to the Exchequer twice in an hour simply to check the numbers."

"And he is doing all of this with King Richard's approval?" I asked.

The chancellor grimaced. "Certainly not with mine, nor, from what I understand, with Lancaster's." John of Gaunt, Duke of Lancaster and in those years the most powerful force in the realm next to King Richard himself. The king's uncle was abroad in Spain that fall, running a small and ragged kingdom from his base in Ourense, a venture supported by several thousand English and Portuguese troops bought or pressed into a sizable army. The massive company had sailed from Plymouth two months before, leaving a void in the domestic defenses even as the French were massing at Sluys. I had heard no good explanations as to how Gaunt persuaded the king to approve the Castilian venture at such a delicate moment, though the damage was already done.

"Lancaster's absence seems to have knocked loose a nail or two," said the earl. "Snell has convinced himself that his artillery is the most important work in the realm. That London, even England, will stand or fall on the power of these new guns. The man's self-regard knows no limit, it seems."

"Vainglory is the truest engine of our souls, my lord," I said.

"Yes." His eyes settled on me. "You know, Gower, you would find the Tower a fitting subject for one of your poetical fancies. It sits there like a great maw between the river and the walls, swallowing iron, copper, wood, powder, chewing all of it to a paste, then spitting out these strange and barbarous machines, pointing them at the future."

"Not an overly indebted future, I hope."

"A new subsidy is inevitable, I'm afraid," said the chancellor with a heavy sigh. "More taxes, more discontent, more force from above."

"And more rebellion?"

He blinked. "If not from the Commons, then from the Lords, I fear."

He looked at Rune, who nodded my way, signaling the end of our appointment. I rose. The earl's face sagged as he received my bow, then he looked aside, and I left his chambers sour-stomached and perturbed.

Rune walked with me to the great hall. We stood at the end of the passage. A droning bailiff descanted from Common Pleas.

I was about to take my leave of the chancellor's secretary when Rune grasped my elbow, closed in. "Snell has isolated himself down there, Gower," he said, his breath slightly foul on my cheek. "This is more than bureaucratic arrogance. The man thinks himself a kind of god, running the armory like some new Olympus. And he never comes out. Nor does he respond to letters, and our messengers have been beaten, thrashed, threatened with knives and swords. All we get up here are bills and rumors."

"The Tower is less than three miles from where we stand," I pointed out. "Surely his lordship the earl or any other of the higher lords could take a company down there with orders from King Richard and simply turn the man out."

"Surely, you say," he responded with a note of disdain. "You cannot think we haven't considered it, plotted it, mapped it all out? The truth is everyone is so terrified of the man, no one wants to confront him — not with Gaunt and our most tactical military men out of the country, and France massing for an invasion. Snell has himself and his guns and his men bulwarked all along the northern walls, practically daring us to come in and uproot him. A dragon sitting on his hoard. The castle that is supposed to be guarding our city has instead become its greatest vulnerability."

"So what do you suggest, Rune?" I said, hiding my surprise at this show of royal weakness. "Should we commission an actual dragon or two to fire the place? Or hire a mercenary army from Italy, perhaps Hawkwood and his company?"

He turned his face to me. It was stony, free of passion. "Jest if you wish, Gower. But there is more at risk here than you can possibly know. We need every ally we can maintain to help keep the Tower in line. And on the subject of allies, what of Brembre?"

I answered him cautiously. "The mayor is showing some reluctance to pursue the Walbrook murders." I watched Rune's eyes. They narrowed at the edges.

"That is disturbing news, Gower. Shall I confront him myself?"

Rune could sense my hesitation. Though the chancellor and the mayor were both in the king's faction, they had very different interests at stake, and I hardly wished to unsettle relations between the two powerful men. Never stir waters that need no stirring, as my father liked to say. "Nicholas Brembre is no weak-kneed baron, eager to protect an unspotted reputation," I said. "Give me time to lift a few leaves, Rune. If I need another hand pushing on this I will let you and the earl know."

"Good then," he said, looking somewhat mollified. Rune palmed my elbow and shared one last thought. "You will be doing the lord chancellor a fair favor if you can find a way to rattle Snell. Pull him from his moorings down there, put things right. Discover who committed this atrocity, Gower, and the extent of Snell's involvement. It would be a great help at Parliament time should things up here grow . . . dangerous."

So there it was. With one finger in a hornet's nest I was about to shove in an arm, and damn the thousand stings.

CHAPTER 8

Stephen Marsh peered down at the swirled
width of mud far below, the very bottom of
the wide ditch separating the Iron Gate
from the old Well Tower, which stood as the
first-built sentry to the great complex
sprawling to the north and west of him. At
Stephen's insistence his entry to the Tower
late that afternoon would be from the east
rather than from the heavily trafficked
entrance off Tower Street, always crowded
with Londoners seeking alms, favor, and
news. One of Snell's men, after meeting him
at the stairs below St. Katharine's wharf,
had led him up and over this, the narrowest
of passages, to the curtain wall, where he
now stood alone, waiting for his audience
with the king's armorer. It was a glorious
day, crisp and clear, and as he smelled the
autumn air his gaze wandered toward the
river. At the far end of the ditch, where the
moat fosses met the Thames, a brave clutch

of morning bathers sprawled on the wide quay, daring the guard to descend and try to take them. Beyond the swimmers two royal balingers stood out on the river, flashing colorful banners from yardarms and mastheads.

"This way."

Two new guards, one beckoning for him to follow. They walked north, away from the river, over the walls and through several towers. The whole perimeter bristled with men and spears. The sentryway then took them east before their descent through the Bowyer Tower just down from St. Peter ad Vincula, the parish church that lay within the Tower grounds. The guards led him to that end of the wide yard, currently occupied with a hobelar company. Yorkshiremen, judging from the banner held by one of the front-most riders, and though Stephen had always appreciated the vastness of the Tower, he was surprised to see such a quantity of horses at work among the towers and walls.

The guards left him in the yard and disappeared through a low door in one of the wide, squat buildings set against the inner wall. Marsh turned to watch the light cavalry at their martial labor. Champing and impatient in the mellow sun, the horses were agile, well muscled, light on their feet, their riders showing off for the king's archers watching from a side rank. As London had armed itself over the preceding months it had pressed whole hosts of brigades from the shires, regional forces brought in to augment the defenses of the city and the Tower. A mongrel army, was the talk, with little overall discipline, reliant on these pockets of ferocity and skill to engage an enemy of sprawling numbers and unknown strength.

"Forward!" the captain shouted. His board-straight back was to Stephen, his gaze sweeping the company, advancing in three unequal ranks. Four in front, then eight, then twelve. A wedge, as Stephen saw it, the first meant to penetrate the enemy's ranks, with the subsequent lines pouring in behind. The captain backed his horse as he surveyed the moving lines, barking directions here and there.

"Marsh."

Stephen turned to see William Snell standing calmly behind him. He performed a half bow that was answered by a slight nod from the armorer, who assessed him through narrowed eyes birdlike and quick. Snell was a short man, yet taut and muscled, seemingly compacted from the same iron and rock making up the engines and walls around them. As in the tavern a few nights before, he was dressed with little regard to fashion or station, with a laceless and undyed coat thrown over his shoulders and fastened with a belt of twisted wool. The sleeves ended at his elbows in ragged hems, showing strong forearms that ended in thick wrists and fine-boned but coarsened hands.

He caught Stephen looking at his attire. "I am a workingman, Marsh, like you and your men, not some ink-stained scrivener polishing his arse all day in the chancery. Come along."

Turning past the church, Snell took him along a path between the edge of the yard and the low buildings against the north wall, which were joined by a cloisterlike covered walkway built of rough beams and boards. Once inside the airy passage Snell led them from storeroom to storeroom, pausing at every turn to allow Stephen to marvel at the quantities of arms kept by the privy wardrobe. Whole chambers were given over to infantry armor and helms, all glistening with a pungent grease to ward off moisture and rust. Plated shields were stacked by the dozens from end to end and from floor to ceiling, their straps and braces removed for ease of storage and stuffed in bulging sacks suspended from the beam ceiling. The next room was a forest of whittled wood and low skeins of hempstring for the making of bows. Another consisted entirely of cross-bow bolts. These were wrapped by the score in leather and thongs, the bundles stacked to the ceiling in the hundreds. Four, perhaps five thousand bolts, by Stephen's estimation, all neatly stored for easy removal when war finally came.

Now the guns. Snell guided Stephen to the base of one of the larger towers in the complex, looking back at him with a flicker of quiet pride. They stood before a long, narrow portion of the main yard glistening with gunmetal. A team of carpenters was at work fitting the area with an addition to the sloping roof, fixed with notched rafters extending from the lower south wall to the higher tower wall on the north side. Only half the structure had been completed, leaving twenty bare beams jutting like bent masts from beneath the boards.

Snell placed a hand on Stephen's back. "The guns themselves are just metal, of course," the armorer said. "Without powder and shot they are no more than water pipes. We have laid in enough shot — iron, lead, stone — for the defense of London. Of twenty Londons. Look there, and there."

Piled in this portion of the yard were projectiles of numerous shapes and sizes. Pyramids of smoothed stones, crates of iron balls, purses of lead shot, as well as several pairs of casting molds leaning against the stone and answering to the large foundry arrays positioned along the wall. In another temporary room off the yard Snell showed him the strange tools and mechanisms crafted for the charging of the brutal weapons: drills and firing pans, rods and touches.

A cluster of long and narrow tubes sat against a corner timber. Stephen's steps slowed. "May I handle these, Master Snell?"

"At your pleasure, Marsh," said the armorer, looking pleased.

Stephen hefted one of the peculiar guns, inspected it top to bottom. Hollow for its full length, but capped at one end and flared at the other, with a small hole bored through near the capped end. He fingered the hole, guessing at its purpose.

"Come," the armorer said.

Two sentries stood to either side of a heavy wooden door, crossed by strong widths of dulled metal. Six separate locks were positioned along the sides, two of them fastened through eyeholes at either end of an iron bar. Each sentry held the keys to two of the locks on his respective side, and opened them at the armorer's order. Snell worked at the two bar locks, struggling to lift the heavy rod crossing the whole. It fell to the floor with a loud *clong,* bringing another guard hurrying around the corner from the yard. Snell waved him off.

"And here, the heart of the Tower," he said to Stephen. "The heart of England, some would say."

The door groaned open to reveal a modest chamber, no larger than the streetfront room back at the Stone foundry. There the similarities ended, and Stephen could only gape in the half-light cast by the barred window. At least one hundred kegs, each the height of a small child, all banded with iron and tightly sealed. The air was sharp, tinged with the thousand or more pounds of gunpowder sealed in the close chamber. Marsh's eyes watered, his nostrils burning in the acrid air.

Snell scrutinized him. "The most dangerous room in all England."

"Aye, Master Snell," Marsh rasped, imagining what a single coal could accomplish in this enclosed space.

"It's taken a few years to build up an adequate supply," said Snell, a touch of fatherly pride in his voice as he surveyed the lethal store. "Endless shipments of saltpetre. Carts and carts of sulfur and coals, the piss of a hundred bishops." He laughed. Stephen smiled. "But well worth the effort, and we have learned of late how to mix a more stable powder, with a purer burn. Let the forces of France and Burgundy only try to take this fortress. Let them assault this city and its walls, and with everything they have. I shall welcome the challenge, Marsh. Welcome it. From any quarter."

Stephen imagined such a scene. Rivers of blood, brains and offal, limbs blown across the Thames, all from the power of guns.

Snell closed the heavy door, supervised the replacement of the locks, then led Stephen to a quiet corner of the wardrobe complex. They climbed a flight of stone stairs to the upper level of a two-story structure built against one of the northwest towers. In the chamber were a low table and several chairs, a stack of ledgers, a few candles and lamps. A long sword and a battered shield leaned by the door. Along the western wall hung a map of the Tower, ruled and sketched on two thick widths of calfskin sewn roughly together and nailed to the boards behind. A window looked out on the whole of the yard, giving the armorer an impressive view of his domain. The room smelled of damp timbers and sawdust, a welcome change from the acrid wisps of powder still tickling Stephen's nostrils.

Snell started to shut the door to his chamber behind them. It caught on the latch. The armorer had to pull for a moment before the door came closed. "Must have that repaired," he mused as he gestured Stephen toward one of the chairs. "Sit," he said.

Stephen obeyed as Snell took the other chair.

"War is all about logistics, Marsh," the other man began when he was seated. "As the king's armorer I've learned a great deal about the intimacy of war and bureaucracy. A good supply line is every bit as important as a capable company of archers. More important, in many ways, as fighting the Scots taught us last July."

Stephen recalled the news spreading through the city the previous summer. It was little over a year since King Richard had returned from the disastrous campaign in Scotland, provoked by news of a French admiral landing a sizable force at Leith and providing arms and munitions to King Robert. Though the English army had destroyed a few towns and held Edinburgh for a short while, the Scots refused to engage Richard's forces. The result had been a desultory campaign of pillaging and burning that gained the crown little in the way of spoils, and lost it a great deal in prestige.

"We had twelve thousand men mustered at Newcastle for upwards of three weeks," said Snell. "Twelve *thousand,* Marsh, arriving by land and sea, crowding into the streets, camped around the walls, filling the fields, and all of them prattling in their different tongues. Bohemians, Picards, Welshmen, some unhappy Scots. The plain of Babel, spread before the Newcastle keep. It was a contract army, you see, most bought with indentures, and led by a hundred and fifty captains. Half of them had as much business taking men into war as my new daughter."

Stephen smiled at the thought. "War gives you much to consider, Master Snell."

"You have no conception." He coughed loudly into his palm, then settled his hands on his knee. His legs were crossed, and there was a lustful glint in his eyes as he turned his full attention to Stephen.

"Efficiency. Doing more with less. Less food. Less coin. Less powder," he said. "And ultimately, Marsh, less gun."

Less gun. His own words, now coming from the mouth of King Richard's armorer.

He blinked.

"You are a talented man, Stephen Marsh."

"You are too kind, Master Snell."

"Some of the greatest bellfounders in the realm are also some of its greatest gunfounders. Those bombards just there?"

He pointed out the low window, opened to the autumn air. Stephen leaned forward and looked into the yard, where a pair of great cannon stood gaping toward the walls.

"The calibre is forty inches, Marsh. Forty inches! Shoots quarrels the size of a man. These ones are modeled on the guns Artevelde used at Oudenaarde a few years back. Poured at John Feel's foundry, though I wouldn't let Feel stamp the barrels himself. These are the Tower's guns, with the stamp of the royal wardrobe."

John Feel headed up a foundry in Tower Ward. A rival to Stone's, known for good, solid work. "If you have Feel's with you, why do you need Stone's?"

Snell tilted his head. "It is not Stone's I need, Marsh. It is you. Your mind, your skills. Your magic with the metals."

Stephen breathed deeply, feeling a nice surge of pride.

"The Tower has become a teeming bitch of cannon, Marsh. It is a — why, it is a *womb* of guns." The armorer turned and fixed Stephen with iron eyes. "And I want you to train up a new litter for us. A secret litter of guns, fashioned outside these walls."

Stephen looked at the etched calfskins on the wall, the immense sprawl of the royal hold. "Such a prospect would be welcomed by my mistress," he said cautiously. "With my master's death, a royal commission would make all the difference for the stability of the foundry."

Snell barked a short laugh. "Don't play the knave with me, Marsh. This is not a commission to Stone's, for entry in the good widow's ledgers, or prattling among the parish gossips. This is an individual assignment, to you and you alone. Hawisia Stone is to know nothing of it."

Stephen fought against a frown, mindful of Hawisia's sullen mistrust. "If this is to be done at Stone's I'll be forced to fire and forge behind her back yet under her widow's nose. I fear she will catch me out at it and drag me to the wardmoot or the Guildhall. My sentence is already enough of a burden." Ten years. *Ten years.*

"Fear is a distraction, Marsh. One I don't covet this season. I ask you to remember that I am giving you an opportunity here. A chance to serve your king and your country, in an hour of great need." Snell leaned forward to place a hand on the younger man's knee. "We are facing war. The French are massing at Sluys once more, Lancaster is abroad in Castile. Men of talent must band together, give their best to the realm." He smiled broadly. "Besides, everyone knows you are the muscle and mind of that operation. Why you never struck out on your own while you had the chance is a mystery, at least to those I know in your craft. Surely you will find a way to work around her suspicions."

Stephen felt himself nod, his confidence returning. "Aye, Master Snell. I surely will. I will, or the devil take my body and bread."

"Another oath!" Snell's eyes flashed a greyish red in the streaming light. "Good fellow." The armorer patted Stephen's leg again. "You'll learn that I am a hungry man, Marsh. Hungry for progress, for innovation."

"What sort of innovation?"

"You will be working on a new kind of gun, Stephen, and in the process helping me solve a problem that has been perplexing me for some months. A problem of efficiency that only you can solve. It will take many tries, many failures, yet I am confident your mind and hands will find the answer for us."

Stephen reached for one last objection. "Cannon are hard to hide in a foundry, Master Snell, even one as large as Stone's."

He shook his head. "You needn't worry about concealment. You won't be making cannon for us. Nothing as large as a bombard."

"What, then?" Stephen asked.

A long silence followed. Through the window came the blare of a trumpet, the muffled calls of the captains out in the yard, a lion's roar from the menagerie.

"Handgonnes, Marsh," Snell finally said, a finger clawed over his lip. "The future of war. The future of death itself, perhaps."

Handgonnes. A word delicious on the tongue, though coming from the armorer's mouth it rang with the virtues of his office and the guiding spirit of the Tower itself.

Efficiency.

Precision.

Less powder.

Less gun.

Handgonnes.

"Last month I had a vision," said Snell, rising at last from his chair. Stephen was able to breathe again, though also he felt a keen longing to remain with the man in the confines of the Tower, to do this work here, with the fine tools and hot forges of the crown, rather than return to the bleak drudgery of Stone's foundry.

Snell had gone to the window and now looked out on the width of the Tower yard. "I saw a city on a plain, ringed with fire and belching smoke. A battle, one conscripting every man, every woman, every child within its walls to join the great fight. Every last soul."

His voice softened, and he spoke the next words as if recounting a saint's miracle witnessed with his own eyes. "And they all had guns, Marsh. The women, the boys, even the littlest of girls." Now a whisper, a soft breath of wonder. "They all had guns."

There was a low aperture beneath the eaves of the building, above the window now filled with the armorer's sturdy frame. Through this upper opening came a hazy gleam, the late hour of a dwindling day. Snell's head appeared to Stephen's eyes within a blazing circle of fire as the armorer began to expound on this new world of guns and shot.

"Let me tell you my dream."

CHAPTER 9

Poison, gallows, sword, hammer, faggot, gun, knife, arrow, tub, cross; berries, wood, hemp, iron, sulfur, river; earth, air, fire, water: man, it seems, is capable of fashioning nearly anything into an instrument of death. Four tired nags too old to plow a field can pull a living man apart. Samson slew an army with the jawbone of an ass. The earth is a verdant field of weapons.

Michaelmas, and as a small goose roasted in the kitchen I spent that morning in my study, sifting through what Chaucer had sent me from his house and offices in Greenwich. The package had reached me by means of a parliamentary messenger riding from Kent on his way to Westminster, stopping off in Southwark to deliver a letter and its accompanying matter. A leather packet, thonged and sealed. Recognizing the impression, I broke the wax and unstrung the parchment threading. Always an ambivalent pleasure, our trade in poetry, and I was in no mood for the frivolous or the bawdy.

I needn't have worried. Inside was a thin quire of eight folios, covered by a brief letter from Chaucer.

To the worthy and right worshipful sir, John Gower of St. Mary Overie in Southwark

Worshipful sir, I commend to you this humble quire, inked with sixteen tragedies that we hope will be pleasing to your ears, if not your eyes — for which I daily pray, old friend. Send us your own offerings when committed to sheepskin. We also appeal to your great courtesy in asking that you delay no longer in visiting us in Greenwich, home to many a shrew, and scoundrels aplenty. A man of your habits and skills would feel quite at home in these village precincts.

Leave aside your dark matter for a few days, John. London can surely spare your lurking presence.

Your prideful servant,
Geoffrey Chaucer

The invitation worked at my conscience, and I recalled our last exchange at Aldgate before Chaucer's final departure from

London. For months I had been meaning to take a horse or a walk to the Thamesside village, a short distance from Southwark. Chaucer had vacated the city so thoroughly since the last autumn that it could often seem as if he had never lived here at all.

At least I had his verse. I sat to read, adjusting a candle at each side of the quire, lined with one of the tales that would go into this pilgrimage collection he was sketching out. I had read several others in the past two years, every one of them peculiar, distinctive, uniquely his own. Romances, fabliaux, moral fables, tedious sermons, lives of the saints: he was building a strange mélange of stories, to no purpose I could yet discern.

This tale, to be told by a monk, sang more darkly than his usual fare, whispering of the many dead. It had been divided into a series of smaller parables, all concerning great men who suffer a hard and inevitable fall. Chaucer had written it in eight-line stanzas, ten syllables to the line.

> I would bewail in manner of tragedy
> The harm of them who stood in high
>   degree
> And fell so far, there was no remedy
> To rescue them from their adversity.

163

> For know this: when Fortune wishes to flee,
> No man may her delay, nor fate withhold;
> Let no man trust in blind prosperity.
> Beware of these examples, true and old!

A monkish sentiment. Even the highest men must drop like stones, to settle in the mud. What followed were brief accounts of sixteen men who met their deaths in some form of misery: exile, murder, deposition. Chaucer included among the monk's examples both the ancient and biblical — Adam, Samson, Hercules, Caesar — as well as contemporary greats only recently deceased. Pedro of Castile, Hugh of Pisa, even Bernabò Visconti, the lord of Milan who had passed away in December.

We know we are writing tragedy, I once heard Chaucer say, *when our verses weep for Fortune's assault upon the proud.* Chaucer, one of the most blindly vain men I knew, loved nothing more than attacking the vice of pride in his own verse, yet beneath the particolored skein of this monk's stories I discerned a subtle warning to certain magnates of the realm. King's favorites all, and Richard kept them in subsidies and baubles, created them earls and dukes with no counsel from the wise. Men whose hold on power seemed always on the edge of collapse, yet who managed to survive the various turns in royal favor.

Nor was I alone in sensing a quick and lethal shift afoot in the realm, its traces winding stealthily through Chaucer's pretty tales. Whispers of discontent, of angry lords and weakening wills, of a sinking softness at the top. The tense truce between King Richard and the Duke of Lancaster had held for several years, notwithstanding some notable gaps. Yet Lancaster was in Spain that fall and would remain there for many months, leaving behind a void that other magnates seemed only too eager to fill with their grudges and cavilings.

A monk's warnings are not to be taken lightly, even if voiced by a poet toying with his oldest friend. Sixteen deaths indeed, I thought grimly. *Watch yourselves, my lords,* this monk's tale warned the realm, *or you too shall suffer a long fall, and meet your end in a sewer.*

"Another messenger, Master Gower." Will Cooper, appearing in mid-stanza. "This one from Heath, concerning a new prisoner."

Lewis Heath, a beadle of Lime Street Ward. I had several men there, as I did in most of the wards, paid to bring me news as it arose. Anyone above a common laborer brought into the city gaols and I would likely hear about it.

"It is Peter Norris," Will continued, his voice somewhat strained. "He has been taken for theft, and jailed at the Counter." One of the city's three busier gaols, holding pens for criminals of all varieties.

"Which?"

"In the Poultry," said Will. "He is to go before the Mayor's Court Tuesday morning."

The news came as little surprise. For a habitual thief like Norris there was a short ladder from the stocks to the gallows, despite his former prominence in the city government.

"Will?"

"Yes, Master Gower?"

"Did you learn what he stole?"

He hesitated, knowing the implications. "Gold wares, Master Gower. A cup, I am told, and a girdle of purses. He had them in hand when taken."

I sighed. Steal a pair of breeches and Peter Norris might have returned to the stocks, perhaps lost a foot. But pinching items like this meant he would need some extraordinary luck not to hang.

On the Tuesday I went across the river for Norris's trial, with the likely futile aim of

166

learning the name of his witness. The Guildhall always stank on court days. Though the building's large main chamber normally felt airy and spacious, the ritual of gaol delivery would empty the city's prisons, their inhabitants led over to be crammed into the northeast corner, screened off from the trestle tables at either end that served as the mayor's and sheriffs' benches for the twice-weekly sessions of the city courts. There they would stand until their matter was called, a thicket of dirt and fleas, the itchy scent filling the hall, with no breeze to mitigate the foul air. Some of these poor souls had lain in the Counter or Newgate for weeks, fed little more than crumbs, and showing it: gaunt faces, thinned limbs, bones protruding from shoulders and cheeks.

On that day a dozen prisoners awaited their turn before the city court. The accused were mostly men, though a few women were mixed in, all of them visibly aware of the sad spectacle they had become. They were a striking contrast to those at the Guildhall on civil matters, which would be heard before the common council. All men, most with self-important airs about them, seated in a double row around the open square of tables formed by the mayor and aldermen, awaiting their moment. One of Brembre's recent and more controversial innovations, this allowance for spectators at the city courts seemed to me little more than a show of power, of a piece with the man's preference for elaborate and expensive ceremony at every opportunity. I found a seat along the low cabinets by the Guildhall's northern wall, allowing me to watch the proceedings at the bench while keeping an eye on the prisoners.

Peter Norris stood at the end of a loose middle rank, angled against the wall, his eyes downcast, his shoulders slumped, a man already resigned to his fate. His cheeks and chin had been shaved to the skin. The hangman likes a clean neck.

At the west end of the hall was the mayor's bench, positioned on a movable dais raised several feet above the floor. Brembre himself sat in the middle, with the city's aldermen stretched beside and beneath him along the adjacent tables, all gazing down at the lower benches and the accused, who came forward to the bar one by one to answer to the charges or suits against them. The area before the bench was separated from the crowd by a low wooden barrier extending around the three sides, keeping the rabble at bay.

Always some useful surprises in the mayor's court, and in former years I had attended nearly every week, eager to gather what buds I could, though that day the civil matters offered little that was not routine. Aliens admitted to the freedom of the city, a dispute over the capture and cooking of an errant street pig, a wife and husband sent to the pillory for tearing a neighbor's hood. The parties and the witnesses were demonstrative, and the arguments could be heated, but the court's decisions brooked no argument. The matters heard in the first hour were all too minor for any kind of appeal, with the mayor's judgment taken as final. Brembre looked both bored and in a hurry, surely eager to return to the more significant matters under debate up the river in Westminster. Parliament had opened the day before, and the mayor had little patience for the squabbles of ward and parish when the future of the kingdom was at stake.

It was nearing the hour of eleven by the time the court came to the criminals. The bailiff called out the names of the jury members, gathered from various wards for that week's service, with the sentences tailored to fit the crime or violation in question. A grocer accused of leavening his spices would forfeit his shop to the city for the space of a year. Others would go to the pillory for the minor theft of an egg or the selling of bad beef.

Yet for certain of these Londoners life and limb were at stake. The Guildhall's work here was quick and cruel, despite the moderating influence of the jury. Two horse thieves would hang that very afternoon, while a Dutchman who had twice escaped from Newgate was sentenced to the severing of his left leg below the knee. Still another man, a blacksmith barely out of his apprenticeship, would lose his hand, and with it his livelihood, for striking the alderman of Cripplegate Ward in a dispute over a property boundary. The alderman preened happily at his victory, and the thought of the axe.

The saddest aspect of the law's application in such cases, sadder to me the older I grow, is the pathetic reactions of the families of those convicted. You could hear their sobs, the loud anguish from Guildhall Yard as each sentence was delivered within and announced by the mayor's caller outside. The mother of one of the horse thieves, rushing for her condemned son, held back inside the door by a ward constable and struggling in his arms. The fresh young wife of the smith, a hooded rose who would never again feel her husband's strong grip at her waist. The Guildhall practiced a justice of arbitrary cruelty, made worse in the last year by a departing mayor with something to prove.

Eventually Peter Norris's matter was called. The tension increased, the aldermen exchanging looks around the bench, as Norris's former position in the city government was well known. The bailiff read out his offense in his bureaucrat's dull hum.

"Be it known to all present that on the Thursday last, the eve of Michaelmas, in the tenth year of the reign of King Richard II, Peter Norris, vagrant, did feloniously remove two gold cups, a silver ewer, four purses of nobles and half nobles, and other smaller goods from the shop of Master Henry Gibbe, guildsman in the parish of St. Michael Paternoster, and that upon being spied by the curate of that parish, viz. Richard Hering, said Peter Norris, vagrant, did then flee through the streets, with four men of the parish in pursuit, viz. Peter Blome, John Braham, John Refham, and William le Tabler, and that upon reaching Bishopsgate said Peter Norris, vagrant, was apprehended by said men of the parish, with said gold cups, ewer, purses, etc. on his person and in his possession, by which evidence . . ."

The bailiff's account went on to detail Norris's arrest and imprisonment, along with his futile repentance before his jailers. In addition to the theft, Norris was being pinned with vagrancy: the ultimate insult for a former ward beadle, and a charge that would render any leniency on the mayor's part all the more unlikely.

The proceeding went quickly, with the curate and two of the four parishioners giving their testimony. No facts were in dispute, the verdict rendered with little ceremony. Norris's face had gradually whitened as his doom became clear, and when the time came for him to speak he had been reduced to a quivering mess, his skin an ashen grey, his voice rasping as he attempted to utter some words of regret. He stammered once, again, then clamped shut his lips and eyelids.

"Speak up then," said the bailiff, poking Norris in the gut with his rod. "Have you any words to say for yourself, Norris?"

"Only, my lords . . ." His head swiveled from side to side, owl-like, though his eyes remained closed. "Only that what I did was done of out the barest need, and done for my son, though I am dreadful sorry for the theft, dreadful sorry, my lords. But I

172

couldn't let him starve, not young Jack. Couldn't bear to see him —"

"We are no fellows of yours, Norris," said Brembre, half standing and leaning forward from the bench, unable to resist a final show of superiority over the diminished man. "Regret will buy you nothing here."

Norris lifted his chin. "Then perhaps I might use another coin, your lordship, for I have information for the aldermen of the city," he said quickly. "It concerns the recent killings, the bodies in —"

"We'll hear none of your lies, Norris," said Brembre.

"Yet I have a witness, my lords!"

"You have *nothing,*" the mayor snarled, and the chamber went silent. Brembre spoke into the quiet. "Now still your tongue or it will be sliced from your mouth this very hour."

Another moment of silence, then, "With respect, Lord Mayor," someone said from the dais, "should we perhaps listen to what the man has to say?"

All heads turned to the speaker. He was, I saw to my delight, William Rysyng, prior of Holy Trinity and the alderman of Portsoken Ward. It was a peculiar arrangement, though one in effect for many years: ever since King Henry I had granted the entirety of Portso-

173

ken to the priory by the city's east gate, the prior had served ex officio as the ward's alderman. While Rysyng's two most recent predecessors had designated worldly men to serve in their places, deeming the civic office unfit for the sober life of an Augustinian canon, Rysyng had embraced his urban duties, involving himself in city affairs with an almost perverse glee. He was the only clergyman among the city's aldermen, who generally served shorter terms. Not Rysyng. Going on his ninth year in office, the prior was a fixture at the Guildhall, exercising a power within the city bureaucracy surpassed only by the mayor's own.

The prior was seated to the mayor's left, his hand held up to delay the proceedings. It was not uncommon for such ripples to move through the mayor's court for one reason or another: a clerical question, a technical knot, a last-minute bribe.

Brembre turned on Rysyng with a dog's snarl. "Not in this hall, Reverend Father. Not while I am mayor of this city. Is that understood?"

Rysyng kept his head high. "It is, Lord Mayor," he said.

"Good," said Brembre, though as the mayor brought his glare back down upon Norris I saw Rysyng exchange dark looks with several of the other men around the tables. Excellent, I thought. Rysyng was one of three or four aldermen on whom I held quite damaging information, though in his case I had yet to use what I possessed. I would visit the priory by Aldgate tomorrow.

As the cursory trial continued I looked over and across the bench, my eyes alighting on a slouching figure wedged against the far end of the bar. It was young Jack Norris, Peter's son. The Earl of Earless, as the taunts named him, and he made a pitiful figure there in the depths of the Guildhall, his close-spaced and mournful eyes watching the proceeding unfold. His father's short trial was soon concluded, the sentence pronounced. Norris would hang.

This mayor tolerated no delay in the execution of London's convicted. Peter Norris and the two horse thieves were to be roped immediately — not at the Smithfield gibbet but out at Tyburn, as Brembre liked to keep the city free of corpses during Parliament time. The Guildhall was already emptying for the trek to the gallows, a choir of Londoners processing to sing the city's crude office of execution. I rose with them, intent on getting a name out of Norris before his departure for the scaffold. Though the mayor's court was still in session, the crowd had massed at the Guild-hall's south door, where I joined the depart-ing throng.

I hurried from the Guildhall, crossed Al-dermanbury, and jogged down to Cheap-side, where the procession had slowed and lengthened considerably as it picked up interested spectators. Norris and the horse thieves had been stripped and thrown into a long, narrow cart drawn by two nags, led by a smirking young man strutting importantly at the head of it all. Along each side of the cart walked two of Brembre's armed pur-suivants, noses up, searching the crowd for the cantankerous and drunk. Another kept up the rear, just to the back of the rickety contrivance. The expanding mass of Lon-doners was raucous but not disorderly, humming with the lurid excitement of the multiple deaths to come.

London is a forgetful, even forgiving city. Only five years before, in the wake of the Rising, the crown had erected gallows across the city to string up hundreds of rebels, many of them surely kin to some of the slavering crowd now panting after the noose. Memory, I mused as I walked, will lose out to oblivion every time.

The procession had passed over the Fleet before I managed to catch up with the cart.

I slowed now, and handed the rearmost guard two groats to let me take his place for a moment. He edged to the left, leaving me just feet from Peter Norris and the other thieves.

The three condemned men sat naked in the cart, legs entangled, hands bound with rope, heads lolling along the splintered rails. Already dead, in all the ways that mattered.

"Norris," I said.

Nothing.

"Norris," I said more loudly.

His eyes, grimed and smeared, fluttered open. His head rolled to the side. He gave me a tired scowl.

"Forget about me, Gower," he said through the noise. "It's too late for your contrivances and connivings. We both know it."

One of the thieves looked up for a moment, took us in, then let his chin sink back to his chest.

"About Jack," I said. The constable gave me a warning look, fingered his thumb. I slipped him another coin.

"What about him?" said Norris, looking off to the side. The procession had reached the far end of Holbourne, where the road narrowed and bent northward, leaving the city's last outskirts behind. Before us stretched the parish of St. Giles-in-the-Fields, the broken spires of the leper hospital rising above the fallow plain. I heard song, faint and unenthusiastic. I looked at the sun. The brothers in the hospital chapel, intoning the work of God.

"Have you spoken to anyone about taking him in?"

"He'll be a ward of the city, now I'm gone," said Norris. "Your friend Strode will see to that, I suspect. Unless you want the little brigand for yourself." A weak laugh, fading quickly. "His father's son, that one."

"Wardship is reserved for the moral and upstanding," I said as the cart creaked on. "But your son is a cutpurse and a rising felon, with a mutilated head. He will be turned out of the city if he's not hanged like you first. You want that for him?"

He twisted in the cart.

"I will set him up nicely, Norris," I said. "He won't lack for meals and shelter, I can promise you."

His scowl deepened. "Why would you do such a thing, Gower?"

I took a step closer, risked leaning over the edge of the cart, and whispered, "Your witness, Norris. His name —"

Just then a new murmuring went up from the crowd. A postern door along the north

178

wall of St. Giles had opened to reveal a gaunt figure limping from the hospital churchyard. A large hood flopped sloppily around his head and his thin neck, hiding his face. Behind him walked a brother of St. Lazarus, hale enough, to judge by his appearance, bearing a bucket and dipper. The crowd parted for the two denizens of the hospital as they neared the cart, which slowed to a halt for the dreary ritual. The lame man looked up at the prisoners, and I caught a glimpse of his face. Scarred, slashed with crusted pustules, though not with the signs of leprosy. One of the crown's decayed domestics, I suspected, and a late case of the pox.

One of the constables took the bucket, the other the dipper, and final ales were served out to the condemned. The three men sipped eagerly, as if some grain of salvation had been fermented into the heavy brew shared among the doomed. I waited as the constables finished the remaining drink. One of them returned the bucket and dipper to the St. Lazarus brother, who led the afflicted man back into the hospital grounds. With that, the procession began anew.

"A name, Norris," I said as the cart groaned along. "All I want is a name. Why did Brembre keep you from speaking it at the Guildhall?"

Norris's eyes had closed again. I reached out and pressed his bare arm, hanging loosely against a cart rail. My hand nearly recoiled. His skin was cold to the touch, clammy, despite the full sun. He looked down at my fingers, then at me.

"Brembre, you say?" His eyes flashed, suddenly alert. "That scabbed swindler! You tell Nicholas Brembre I'll be back for him, back from the grave. You tell him that for me, John Gower."

"Think of your son, Peter. Young Jack."

"A son, a sack of coin, the things we leave behind." He turned and spat over the side of the cart. "All the same in the end, isn't it?"

Now a new agitation. His hands struggled against the shared ropes, drawing low moans of protest from the other prisoners, whose limbs moved in tandem. "Save his hands, Gower, if you can," said Norris, his eyes flashing with new awareness, as if he had suddenly woken from a stupor. He strained to lean back toward me. His mouth gaped, and he whispered hoarsely, "First the boy's ears, and next they'll take his hands. You must save his hands, John Gower, you must!"

"A name, Norris. Only a name, and his

hands shall be safe. Your witness, Norris."

He looked up at the clouds, then at me. "Jack," he said, with the saddest of smiles. "Jack's his name, isn't it?"

Those were his final words to me, and it was clear I would get no more. It was enough. I slowed my steps as the cart pulled forward and the press thronged in.

A labored trudge up the Oxford Road brought us to the Tyburn Tree, freshly cleared of its most recent danglers. The crowd pooled almost luxuriously around the triangular scaffold as the cart creaked to a halt. The constables moved quickly to remove the three condemned. They were pitiful in their nakedness, their backs bent, their forms huddled forward as if to clutch at what dignity remained to them as they faced the high beams looming overhead.

To watch a man hang is like nothing else on this earth. For no other violation puts the body through such strange paroxysms, nor reminds us so starkly of what life is and what it is not. The quickness and quality of death on the noose depend in part on the relative talent or perversion of the hangman. Just as often, though, they are a matter of luck.

The horse thieves were fortunate that day, their necks snapping as soon as the rope tightened, their bodies swaying gently before us, disappointing the spectators.

Peter Norris's death was of another order, and far worse than most on the gallows. The drop, a jerk of his head, a heave of his full frame, the silence lengthening, and I thought it was done. So did he, it seemed, until his expiring mind awoke to his predicament. His frame jerked. His tongue shot from his mouth. A river of drool slathered his chin. Above it all his widened eyes bulged outward from their sockets, as if his skull were a bagpipe bladder invisibly squeezed.

Worse was what happened below, as it will sometimes do. His bowels emptied in one loud and liquid rush, soiling his legs and feet and leaving him a dribbling mess. His member, a flaccid nothing amidst the thick bristles of his lower hair, became stiffened and engorged, jutting obscenely outward as his body endured its final convulsions. This last indignity inspired a round of delighted shouts and claps from the assemblage, which treated the rude spectacle of Norris's passing as they might the performance of a shrewish Noah's wife in a mystery play.

Finally Norris's soul had had enough. It abandoned his ruined flesh without a whisper, leaving just this dangling thing, man no more but spiritless flesh. I closed my eyes, said a prayer. When I opened them again the crowd had already started to disperse, its attention seeking new diversions, and turned coldly from these three dark drops against the cloudless sky.

Only one other remained in the gathering silence as the crowd made its way back to the walls. He stood directly across the Tyburn green from my position, his face small, round, pale. It was Jack Norris, watching his father's ruined body swing and twist in the gentle breeze. The boy — the witness — had lost his cap, leaving the stubs of his severed ears plainly visible beneath the strawlike thatches of his hair. His features were still, his eyes expressionless. What had those eyes seen, what knowledge lurked behind them in that cutpurse's brain of his?

"Jack," I said. He swiveled his head. His eyes widened when he saw me. I took a step toward him. "You remember me, Jack." Another step. "We met in the yard, before Ludgate." Two more. "I bought you pies."

Speaking to children has never been one of my stronger skills. Feeling like a fool, I could only watch as he turned and sprinted off toward Holbourne, reaching the edges of the crowd before I had even left the Tyburn round. He looked back just once

before being dissolved into the press of
Londoners fresh from the killing of three of
their own.

CHAPTER 10

A clouded moon that night, though the dark hardly helped. In the smallest hours Hawisia, assaulted by the pounding kicks of her unborn child, rose to take turns around the upper rooms. She bent against walls, stretched her sore legs, and in the end descended to the larder for a little something to stave off the hunger. A wedge of cheese, some cider, a hunk of rough bread. The walking helped, though less than it had a few weeks before.

The climb back upstairs tired her further, moistened her face. She turned into the narrow cutout between the upper bedchambers and paused at the window, pushing open the shutter to get a bit of air. As she leaned out into a chill breeze her gaze wandered from the stars over the city rooftops and down into the foundry yard, cast in a darkness complete but for a narrow smear of light coming from the far side.

Well, that wasn't as it should be.

She peered down across the darkened yard at the smithy, a half-roofed, squat structure that occupied one corner of the Stone complex. From beneath the eaves on the building's west side shone the cone of lamplight she'd spied from the window. She listened, palm cupped at her ear, and caught the faintest sound of metal on metal, metal on wood.

Tap tap. Scrape.
Tap tap. Scrape.
Tap tap. Scrape.

Night work in the smithy, her own smithy! A practice strictly prohibited by the guild regulations, had been for an eternity, and there wasn't one man in the whole Stone operation who didn't know it, who hadn't had that unbending principle of the craft ground into him in his first weeks under the foundry roof. Smithing at night produced inferior work, when you were more likely to slip weak metals onto the forge, make infernal sounds that would wake the parish, goad its fury like nothing else.

Hawisia stomped down the back stairs and through the house to the yard door, where she reached for the heavy wooden club kept leaning within. Mostly for shooing away slaughter beasts escaped from the shambles, or beating off hungry dogs, or going after the occasional thief on the prowl for copper or tin. But a reliable weapon, and it would do fine for the wayward apprentice or guildsman risking a large fine under Stone's roof.

Once in the yard she silenced the door behind her and hefted the wooden club, feeling its weight, intent on delivering a well-deserved beating to whichever of the foundry's workers might be violating the ordinances and risking her livelihood.

As she left the house behind she felt another stab of anger. Even from across the yard she could tell the forge was lit. An infernal glow came from the bed of coals, while smoke rose from the chimney to curl around the brighter stars. Hawisia could not tolerate such defiance in her shop. Fire or no, the night work would have to stop, and it was up to her to see that it did. She stopped some twenty feet from the near edge of the smithy and peered beneath the eaves.

Stephen Marsh. She could make out his broad form, shoulders bent over his work. He stood between the anvil and the finishing table against the tool wall. She shivered, furious at him for swatting away the house's rules yet reluctant to interrupt him, intent as he was in that moment. The man had been sullen for days on end. Hawisia needed him working and working well. If the night was what it took to get his craftsman's blood flowing its fastest, should she allow it?

Their difficult relations aside, it was always a thing of fascination for Hawisia, to watch Stephen Marsh at his rough magic. His hands gliding from wall to bench and back, taking one tool, then another, replacing each before lifting the next, all done with the deftness of a limner switching out his brushes. A file, an awl, pliers, a hammer, another file, the awl. Every now and again he would pause in his tinkering; lift the piece of metal before him in the lamplight; heat it on the coals; move his hands apart, then together, testing out the product of his subtle labor.

From her angle Hawisia could not make out what the object was, just that it seemed to be small, precise, crafty — and worth the skulking secrecy of the dark.

Ignoring the shooting pains down her legs she watched Marsh for an hour or more, her heavy middle brushing against a post, her weight shifting every little while to keep the blood running. The club was drooped at her side, forgotten as she kept this strange vigil.

At some point in the still night Stephen put a hand to his lower back, straightened, stretched, and yawned, then started to put away the tools and neaten the bench and wall. Before he extinguished the lamp Hawisia watched him reach up, rest a knee on the high bench, and place the object of his labor on the topmost shelf, a plain board otherwise bare running across the width of the bench. She turned quietly for the yard and bed, her limbs screaming for rest, her mind grasping at the riddle she'd witnessed.

The next morning she woke before the sun and stole across the yard, reaching the smithy before any of the apprentices left their shared rooms at the far end of the foundry to start the fires. Once beneath the eaves she pulled over a stool. One foot up, the other on the bench, and with a hand on the lower shelves she hauled herself upright, finding a dangerous balance between stool and bench. She reached up and over, searching blindly with her left hand, first here, then there, then —

There.

Smooth, curved, cold to the touch, and when she brought it before her eyes she could scarcely believe that Marsh had risked those night hours and her own wrath in fashioning such a little nothing — nor that she'd risked her babe and her neck to discover it. The thing could have been a child's bauble, this light length of metal. It gaped open at one end to show four prong-like teeth, then curled majestically to the side and back, and ended in an extravagant coil of spirals that left just enough room for the easy insertion of a finger or a thumb.

Yet the gadget was more cleverly made than it first appeared. On its underside was a narrow rod, and at the bottom of that a subtle hinge, as if the contraption were meant for attaching to some other, larger device.

Hawisia reached up and returned the object to the upper shelf. She left the smithy more bewildered than angry, and spent the whole of that day puzzling over the nature and use of what she had seen and touched, this sinister thing Stephen Marsh had fashioned in the dark of the moon.

A serpent.

PART II

CHAPTER 11

Another byway on the road north, another common hostelry, another night with him, and yet the miles of travel, she found, had not weakened but strengthened her. Margery's arms felt steady and firm at the reins, the muscles in her legs and buttocks were finding new reserves of endurance, and her middle was tightening into a hard circumference of muscle and effort. There were worse things, she supposed, than a week on one of the safer roads, the autumn sun on your face and an October breeze teasing the hair out from beneath your hood, riding it up to curl around your ears, down to whisper against your lips.

Much worse things. Like a hanging, or a season in a cell, or an iron ball in the heart.

He too sat taller on his new horse, the roan mare taken as a replacement from the inn now some days to the south.

Robert Faulk rode well for what he was.

She hadn't told him so, as every time she paid him a kind word his cheeks reddened, and he stammered and hawed in ways she didn't like. It was true, nonetheless, and she felt silently grateful for the willingness he had shown to adjust. Like a poor orphan given over to a wealthy ward, finding a new way and its unfamiliar patterns.

Unfamiliar patterns. As their company turned for the waiting stableboy, come out to greet them from the inn's barn, she felt it again. That tightening, a tensing of something deep within her. It had been like this for the last several days, since that Westminster messenger had nearly sent her into a fit. There was no explaining it, really, though she suspected it had little to do with Robert and everything to do with their flight.

Why, who would find it surprising that such a harrowing adventure would lead to new twinges here or there, as her mind and her flesh molded themselves to the stark realities of this unwonted exile from the dreads of her former life? It was only natural that she would feel a slight tingle as this man handed her down to the mounting block, his skin rough and dry on her palm, his eyes respectfully averted from her feminine form, as was proper.

Yet why did this agitate her further? Why

was she craving the touch of those eyes, the grip of those callused hands? She pushed away the unclean thoughts and allowed the boy to take her horse.

With their beasts stabled they followed the company into the front eating room. There was no separate chamber for gentles at this less spacious inn, and she found it a relief to mingle with the others, to dine without the close intensity of his singular presence.

It was a diverse array that had set out from the Bethlem Priory, just north of the London walls. Seven men, five women, twelve all told including themselves, and as she sat with the women, listened in on their talk, she learned what had brought them there, what circumstances of life and longing had provoked them to make the long journey to Durham and the holy bones of St. Cuthbert.

Two were sisters, Catherine and Constance. Widows both, husbands years in their graves, and a more accomplished pair of pilgrims would have been hard to find.

Yes, we have been to Jerusalem, they boasted loudly, walked in the footsteps of our Savior Jesu, trod the stations of His Passion, prayed on the hill of Calvary. They had taken in St. James at Compostela along

195

the way, as well as Rome, where they enjoyed an audience with English bishops and a cardinal at the Curia, receiving blessings and pilgrims' alms from all. Weeks on an old hulk in the great sea, a month in the blood-drying heat of the Holy Land, then home again, and who was to say they wouldn't attempt the journey again before they died?

"And Canterbury?" someone asked. "Have you made the journey to Becket's tomb?" There followed an uncomfortable pause, which Constance broke with a light and condescending laugh.

"Why yes, my lovely, we have been to Canterbury once or twice, have we not, Catherine?"

"Oh, twice or thrice, I'd wager, twice or thrice," said her sister, her eyes sparkling with amusement. "Though never Durham."

"No, never the Palatinate," Constance allowed. "So here we are, filling a little gap!"

The next woman, Evota, a pert young wife with a wandering eye and a rich liking for gossip, was traveling with her new husband, "the slight fellow with the yellow face and that lovely lump of suet on his chin," as she described the poor man and his unfortunate carbuncle. He was yeoman to an Austin canon of Durham, to which they were returning after a sojourn in London to retrieve the inheritance left by her late departed father. "Sixteen pounds, and a silver ring," she said, holding it up for them. "Tried to leave me his cooking pots as well, though we sold them to the peddler for a few pence rather than haul them along."

Maud, the fourth, was also young though great with child. "With a bastard, I'll warrant," Constance had loudly opined. This seemed to be the case. Her father was a tight-lipped mercer of Queenhithe Ward. The talk was that the pair were bound for Durham to rid the family of the child's stain.

Margery was the last, and she answered their questions with the same lies and half-truths she had spun in her mind from the beginning. We are from a village on the Sussex coast, up from Brighthelmstone. Our only child, a girl of six days, gone to her grave, and before her mandated baptism. The fever. How to assure her eternal rest, to save her unblessed soul from the fires of purgation?

A pilgrimage, they had decided with the parson. To what shrine? Durham in the Palatinate, he had advised them, and the shrine of St. Cuthbert. For old Cuthbert is the saint of incorruptibility, a reminder of

God's triumph over death. Let this long journey north along the length of all England serve as a pilgrimage of thy soul to sweet Jesu, and soothe thee and the soul of thy babe in the balm of His eternal and undying love.

"So we departed," she said softly, "our little Alys dead only a fortnight, and it is all my Antony can do to stay on his horse, his heart sits so heavy in that strong chest." The women all looked over at that strong chest and the ruddy face above it, cooing in sympathy as they imagined the sorrow of this bereft father, pictured the ways he might be comforted.

This was the story she told them, to some moist eyes and pats on the hand, for how could she tell them her true tale, the sum of all that had brought her here?

A husband may do what he wishes with the flesh and flower of his wife. Walter had always liked to remind her of this, quoting canon law as he smacked her face, broke her ribs, ruined her inner flesh front and back, and it seemed that was the only sentence of the church's decretals that meant anything to him. He'd had two years at Oxford in his bachelorhood, failed miserably reading theology, then he returned to Kent to suck once more at the small teat of his father, a gentleman of modest means albeit well respected in the shire — despite his wastrel of a third son. By the time Walter married her he'd become a bitter, sullen man, often drunk, full of foul smells and ugly noises. From the start he had treated her like one of the deer carcasses brought back from his slovenly hunts. There had been no escape, it seemed. Until there was.

Margery felt a hand press her arm. It was Constance, leaning against her. "Bear up, dearest. Eleven children I bore, and but six live now, the rest sleeping with God. It is our woman's lot, such suffering, daughters of Eve as we are. St. Cuthbert will comfort your soul, you shall see."

"Aye, he will that," said her sister, Catherine, with a pious nod, and a sober quiet settled around the board.

The men, hearing nothing of the exchange, were as loud as they liked, relieved to be off their tails for the day, installed around a table with ample ale to dip and share from the common cask. As the women resumed their own conversation she caught his eye, as a wife does, smiled openly at him in the candlelight. His own eyes widened in surprise, thrilled her with a gleam of unspoken want.

Over the following hours the room filled

with villagers, there to mingle with the pilgrims passing through, and to hear the news from London and beyond. A large crowd, at least forty strong. Out here there was little of the rough trade she'd heard was common in the city taverns. In London a gentlewoman like her would not be seen in such a place, yet here she felt unobtrusive, welcomed by the diverse company.

Margery found herself more at ease that evening than she had felt for many months. Robert seemed content as well, happily playing the lower gentleman's part, drinking neither too much nor too little, affecting an air of light condescension toward men who were surely his betters. He was easing into this strange role circumstance had forced on him, and playing it well.

Someone in a far corner began to sing. A ballad from the north country, one she had never heard, and a dark song it was, with a haunting, warbling tune that matched the eerie matter.

Sir Aldinger, steward to King Henry, is smitten with Queen Eleanor, who refuses his advances. Furious and ashamed, Sir Aldinger vows to watch her burn. That very day a leper, on the verge of death, limps into town. Sir Aldinger, seized with a plan, lifts the sick man onto his back and carries him into the castle, promising him his health will be restored if only he will obey the steward's commands. While the queen sleeps, Sir Aldinger places the leper in her bed, swearing him to silence, then rushes off to find King Henry. The king, upon being led to his wife's bed and spying his queen lying with a leper, pronounces a sentence of death upon the corrupt lovers.

A pair of new gallows shall here be built,
Thou'll'st hang on them so high.
And a fair fire beneath be lit,
To burn our queen thereby.

The sentence sent a thrill through the assembly, all eager to learn how the queen would elude noose and flame. Sensing the ardor of their audience, the singers slowed, hummed, mouthed a string of *lee-dee-la*s and *lee-dee-loo*s in place of words, dilating the story as long as the company would tolerate before relenting.

They had begun the next verse — *Forth then walked our comely king, to meet our comely queen* — when the outer door burst open.

There was a shout of alarm in the courtyard, the scuffle of feet on dirt, then six strangers clambered through the inn's door.

201

Two of them bore a child in their arms, a boy of seven or eight. The nearest table was cleared, the boy stretched on the board, water and cloth requested by one of the men who had carried him within. She could see little, as she sat on the far side of the room, though she could hear the low moans. She caught a glimpse of the boy in the candlelight, his dirt-streaked face divided by a deep and oozing gash.

As three village men rushed off to ride for the nearest surgeon, the story was quickly told. Another, smaller group of pilgrims, a Kentish fellowship from Canterbury, had been riding along the highway, bearing for this very inn. They reached the outskirts of the village later than they had intended, and just before emerging from the woods were set upon by a gang of brigands in the night. Though the thieves were well armed, one of the company, the father of the wounded boy, had resisted, drawing on the band of criminals and provoking them to unsheathe their short swords and assault the would-be defender.

A brief but vicious struggle ensued, bags and purses violently cut and seized by the brigands, ending only when the man's son, mounted before his mother, leapt down from his horse, raced to his dying father's side, and received slashes to the neck and face for his troubles. The boy's screams had frozen both companies in place, until the shame of an injured child caused the brigands to flee with their spoils — including two of the victims' horses.

The father's body had been thrown over a remaining horse, the rest of the company double mounted for the last push to the village. Now the mother, this new widow, stood leaning over her son's prostrate form, weeping for his wellness. In low voices everyone began to describe his worst wounds seen, suffered, or tended. All had witnessed much worse than this, as the slash to the boy's face was shallower than it had at first appeared, and it was generally held that he would survive.

The talk then turned to the conditions of the highway. Some recounted prior incidents of robbery, others cursed the sheriffs for inadequate patrolling, though all agreed that it was best to leave even the safest of the king's roads well before nightfall.

The boy stirred on the table. She heard a cough. He asked for drink, prompting sighs of relief. The mother collapsed against a bench, and the keeper's wife directed two other women to help remove her to a room. As the distraught company settled into the relative safety of the inn the subdued chatter resumed.

Once the room had calmed, Robert stood to leave, swishing past her back. She watched him go out a side door, to the privy, she assumed. In a few moments he returned, though not to his table. As he slipped past her he placed his hands briefly on her shoulders, then went to the hearth. He stood there, unmoving.

She felt his stare but could not return it, afraid she would betray how it had moved her, this new firmness of his touch. Finally she turned her head, looked straight at him, her eyes blazing with invitation — and saw the fear in his own. His face was ashen and drawn.

The sounds around her faded. She heard only the pulse in her ears as she rose slowly from the table and walked to him, feigning unconcern. She touched his hand.

"What is it?" she whispered.

"We must go, Elizabeth." His voice was soft, barely a whisper. His neck was bent, his lips just inches from the hollow of her neck. She felt it throb with his nearness. "That mother."

"What about her?" she said.

"I had to see her more closely to be sure. I went back to the rooms. She was there, with her son. I saw her face in the candle-light." His voice caught. "Now I am sure."

She looked over her shoulder to where the mother had wept for her boy. All was as it had been before, no trace of the diminished family, and the others in that company had mingled with the evening crowd. She turned back to him, her mind astir with new concern.

She pressed his wrist, wanting to comfort him, though unsure how to begin. "Come." They made their way between the benches. She nodded good nights at their fellow pilgrims, received knowing smiles from Constance and Evota in return.

Outside they strolled to the street wall, a husband and wife taking a turn before going in to bed. The night air carried a spreading chill. The first week of October, yet they had traveled far already, nearly into the north country. Tomorrow they would cross the Trent at Newark.

"Tell me," she said, her hand a ball of heat in his ample palm.

He told her.

CHAPTER 12

"I had thought Satan's minions were leaving us in peace, at least for the season." William Rysying, alderman of Portsoken Ward and prior of Holy Trinity, looked at me over the pious arch of his joined hands.

"This is a special advisement, Reverend Father," I said, unsurprised by the prior's dry greeting. "He unchained me for one afternoon only."

Rysyng stood and gestured for me to precede him from the almonry, unwilling to tolerate my presence within the priory. He led me briskly away from the Holy Trinity gate. The prior's head was down, a grey cowl bunched around the neck of this short, angry, ungraceful man. A piggish nose flattened above thick, dry lips. Eyes closely spaced and incurious, of no memorable shade. Hair too thin for a proper tonsure at the front, though overgrown into greasy, almost boyish ringlets where the circle met the shave. He smelled that day of sour cheese and smoke, though the priory's seasonal laundering had left his wool habit unsoiled, scented with lye and rosemary. We skirted the priory's western face through the great court up to Bevesmarkes, and walked with the looming bulk of the walls to our backs.

"You wished to speak with me, Gower," said the prior. "So, speak. You have come to buy away our cartulary, or extort a measure of gold, I suppose?"

"No, Reverend Father," I said. "It is city business that concerns me."

"City business. So you are here to see the alderman of Portsoken Ward, not the prior of Holy Trinity."

"Correct."

"By whose warrant?"

"Father?"

"By whose warrant are you here?" He lifted his chin. "For you are not a freeman of London, Gower, nor even a resident of the city. You are a Southwark man, as Southwark as those maudlyns coining away their queynts in Rose Alley. As prior I serve my house and my order. As alderman I serve the men and women of my ward, and his lordship the mayor. What I do not serve in either capacity is the disordered population of Southwark. Move to London, purchase your freedom of the city, and buy a house in my ward, Gower. There are fine tenements just without Aldgate, and along the ditch above the Tower postern. Or you might pitch a tent in the green and live with the soldiers. Until then I'll have no doings with you."

The prior stopped in the street. His left foot had found a mud clod, which he kicked to the gutter. His eyes gleamed with righteousness as he looked at me, tensed to turn away.

"A pleasing homily, Reverend Father," I said quickly. "Would that a scrivener were hard by, inking it on a bill. I'd happily hang it up on the gate of Winchester Palace, for every Southwark man to see and admire." The bishop of Winchester, a neighbor of mine across the river and recently become an ally, was fiercely proud of his Southwark domain, claiming that our growing suburb embodied the future of London.

The prior scoffed unconvincingly. "I am not afraid of Wykeham. The bishop has larger things to concern himself with than the doings of a house such as ours."

"Perhaps," I said. "Though the doings of its leader could bear some episcopal probing, don't you think?"

His lip quivered. "Whatever do you mean?"

As we delayed there in the street I told him. It was a piece of information I had held on Rysyng for nearly a year, waiting for the right moment to use it. A series of liaisons with the daughter of a fellow alderman, the young woman put away to birth the prior's child — and much worse, the purchase of a position for her in a sister house under the sworn pretense of virginity. The child was now a ward of the city of London, under the care of a Cheapside chandler.

"A whisper to the bishop, and you will be expelled from the order, lose your office and your livings."

"You wouldn't — you wouldn't dare."

"Oh, but I would, Reverend Father. I would, and with no small pleasure."

His face reddened, his jaw shook, his head acting like an abscess about to burst. Then his eyes closed, and something resembling peace settled into his features. It is often like that at these moments, as men confront their hidden lives anew in this quick and brutal form of confession I offer. With acceptance and submission, relief displaces fear.

"What do you want?" he finally said, resuming his walk along the walls. We were

209

nearing Bishopsgate, our paces slowing.

"The last court session, at the Guildhall."

"What about it?"

"You and several others seemed quite intent on hearing out Peter Norris. He had something to tell the court."

"So he claimed."

"Why wasn't he permitted to speak?"

"The mayor was convinced he was lying. Trying to purchase his freedom with a convenient bit of deceit."

"You didn't believe him either? Norris, that is?"

His eyes shot toward me, then away. He turned, and we started our walk back toward the court and the priory. "None of the aldermen know what to believe."

"He claimed to have the name of a witness."

"Yes."

"To the dumping in the Walbrook."

He nodded tightly.

"When did he first speak of it?"

"After his previous arrest, a fortnight ago," he said, looking around cautiously as we went along. "He started chatting about it his second day in the stocks, going on to the sheriff's boys on his return to the gaol each night. No one paid him any mind, everyone thought he was raving. Then the bodies were found. One of the serjeants told Brembre what Norris had been saying. At first the mayor was after speaking to Norris right away. Then something changed, and he refused to hear or even see the man."

"And then?"

"Then Norris's sentence ends. But he robs again. After the second arrest Norris was taken in by my men and thrown in the Counter." A city gaol in Rysyng's ward. "The next morning he started larking again, this time to my beadle, who told one of Brembre's sheriffs, who told the mayor. And then —" He shrugged. "Then Brembre intervened. Norris's trial would be held before the Mayor's Court the next day, he ordered. The Guildhall would hear nothing about this other matter. London would have done with Peter Norris. And so it was. A quick trial, a quick hanging —"

"And any memory of a witness to this greater crime dies with him," I said.

"Yes."

"Why was Brembre so intent on keeping Norris silent?"

"Perhaps his witness saw something. Something damning, or at the least inconvenient."

"Does Brembre know who was responsible

for throwing the bodies in the channel, then?"

A short sigh, almost a gasp, as if Rysyng's throat were reluctant to release its owner's words. "He may."

"And do you believe Brembre himself killed these men, or had some role in their deaths?"

The prior shook his head with confidence. "He did not, Gower. Of that I am certain."

"How can you be so sure, given how the mayor has been acting since the killings?"

His swaying head jellied his cheeks as he walked. "I've told you all I know."

I observed him from the side. "You are hiding something from me, Rysyng. What is it?"

His chin tilted up.

"Very well," I said, stopping in the street once more. "I will visit the bishop tomorrow. I trust you'll hear from him shortly thereafter."

Rysyng stomped a shoe and wheeled on me. He puffed his reddened cheeks, then blew out a long, wheezing breath. "There was a piece of evidence," he said. "Something found with the bodies. Brembre had it taken from the scene and ordered destroyed before the coroner's arrival."

Strode had hinted at this, though he had

known none of the details. The coroner would have examined the bodies shortly after their recovery from the Walbrook, while Strode hadn't been pulled in until the day after the inquest.

"What was it?"

"Strips of a livery banner, used to bind several of the victims' hands."

"The mayor ordered them removed?"

"And burned, or so I understand. All prior to the inquest, which was a cursory affair in any case."

Nothing unusual there. The office of the king's coroner lived on bribes, and if Brembre had wanted a cursory inquest he could have purchased one readily. "Could the heraldry on the banner be discerned?" I asked.

He hesitated. "Yes. Early that first morning, when the bodies were spread together on the ground, one of the sheriffs removed the silk strips from ten pairs of wrists. He laid them out together, and there it was."

"Describe it."

He made a decision, then, "Twin swans gorged, their necks entwined," he said while closing his eyes. We both knew what this meant. The entwined swans distinguished the favored livery of Thomas of Woodstock, Duke of Gloucester, uncle of the king and leader of the appellant faction of lords opposing Richard. The man Michael de la Pole had invoked with such hatred at Westminster a few days before. The lord in whose household William Snell had labored before his appointment as king's armorer — at the duke's request. In that moment I felt something wobble on an unseen axis, as this inquiry into a London crime took on new weight and width, stretching itself beyond the city walls, reaching into the uppermost ranks of the realm.

"What can it mean?" I wondered aloud.

"Who can say?" Rysyng replied. Too lightly, I thought. "The duke, leaving his mark in the privy?"

Or an enemy, leaving the magnate's livery on the victims. I wondered why the mayor would destroy such a telling piece of evidence, and what else Rysyng knew. Gloucester was Brembre's sworn enemy. Anything damning of the duke should have been a treasure in his eyes. Yet something or someone, perhaps Gloucester himself, had got to the mayor following the recovery of the corpses.

We had made our way back to the priory's almonry. Rysyng appeared eager to return within. I looked at him closely. "Why would Brembre do such a thing, Reverend Father?

What kept him from publishing the duke's banner far and wide, and thus casting his enemy in a foul light?"

"Perhaps he is being discouraged from pursuing an inquiry against Gloucester," he said hintingly.

"By whom?"

An arch smirk. "You are not England's sole trader in damning secrets, Gower, much as you like to imagine yourself so."

"Only the most skillful," I said wryly. "Now tell me."

His face assumed a distant sadness. It lasted only a moment, then he said, "I must be free and clear of this matter, Gower. No more threats and extortions, do you understand?"

Not the murderous Walbrook affair, I realized, but his own, more delicate transgression.

"Tell me what you know, Reverend Father, and the history of your calamities shall be scraped from the tablet of my memory," I said. "You have my sworn word."

Though he had no reason to trust me the prior looked relieved. With relief came words. "I've heard only rumors, though believable ones. Several months ago the mayor's name came up during a proceeding at the Guildhall. A routine interrogation by the sheriffs. The mayor himself was out of town."

"Whom were the sheriffs questioning?"

"I wasn't informed, though I'm told the subject was an embarrassing one for Brembre — quite dangerous as well. When Brembre returned to London he heard whispers of the interrogation and went into one of his rages. He threatened those involved, then seized the transcript of the interrogation by force before it could be copied into the rolls. Ripped it out of the scrivener's hands, by all accounts."

"If Brembre has the record, how is it being used against him? He would hardly fear idle gossip."

"You assume he still holds it," said the prior with a tight smile.

I stared at the almonry wall. "Gloucester," I said softly.

"The record came into the hands of the duke soon after the proceeding at the Guildhall. No one knows how he laid his hands on it, nor will anyone say what it concerns for fear of Brembre's swords."

"Who else knows about this?" I had no inroads to the Duke of Gloucester's household, yet if what Rysyng had told me was true, Woodstock was at the foul center of this whole business. It was a humbling thought, to imagine my own craft being practiced so far above my head.

Rysyng smiled. "You might speak to the Lady Idonia." Brembre's wife. Noting my surprise, he said, "The mayor is a venereal man, Gower. All anyone will say about his transgression is that it somehow involved his wife. She has been heard cursing him openly. She surely knows the nature of his offense."

The prior turned into the almonry, the door held open by a novice.

"One last question, Reverend Father." Rysyng had proved himself a goose well stuffed that day. Perhaps he held one morsel more.

He paused at the opening, his back still to me. "What is it?"

"Peter Norris's son, the earless one."

"What of him?"

"Norris was a man of your ward. I need to find the boy."

He turned around, looking amused. "What can you want with a mutilated cut-purse?"

"The boy is an orphan. He needs the city's charity."

The prior scoffed. "Is John Gower going downy?"

"Merely a gallows promise to his father

that I would see to Jack's wardship."

Rysyng's reaction to my half-truth was bland and convincing. "I haven't seen the boy since his father's sentencing at the Guildhall. I'm sure the constables will net him soon enough, then they'll take off his hand. Can't help you on that one, Gower, no matter what scandals you threaten."

With that he left me at the low door through the almonry, and as it closed behind him my vision was engulfed with the most frightening darkness I have ever experienced. The world went black, as if some shade had stolen out of the underworld to tear across my sight. This sensation of utter blindness was accompanied by a deep pain in my skull, a stab followed by a continual throbbing that left me weakened in my limbs, sickened in my gut.

I fell back against the priory wall, to the side of the door. My face and arms had broken out in a profuse sweat, drenching my clothing through to my cotte. My hands clutched at the wall, searching for purchase on the rough stone. Shallow, panicked breaths, no sensation in my legs or feet. I nearly collapsed.

Slowly, as I bent forward over the wall-side gutter, my sight started its return, though in a manner that I found if anything more alarming than its initial loss. A flicker, a brighter flash and then another, and soon a thin halo of daylight began to gather above the void at the center. The glow widened to reach around the darkened middle. Now two concentric circles, the outer a nimbus aglow, the inner an unlit coal. The glow gradually thickened, pushing inward against the blackness, now melting like a disc of ice in full sun.

During all of this my skin had cooled to near numbness. Now feeling stole back into my limbs. I risked a shallow breath, then a deeper one, the pure and saving air filling my lungs, and with it came the realization that I still lived. That I could see. My very ribs seemed to open once more to the world. I looked up at the looming west face of Aldgate, where a bored guard observed my plight from a great height over the hoarding-walk. Another breath and I felt ready to move, slowly at first, then with more confidence as my sight returned to its full if weakened capacity. I went through the city to the bridge with a new aim in mind, my affliction winning out against my pride and fear.

CHAPTER 13

When did I first sense this creeping blindness? For the longest time I felt it as a dog suffers a single flea: an occasional nuisance, rarely acute, beneath notice or mention. Only in the last five years had it interfered somewhat with my everyday life, and only in the last three had it forced me to alter old habits and find new crutches: a head turned slightly to the side, additional candles on the desk, a hand more often raised against a brightening sun. Since Sarah's death I had taken particular notice of the fully blind, those old men sticking their way along the pavers, rattling for alms. There goes John Gower, I would think, a few years hence.

The surgeon Thomas Baker was letting a pair of rooms atop a grocer's shop in Cornhill, one for his accommodation, the other for procedures. The grocer, George Lawler, had purchased a grander house in the Mercery, returning with his wife to the shop along Broad Street only on select days of the week to sell spices and dried fruits to the wealthier denizens of the ward. On the afternoon I visited Lawler's the shop was closed, so I walked around back and took the outer stairs to the surgeon's rooms on the third floor. As I neared the top a woman's high and muffled moans could be heard, a keening sound that nearly chased me down again.

Baker's door stood open, allowing the surgeon to perform his grisly work in the morning's full light. At the moment this consisted of the draining of an abscess from the bound leg of a young woman, who lay writhing on his table and grinding at a rag between her teeth. Trembling limbs glazed with sweat, grunts of pain and effort, Baker's apprentice and another man pinning her arms. Not wanting to interrupt or subject the woman to any further humiliation, I descended and ran a few errands in the district, returning an hour later to find Baker's apprentice mopping up the last remnants of blood and bile from the floor. He tossed the rags aside and took up a bucket of sawdust and ash, which he sprinkled in a thin layer over the surface. The room on the whole was crowded but neatly and efficiently so, with an operating table angled across the center, a bulky chair by the door, and several shelves and tables laid neatly with the tools of the surgical craft. On a high stand by the table a thick volume lay open to a center folio, its opened pages spattered with old blood.

"Is Baker about?" I said to the apprentice.

He nodded slightly, then glanced at the door, where Baker had appeared bearing a bucket of surgical tools.

"Why, Master Gower. Good welcome to you."

"And to you." I blinked, agitated. "I am here about my eyes."

"Ah," said Baker, placing a hand on my arm. He gave the bucket of tools to his apprentice and guided me toward the large chair near the door. His grip was firm but gentle, as if he were leading an old man already blind. "Chaucer told me to expect you."

"He did, did he?" I sounded haughty, even to myself.

"He is a great friend to you, I can see this. Please, sit here."

Baker pushed around the heavy examining chair to take maximum advantage of the light. I sat and adjusted myself to the unfamiliar arrangement as the physician and his apprentice placed a table and tools to each side. The chair's joint between the seat and back had been constructed so as to allow its user to rest at various angles, with pegs to adjust the position of both. Baker took a high stool to my left, while his apprentice stood to my right — his sole task, it seemed, to keep my eyes from shutting at all cost. For this he used a pincer-like instrument with rounded ends, which pressed into my eyelids and separated them for the surgeon's convenience. The sensation was not unpleasant, as the touch of the metal was cool and smooth, and I appreciated the sharpness and clarity that came with widened eyes.

Once the apprentice had performed this opening procedure on my left eye, Baker used a small hook to pull up the lid, then a flattened metal plane to scrape gently along the inner rim. He looked across my prostrate form at his apprentice. "No ungula or pannus. Do you see?"

The apprentice nodded. *"Sì."*

"What about cataracts?" Baker asked, keeping my lid stretched forward.

The young man leaned over, peering carefully. "No sign of cataracts, master," he said.

"Bene. Now the right." He switched eyes, placing his thumb and forefinger gently on

my cheek as the apprentice spread the skin. The right eye having garnered the same verdict from master and apprentice, Baker lifted a tubelike device from the table at his side and used it to peer into the depths of the opened eye. His apprentice moved a lantern above my face, shifting it slightly back and forth at his instruction until the examination was complete.

"That will be all, Agnolo," said Baker, his hand at my elbow. "Now see about those new chisels, will you? And we have a case of earworm tomorrow. We'll need juice of honeysuckle and calamint and we are depleted of both. You know where to go?"

"*Sì, signore.*" The apprentice left us, clomping down the rear stairs.

When he had gone Baker helped me sit up straight, and I swung my legs off the chair. He leaned back and regarded my face. "I see no external evidence of a disease or injury, Master Gower. No cataracts, no webbing on the eyelids nor excessive phlegm in the pouches. No floating matter or obstruction in your eyeball, either. How do you find reading?"

"Still bearable, though more difficult by the day," I admitted. "It was once pure pleasure. Now it is something of a labor. I find myself avoiding it sometimes." Like a dog veering from the room where its master died.

"And generally? How would you describe this gradual loss of sight?"

"It feels to me that my world is growing smaller," I said, hearing the weight in my voice. "Dimmer as well, as if a series of thin veils were being lowered before my eyes. Every month or so I will realize a new veil has come down, as things I once saw clearly appear blurred or dull. The streets of London are not as colorful as they once were. The faces of friends grow indistinct, hazed."

"You speak like the poet you are," said Baker, smiling kindly. "You have thought a great deal about your encroaching blindness."

"Blindness," I said, feeling the weight of it. "A bleak word." And a commonplace figure: for stupidity, dumbness, ignorance in all its forms. How often had I used the device in my own verse, attempting to capture the felt condition of man's distance from God, from love, from grace? To imagine that I was coming to embody such unseeing oblivion seemed impossible to accept.

"Your condition will grow only worse, I'm afraid," said Baker. "If you were showing cataracts I could help you, but in a case like this, where the cause of deterioration is hidden, surgery would be foolish."

"There is nothing you can do to arrest it, no procedure to perform in a case like mine?"

"A lancet peeling your eye, is that what you would like, Master Gower?"

"If it would help."

Baker folded his arms. "One could operate on your eyes, I suppose. Perhaps relieve some pressure on the engines, retard the further deterioration of your vision, whether for a month or a year we can't know. Yet the risks are quite severe. I have watched hale and healthy men put their eyes under the blade for mere cataracts and emerge entirely blind. There are barbers in this very town who would be only too happy to take your coin and slit your eyes." The barbers, those blood letters and tooth-drawers plying their rusty tools around the city's hospitals and tenements. A barber, or so surgeons like Baker were fond of saying, would slice your throat to treat your toe.

"With no hope of a cure?"

"One does not cure encroaching blindness of this sort, not in my experience. Temporary relief at great risk is the best we can hope for." He placed his hand again on my arm. "What you describe to me is a gradual process of deterioration, Master Gower. *Gradual.* There is no reason to think you will be entirely blind in six months, or even three years. You have two choices, as I see it."

"And they are?"

"Stay on your present course and you will be a seeing man for as long as your vision lasts, and eventually a blind man. Or save yourself time by submitting to a painful, messy operation that will blind you now."

A sentence devastating in its inevitability. "I understand," I said, a little proud of myself for keeping my voice from hitching.

"However," Baker said, his face brightening, "I can certainly help you in the shorter term with your reading and writing."

"Oh?"

"Are you familiar with spectacles?"

"I have heard of them. A clerk I know at the Guildhall tells me that one of his former colleagues possessed such a device. You recommend them?"

Baker rose and went to a cabinet along the near wall. A drawer slid open, and he removed a tray that he brought over to me by the door. On the tray was an odd device that the surgeon held up for my inspection. Two circles of glass, each within a leaden teardrop, with the narrow ends of the oblong shapes hinged together in the middle. Baker lifted the device from the tray. Positioning the notch formed by the hinge over the bridge of my nose, he brought the glass toward my eyes. He took his manual off the bookstand and placed it in my lap.

"There now," he said. "Here is a book of surgery purchased in Genoa. Give that a try."

I am not a weeping man. Yet as I sat there in Thomas Baker's peculiar chair I could feel the tears gathering in the corners of my eyes. They pooled beneath the odd lenses the surgeon had placed on my nose. I felt one trickle down, and before I could thumb it off, it dropped to the surface of the book. I wiped the parchment dry, felt the smooth flesh of the leaf.

For the first time in years I was able to see and read a line of writing with all the clarity I recalled from my earliest lessons in grammar. It was as if the page came newly alive before me, the script enlarged to span across my field of vision, the hand rendered in its full and worthy complexity: the flourishes reaching out from certain letters, the marks of punctuation in the Italian style, the liberties taken with uppercase vowels. I am sure now that there was nothing special about this hand, though in the moment I regarded the nameless scribe as a kind of god, capable of filling a folio with this ingenious invention of readable script.

This immediate sensation of miraculous clarity was short-lived. When I looked up — across the room, out the door, into Baker's kind face — the world suddenly blurred.

I reached up to claw at my eyes. Baker grasped my forearms. "Simply remove the spectacles," he said patiently.

I did, and focus returned, or at least the semblance of focus to which I was accustomed. My pulse slowed, and I breathed deeply.

"The spectacles are for reading, and only reading," said Baker. "They will enlarge everything within two feet of your eyes. Beyond that they are less than worthless."

The spectacles sat heavy in my hand. I fingered the frames, the clever hinge that joined the two lenses in the middle. "What sum for a set?"

He named a price, which I happily paid after selecting an additional pair from his collection and trying them out again on the manual. The apprentice had returned from his errand, and went about the room neatening up, placing the optical instruments in their proper order.

Baker led me to the door. It was nearly dusk, the coming evening settling on the city like a soft veil on an aging nun. We stood on the small covered landing outside, looking down on a neat courtyard formed by the grocer's shop and three houses on each side of the square. He glanced at me kindly as I fingered the spectacle cases and slipped them into my inner cotte pocket.

"In some ways blindness could be a sign of God's grace, you know," he said. "It will save you from seeing things a man is not meant to see."

I returned his look, thinking of the array of corpses in the St. Bart's trench.

"Londoners have been killing Londoners since the Romans arrived, I suppose," said the surgeon, looking out on the jumble of rooftops below Cornhill. "Yet the city has changed in the years since my first departure for Lombardy. It murders more brutally now."

"And with new weapons."

"Old ones as well. You have heard about this carter?" He half turned to me.

Something scratched at my memory.

"Stabbed," Baker went on. "In the throat, the heart, the stomach, the back. Repeatedly and savagely, then dumped in the Walbrook."

"Where?"

"Same spot as the others."

"Who was he?"

"I did not hear the man's name," said Baker. "But he was a carter, that much I know. From the parish of St. Nicholas Acons, where my mother still resides. It was she who told me. A good man, his woman with a new child."

St. Nicholas Acons, a parish in the ward of Langbourn, and for the second time that day I felt blinded as Piers Goodman's words unfurled across my inner sight. *And had a carter of Langbourn Ward up here — oh — last week? Weeping mess he was, too, with a sad sad sad sad story to tell about his cart and his cartloads. What's in his cart and cartloads, Gower, hmm, what's in his cart and all his cartloads?*

My face had whitened. Baker noticed and reached for me, thinking me ill, though I shook off his comforting hand this time and turned for the stairs.

"What is it, Master Gower?"

I murmured something, waved the physician off, and descended among the Cornhill throngs to begin one of the longest walks of my life, through the mids of London and the turn for Cripplegate, feet not feeling my stride, as if I were floating above the pavers

231

even while weighted with an impossible burden, my skin clammy and cold, chest tight with dread.

A lone sentry stood before the narrow walkway to the hermit's cell. As I tried to ease past him he clutched my arm. "No passage here, sire."

"I'm here to see the hermit."

"What hermit is that, sire?" His cold look told me everything I needed but feared to know.

I straightened to my full height. "The hermit of St. Giles-along-the-Wall-by-Cripplegate." There was a certain dignity in speaking Piers Goodman's florid title for perhaps the last time. "The hermit who has blessed this sector of the London wall for as long as you have been alive."

The soldier said nothing.

"I want to see his cell." I fished a quarter noble from my purse. He looked at it, took a glance in either direction and then the coin. His head angled slightly toward the narrow walkway.

"Have your pleasure, sire. I've not got the key, but you'll see all there is to see through the bars."

As I rounded the tower the smell hit me. Not the accustomed stench of the hermit's filth, but a mingled air of burned wood and cloth. Beneath it was something darker, animal in its intensity. A lingering smell of cooked flesh.

The day's light was fading, though enough remained to illuminate the chamber behind the barred window, where I knelt as if at prayer. Scorch marks were visible on the sides and top of the small opening and along portions of the inner walls, which were marred by several blackened patches. One of them was a blurred handprint. Yet the cell itself had been emptied and cleaned, Piers Goodman's meager belongings removed. In their place, along the far wall and protected from the weather, now stood a dozen powder kegs, banded and marked with the livery of the king's wardrobe at the Tower.

Back at the crossing I slipped the guard another coin. "Tell me all you know."

He glanced over his shoulder, gave a slight shrug. "Not overmuch," he said. "Got shuffled up here from the Newgate guard only this morning. The old fellow died, is what he did, and they hauled him to St. Bart's or Spitalfields. Would have been two, three days ago. Burned his things in place rather than deal with the scent, then cleaned out the room and loaded it with powder."

One of the city's most durable hermits,

tossed in a pauper's grave. "Who burned him out?"

The guard's eyes widened, then narrowed as he caught the implication of my question and the tone of my voice. He sucked in his lower lip and turned slightly to the side. His head bobbed in the direction of the next tower along the wall. "See that fellow up top?"

"Yes," I said, pretending to discern the distant guard against the darkening sky.

"That's Burgess there. He saw it all. Heard it, too. Ask him."

Burgess, thankfully, was a guard I knew, a solid and trustworthy denizen of the London walls who'd sold me any number of useful scraps over the years. Soon after leaving the crossing I was climbing the next tower, the highest between Cripplegate and the postern below the Moorfields. As I came to his side he turned to greet me with a nod and a tightening of his lips. He waved away my coin. "You're asking after our Piers?" he guessed.

"I am," I said. "What did you see, Burgess?"

"A pack of Tower dogs done the thing," he told me, his jaw rigid with his indignation. He gestured me to a crenel at the edge of the parapet. I gazed through the gap in

234

the stone. Piers Goodman's former home was situated below us and to the north, the scorched window clearly visible from where we stood.

"Seen it all from right here, this very spot," he said. "They wedged the door from the outside, then shoved a clutch a torches and an armful of faggots through the bars. Poor old fellow never had a chance, did he?"

"And they were Tower men?" I asked him. "You are quite sure of it?"

"Sure's a man can be," he said. "One of those badged gangs. Wardrobe men, a dozen strong."

It was one of the emerging divisions within the military ranks, increasingly sharp as England prepared for war with France. Though the soldiers manning the nearly two miles of city walls could be a proud bunch, the London guard was generally considered a lesser station than the Tower garrison. Even within the Tower itself there were fiercely guarded distinctions among the regular infantry squadrons and several more elite units of highly trained men charged with special missions and duties for the king, and regarded with an accordant mix of fear and awe. At the top of this latter group were the guards of the Tower wardrobe, a handpicked company of elite fighters whose particular duty entailed the full and final defense of the great stores of wealth and instruments of royal power held in the treasury and the armory at the Tower: gold, jewels, the royal mint, the privy seal, gunpowder. It was one of these companies, I suspected, that had descended upon Piers Goodman's filthy lair to torch him from life.

At an odd sound from the soldier I looked back at him. His voice hitched as he tried to speak. Tears spilled down his young cheeks. I waited for his words.

"Piers, you know, he — he never screamed," said the man. "Nor never cried out when they came for him and cooked him, even when the flames and smokes were pushing out that window there. Piers, he just chanted that bit of foulness he'd always be sparrowing through his bars."

The soldier smiled sadly at the recollection, then, to my surprise, started to sing, a weak warble from his tongue at first, a faraway look in his hardened eyes as he chanted words I had heard a dozen times from Piers Goodman's raving lips. *"I loved and lost and lost again, my beard hath grown so grey —"*

From somewhere below us another voice took up the tune. *"When God above doth ease my pain my cock shall rise to play."*

A second guard at the lower parapet, adding a strong burden to the hermit's tune. The two of them continued with the next verse.

Merry it is while summer lasts,
Though autumn bloweth cold;
When God above doth calm these blasts
Shall hermits pricketh bold.

By the end of the verse two more guards had joined in, and as if by silent assent the four of them, then a fifth, then a sixth and a seventh began the hermit's song anew, and soon the rough and growing choir of city guards and gatekeepers had become so many links in a sonorous chain stretching into the distance, as far as a man could hear.

It was as if the entire northern wall of London were come alive to breathe the hermit's song, to throw its stony echoes off dozens of churches and inns, to bowl its tuneful hopes down the narrowest alleys and along the widest streets of ward and parish, to fill the great city beneath the early stars at dusk, and to soften a hard, impregnable wall with this rough requiem for its most durable inhabitant.

I loved and lost and lost again,
My beard hath grown so grey;
When God above doth ease my pain
My cock shall rise to play.

Merry it is while summer lasts,
Though autumn bloweth cold;
When God above doth calm these blasts
Shall hermits pricketh bold.

As the bawdy song of Piers Goodman filled the gathering dark I found my own lips shaping the hermit's peculiar words, my tired lungs filling and emptying with his melancholy chant, like a creaky bellows gladdened with unfamiliar air. Dozens of soldiers were visible from our high parapet, their solemn faces down above Cripplegate and beyond lit with torches and lanterns against the coming of the night, as together we sang the death of the kindest, maddest, most selfless man we had ever known. A man who gave his life to God and to our city, burned to death in recompense.

Yet there was more than a shared fondness or melancholy intoned among the singers that night along the walls. Beneath the voices of these men, London soldiers all, was intermingled a note of defiance, a faintly mutinous undertone of discontent at the Tower's wanton destruction of a harmless, joyous man.

To kill a hermit is a serious thing indeed. To burn a hermit alive, though, to trap him like a caged animal and crackle the very fat and flesh from his bones — this was something else. This, we all of us proclaimed in Piers Goodman's fading song, this was evil.

CHAPTER 14

Neither slept that night nor the following, and though they remained in their separate spaces, between them there grew a new, unspoken intimacy, born of desperation and fear. There was no question of leaving the inn and their company, of venturing out along the roads alone, not after hearing of the highwaymen who had injured the boy and killed his father. Nor could they simply let chance take its course. A decision had to be made.

Though not this very hour, perhaps. "Tell me of your crimes, Robert," she said into the dark.

His breath stopped. "My crimes?" he said from the floor.

"What put you in the Portbridge gaol?"

"That. Well." He sniffed. "A hundred pigeons, a dozen hinds, a boar, a faun or two."

"Yet you are a cook," she said.

"I am."

She propped herself up on an elbow. "Then by your station you are naturally accustomed to dealing in beasts and fowl for your lord. Why would such things put you in gaol?"

"I am a poacher, aren't I. No problems stewing harts and peacocks from those given license to shoot 'em, like m'lord on his hunts. But shoot 'em myself, to coin off the meat and hide and feathers? A gallows stands at the end of that road. They rode me on a pillory wagon through half the villages of Kent before tossing me in the gaol at Portbridge. Would have been the king's justice at Westminster but for the guns."

"Was this your first arrest?"

He laughed softly. "Hardly. Was my tenth, eleventh. They'd finally had enough of Robert Faulk, that's sure."

She thought about this. A common criminal ravishing the hunting grounds of dukes and lords, likely going after the same hinds and boars pursued by her husband, though with much more skill and cunning. Yet in his work he was no better than a butcher. To Margery there seemed little difference between taking a hart in a royal wood and cutting up mutton in the kitchens. To put a man to death for the crime of killing a deer?

"In the woods," she said.

"Yes."

"You shot like a royal archer. It is why we are alive."

"You are why I am alive."

He had said it simply, instantly. She felt a rush of desire.

"You spared me, Dame Marg—"

"No."

"You spared me, Margery. I saved you. There was no choice in the matter."

Some minutes passed. From far off in the hills came a long and lonesome wail, followed by another. She moved her elbow and settled back into the pallet, listening to the plaintive song of the wolves.

"And your crimes, Elizabeth?" he asked softly.

She'd thought he was asleep. She considered her reply. "I am also a killer of beasts," she eventually said. "Well . . . one beast."

At dawn, as the low bell tolled from the small parish church down the road, she woke to find him staring at his feet in the rising light. He sat on the floor of their room as if frozen, his long body angled against the wall. At the inn's waking bell, when companies on pilgrimage were to gather in the hall, he refused to come with her. She willed him to find the strength, urged him to rise. He would not move.

"You cannot remain in this room all day, Robert," she pleaded.

She looked at him, willing that new confidence to return from wherever it had fled. He would not meet her eyes. She left him there, bent and afraid.

In the kitchen the keeper's wife shredded greens. The curly leaves went in a heaping basket, the stalks in a pail for the hogs. On the long, narrow table dividing the room was a basket of pears, blushed a deep red. "May I take one, please?" she asked.

"Course, mistress," said the wife, offering her the lot. She took one of the fruits. Softened with ripeness, the pear's skin gave beneath her thumb, spreading a thimble's worth of juice along her skin. She wiped it on her sleeve.

In their room she handed him the pear. Its light heft and perfect ripeness seemed to enliven him. From a pouch at his side he pulled a knife. He looked up at her from the floor, holding the fruit between them.

An offer. She nodded and sat.

First he cored it, plunged the big knife in from the bottom and drew forth the seeds and stem in a single movement. He set the core aside, a short length of stick, flesh, and clinging seeds. Then, more slowly, he separated the peel, curling it from the flesh in one long, delicate spiral. His fingers were quick like a child's, nimble despite the size and strength of his hands. He palmed the quartered pear. She took a wedge. The sweet juice moistened her lips, dribbled to her chin. She moved to wipe it off with her sleeve but his hand had risen to the task, though he withdrew it before he touched her. She reached daringly for it, brought it to her face, moved his thumb across her chin, her lips, her nose. She kissed the pear juice from the rough pad, then pushed his hand back to his crossed ankles.

She returned to the common room to find the other women in their company already gathered around a table.

"And where is your man of sorrows, Mistress Elizabeth?" said Constance, nudging her sister's arm.

"Swinking off his debt through Nocturns, I hope and expect," Catherine chimed in.

Margery gave the sisters a coy smile, raised her brow slightly, let them think what they would. She joined them at the common table. The food was simple, a spiced rye gruel with cream in a trencher of heavy, dark bread. She sat and ate, hardly tasting the meal as the mixed companies held forth in subdued conversations around the front room.

Eventually the keeper came in to stand at the hearth and speak to his guests about their wishes for the day and night. The burial of the brigands' victim would take place that afternoon in the parish church-yard, he said, with four shillingsworth for the parson and the sexton's diggers. A cup was passed around, purses opened, bright clinks of pennies and groats. She put in a half noble, a gentlewoman's share. After a brief consultation among the men, the decision was made in her own company to stay on in the village for a third night, out of respect for the widow and her son.

The keeper stepped down from the hearth and made way for a stooping, bashful man who had arrived at the inn with the smaller Canterbury group. He fidgeted and hawed for a few moments, then voiced his request. "We would like to join ourselves to your fellowship, good gentles, if you will have us. The road north to Durham is long and, as we have already known, perilous. We have a widow and her child among us. The pall of death hangs over our sacred purpose. Yet there is safety of body in higher numbers. Good fortune in newly joined hands. Will you have us?"

Their own company huddled and conferred in a corner. No one could find a strong reason to object to joining the second pilgrimage to their own. True, a larger company made for more difficulty in finding lodging — though they would be on main highways the entire journey, with many inns along the way. The presence of a child might complicate things — though who could deny this bereft boy and his grieving mother the gift of greater fellowship?

Margery listened silently. Saying something contrary would only arouse suspicions. The decision was made with little delay. Afterward the mood in the room lightened despite the coming burial, as the two companies mingled and met, swapped bits of their lives and stories, becoming one. They would be twenty now, a full and merry group for the still-lengthy journey to Durham.

She sat alone, weighted by the decision. They had hoped for a clear separation from the Canterbury group, assuming the other company would stay behind for the burial. Now it seemed inevitable that this widow would see Robert. Perhaps know him.

In their chamber she told him the news. His eyes grew wild, unfocused as he paced the floor. He glanced out past the shutters more than once, as if planning to flee.

She stood in his way. He looked down at her, his breaths coming quickly. She put her hands on his face, tangled her fingers in his thick beard, and made him look at her. "Sit just there," she said, gesturing to a place along the wall. "Wait for me." He sat.

Back to the kitchen, where she procured a basin of heated water from the keeper's wife, who also slipped her a clump of wood lye mixed with honey — a soap we keep only for our gentle guests, she explained.

In their chamber, seated before him on the floor, she warmed the soap with the water and lathered her hands. The lye filled the air between them with a sweet and homely scent, reminding her of another, less trying time.

"Your knife," she said. He reached behind himself for the knife, which he placed on the floor between them.

First she worked the soap through his beard. The hairs were not overly long but dark, rich, thick with the scents of woodsmoke and travel. Their rough ends abraded her fingertips like sand or soil. His cheeks moved beneath them, bulging up to his surprised eyes, lowering to thicken his jaw. She reached for more soap and spread the lather on his neck, used her palms to smooth the creamed lye down along the gentle slope to the top of his chest. She rinsed her hands, dried them on her dress, then reached for the knife.

Her hands hesitated before his face. Yet how difficult could it be? She pictured Thomas, the barber-surgeon who shaved her father over all those years. Twice a month he would arrive with his straight knife and his gangly apprentice, to stand out in the manor foreyard, beneath the small elm, and service the whiskers of his lordship, who had always preferred the blade to the pumice stone for his shaves. He would sit in his great hall chair, brought outside by two servants for the occasion, obeying Thomas's instructions to tilt his head to the left, to lean back, to raise his chin. It was the same Thomas who would cut open her mother, saving her last child while leaving her to die of flux in the wake of the birth. Part of her hated the man after that, but the shavings continued without a pause. She remembered the quick and expert flicks of the blade, the pleasing rasp as steel met skin.

Her own hands moved slowly, inching the flat edge of the blade along his cheeks, gathering hair and lye in a humped line, like a row of raised dirt between furrows. She stretched his skin, scraped his neck, fingered his ears. His eyes never left hers as the knife discovered those angles and dimensions of his face she had not yet noticed, much less appreciated, but now had time to sculpt and clean.

She cut him twice. A nick below his left ear, easily stanched. Another above his upper lip, to which he held his sleeve as she cleaned the blade. She looked at him. Without his beard he appeared if anything more of a gentleman, not less, despite the current fashion. A high brow now fitting to his face, eyes that could look both kind and severe, a strong jaw keeping a rigid course to below his ears before angling up to frame his lower hairline.

He flexed his jaw as she inspected him. He took her hand. "A while longer, Elizabeth," he said to her, in that new voice he'd learned. "Give me the smallest while, then I shall join you out front. Go now."

He emerged from their chamber in the middle of the afternoon, his back straight, his eyes clear, his chin right where it should be. He said nothing to the widow, keeping a distance from the new pilgrims joined to their company.

From the next bench she watched him eat

a sop. The morning bread was gone, so he sipped the thin broth from a shallow tin bowl. The tendons along his newly clean neck pulsed with his generous swallows, hardly tentative yet not too large for a gentleman. She admired her work.

Early the next morning, with the dead pilgrim in the ground, the joined companies gathered in the yard, where the din of departure brought the keeper's dogs from the barn to nuzzle and sniff for scraps. The inn's stableboys led the horses to the blocks, then locked hands and pushed their guests' feet to get everyone mounted in turn. As she adjusted herself on the animal's back her own helper stood by, his young eyes aglint with hope. Once astride she pressed a penny into his hand, and almost flinched at the touch of his skin, which despite the boy's youth was the texture of *his,* and jolted her accordingly.

The boy or someone else had stuffed her saddle well. It filled the width between her upper thighs with a pleasing firmness, rubbing her just there as the horse's muscled back worked beneath her and a confessor's old injunction sang in her mind. *The saddle of thine horse shall be patience and purity, that thou may be patient in adversity and pure in the flesh.* Not my saddle, she mused as she followed Robert through the wooden gate, thrown open to the road for the company's departure. The saddle of mine horse shall be lust and want, that I may be quick in swinking and sated in the bed. She shuddered, let out a held breath.

They left the village at the stroke of seven, twenty pilgrims strong. A few last houses, thatched roofs and low-cut hay, a sheepfold spilling onto a heath; groan of leather adjusting to new use, clank of pans on the cook's packhorse.

The widow shared a nag with her son, and as the company rounded the first bend in the road Margery turned to look at the woman's face, wan and sad. All that day she watched the widow carefully, observing the ways she tended to her son, now able to sit up on the saddle against his mother. Their occasional weeping was a sad music to the fellowship as the diminished family mourned the loss of a father and husband to a highwayman's blade.

It was the boy who gave them away. The pilgrims had stopped for a rest and refreshment, just short of a wide area where the road had been washed out by a crossing stream. The horses were led to the water, and the women spread food on blankets up along the higher bank. Later, as they remounted and rode from their rest, the woman and her son started to edge closer. The boy was whispering to his mother, his eyes on them. On him, Robert.

The company forded another, smaller stream. A step, a light jump, the horses having no trouble managing the crossing. Once on the far bank the widow and her son closed the distance, and when they were alongside she looked him full in the face. "Why, you are Faulk! I *knew* it," the widow said, too loudly. Several of the other pilgrims turned toward them, their curiosity sparked by the widow's first words in hours.

"Mistress?" he said with a frown, his smooth chin raised, his gaze fixed on the road ahead.

Margery watched the exchange, pondered how to stop it.

"Robert Faulk, as I spit and kick," said the widow, inching her horse closer. "Why, you been the cook in Bladen Manor for nigh on ten years, and here you be, astride a fancy saddle in rich jet, acting a gentleman's part."

Margery watched him. *Do not flinch.* He remained impassive as he said to the widow, "You are mistaken, mistress."

"Mistaken?" she scoffed. "Don't you twist words with me, Robert Faulk. Why, you're a famed poacher in our parts, a bowman to match a king's archer you are! Selling your coneys and your hinds, the hides and the meat, door to door up and down the shire. 'Twas my young Will here, was he knew your face."

"That's Robert Faulk, sure," said the boy, looking shyly up from beneath his hood. "Well met, Rob."

Margery edged her horse forward, coming between Robert and the widow. "I am afraid you have mistaken my husband for another man, good mistress," she said, trying to sound kind, reaching to place a protective hand on his arm. "He is Antony Brampton, an esquire *en service* of Sussex." A condescending smile to put a nosing widow in her place. "Hardly a cook, I should think."

"Though I do admire the craft of cookery greatly, my good mistress," he said seamlessly, his voice almost jovial. Margery looked at him in awe. "My father's family has employed a long, strong line of cooks in the manor kitchens for many generations. Their surname is Bolt, and there is a story about one of them from King Edward's reign that your son here might enjoy. What is your name, young fellow?"

"I — I am called Hugh, if you please, sir."

"Well, Hugh, in those days, before the great pestilence, there was a young maiden, a reeve's daughter, living on the next manor to ours. She was a remarkable beauty, and in all the shire it was agreed that she would make a splendid match, bringing glory to her father and her family." And he went on for nearly an hour, spinning a delightful tale of love, nobility, tragedy, and retribution that soon enough had several of the other pilgrims in the company listening in, nodding and laughing at the appropriate places. It was masterfully done, without a single lapse in voice or word, and thrilled her to her bones.

Later, with the story concluded, he nodded toward the front. "Let us ride ahead, Elizabeth."

"Yes, my lord husband," she said, and lifted her leg to kick lightly at the mare. From behind her she heard the widow's soft mutter.

"It is a remarkable likeness, by Jesu's blood. Truly remarkable."

She allowed herself a private smile, her shoulders to settle. It had been the correct thing to do, the only thing, to escape the way they did. To fight, to flee, to deceive. Now to survive.

Yet how had he done it? A question nagging at her for days, as they had made their way from a clearing in a Kentish wood to this road so many leagues north of London, all the while pursued by the malevolence that sought to end them both. It had been Margery's idea for them to travel together and take on the public semblance of marriage. Robert had gone along only reluctantly, yet had quickly become a master imitator. How had he managed to feign a gentleman's voice and bearing so naturally and with such ease? She asked him.

He smiled almost shyly, still looking at the road. "There. You have stumbled upon my greatest secret, fair wife."

"As unpublished as your poaching, my lord husband?"

"Indeed. And here it is." He leaned slightly in her direction. "In my parish, at New Romney, I am renowned as an actor of great note."

"Truly?"

"The church there performs an interlude of Jesu's Passion every Whitsuntide. For two days entire the parish and town are given over to the wagons and costume, with the players picked out from households in the surrounding hundreds, high and low alike. When I was young I would seek out every

255

moment of the plays, and rehearse them at home before the hearth or while peeling beets for Father. One day I was overheard by a playwarden, a fellow who fancied my elder sister. He pressed me into the willing service of our players. There was no role I wouldn't take on. Herod, Herod's wife, the figures of Mischance and Evil Grace. Pontius Pilate became my favorite. 'Sire, what say you of Barabbas, a thief and traitor bold?' Or, 'There be no man here who will vouch you king, Jesu, but you be a lord or a gentleman.' You see? Pilate is all in the song and the shoulders."

"A lord is nothing more than a lofty voice and a heavy purse then, methinks," she said furtively.

"And a title, and lands to his name, and a firm hand, and a whip," said Robert.

He did not see her cringe, his words summoning the violence of her dead husband. She regarded him in a different light after this disclosure, admiring anew the deftness of his dissembling, the devilish magic he worked on the company they shared.

That night, in the common room at yet another inn, she sat among the women and the flickering candles as a company of minstrels sang for pennies around the hearth. A long tale of Guy of Warwick, the beautiful Felice, battles with giants, dragons, boars. At one point, as Margery listened with the others, she dozed off for a while, awakening to the sound of claps and laughs as the story reached a moment of absurdity. Yet her eyes fluttered open on a vision of the purest malice, a widow's cold gaze on her lover's face.

CHAPTER 15

Taxes and treachery were the subject of the day when Michael de la Pole, Earl of Suffolk and chancellor of the realm, opened Parliament that year. The lords had assembled that Monday morning in the chamberlain room near the Painted Chamber to hear the earl's declaration of the causes of their summons to Westminster. The chancellor's first move was to demand a crushing war levy of four tenths from the towns, and four fifteenths from the counties — such an excessive portion that talk of impeachment began almost immediately. The treasurer and the clerk of the privy seal were also in jeopardy, and the succeeding days and weeks would see a flurry of charges and countercharges, challenges and refusals as the Parliament worked itself into a bitter frenzy against King Richard, who would ride angrily to Eltham with half his household and refuse to hear petitions from the

Parliament's envoys. Everyone could see that the lord chancellor had made the wrong move in those first hours, and that his days in high office were numbered. Despite a political acumen that had kept him at the center of power going on thirty years, the earl never saw the dragons coming, and from every corner of the realm, until he stood within their flames.

All of this I gathered over that first week of Parliament without spending a farthing, as the taverns and shops of the royal capital throbbed with talk of the great events that would shape the realm for years to come. My own business in Westminster on the eighth day of the month was less public, as I needed to see a Shropshire chaplain in town with his lord for Parliament. We met in the hall near Common Pleas, traded the whispers and coin we had come to trade, and I left the palace and walked toward the river, my intention to hire a wherry back to London, where I hoped to find Ralph Strode at the Guildhall. Too much had transpired to keep him uninformed for any longer, though I had yet to decide how much to reveal. Rysyng's revelations about the mayor bore further investigation, and Piers Goodman's death had chilled the bones. Strode's reaction would be loud and violent, I feared, and I had little desire to risk his ire without sounder information.

Strode, it came about, saved me the float. Walking past the narrow line of vicars' houses fronting the river I saw his distinctive form up ahead, standing on the pathway above the royal docks. He looked to be dawdling, waiting for someone. I was about to hail him when one of the south side doors to the palace flew open and out stepped Brembre himself, his company a dozen strong and including Strode, who fell in at the mayor's behest and joined arms with him as they went along.

There was always a certain smugness about Nicholas Brembre, a sneering confidence in his own invulnerability. Not pride of blood, as with a higher lord, but the kind of stony façade one sees in those sorts of men who have worked and fought their way up from low places. In Brembre's case this place was a tenement house in Bread Street Ward, where his father had been a humble cordwainer, shoeing his betters with the finest leathers to be had in London. The son came into the business with a ruthless eye on his future, somehow managing to buy himself into the Worshipful Company of Grocers and establish a successful shop that grew quickly, whether through cunning, corruption, or both. Within a matter of years he had ascended to alderman of his father's ward, then began his first term as lord mayor of London a few months before old King Edward's death. His greatest triumph came at Smithfield, when he stood with King Richard against a rebel force five thousand strong, then was knighted for his stolid loyalty.

A false knight, certain lords would always insist on calling him, though he seemed to embrace the accolade rather than spurn the slander. He was Sir Nicholas to his face, Nick the Stick behind his back, and he wielded many rods against his enemies real and imagined. During his most recent election he'd had an opponent killed, knifed in the street, without a thought of penance or guilt.

Nicholas Brembre, it was whispered, could purchase your murder for half a groat.

Yet in Westminster that Parliament day Brembre was greeted like the king himself, the fawning masses delighted that the powerful mayor had deigned to step outside the walls for the occasion. He liked to surround himself with hard, armed men, who formed a diamond wedge that hustled him quickly through the crowd. The press deferred to him, parted ways for him, as if

Lancaster himself were moving among them, though without the pomp and blood.

Slowly I closed the distance between us, pushing my way through a river of watchers and hucksters, drunks and whores, all stretching for a glimpse of the famed or a brush with the vulnerable. Brembre had ordered a pause, his apparent aim to speak with someone who had called to him from a gap between two of the cottages. His men spun around and stood forth, watching for a blade or a dart. Brembre and Strode turned toward the river, and as I neared their position I saw that the man who had hailed them along the vicars' walk was Chaucer.

I spoke to one of the mayor's guards. He got a nod from Strode, allowing me to join the three men. Though I stood half a head taller than Brembre, it was impossible not to feel diminished in the man's presence. Taut, broad-shouldered and thick-necked, he was both knight and grocer and never let you forget either role. A lofty figure in the king's affinity, yet the sort of man who was unafraid to pitch in and help load a wagon with barrels or boards whenever another pair of hands was needed. Brembre commanded more personal loyalty than Lancaster and the king together, and though a committed member of the royal faction, he had established over the years a fierce and widespread devotion from nearly every quarter. The mercers hated him, which in my view only burnished his reputation.

As I quickly learned, the three had been discussing the Court of Chivalry and an ongoing dispute over livery. Chaucer flashed a rueful smile.

"As I was telling the lord mayor, John, I am to be deposed here in Westminster, one week hence, on this Scrope-Grosvenor matter. You have heard of it?"

"Not a man in England has not, Geoffrey," I said. An exaggeration, though not by far. For months the earl marshal's court had been traveling around the country deposing the cream of English chivalry in hopes of resolving a standing dispute between Sir Richard Scrope, a Yorkshire baron and onetime chancellor to King Richard, and Sir Robert Grosvenor, a Cheshire knight of limited influence in Westminster, over the right to a particular coat of arms. Despite the seemingly trivial subject of the dispute, many feared that blood would soon be spilled. Lords took their heraldry as seriously as their rights, investing a large portion of their honor in the disposition and protection of their arms.

"The fifteenth of this month," Chaucer continued. "In front of Derwentwater himself, and possibly Gloucester."

"I am to appear the same day," said Brembre, with an ostentatious roll of his eyes. "As if a man doesn't have better to do."

"You must be thankful then, Lord Mayor, that your duties will soon be lightened," I said.

Strode shot me an admonishing look, but the mayor laughed at my allusion to his coming departure from office. "I am more than happy to hand those duties on to Exton. The customs are keeping me busy enough. In fact I will be out at Gravesend for the next several days to see about these smugglers." In addition to his duties as mayor Brembre was controller of customs for the crown, a position that would allow him to slide seamlessly from power to power upon Nicholas Exton's inauguration at the end of the month.

"You will take the ferry?" Chaucer asked.

"My own barge," said Brembre with a sniff.

Without a thought I asked him, "Will Lady Idonia be accompanying you, Lord Mayor?"

He turned to me, looking amused. "She's currently at Peltham, our house in Sussex.

But she will be here later in the week. Not a happy traveler, my Idonia."

"Too true, my lord." Strode shook his big head. "I recall a particular journey to Oxford during your first term, when the lady —"

"Chaucer, what did you need?" said Brembre.

Strode, looking stung by the mayor's interruption, turned away, his heavy jaw clenched shut.

"I've heard from Middleburgh, Lord Mayor," said Chaucer. "The staplers are as restless as they are conniving, and there are some things you need to know before your departure. May I ride with you to the Guildhall?" Brembre had been collector of customs and thus Chaucer's immediate superior during his time at the custom-house. The two still consulted frequently on matters of the wool trade.

"Come along, then," said the mayor to Chaucer. "Ralph, I will see you shortly at council."

"Yes, Lord Mayor," said Strode, with a stiff and ungainly bow. Chaucer gave us a wink before turning away. In that moment after the mayor's departure Strode looked aggrieved, as if put off by Chaucer's sudden appearance and Brembre's decision to curtail their appointed exchange.

"Where do things stand, John?" Strode asked, staring after the mayoral company folding into the crowd, with the guards closing around them. "What have you learned?"

How much to trust him? Though our friendship was long, Ralph Strode was a mayor's man thick and through, his first loyalties owed to the Guildhall. I decided to tell him only what I suspected most strongly.

"Not as much as I would like," I finally said. "Though what I do know is more than alarming. You heard about Piers Goodman?"

"The hermit up by Cripplegate?"

"He is dead."

"A fire in the tower. Unfortunate."

"Set by the Tower guard themselves. Piers never had a chance."

He turned to me, his rheumy eyes closing with the news. I gave him a few more details gathered from my inquiries, then my most important finding. "What I believe now, Ralph, is that the victims of this slaughter may have been Welshmen. 'Welshmembers,' poor Piers called them in his lunatic's cant. He saw over a dozen of them come into the city a few nights before the bodies were found. They were brought in by the St. Giles parson, for reasons I have yet to discover."

Strode stared at me for a long moment. "A crew of Welshmen, you say, entering by Cripplegate?"

"So Piers claimed. He also mentioned a Langbourn carter, perhaps the fellow thrown in the same privy. How the two are related I don't yet know. Thin enough at this point, Ralph, but there it is." Gloucester's unknown threats to Brembre, the destroyed evidence, the identity of Norris's witness: all this I kept to myself.

Strode's heavy sigh was a whistle through his nose, his lips pressed tightly together. "Come with me, Gower."

Turning from the palace Strode led me between the cottages and down to the bankside. We turned west and walked upriver a few hundred paces until we came to a position east of the royal pier, where an enormous jumble of boards, timbers, and stones sprawled fifty feet inland. The sight was a familiar one, a temporary blight on the king's embankment during a major expansion of Westminster's main point of access to the Thames. Three rows of new piles, eighteen in all and thick as masts, rose from beneath the water level, ending four feet above the river's surface in iron shoes specially crafted for the purpose. Surrounding each length of timber was a large mass of stones, stacked artfully in a conical shape around every pile to reinforce the verticals against the flow of the tides. Soon the pile shoes would be connected with strong timbers, which would in turn be laid across with hundreds of boards to create a new platform several feet above the river. The effect would be a new artificial peninsula of considerable size and strength, befitting King Richard's designs on the river.

Though the keeper of the king's works generally called a labor halt at Parliament time, such was not the case for this job. A crew of fourteen or fifteen men had just completed a morning shift and were now ambling toward a warehouse to the rear of the wharfage.

"Dangerous work, this pier enlargement," said Strode.

"I would think so," I said, wondering why he had led me here.

"A week ago they were working on London Bridge, fortifying the starlings. Now they're here." He sighed. "These men are slaves, really. The keeper of the works has had more than one worker crushed by stones as heavy as ten men, he tells me. Several drownings. For a perilous job such as this you want outside men. Men willing to work long hours for little coin, and without wives and children in the city to feed or mourn."

We reached the streetside door of the warehouse. An alewoman had come in and was standing among the men, filling and refilling three tin cups passed from hand to hand, lip to lip as they shared loaves and hunks of cheese among themselves. The men were haggard, worn down by the labors they had been forced to endure — though very much alive, and speaking in a tongue vaguely familiar to my ear.

"Here are your Welshmen, Gower," said Strode, and now I knew why we were there. Piers Goodman's "Welshmembers," a crew of foreign laborers pressed into the most dangerous work to be found in London and Westminster. Yet these men assuredly had not been brought to the city for slaughter. I was left no closer to identifying the victims in the Walbrook than I had been that morning in the St. Bart's churchyard.

We exchanged few words on our short and sobering walk back to the palace yard, where Strode left me for another appointment in the hall. Curls of smoke rose from two rubbish fires burning in the middle of the space, and a bank of heavy clouds was rolling in distantly from the west, threatening rain, though not for several hours. Feeling the need to clear my head after what I'd just learned, I decided to return to the city by way of the Strand, which would take me past the grand houses along the royal way.

As I neared the crowded mouth of Queen's Street and the vintners' stalls clustered there, I sensed a presence at that end of the square. I turned to see the pale face of Jack Norris, if anything thinner and more drawn than the last time I'd seen him. The boy was looking out over a long row of wine barrels, fixing me with a gaze both fearful and forlorn.

"Jack!" I called out. "Jack Norris!"

He continued to stare as I lunged through the crowd toward him, intent on netting him this time. Well before I reached him he pivoted on a foot, turned away, and slipped up Settler Lane, a narrow and tightly crowded way angling northwest from the square.

By the time I moved thirty feet along Settler Lane myself he had already disappeared into the thick press. By that point Norris could have been anywhere, and I knew better than to attempt a pursuit, not with these weak eyes and unyouthful legs. I thought of him many times over the remainder of that day, haunted by the boy's face, the earless

head of a new orphan, his life no better than
a rat's.

CHAPTER 16

A light morning shower was passing as Stephen Marsh went out from the city through Bishopsgate. The slickened stones along the lower end of Ermine Street spat up an ugly spray that wet and cooled his legs, helped to calm him as he left London behind for this first and perilous test. The way quickly thinned, a few last foot vendors barking for coin, and soon the urban street gentled into the dirt and gravel pack of the road north, though he wouldn't travel even as far as Ware that day. Beneath him the mare relaxed into a steadier rhythm as any signs of the city receded with the gentle descent into the valley below Hornsey.

This part of the ancient road was well patrolled and safe, at least in the daytime hours, crowded with cartloads of grains, greens, and fruits, all bound for the gates and the many mouths between the walls, and Stephen had little worry that he would be waylaid by highwaymen. He left London less than twice a year, though each time he did he vowed to make such sojourns a more frequent part of his life, which was too often consumed by his work and its demands. Founding, forging, bending, banding: metals and ores ran in Stephen's veins, yet they were not all of his heart, and with this October sun on his face, these first nips of autumn in the air, his thoughts could turn for a while to the purer beauties of the natural world around him.

It had been less than two hours by the sun when he reached the top of the rise he remembered. As Stephen knew from his last trip up this way, the fields on either side afforded an excellent vantage on the surrounding countryside. To the east of the road spread several long and narrow fields, all dead flat and several of them neatly furrowed, a line of tenants in the far distance likely sowing winter rye. Beyond the next furlong stood a manor house, with one of the new and higher chimneys of eight sides crafted from a lighter stone. To the west, a fallow field, then a wooded copse, perhaps a mile distant from where his horse stood, and leading to it a winding path partly obscured by the brush.

Stephen looked back to the south, toward

London. A quarter mile behind him the road cut sharply right. No traffic between here and there. Same to the north, where the way ahead went gently downhill before disappearing behind a high hedge. No one would see him leave the road, and with a bit of fortune, Stephen might even make the woods without being observed.

A tug on the reins and the horse was cutting down the track, which soon met the course of a creek flowing along the edge of the field. No huts or houses in sight, and his progress was quick. At one point he heard the faint tinkle of bells from behind him on the road. He slowed his mount and turned in the saddle to look back up the track. A company was passing, five strong, merchants or tradesmen. Men's voices, mingling, laughing. Marsh went unnoticed, and when they had gone he turned for the copse.

At the far side of the small woods the land dropped sharply away over a stone cliff. The ground here was still damp, though he was able to gather enough dry brush and wood for his purpose. Lighting a fire took little time. Soon he had a small blaze crackling merrily beneath the trees, and all the while the question wormed through his mind, shaping and consuming his every thought.

Will they work?

For it was all very well to imagine such a clever firing device as he had created, to design it and craft it in the familiar safety of Stone's. And it had been all very well to make these four simple handgonnes, two forged of iron and welded at the seam, two founded of bronze in a single piece. Yet to fix snake to gun and actually deploy it, with all the shot and powder and flame this required — this was something else entirely.

Stephen started to prepare one of the iron guns. First he attached the serpent device in its proper place along the barrel, testing the hinged mechanism with his free hand. Then a measure of coarse powder procured from Snell, poured down the barrel and shoved to with a parchment wad and a drivel fitting the width of the barrel. No ball for this first firing, he'd decided, as he wanted to test the soundness of his weld before adding a projectile. Next the matchcord, a simple length of rope soaked in saltpetre and oil, dried, and cut to a few inches. Stephen carefully lit the cord at the fire, then clipped it into the upturned mouth of the snake. The snake's mouth would bring the smoldering end of the rope into the firing pan, a small metal semicircle affixed to the barrel that would carry the flame through the touchhole and set ablaze the powder in the barrel, which would in turn fire the ball. Holding his breath, he filled the pan with a final tap of powder.

He gave the loaded gun a close look, end to end, and thought through the firing. Left hand braces gun against chest. Right hand raises tail of snake. Snake's mouth brings flame to pan. Pan lights powder in barrel through touchhole. Powder shoots ball.

Simple. Efficient. Beautiful.

Stephen grimaced. The matchcord, he saw, was cut too long, forming an awkward curve away from the pan. He could straighten it, though then he wouldn't know how far the snake would have to travel to light the powder. As he pulled on the matchcord, still lit, to shorten the inner length, Marsh's hand jostled the snake. The mouth dipped, the ember touched the pan, and — *crack!* — the gun fired, throwing a spray of flame at his face.

"By *Jesu*," he cried, slapping at the scattered powder and reaching for water. He splashed it on his left cheek, where a flame had licked at his skin and caused a burn. The noise had astonished him, and as his ears rang with the report, his good sense told him to abandon his guns and powder and flee, so certain he was that the strange noise would bring unwanted attention, perhaps a pursuit.

He jogged to the other side of the copse facing the highway. No movement on the road, and as his breaths lengthened he appreciated the security of his situation, at least for the moment. The gun's report, though unfamiliar, could have come from anywhere, and no one curious about the alien noise would think to look in the copse. He would need to be cautious, however, and limit his test firings.

Stephen was more careful with the next loading, as this time he would shoot one of the molded balls provided by the armorer. The barrel was fouled with powder, so first he had to spend some time cleaning it out with the drivel. Once the gun was loaded he kept the smoldering cord well away from the powder until nearly ready to fire. When all was prepared, he brought the stock up beneath his left arm, steadied the gun, and lowered the barrel. His target was a broad elm about thirty yards away, wide enough that he could reasonably hope to hit it, yet sufficiently distant to present a real challenge. A deep breath, and his right hand slowly lifted the snake's tail, allowing the curved neck and the head to descend toward the pan. He whispered a prayer, then touched coal to powder.

Crack.

The gun's slight jump raised his head, though his gaze remained steady enough to see a spray of wood fly from the elm. With the gun still in hand he darted toward the tree.

A hit! And from his own gun!

Not in the center of the trunk, but the ball was now embedded in the thick bark to one side. He fingered the splintered wound, marveling at the power of metal and fire to cause such damage to a surface so unyielding to the touch. A knight's shield would be useless against these weapons. Even plate armor would be vulnerable to the new guns.

For the next hour or more Marsh remained in the wooded rise, trying out the four guns, fixing the snake to each of them in turn. Every handgonne, he discovered, sent its missile in a slightly different direction and kicked with its own degree of force. Yet he quickly mastered their oddities, taught himself how to aim so the balls would follow the truest possible course to their target. He noted the results of his test firings on a small wax tablet brought along from the foundry and carried at his belt, one he normally used to record bell soundings but suited his present purpose well.

Depth of impact, trueness and angle of aim, ideal length of cord: all these factors had to be calculated into the effectiveness of each weapon. For these handgonnes, Stephen came to understand, were a marvelous, demanding art in themselves, and his imagination soared with the many new innovations and inventions he might introduce to their manufacture and use.

By the time he had taken six shots with each of his four guns, the elm's lower expanse was ribboned into a marvelous wreck of slivers and burned gashes, and Stephen knew his weapons like he knew his own limbs. He gave them dragons' names. Ironspitter shot high and right, and needed a touch of extra powder in her priming pan. Firebreather shot low but straight, though Stephen hadn't fixed barrel to stock tightly enough, and she wanted a firmer embrace beneath the arm. Torchtongue was a girlish mess, her barrel too wide by far, firing her ball in no predictable direction.

And then there was Flame. His beautiful Flame. A nearly perfect handgonne, her bronze barrel smooth and sound, her aim so true you could sight along her length and she'd spit her ball right where you wanted it to go. It was often like this with metaling, even when you were making ten versions of a thing that were supposed to be identical. One of them always stood out from the others, with superior lines and balance, a congruence and a kind of inner harmony that could be achieved only with great patience and greater luck. If every handgonne could fire like Flame, how his fame would grow!

The sun was starting to lower in the sky. Time for his return to London. He cradled Flame in his arms and fed her a final meal of powder, slipped a patch into her barrel, driveled her good, checked her cord. He stood, this time seeking out a more distant target, a harder test for her, a tree another thirty feet beyond the ruined elm. He raised Flame to his chest, tucked her stock beneath his arm, and took his aim. His finger touched the serpent's tail, lifted slowly —

Then, behind him, a rustle of leaves.

Marsh spun on his heel, the snakehead dropped —

Crack.

The barrel exploded in his hands just as the face of a young woman appeared in his line of vision. It happened all at once, a crimson burst from her neck, his hands releasing Flame, the dull thud of a milkpail dropped on leaves.

The smoke cleared and the powder

burned in his nose. Stephen stared at the young woman's crumpled form.

He walked slowly toward her, then went to his knees. She writhed, looking up at him with the widest eyes, blood pouring from her neck to mingle with the milk seeping into the forest floor, her mouth moving in vain gasps to choke out breaths already gone.

He reached forward, lifted her head. With his other hand he palmed the miserable wound, still pulsing out her life. The blood gushed through his fingers. It reddened his wrist. It moistened the end of his sleeve. Her limbs shook. Her gut buckled. Soon she was still, her eyes fixed on her killer's face.

Stephen rested the limp head on the leaves and staggered to his feet, looking down on this fair innocence he had ended. She was a poor tenant's daughter, it seemed, in a rough dress of undyed wool, cinched with a belt of hemp. Her head was uncovered, her hair trussed at the back of her head and now matted with the leaves it had gathered in her final throes. Likely she had been delivering milk to a neighbor, only to hear one of his earlier shots. Girlish curiosity, and a ball in the neck.

At a certain point in his dazed circling of

her body Stephen stopped. His heart continued to race, yet his mind was already
reckoning the consequences of what he had
done. A gun, a shot, a girl, a death. There
would be consequences, and deadly ones.
Accident or not, he could see no way to
escape the noose, nor did he deserve to. And
yet —

Yet for the moment he remained alone
with the woman he had slain. Stephen
stepped out from beneath the tree cover and
looked off the cliff. Empty fields, the path
continuing its course until it merged with
the unpeopled landscape at the far end of a
distant pasture. No hue and cry, no rush of
hooves pursuing a murderer through the
wooded copse.

No one. Nothing.

He looked through the trees at the corpse.
She seemed so small against the forest floor,
almost hidden even in her present position.
He surveyed the landscape once more, then
pushed back through the lower branches
until he reached the young woman's body.
Gritting his teeth and clutching her by the
wrists, he dragged the load deeper into the
woods, not stopping until he had her concealed beneath the thick branches and stems
of a hawthorn stand. Loose limbs, several
armfuls of leaves, and a few sprinklings of

dirt served to obscure those parts of her body and dress still visible from beyond the shrubbery. The milk pail he threw into a deeper part of the woods.

He walked backwards, evaluating his work. Anyone coming by would surely miss her there in the brush, thinking of the slight mound as a buried log if they thought of it at all, which they likely wouldn't.

With the grim task accomplished, Stephen returned to the elm to gather his things. His hands shook as he wrapped his guns in their sailcloth, tucked away the remaining powder and shot, and led his horse from the woods. At the stream he stopped to scour blood, soot, and soil from his hands and sleeves, plunging his head beneath the water to cool his skin and calm his fear. He joined the road back to London behind a merry company of Cambridge clerks, robes doffed, sporting the colored silks of the season, yet a girl's ruined body was all he could see.

CHAPTER 17

Crack.

Crack.

Crack.

Finally the hazelnut split beneath the hammer. Iseult reached for the meat, splayed on the stone.

"Non non!" Her father scowled, slapped her hand, but not before she had her treasure. Nutflesh, earthy and rich on her tongue. She mashed it up against the roof of her mouth and wriggled it around to gather the most texture and flavor. She'd always liked the raw ones over the roasted ones; why she couldn't say, but it was a purer taste somehow, a greater challenge to extract.

She spit out a fragment of shell, then dashed off toward the horse line to find her husband. Well, her future husband, Donard.

Iseult was eleven, and her hair could still be allowed to fly without a bonnet or a bothering hood. But Donard was twelve, and together they would rule all France, and England, too, and Donard would be king, and Iseult would be his queen, and there would be endless cream and meats and spices and capons and no wars or hangings and no burning fields and no church and every day would be a loveday like today, with an October sun sharing its glow and promise over the fields and shadowing her favorite nook amidst this colorful sprawl of market day up against the walls of Desurennes.

At least a hundred folks from town and tenantholds alike were gathered for market, though to Iseult they might as well have been a thousand, or ten thousand. She liked to imagine the world bigger than it was, so her mother said, bigger even than God made it, and on days like this it was impossible to think the world had any limits. The air was crisp, the last week's rains had passed, and spirits were high.

She found Donard in the paddock, where he worked on market days tending the visiting animals along the horse string. Always with the horses, her future king; he smelled like a horse more than a man she sometimes thought, but that was fine with Iseult. She liked horses, too.

Though his father was a farmer, Donard was a smith's apprentice, richest smith in Desurennes, not that there were a lot of smiths in Desurennes, one in fact, but he was a good man and Donard was a great man and would be a great smith before he was king, and he *would* be king, and she queen.

He was looking at an unshod hoof, had it shoved up between his knees that way he did, studying it like a book, as his master told him he must. Know your horses, know your hooves, Donard's master liked to tell Donard.

She sneaked up behind him. She was too quiet for his ears but the mare saw her coming, blinked its big eyes at her, didn't move. *Good girl.* She gave the pretty beast a wink.

Donard was about to set the hoof down when she chopped him in the sides. He jumped a foot at least and the horse stepped away. She laughed, and when Donard spun, there was a cross look on his face that melted right off when he saw her, as she knew it would, and now the kisses.

He got her on the right cheek, then the left, then the lips. She loved that, the warm and wet he gave her, the downy tickle of his upper lip here in private, between the big animals.

She closed her eyes, and when she opened them she saw Donard's eyes up close, that deep berry blue, and that was when she noticed the gathering men, at the edge of the woods beyond the market.

There was nothing odd about strangers lurking around on market days. Desurennes sat at a crossing along a main road from the coast, and even with England and France at each other's gullets there was always a deal of traffic, with frequent visitors to the lord and lady of the manor. Market days saw good crowds spilling into Desurennes from the surrounding villages, towns, and farms, as the people flocked to sell and trade.

These men, though, showed no interest in the market. They had appeared somehow from within the thick woods, fifteen or twenty of them, their horses left along the nearest stand of trees. They carried themselves like soldiers, though they weren't heavily armed, not that Iseult could see. Swords and knives, but no armor, no lord's banner to mark them out.

They all bore long leather bags strapped from their shoulders, some as long as the men themselves. What was in them Iseult couldn't see, and didn't much care, though she was curious about the look of these fellows. English, she thought. She would go to

England when queen, she and King Donard, take it back for France, as her father whispered, and they'd see London and Westminster and all of it.

After a final kiss she left Donard with his horses and walked back into the market, where she rejoined her parents in among the vintners' stands. Lots of talk, mostly about the wines, though as always in the market there was news being swapped, stories from close by and abroad, a lot of boasts and lies.

Others had noticed the men, too, and word soon spread. They were an arm of a garrison, it seemed, sent out by the captain of Calais at rumors of invasion from King Charles. Every village in the Pale was getting a company, someone grumbled, a small group of men to watch the roads and fields, stay alert for marauders, for chevauchées from Burgundy and France.

We Desurennes folk, we tolerate the English, yet not for long, her father and the other men would mutter. They lay siege to Calais, empty it of its native inhabitants, ravage the countryside and its villages, and all over a false claim to a throne already occupied by the rightful King Charles. War, they said. War and rebellion is what the English need.

Iseult had heard the stories of brutality from both sides, of townspeople slaughtered in their sleep and on their streets, in Crécy, Quimper, l'Humeau, towns she knew as well as she knew London itself, which was not at all. Yet who could say which stories were true and which false? Besides, Iseult had met a few of the English in the past. They seemed perfectly friendly to her.

Her father was trying to sell another cask to a steward from out by Béthune. Voices were raised, though the bartering stayed at an amiable pitch.

She looked across the field. The men had made a fire at the base of the hill, a drift of smoke idling to the sky.

Odd. It was a warm day for October. Why a fire on a market morning?

Now they were slinging the long bags to the grass, arranging them in lines along the ground.

She tugged her father's sleeve.

"What is it, gosling?" He turned from the steward, whose lips were smacking a possible purchase.

"What are they doing?"

"Who?"

"Those men."

Her father looked up at the company, milling on the hill. He shrugged, his attention

289

on his work. "A patrol out of Calais, my chick, come to protect us against ourselves. You know the English. Naught to concern the little likes of you."

Her mother's stare lingered on the soldiers as they began unpacking the elongated bags slung at their sides. Then she too looked down at her work.

Iseult watched the men as they tarried by the fire. From each of the bags a soldier removed two sticks. Not wood, as they gleamed dully in the full sun. Metal of some kind, like pot iron. They were handling them now, inspecting their length, shaking them and tapping them on the ground as if to conjure spirits from the lower earth.

Several villagers had gathered a respectful distance away to watch them at their mysterious toil. Yet the men themselves made no secret of their task. Every soldier had brought two of the rods in those strange bags. The rods were not long, no lengthier than a grown man's arm. They looked heavy, though, unwieldy as the men tested their weight on forearms and shoulders, patted the backs of their fellows, made adjustments here and there.

Curiosity nipped, and so Iseult slipped from her parents' station, through the crowded makeshift lanes of the market, and approached the visitors. One, two, three . . . thirty-one steps to the top of the low rise, lifting her dress above the dirt and clumped grass.

One of the strange men saw her coming. He murmured something to a fellow, then squatted in the dirt before her.

"Yes, little mother?" he said.

She wrinkled her nose at his speech. "What are those sticks?" she asked him, pointing to the rods. One was in his hand, the other on a rough blanket. Next to the second one sat a small horn, polished to a gleam and with a spill of black powder of some kind visible along the lower rim.

He looked up at a companion, back to her. "They are fire sticks."

Bâtons de flamme. "Fire sticks!" She laughed. "But what are they for? What do they do?"

He laughed, too, pointing to his ears. She looked up at his companion, a huge fellow, big as a tree. The man's face was unmoving, his gaze fixed on the first man. He would not look at Iseult. She glanced back at the friendlier one.

"Will they letting you up big walls, my pretty mother?" he said, pointing to the city walls behind her.

His wretched French tickled her. "They

291

will," she boasted, thinking of the last time she was up there on the town walls, with Donard. More kisses and love talk.

Then a few low calls from the other men, words she could not comprehend, English words.

Her soldier stood and gave a signal to the company behind him. He turned back to her. "Allow me seeing you waved," he said. "That place there from."

He pointed to a spot along the gate parapet, where two town guards stood watch in the crenels. She understood what he was asking and felt a flush of excitement. She looked over her shoulder, saw her mother and father down below. They were watching Iseult's talk with the soldiers. So were a number of other villagers now, all looking warily at the girl's exchange with these Englishmen.

She glanced back to him, unconcerned. "I will do it. Wait just here."

"Not yet," he said.

She looked at his mouth.

"Do you like swans, little mother?"

"I like all birds," said Iseult, lifting her chin.

He reached his right hand up to pull at a portion of his left sleeve, uncovering a band wrapped around his forearm. On it was an embroidered badge. Two swans, very pretty, with their necks entwined about a rod or tree and wrapped with a chain of gold.

"Remember the swans, little mother," said the man, patting her lightly on the head. "Will you remember the swans?"

"I will," she said.

"Now go," he said.

With a quick smile she turned and glided down the rise, rushing through the market murmurs.

"Iseult, come," her father called as she swished through. She ignored him.

Once within the gate she darted to the left, then slipped into the western tower and up the stairs, feet pattering on the stone, breaths coming heavy, heart lifting as she neared the parapet.

Sunlight flooded the top of the staircase and now she was above the Desurennes market, leaning across a crenel, the breeze rustling her hair and cooling the light sheen of sweat on her face.

Iseult loved it up here, high above the loud press of the crowd along the walls. On market days it was as if a lord's chess table were arrayed below her, with all the wagons and carts and stands on the outer edge opposing the fixed stalls against the wall, the colorful slashes of cloth and fruits in their bins.

She looked across to the rise and saw the English company. They were standing in a rough arc now, no longer jumbled together, and she could count them. *One, two, three . . .* there were twenty-two of them, bunched in groups of two along the length of the arc. In each group one man carried four of the tubes while the next held a torch, lit from the fire by the woods. Two men, one at each end, bore neither tubes nor torches, though they had bows slung over their shoulders.

She hadn't noticed the bows.

Iseult found the friendly soldier, waved wildly and hopped twice to get his attention. He looked up, his gaze lingering for a long moment; then he leaned over to speak to his fellows. The company advanced toward the market, slowly down the gentle rise.

Iseult searched the soldiers' faces. No lightness or laughter now, only a line of ugly frowns, the men's eyes fixed on the market crowd before them. The friendly one glanced up at her, a last, bright glimpse. She smiled, started to wave again.

No smile this time. His face was sad. He shook his head and looked away with a strange grimace. He looks, she thought, ashamed.

Iseult felt her arms pimple, suddenly cold. Something was wrong.

A glint of color, off to the right, from the horse string. It was Donard, passing by the stalls to look for his father, who came to the autumn markets selling beans and greens from a cart. Donard reached the cart and, after a whisper from his father, turned and found her on the wall. He spread his arms in a question. What are you doing up there, my only love?

She pointed to the line of soldiers, now less than fifty feet from the edge of the market. He frowned and turned away. Iseult would forever remember that last pale flash of his face, the wisp of golden hair tumbling over his left eye as his head spun from her a final time.

The din quietened as the soldiers reached the outer edge of the market, everyone now aware of the company's march. With a deft swiftness that surprised her, the two soldiers on either end of the line spun their bows from their shoulders, nocked arrows, took aim, let fly.

A hiss to her left, an ugly spit. She turned to look. The guard closest to her fell forward, collapsing against a merlon. An arrow protruded from his neck.

At the far end of the parapet the second guard fell backwards, two arrows in his chest. A third missile whistled over the gate tower.

Before she could scream Iseult heard a series of loud pops.

Crack.

Crack.

Crack.

Crack.

Crack.

Something came hissing through the tents. Fruits jumped and popped, throwing pulp and juice across the wagons.

Iseult's body clanged and shuddered as if a devilish bell had rung inside her. She wet herself. A stream of piss ran down both legs. Where was Donard?

She looked through the crenel, her head a mush of sound, too muddled to think of her own protection.

There he was. He had put a necklace on, a ruby shining from the center of his neck. Was it for her?

Her ears rang with more hisses and cracks and pops. By the time the second round was fired, her ears were too full to hear the screams, though she saw the open mouths, the clutched chests, the ravaged limbs.

At the center of it all she saw Donard, her once and always king, bleeding and ruined on the ground.

CHAPTER 18

Idonia Brembre, Queen of London.

The daughter of a prominent vintner, the mayor's wife was as strong and intimidating a London presence as ever during those last weeks of her husband's final turn at the head of the city. A series of coerced elections, silent bribes, and brutal struggles with Northampton had left Brembre in a precarious position upon his last assumption of the mayoralty, and the wagering then was that his rule would last mere days or weeks rather than the full mayoral term. Yet Idonia had weathered every crisis standing by her husband's side, giving him a pillar to lean on and a shelter from political storms both powerful and relentless. At the Guildhall her name was whispered in mingled tones of fear and submission, and more than one dispute among the aldermen and guildmasters had been resolved in her household chapel. It was often said that what little

Nicholas lacked in iron, Idonia made up in silk.

The Brembres inhabited a fine three-story house in Bread Street Ward near Gissor's Hall and the church of St. Mildred. The way widened somewhat at that point, inspiring Idonia to commission a low-walled fore-court to be built onto the front. Pushing out into the street nearly fifteen feet, the structure had the added virtue of forcing passersby to move across as they went along and thus take in the full view of the Brembre domain from the far side of the lane. Idonia saw to making this view a colorful, even splendid one, with fresh paint and wash every season, gilt trim along the jambs and sills. There was always a crowd gathered out front when Nicholas was at home. When I arrived that afternoon I was happy to note the absence of that usual press of fawners and flatterers all waiting for a taste of mayoral largesse. I wanted to speak with Idonia alone, and without being observed.

I approached the forecourt door, a bur-nished span of dark wood embossed with the Brembre arms of three sable rings and mullet, and was stopped by an idling guard. Initially he refused to hear my request, claiming the lady of the house was still out of town, though my purse convinced him to relent.

"A moment," he said, then unlatched the door and went within. He was back quickly with Brembre's yeoman, who ran his city house during his steward's travels with the mayor.

"Lady Idonia is completing a letter," he said as he gestured me within. "She will see you in the parlor."

I followed him through the screens passage. Such letters were a peculiarity of Idonia Brembre's reign as the mayor's wife, part of a more general effort to nose out and manage every detail of her husband's jurisdiction. At least two or three times a week she would send out a clutch of written instruments in her own name, and sealed with her ring. "Idonia's snowflakes," these missives were not so fondly called, their various cajolings, commands, and commendations delivered to their recipients with all the ceremony of a royal patent.

I had received one of these letters myself several years before, during her husband's second term, expressing gratitude for a minor difficulty I had helped to resolve on the mayor's behalf, while also requesting that I avoid any future entanglements with the Brembre household. *Women and writ-*

ing? Not a happy mix, the bishop of Ely had once observed upon finding himself in receipt of one of Idonia's terser missives. In Idonia's case the mix was an unusually potent one.

The oblong parlor spread out from the hall door along the north side of the house. A servant guided me to the far corner of the room, where Idonia sat at a writing table. The mayor's wife had a narrow but not unattractive face, festooned that day with a coverchiefed hat of heavy ground and elaborate decoration. Her nose, quite sharp, looked out of place on a face and head so delicate, though the unnerving radiance of her eyes drew the viewer's attention upward and inward. She rarely blinked these eyes, yet they seemed to remain watery almost to the point of tears while she spoke.

"Gower," she said, staying seated but gazing at me moistly. She looked uneasy, as if I might be about to pull a blade on her.

"Lady Idonia." I stood by her writing table. It was littered from one end to the other with parchment and paper in haphazard piles.

"What can you want with me?" she said. "My husband the mayor is out at Gravesend. Surely it is my lord with whom you wish to converse." Precise speech, her diction well above her natural station as a vintner's daughter.

"What I have to say is not for the mayor's ears, Lady Idonia. He would surely object to my presence here, though I hope once you hear what I have to say you will prove more solicitous." I waited for a reaction, saw the smallest flicker in her steady gaze. I imagined myself taking a deep breath, casting in the dark, then said, "You and your husband have a difficult situation that needs resolving. I have come to offer you my assistance."

She squinted at me, in a way that suggested the need of spectacles. I was tempted to offer her my own, though kept my generosity at bay.

"What exactly is it that you *do,* Gower?"

The randomness of the question surprised me. "My lady?"

"What do you do with your time? You are neither a merchant nor a knight, nor do you practice the law in any official way. You slink about London and Westminster like a rat with a florin in its gut, expecting everyone you meet to scurry down your throat to find it. Yet I cannot comprehend how you maintain your station and status in our city, nor from where your evident wealth derives. So I ask again. What is it you *do*?"

Insulting, imperious Idonia. The first bell sounded from St. Mildred. "I find things, I suppose," I said in the space before the next clap. My clouded gaze lingered on the window, then turned slowly back on her. "Then I sell them. Or use them."

She quivered, like a frightened doe at a rustle of leaves. Another stroke rang out, then dissolved in the parish air. Her narrow frame was shifting on her chair, and in her body's unease I saw her acquiescence. "Well then," she said, trying to smile. "Well then, I hope you might use these skills in finding something for me, and for his lordship the mayor. The peace of the city depends upon its safe recovery." Her unblinking eyes finally blinked.

"What is it you hope me to find, my lady?"

"A letter."

"What does it concern?"

"Merely the purchase of some yellow silk for a set of new dresses I desire."

I sensed even in her condition the toying amusement she was taking with me. "Surely there is more to this letter than yellow silk."

"My own letter holds no peril for anyone, Gower, let alone my husband. The overleaf, on the other hand . . ." She looked away, seeming confused, her hand agitating the cloth at her lap.

Her suggestion fit with what I knew of her epistolary habits. The thrifty Idonia was known to reuse numerous specimens of writing from her house's extensive cabinets of books and muniments, never wanting a good piece of parchment to go to waste. Shop inventories, account books, old court transcripts, even leaves from disused prayer books: all were fodder for her missives. Recipients of her correspondence, myself included, would often find one side of a letter lazily scratched or blotted out, the other filled with her peculiar commands. In this case, it seemed, she had salvaged a piece of writing she shouldn't have.

"Did you read the overleaf yourself, my lady?"

"I did not, nor could I have done, as it was written in Latin. I simply wrote what I wished and sent it off with a servant, who gave it for delivery to a page, who was beaten to within an inch of his life for the transgression. The letter was intercepted, by whom I do not know, and now Nicholas claims it has imperiled his office, his station — his life."

"So you are ignorant of the nature of the document that prompts the lord mayor's concern."

She huffed. "If I weren't, I certainly

wouldn't tell you, Gower. The distaff only hits so hard on a poor husband."

"Would it surprise you to learn that it was an interrogation record?" I asked her.

She looked away.

"Your husband was implicated in a crime or scandal of some kind, yes?"

The slightest of nods.

"And now someone is holding it over him, playing him like a glove puppet."

Another nod.

"But you don't know who this is."

A shake. I waited for her to turn to me before telling her. "Lady Idonia, the interrogation record is in the hands of Thomas of Woodstock, Duke of Gloucester." Her eyes went wide. "The only way I can help you and your husband is if I learn the nature of the mayor's offense — and the name of the party questioned at the Guildhall. Before approaching Gloucester I need as much on this matter as you will give me. The mayor, as you are quite aware, is saying nothing."

Her hand had moved to her lips, her face gone the color of new vellum. She blinked several times, then clasped her hands in her lap. "It was a maudlyn, Gower," she said. "A common whore of Gropecunt Lane, and Nicholas one of its most frequent jakes. I

305

don't know its name."

"I see," I said. Though Idonia had been understandably humiliated, the information was deflating. Half the grown men of London frequented the precincts above St. Pancras Soper Lane. A loosetongued maudlyn would hardly imperil a man as powerful as Nicholas Brembre. Before I could explain this gently to Idonia she told me more.

"This was not just any maudlyn, Gower."

"Oh?"

"It — she — he — is a swerver."

I felt myself recoil. "So Sir Nicholas is —"

"A sodomite. The abominable vice, practiced with glee and regularity by the honorable lord mayor of London, paying a man to take a woman's part."

And with a sworn record of confession to prove it. Though the crown and city did not prosecute sodomy as a civic matter, such a document could subject the mayor to an ecclesiastical tribunal before the bishop of London, who would surely relish the chance to humiliate Brembre in front of the city's most prominent clergymen. Excommunication would inevitably follow. The mayor stood to lose everything: his office, his livelihood, his parish, and likely his wife, who would surely be granted an annulment as a result of her husband's vice.

I leaned to look through the screens passage toward the door, then turned back to Idonia. "Why did Sir Nicholas not destroy the record after seizing it, given its obvious dangers? He is not a reckless man, in my experience."

She narrowed her eyes. "I asked him the same question. He claims other men were named in the document, and that destroying it would rob him of information on them. So he put it in the chest in our bedchamber, along with piles of meaningless scraps from the Guildhall scriptorium. Some eight weeks ago I was out of parchments, so I fished one of them out, wrote my letter, and the rest of it you know."

Keeping the interrogation record was understandable on the mayor's part, if foolish. Better to forestall your own damnation than hold another man's ruin in your hand. Yet Brembre had made a very large wager and lost badly, leaving his wife shamed and his own reputation hanging by the thinnest of threads — threads I fully intended to pull.

CHAPTER 19

"I give you the greatest commission of your life." William Snell's voice had lowered to a soft threat. "A chance to forge and shape your infernal metals on behalf of the very king of England, to craft some new invention from the veins of the earth. And what do you bring me? A little *snake*? A *child's* toy, tapped out in the smithy?"

"It is hardly a toy, Master Snell." It has, after all, killed a breathing body, Stephen did not say. One false word, he suspected, and Snell would have him tossed over the wall. Yet with the lethal accident in the woods still numbing his mind, Stephen would not allow himself to cower before the armorer's rising wrath. His gun worked, worked all too well, and he was at the Tower that day to prove this to the man who had commissioned it.

"The shape is serpentine, yes, and I will admit to taking special care to the design and crafting of its outer appearance," he said. "But the snake is merely a disguise. A trick of the eye, meant to deceive anyone who discovers it, and hide the nature of your commission to me. As to the function and purpose of the device — to these, the snake is incidental."

"And now you confuse me with all this metalman's cant." Snell threw up his hands. "Can you not speak plainly to me, Marsh, and tell why you have mocked us in this way?"

"If you will allow me —"

"Allow you *what*? Further patience or forbearance? Not from this quarter of the Tower, Marsh."

"Yet if you will only let me show you, Master Snell. I believe you will be more than pleased. I ask merely for a demonstration on my part, and an observance on yours."

Snell stood there, chewing on a jutting lip. "An observance."

"A matter of minutes," said Stephen.

The armorer sniffed. "Very well, then. Prepare yourself."

"Aye," said Stephen. Without further delay he took the bundle from beneath his arm and unwrapped the four weapons he had brought along for that day. He lifted Flame, the greatest and deadliest of his guns, the straightest in bore, the truest in aim, the elmwood stock as smooth against his palm as a woman's flank.

"What do you have there?" Snell demanded. "One of our handgonnes, stolen from the Tower?"

"Not the king's gun, Master Snell, but a smaller replica," said Stephen, dismayed that his imitation could pass for one of the armorer's rough originals. "A shorter barrel and stock, a lesser weight, though the same width of shot." He handed the gun to the armorer. Snell hefted it, turned it about in his hands, palmed the barrel and stock. He gave it back to Stephen.

"A well-made gun," he said, with some reluctance.

"Aside from size and weight, the sole difference between this gun and your own lies in these three holes I have drilled into the barrel several inches back from the touchhole. Do you see?" He showed Snell the small bores placed in a tight triangle just where the stock met the barrel.

"Their purpose?" the armorer asked.

Marsh swallowed. The moment had come. "I have carefully observed the usage of these weapons, Master Snell," he said. "I have seen how your soldiers prepare them and fire them. There must always be two men, each working toward a single firing of the gun. One steadies the gun and takes aim, the other prepares the coal for the touch. One holds the gun in place, the other lowers the coal to the powder. The gun fires, and the process begins anew, the same two men laboring over a single weapon and the multiple tasks required to deploy it."

"What is your point, Marsh?"

"My point, Master Snell, is efficiency."

Stephen saw it, that flash of bureaucratic longing in Snell's eyes. "Explain yourself."

"Take your archers," he said, sweeping a hand in the direction of the armory, where so many thousands of bows, bolts, and arrows were stored. "Picture a company of fine English longbowmen, engaged in battle, the sky bristling with arrows at each volley. Fifty archers, fifty arrows hurling toward the enemy in one fell rush." He paused to allow the scene to play out in the armorer's imagination. "Now cut that number in half. Imagine the spectacle such a scene would become if every bowman were dependent on — on an *arrowman* for the loading of his bow."

"An arrowman?"

"An arrowman," said Stephen, with new confidence in the comparison. "Each time the archer readies his weapon, he must depend upon an arrowman to fit nock to string, shaft to knuckle. Your arrowman stands next to your archer for the duration of the battle, pulling arrows from his quiver between shots, assisting the bowman in the laborious task of mounting the arrow or fitting the nock, or — or releasing the string. Imagine it, Master Snell. Imagine if your bowman were incapable of releasing the string himself. If the technology of the bow were such that another man's hand was required to perform the crucial task of releasing the string and sending the arrow on its way. What would be the effect in the field of battle?"

In the narrowing of the armorer's eyes Stephen saw the first glimmer of discernment. "Fewer arrows."

"Correct," said Stephen. "More men, yet fewer arrows in the air. To get the same number of arrows presently shot from fifty bows by fifty men, your company of archers would have to be doubled in size. More men, more mouths to feed, more horses, more supplies —"

"Yet less death," the armorer mused, bringing a hand to his mouth. Snell's words raised a chill on Stephen's arms. "Go on, Marsh."

312

"Now, Master Snell, consider these handgonnes of yours redesigned in such a way so as to mimic the self-sufficiency of the longbow and the arrow, or the crossbow and the bolt. Rather than seeing a company paired along the line, two at each weapon, you would have in battle a solid wall of gunmen, each capable of loading, aiming, and firing his own gun, from beginning to end. We remove the need for a companion to touch the flame to the powder. Give the gunman himself that capability, and thus the power to hold, aim, and fire all on his own."

"And your snaky device here promises this innovation?"

"It does."

Snell's eyes narrowed. "I shall be quite impressed if this proves true."

Marsh bowed slightly. "There is more."

"Yes?"

"This design promises two increases in efficiency, the first of personnel, the second — and perhaps the more important — of portability."

"Explain."

"It is one of the great barriers to efficiency presented by these weapons. In order to fire the powder, you must have a ready source of flame. As I have observed in the case of the Tower's guns, a coal or stick is placed in the fire, then lifted and held to the pan. Anyone who wishes to deploy a gun in battle must be positioned next to a fire pit, and must fight from a stationary position."

"Yes, the evidence of warfare bears this out," Snell mused. "The guns deployed at Aljubarrota last year could only be fired in place. Their use on the battlefield was quite limited. They were wielded by immobile infantry rather than riding cavalry, to the detriment of the Castilian effort — though it must be said, they struck terror in the heart of Lisbon. Until the cursed barrels blew apart." He looked closely at Flame, reached out to stroke her stock. "I have wished for a means of rendering these guns portable. What do you propose, Marsh?"

"What impedes their use on horseback, or even by infantry at a run, master, is the matter of fire," said Stephen. "A burning stick will expire in the wind. A hot coal cannot be carried for long in the hand. The only means of getting adequate flame to the task is for every gunner to have a fire near at hand — and no soldier is capable of carrying fire with him into battle."

Snell scoffed. "You've not heard of torches?"

A question Stephen had expected. "It

314

would be difficult beyond reckoning to hold a torch, light a match from it, and aim and fire a gun, all with the same two hands. The need for a torch, and thus another man to bear it, only brings out all the more clearly the problem of efficiency."

"I happily concede the point, Marsh."

"What is needed, then, is a means of firing the powder in the pan with a tool ready to hand. A carried flame, able to be deployed near and far, whether mounted or on foot. More than this, an ability to fire more quickly than ever before." He held up a short length of twine. "Each gun, I believe, should be equipped with one of these."

Snell took it from him, fingered it, held it before his nose. "What is it?"

"Simply a cord soaked in saltpetre, then dried and cut to length. Saltpetre burns slowly when not mixed with charcoal and sulfur. This cord will glow happily in place or at a run, and even in a fearsome wind. When affixed to the device I have created, it will light as many as a dozen pans of powder, with minor adjustments as the shots proceed." He took the cord back from Snell, fixed it within the snake's mouth, then pushed it down and up again, demonstrating the agility of his device.

Snell stared at the mechanism. "One man

to fire, then, and he may move about the
battlefield as he wishes, firing multiple times
from any position — and without the need
for a source of flame."

"Yes, Master Snell. Thus increasing the
element of surprise."

The armorer hefted the gun again, then
sighted down its barrel toward the nearest
span of wall. "Had a hundred Castilians
with such handgonnes ridden against King
John's several guns, Portugal might have
fallen after all. And your snake simply at-
taches to the stock and barrel?"

Marsh took the gun and began to affix the
snake in its proper position. Back at Stone's
he had designed a simple clip to hold the
device in place while the three bolts were
tightened. Once the snake was attached he
removed the clip and slipped it in the pouch
at his side. All was done smoothly, as Marsh
had practiced every maneuver a dozen times
during his half day in the woods.

"Ready for a firing, Master Snell."

"You'll need a target." The armorer signaled to one of his attending guards. He
whispered in the man's ear and nodded in
the direction of the barbican. "The elder
one."

"Aye, sire," said the soldier. He walked
briskly off, signaling to another guard to

follow him.

"It won't be long, Marsh," said Snell, with a sly grin. "Please continue your preparations."

Stephen checked the serpentine for a second time, tightening the bolts, scraping out the touchhole, testing the serpentine's hinge. When he looked up a small company was walking toward them from the direction of the barbican.

"Richard Wolde," Snell murmured to the soldier by his side. "A lover of cats. He swyves with them, it's said."

"And the softest ewes as well," one of his men put in.

Snell laughed from his belly as the strange company approached. Behind them strode a lion. A body impossibly long, the head framed by an immense mane of particolored hair, gold-flecked blacks and browns. Upon its mouth was fastened a stout leather muzzle, the animal's lips and whiskers barely visible beneath the thick straps. The paws were huge, though a rear one appeared injured, as the beast was clearly favoring it. A lengthy tail played in the air as the lion limped along, not, as the beast books claimed, furtively clearing away his own tracks, but held upright and proud, its curled length whipping from side to side:

the part of the great animal that seemed most truly wild.

Stephen had seen the king's cats only once, years ago, during that long season of celebration marking King Richard's coronation, when the Tower menagerie was thrown open to all England for gaping and delight. The animals were so foreign to the English mind, so unlike their unmoving counterparts depicted in the various liveries of the realm. Lions rampant and supine, lions embossed and embroidered: these were as nothing compared with the living, breathing cats themselves.

The man Snell had identified as Richard Wolde stepped forward from the group and stuck out his chest. "By what rights do your men bring this beast from the menagerie, Snell?" Small of bone, nearly dwarflike in stature, Wolde made a comical figure as he confronted the powerful armorer in his domain.

"The beast's time has come," Snell said. "Can't be helped, I'm afraid."

Wolde weakly scoffed. "You are a mere armorer, Snell. I am keeper of lions and leopards for King Richard. This is *my* lion."

"*Your* lion? Hardly. This is the Tower's lion, Wolde, and thus the king's. You know as well as I that our sovereign lord has ordered this old beast to be put out of its suffering. And yet here you are, defending it with all your will. Why, look at the poor fellow."

All heads turned to the great cat. The lion was a sorry spectacle. Bare patches of mange on its flanks, a long and ugly scar running along its left side, a gaping wound at the snout. The animal's eyes were drooped and overly moist, sad smears of phlegm pouched in the lower lids.

"This is an absurdity, Snell," Wolde continued his protest. "An outrage against Lady Nature herself. You cannot put such a royal animal to death with one of your foul tests."

"Enough, Wolde," said Snell. "This is beyond and above you now. I suggest you take your cat-swyving cock back to the menagerie, and leave this task for the true men of the armory."

Snell chinned a signal. Two of his men stepped forward and pinned Wolde's arms behind his back, pulling him away from the lion.

"No!" Wolde shouted, his short legs dangling in midair. "You will regret this, Snell!"

The armorer turned away with another gesture to his men. A guard took the guide rope from Wolde's hands and led the great animal away from its keeper.

"Come along, Marsh," Snell said, softly now, gesturing for him to follow the lion as Wolde's shouts of protest faded. "Let us put your ingenuity to the test."

Stephen followed him blindly, his head growing light and his thoughts distant, as if all this were unfolding in some life he was merely observing rather than living. The lion was tied to an iron stake hammered into the ground, and now stood before the firing wall. This, a high, whitewashed plane of hardwood timbers and boards, had been erected before the Tower's western rise and was already riddled from previous firings. Stephen's gaze roamed up and across the pocked and ugly surface, taking in the holes caused by arrows, bolts, and shot. There were a few brownish spatters that looked like dried blood.

Stephen glanced about for a fire. "I must light the matchcord, Master Snell."

Snell ordered one of the guards to assist. Stephen handed him the saltpetre cord. "Light it at one end only, if you please."

The guard nodded and began to walk to the nearest forge, the cord held lightly between his fingertips.

"Quickly now," Snell said. The soldier took off at a jog. Stephen turned to the lion, watched its tail flick through its last lashes, wondering at the beast's solemn stillness.

The soldier was soon back with the cord, the tip smoldering with a steady glow. With care, Stephen fixed it by the middle within the snake's mouth, careful to keep the hot end free of the powder.

"A moment, Marsh." Snell approached him, asking for Flame. Stephen handed her over.

"The first shot is mine," said Snell. "Show me."

Stephen, hiding his displeasure, demonstrated the serpentine lever, showing Snell how to keep the spark from prematurely igniting the pan. "You may sight along the barrel, Master Snell, though you would be advised to keep the stock well away from your eyes."

Snell asked a few more questions — keen, discerning, with an expert's eye for details — then assumed a firing position. Just before lowering the gun he turned and said to Stephen, "After the ball leaves the barrel I will hand the gun back to you. You'll reload it and fire, and I shall count the time elapsed between shots. My own ball will be well high of the mark, but yours must be true. Do you understand?"

"Aye, Master Snell." Stephen's gut roiled. It would be his lot, then, to kill the lion, and as quickly as he could. A grim reward for a successful commission.

"Good." The armorer turned toward the wall. Steadying the gun against his chest, he craned his head back, sighting along the side of the barrel, then lowered the snake.

Crack!

A fragment of wood flew off the wall several feet above the lion. The beast flinched across its body, then reared up feebly on its hind legs. As the report echoed across the Tower compound, the soldiers gathered round murmured their appreciation, and the lion made a vain attempt to throw off its muzzle. Snell handed Marsh the gun and began to count. "One. Two. Three. Four . . ."

As Snell ticked off the intervals Marsh seized Flame and went to work on unfouling, blowing, wiping, reloading, those hours in the woods coming back to him.

"Eight. Nine. Ten."

A measure of gunpowder down the barrel.

"Sixteen. Seventeen."

A ball.

"Twenty. Twenty-one. Twenty-two."

A good tamp with the drivel to ram it all to — though not with too much force, as only powder leavened with air would ignite; nor with too little, as an excess of the same air would cause a misfire.

"Twenty-six. Twenty-seven."

A small tap of powder in the pan.

"Thirty-two. Thirty-three."

Stephen took his time, as this was the most delicate part of the reloading.

"Thirty-six. Thirty-seven."

All the while Stephen kept the still-smoldering matchcord away from the pan and touchhole, moving gingerly but swiftly as the Tower guard and William Snell looked on.

"Forty-one. Forty-two."

Now he took aim, settled his mind, and stared down the barrel at this beautiful creature, this noble beast.

"Forty-nine. Fifty."

Just as his hand lifted the near end of the serpentine device, the lion turned to him. The beast stared at Marsh with the saddest eyes he had ever seen.

"Fifty-three. Fifty-four."

Cord touched powder. A flash.

Crack.

The sharp report echoed around the walls. A bloom of red jellied the animal's skull. Flame had done her work. Stephen stared through the smoke as the beast collapsed, its mane rippling with the afternoon's full sun. Over it, as if a reflection on the stillest

323

water, he saw the milk-white face of the woman in the woods, the golden spread of her hair against the forest floor.

Stephen swooned.

He would never know how long he lay on the ground, with his senses closed to the world. When he awoke and sat up, he was alone in that portion of the Tower yard. Twenty feet away Snell was clustered with several of his men, all speaking in low voices. Noticing his alertness, a soldier by the near span of the wall pointed. His fellows laughed.

The armorer approached Stephen as he sat up. Snell's hands were spread in exaggerated concern. "You are quite recovered, Marsh?"

"Yes, Master Snell."

"Very well," he said, looking down at him, contempt unmasked. "I shouldn't be surprised, I suppose. Even the greatest of gunmakers may prove the weakest of killers. It unsettles you, does it, to put a ball in a brain?"

"N— no, Master Snell," Stephen weakly said, seeing a girl's ravaged neck. "I am merely fatigued. I've stayed up many nights perfecting the serpentine, the pan, the cord and its clip, measuring the ideal dose of powder and the quality of shot —"

"Never mind that. Indeed I am delighted that you fainted at the sight of a dying animal. It proves a point I have been trying to make about these new handgonnes, though I seem unable to get anyone in Westminster to listen."

"What point is that, Master Snell?" said Stephen. He stood, relieved to have the armorer's attention diverted from his unmanly show.

"Handgonnes are the ultimate weapons of the weak," said Snell. "You have proved it yourself. It would take a skilled archer to bring down a lion with one arrow. A steady hand, a strong arm, a knowledge of anatomy. Yet you felled the beast with a single shot to the head, from a weapon you banged together in your own foundry. Simply point, touch, and a life is ended, with no strength or skill or even courage required."

Stephen wanted to protest, to show Snell just how much skill and knowledge had gone into the making and testing of Flame and her sisters. Why, he had already killed a young and living person with his own gun, not only the already half-dead and compliant beast killed just now.

"Loud miracles of efficiency, these guns," Snell went on. "Soon enough there will be one in every farmer's hand, Marsh, to say nothing of Burgundy's army. It will be up to us to stay ahead of those who oppose us. More and better guns, more and better powder. And that, Marsh, is why you are here. We shall keep three of your four guns and snakes in the Tower for now, and you will continue perfecting this device until I give you further instruction about your next role in this great matter. There is much work yet to be done."

Snell left him there, staring at the lion, the great animal's corpse still leaking on the Tower ground.

CHAPTER 20

From the church of St. Pancras Soper Lane two narrow alleys run northward toward Cheapside, drawing vice from the thoroughfare as twin drains pull filth from a gutter. Popkirtle Lane twists up from the churchyard through a series of ugly bends, while Gropecunt Lane, its near companion, makes a straight line up to Cheap along a row of abandoned horsestalls and old shopfronts. Within London's walls, it is here that a man, and more rarely a woman, can most easily find carnal companionship for two or three pennies, and avoid the public and visible arrangements across the river in the Southwark stews. Though I had never sought out a maudlyn for anything but information, many of my friends and acquaintances saw them regularly, and it was no rare thing to encounter a man I knew emerging from the precincts with a hung head, wiping a hand across his mouth, adjusting his hose.

Joan Rugg, the bawd of Gropecunt Lane, was a dun-clad mound of a woman, with as many chins as words, and a banded hat fitted with seeming permanence atop piles of curling, unpinned hair the color of old hay. We had met the year before during another crisis pitting town against crown. Though she would have no reason to recall me given the quantity of men who sought her services, to my surprise she remembered my name.

"Why, it's Master Gower it is, come to nose out our fine ladies of Gropecunt Lane!"

"I am seeking out only one of your maudlyns, Mistress Rugg."

"Have you a name, good master?"

"I do not, though I believe she fashions herself a swerver."

"Aye, a swerver," Joan said with a knowing nod. "Fancy some of that arse-queynt do you?"

"Hardly," I said, refusing to show her my disgust.

"You'll want Eleanor," she said. "Edgar's how she mans." She looked up the lane and signaled to a fresh-faced young woman leaning against a post. "Get our Ellie, will you, Bet?"

"Aye," called the girl. She went briefly

around the corner and returned with another maudlyn who approached us with a light step, and when she arrived I looked at her closely. Rykener's was a face I had glimpsed more than once on the city streets, one of those hundreds of nameless Londoners a man passes along the lanes and avenues without a thought. Yet there was something familiar about Rykener, and it came to me that she had been among the company of maudlyns at the center of last year's turbulent events. I saw a young man entering a Southwark stewhouse, a broken kitchen door, a clutch of maudlyns avenging a bawd on the flesh of a dying knight.

She recognized me as well, I could tell from a flicker in her eyes. Yet we said nothing about that old business, moving immediately to her minglings with the mayor, which I got out of her with surprising ease. Brembre, it turned out, was one of the more frequent buyers of her peculiar services. Rykener seemed willing to describe their arrangements and couplings in as much detail as I wished.

"Aye, I swerve for my sustenance. Not many like me, not in London at least, though Oxford has a bevy of swervers, it does."

"And your techniques? Do they make it

apparent that you are a — that you are what you are?"

She poked a tongue against one of her cheeks, pushed it out, considering my question. "I got my own particular ways of tricking the fellows. Greased thighs, a pulsy hand." She smiled. "My lord the mayor, though, he wants no tricks, as I told the Guildhall clerk. Arse up and straight in, no fuss and foisting about it."

"Did he seem keen to protect his name?"

"Oh, aye, sire. Has me call him Harry, doesn't he. As if I don't know his face from his Ridings and mayoral entries and such." Her eyes went wide. "Mayoral entries. You catch that, sire?" She laughed.

I allowed a smile, then asked, "Who questioned you at the Guildhall?"

"One of the sheriffs it was. Fierce fellow. Don't know his name."

I thought for a moment. "And who took the deposition?"

"Sire?"

"Do you recall the clerk taking down your words, his name or what he looked like?"

The swerver widened her eyes. "Now, him I remember. Strange face, that sribbling carl, all burned up, and an odd name to match. Pinkhouse or some likeness."

"Pinkhurst?"

330

"Aye, Pinkhurst's what it was."

"I understand you named other jakes in this proceeding."

"Oh, aye. Lords, abbots, your knights, and can't say I haven't swyved a bishop or two in my Gropecunt years. And one abbess, bless her nether lips!"

I was tempted to ask for their names but didn't want to distract the maudlyn. "Why are you telling me all this so freely, even for good coin? And why did you confess before the sheriff? You're not worried about Brembre's taste for his accusers' blood?"

Her eyes went cold. "I don't take nicely to threats. But that sheriff said he'd have my cock off and all Joan Rugg's mauds jailed if I didn't spout the truth." She smiled, her gaze unchanged above. "Sheriff wasn't wagering on the truth I gave him, though. His face went white as a man's seed when I told him Sir Nick Brembre lived a second life in my arse!"

CHAPTER 21

The first part of that day the mother, Mariota, rode alone toward the rear of the company. She had gathered a blanket about her shoulders against the chilling air along this stretch of the road below York. There was a lingering sadness in those shoulders, Margery observed, in the stooped back of the recently widowed.

The boy was doing better, in her estimation, having been befriended by a group of sympathetic men from the London group. They'd even got him laughing by the second day out from the last village, and now were on to snaring coneys and scaling fish, warning him his turn was coming to feed the company's many maws with a good cooked meal.

The mother, though, sat heavy in her saddle, and Margery saw the faint sparks of doubt in those dull and sagging eyes. She decided to stoke them.

How to do it? At one point before the noon hour she slowed, then turned her horse in the road and waited for the widow to reach her. "A bright and cool morning, blessed with full sun," she said once she was alongside Mariota.

The other woman did not look at her. "Aye," was all she managed to say.

"We have had no storms along our way, with the roads free and clear," Margery went on. "Often in these weeks it has felt as if the blessed St. Cuthbert himself were guiding our way, with fair weather, no illness or accident, no sudden strokes of ill fortune —"

Mariota twisted to look at her sharply, fury in her beady eyes.

"Ah!" Margery shook her head, lifted a hand to her mouth. "What a mindless thing to say. You will forgive me?"

Mariota turned toward the front, her lips tight.

"Please forgive me, mistress," Margery said, reaching out a hand. Mariota felt it on her arm, shook it off.

"I am dreadful sorry, Mariota. My — my mind muddles easily since the birth, you see. I often find myself thinking things happier than they truly are."

Mariota squinted at her.

"We lost a babe, you see," said Margery quickly. "Before the pilgrimage began. That is why we journey to Durham."

The other woman nodded tightly, looking eager for their exchange to end, though she was kind enough to give a fitting reply. "Lost two m'self. It's a woman's lot, isn't it."

"It is that," said Margery, letting her face relax into a semblance of melancholy. They passed a fallow field, unusually flat for this region, and watched as two men hauled stones to one of its near corners.

"What was your husband's occupation, Mariota?" she asked softly.

Silence for a while. "We have a mill, don't we," Mariota eventually said.

"And who is watching it for you during your pilgrimage?"

"Left it in the care and running of our John, didn't we."

"He is your brother, or your husband's?"

"Our son," she said. "The elder."

"Ah. Two sons for you then?"

"Two sons, aye," she said. Her chin went up slightly. "And we've a daughter of fifteen, don't we."

"Fifteen and left alone, under her brother's care?" Margery asked in mock surprise. "And a miller's daughter, no less! You don't

334

worry for her virtue?"

Mariota scoffed. "Honest to say, there's more worry for her dowry than her virtue."

"Tell me about the river, then. Is it well situated, and quite beautiful?"

"It takes a fair wide bend for us, doesn't it," Mariota said, turning slightly in her saddle toward Margery. "Narrows above us, broadens below. The perfect perch for a mill, or so my late John's grandfather would say. He's the one what built it there, stone by stone, didn't he, and the house that adjoins."

"And the shire's farmers grow enough to keep the wheel turning?"

"Oh aye, that they do," said Mariota, and she was off describing the lands, the neighboring manors, relations with the lords.

It was a light condescension Margery practiced that day, a woman of gentle birth speaking down to a miller's widow, yet with enough warmth and kindness to keep the widow talking for hours and with an increasing openness about all matters of life.

She saw Robert watching them warily, yet there was little danger in the exchange as long as he was kept from answering too many of Mariota's prying questions. By the late afternoon the two women had become fast friends, or so it seemed.

A steeple loomed ahead, signaling their resting place for the night. Mariota turned to her as they passed an outlying smithy. "Now it be your turn to discourse to me, good mistress. What reason would a gentlewoman such as yourself have t'take up with a scullion such as Robert Faulk?"

"As I have told you already, mistress, my husband is hardly a —"

"Don't give me hardly this, hardly that," she said softly, and somehow the lowness of her voice was more threatening than her screechy accusations days ago. "I'd know Robert Faulk were he traipsing 'cross the face of the moon. You two go together like sop and snakes. You'll tell me what's this about or I'll shout it to our company, I will, every man and woman of them."

Just as Margery had suspected. The scowls, the cold glares, the ugly, suspicious looks. Mariota knew, despite the clever way Robert had sought to convince her otherwise. Yet Mariota had said nothing about the Portbridge gaol, nor about Robert's poaching, let alone about murder. Margery suspected that none of this was yet known to the woman for the moment. That could change, however, and instantly so, depending on how widely and speedily the sheriffs were searching the two of them out.

"Your son," said Margery. She nodded to the boy up ahead.

"What of him?"

"You feel as if you would do anything to keep him safe, don't you?"

"Aye to that, mistress," said Mariota, raising her shoulders a notch. "Nothing I wouldn't do to protect young Hugh."

"Yet you have already lost your husband."

"I have."

"As I have lost mine, Mariota."

"Yet Robert there —"

"Hardly my husband, as you have so shrewdly deduced, Mariota."

"Then what are you —"

"My true husband beat me, Mariota. Used my flesh in every conceivable way. Hammered my ribs, bruised my legs. There was one day when he came home after a week of hunting boar with his lord the baron. He never took a boar himself, but the baron did, on that last morning. My husband had made some drunken wager with another in the party that he would butcher any man's boar killed before his own, so it was up to him to string up the beast, skin it, gut it. No surprise that he made a mess of it. When he got to the manor he was still slathered with gore, still drunk, and he forced me up into our bedchamber in front of our servants, and with our doors and shutters open to the world he set upon me with every weapon in his arsenal. He made me bathe him afterwards."

Margery cleared her throat, spat to the side, wishing the memory would leave her with the spittle. "He would have taken my life had I remained in his house much longer. So on a fair Sunday the next week I hid an axe in my dress. He came into the gallery late that morning. I waited for the blow I knew would come. When it fell I turned away from him, pulled out the axe, and chopped him to the neck bone. Three strokes."

Mariota was staring at her, her mouth agape.

Margery smiled at the other woman. "I tell you my story not to inspire your pity, Mariota, nor to spark your outrage. Consider it, rather, a warning, to you and to your son. I will do anything to protect what is my own. My body, my dignity. My name. *Anything.* You are comprehending my words, Mariota?"

Mariota nodded, the fright apparent in her widened eyes.

"Your husband has recently died. You have a young son with you as your burden and your responsibility. Yet think what awaits you back home. The mill, the river, a grown son to manage things in this hour of sorrow."

She reached over to place a hand on the other woman's arm. "It would be a far better thing, would it not, to return to your home rather than continue on this pilgrimage to the remotest end of England? The road is perilous enough with a good man by your side. Now you have but a weak little boy as your sole companion. So go south, Mariota. Buy a Mass for your husband at your parish. Extol his dying bravery to your neighbors. See that the mill is passed on to your elder son without incident, and that your younger son is provided for. Give a thought to your daughter's betrothal."

Margery sat straight, taking her hand away. "St. Cuthbert was renowned for his patience, you know. His bones can wait until another day for the arrival of good Mariota."

They spent that night in a pilgrims' hamlet midway between York and Durham. In the morning Mariota announced to the company that she would be returning south, for London and Kent. Mother and son would remain where they were and join the next company traveling southward. There were some sad farewells though few tears as the company saddled and mounted.

Margery and Robert waited at the inn gate as the pilgrims departed the village for the way north. Once on the road they slowed their mounts until they rode at the rear of the company, and in the coming days they took what joy they could in the welcome reprieve from the widow's presence. Yet their relief was mingled with a rising dread, neither of them knowing how many days and hours God would grant them to remain free.

CHAPTER 22

The Court of Chivalry moves about England like a lamed plow-horse thinking itself a charger. Though occasionally hearing appeals of treason or desertion from the military ranks, the earl marshal's court spends most of its time plodding through matters of heraldry, deliberating on such subjects as which knight should be allowed to emblazon what kind of lion on his shield, or what magnate may be permitted to display a certain length of unicorn horn on his faction's badges. Presiding over this peripatetic body — in name, at least — were the lord high constable and the earl marshal: Thomas of Woodstock, Duke of Gloucester, and Thomas Mowbray, Earl of Nottingham, though these two lords would rarely condescend to show their faces for the court's routine proceedings. That duty fell to lower men such as Sir John Derwentwater, who sat uncomfortably on a monk's narrow council chair in the abbey's refectory, glaring at his latest deponent, Geoffrey Chaucer, as his clerk inked along at a nearby desk.

I could well understand the knight's hostility. It was now the fifteenth day of October, and for months Derwentwater and several other knights of the court had been appointed to travel around deposing the cream of English chivalry in hopes of resolving the long-standing dispute between Sir Richard Scrope and Sir Robert Grosvenor. Assembled in the refectory that morning were over a dozen men, most of them knights, all of them aggrieved to have been summoned from their gentler parliamentary duties while in Westminster for an interrogation at the hands of the court: Sir Maurice de Bruyn, Sir Edward Dalyngrigge, Sir Robert Clavering, Sir Richard Waldegrave, Sir John St. Quintyn, Sir Bertram Mountboucher, Sir Thomas Sakevyle, Sir William Wingfield, and several others I did not recognize. The depositions had whisked by, all of them from men who supported Scrope, and nearly all identical in their recollections of the baron's arms in years past. Though King Richard had expressed sympathy for Grosvenor, it was known that Woodstock supported Scrope, and in the constable's own court there was little doubt as to the ultimate outcome. Even a higher knight was well advised to avoid entanglements over heraldry not his own.

Chaucer, the day's final deponent and lowest in rank, was sitting on a lone chair in the middle of the chamber. Derwentwater looked at him with an air of fatigue. A long finger was pressed into a pocket of flesh above the knight's cheek, which he pushed up to close his right eye and released to open it, a slow rhythm that marked his own boredom with this procedure he had been enlisted to oversee.

"Did you ever have occasion to witness Lord Richard, Baron Scrope, bearing the arms in question?" he said.

"I did not, Sir John," said Chaucer.

A quick ripple through the knightly throng, which had expected Chaucer to rehearse the identical testimony provided by the day's other deponents. Perhaps the proceedings would yield a twist after all.

Derwentwater's finger stilled on his cheek. "Yet you were called here as a witness based on your knowledge of the baron's right of claim to azure, a bend or. Do you remain confident in this knowledge?"

"I do, Sir John."

"Yet you just told this court that you saw his lordship bearing the arms in question."

343

"Not in question."

"Pardon?"

"He bore the arms not in question, my lord, but on his shield."

I smiled. A discerning knight somewhere to my left chortled through his nose.

"What's that?" said Derwentwater, his finger still paused.

"The azure a bend or, Sir John. On his shield."

"You saw this."

"I did."

Derwentwater's finger continued its nudging work. "When were you first witness to the Baron Scrope bearing such arms?"

Chaucer looked off to the right. "My earliest memory of the Scrope arms comes from my time in France. With the Earl of Ulster."

"Prince Lionel," said Derwentwater.

"Yes. This was shortly before my imprisonment, some twenty-five years ago. We were encamped about the town of Retters. Monsieur Henry Scrope was a great presence in the camp, as he had been the victor in a tournament held for King Edward a few weeks before. No one sat higher on his horse, no back was straighter in the king's army. This was in Lord Scrope's pre-baronial days, you understand, before his summons to the lords. He was Yorkshire stout and Yorkshire strong, a knight of the shire with a fresh new wife and a scare of mistresses cawing for his cock."

This drew titters from the knights.

"And what were the precise circumstances under which you witnessed Lord Scrope bearing azure a bend or?"

"I distinctly remember the occasion." Chaucer glanced up at his questioner. "Though it is rather an involved story, Sir John."

Derwentwater sniffed and crossed his arms. "Tell us the short version, if you please." A few mumbles of protest. "Well . . ." Derwentwater looked up, haplessly shrugged. "The moderate."

"With pleasure, Sir John." Chaucer was off, and over the next quarter hour spun a complex and ingenious tale involving Lord Scrope's entanglement with a grocer, a maudlyn, a tinker, and an apprentice, all unfolding on the lanes of Retters and ending with a sober homily by the baron himself on the origin and meaning of his family's venerable arms.

Chaucer could pull stories from his mind like groats from a purse, and as I looked around the refectory I could see the tale's balming effect on these roiled gentles. If I dealt in coins and cunning, Chaucer dealt in words and figures, which he mingled, cooked, and distilled with the adept mastery of an alchemist. Nor was such invention a ritual of idleness or waste. Every knight in the room would remember the story told that morning, delight in its twists and perversions as he recounted it for his wife, his consort, his men, his lord. Yes yes, it was Chaucer himself who told it to me — no, not one of his poetical fancies, mind, but a true and real account of the baron himself, so Chaucer said; well, the fellow was under sworn oath to the very earl marshal's Court of Chivalry, so who's to doubt the truth of it?

Even Derwentwater sat as if tarred to his chair, his finger at rest on his cheek, his gaze fixed on the face of our yarning bard. When Chaucer had finished, the knight stirred and glanced over at his clerk. "No need to transcribe that last part, Roger."

"Aye, sire," mumbled the clerk, who hadn't bothered, and thus another of Chaucer's numberless tales faded to oblivion.

The deposition resumed with a turn to the other party in the dispute. "Have you ever witnessed or heard of any claim or other such interruption made by one Sir Robert Grosvenor or his ancestors, or by someone else acting in his name, against Sir

Richard or any of his rightful ancestors?"

"I did not. Though — well, not so much a claim as an affront, as I would call it."

"Go on," said Derwentwater.

Chaucer cleared his throat. "Last year, on a Tuesday in September it was, I found myself walking about on Friday Street, minding my affairs, when I saw the arms in question on a new sign, hanging fresh-painted from a hall. 'Why, Sir Richard Scrope is within,' I thought to myself. So I asked a fellow standing there, 'What inn is this, that's taken to hanging out the Scrope arms? Has Lord Scrope purchased a new house in London?' The fellow looked at me with the most peculiar frown. 'Why, those aren't Scrope's arms put out there, my good fellow, nor Scrope's arms painted on that sign. Those, my good fellow, are the arms of a great knight of Chester, name of Sir Robert Grosvenor.' I must admit, Sir John, that this was the first time in my life that I had ever heard mention of the name Sir Robert Grosvenor, or his ancestors, let alone his family's ancestral right to azure a bend or. And those, I believe, are all my relevant memories on the matter."

Chaucer was dismissed, and that day's hearing shortly neared its predictable end. Derwentwater was just speaking the obligatory formulas of closing when the refectory doors burst open and the Duke of Gloucester strode into the chamber with two pages in his wake. All the seated knights rose and bowed as Gloucester went over to Derwentwater and whispered something in his ear.

"Yes, Your Grace," we heard Derwentwater say. Woodstock walked to the clerk's desk and took up a position behind the quivering man, clearly unused to the disquieting thrill of a duke inspecting his scribal work. From my angle I could see the transcript, a loose sheaf of double-sheet parchment on which he would record a rough copy of the proceedings before inscribing them for permanent record on the court's official rolls. The duke leaned over the clerk's bent back, tracing a finger along the transcripts of the day's depositions, murmuring in the clerk's ear.

"Very good," Gloucester said, and stood to his full height. His gaze swept the refectory. "You have all performed according to your duty. I am glad to see that the peerage has been supporting the Baron Scrope's rightful claims to the arms. Who is our next deponent, Sir John?"

Derwentwater looked at the clerk, who consulted his list. "Our next deponent, sire, is to be . . . Sir Nicholas Brembre, knight and lord mayor of —"

"Knight," Woodstock scoffed. "Sir Nick the Stick is no more a knight than my left buttock." He clutched at the muscle in question, and a ripple of flattering laughter swept the refectory.

"He is arrived, my lord," said Derwentwater, a warning in his voice.

The laughter died quickly as all heads turned to the refectory's north doorway, which the mayor now filled. He looked at each face in turn, not a mote humiliated or angered by the duke's childish pronouncement, and most of the knights visibly flinched beneath his gaze. Though hardly a peer, Brembre commanded enormous respect among the lords of the realm. He was the richest merchant of London and a close confidante of King Richard's, with an unrivaled power over the life and well-being of any man who set foot within the city's walls.

"My lord," he said to Woodstock, and gave the duke a proper bow.

"Lord Mayor." Woodstock looked over at the knights with a knowing smile.

Brembre's face was set as he stepped fully into the chamber and addressed Derwentwater. "I am summoned, Sir John?"

Derwentwater looked nervously from

mayor to duke. "Sire?" he said to Gloucester.

The duke tilted his head just slightly back
toward the door. "Your deposition is no
longer required in this court, Lord Mayor."

Brembre paced slowly along the first row
of knights — away from the door — his eyes
fixed on the duke's. "I received a summons
from the earl marshal, and under his seal. It
was delivered to me not three days ago."

"The summons did not come from me,"
said Gloucester. "Nor is Nottingham the
lord high constable."

"Is he in Westminster today?"

"I have no idea."

"Is he aware that Your Grace is sifting
deponents in his court?"

"*His* court?" Woodstock sniffed. "Chivalry
is the lord high constable's jurisdiction, and
only secondarily the earl marshal's."

"An interesting perspective, your lordship.
One I won't hesitate to share with Mowbray when I see him next."

"Do so at your pleasure, Brembre," said
the duke. "What you won't be sharing is
your testimony in the case of Scrope and
Grosvenor."

The two men were now mere feet from
each other, of the same height and compact
build, the small space between them crack-

ling with hostility. I feared the confrontation would come to blows even there, in the abbey's refectory.

"You would forestall my testimony in the face of the earl marshal's direct request?" said Brembre.

"I would."

"You are countermanding his summons, then."

"I am."

"Yet I have pertinent information to share with this court."

"Perhaps you might share it with your wife," said the duke softly. "Though impertinent information seems more her strength, wouldn't you agree?"

The mayor flinched, and suddenly the air seemed to go out of him. His jaw loosened, his arms dropped, his spine visibly sagged. "There is no call to bring Lady Idonia into this, Your Grace."

"No?" said the duke, enjoying himself now. "Yet Lady Idonia brings herself into everything she can. Who are we to deny her own wishes and inclinations, Lord Mayor?"

Brembre, recovering his composure, straightened his back and raised his chin at the duke. "You will regret this, Woodstock."

Murmurs from the knights, for addressing such words to a duke.

"Ah, regret," said Gloucester, unruffled. "The sentiment of the loser and the fool. It's not an emotion I am accustomed to."

"That can change, your lordship."

"Perhaps," said Woodstock, with a little nod. "Though not today, I'm afraid."

Brembre, deciding not to push nor to threaten further, bowed shallowly and turned for the door, striding with confidence from the refectory.

The proceedings were shortly to conclude, though Chaucer discreetly excused himself, and I followed him from the refectory through the door to a side passage and out of the abbey.

"I must ask you for something, Geoffrey," I said in a low voice.

"And I you." He gave me a dark look. "Westminster has many ears. Let's cross over the yard to the market."

We left the abbey grounds, traversed the great yard before Westminster Palace, and entered the Parliament market through the close at Lords Way. When we had a decent amount of space between ourselves and any potential eavesdroppers I took his arm in mine, slowed our steps, and said, "I need you to get me Pinkhurst's ear."

"Master Adam?" he said with amusement.

"What could you want with our pied scribe, John?"

I switched to French. "You spoke with Brembre several days ago. That afternoon along the river."

"Yes."

"How did you find him?"

He looked to the side. "Honestly, John, I've never seen him more distracted or distressed. He put on a brave face for you and Ralph, but once we were alone he could scarcely put his words together."

"He is being threatened over the Walbrook killings."

"Threatened?"

"By Gloucester," I said softly as we passed the booths of the cheese sellers. "The duke has pressed Brembre into thwarting an investigation in his own city. The mayor won't move against him, despite evidence that points to his involvement."

"Whyever not?"

"I will not tell you, Geoffrey. The thing is unmentionable."

He gave me a sidelong frown.

"Believe me, *mon ami,* it is better that you don't know," I said. "For Brembre's sake, and your own."

Only our years of friendship and mutual trust could have persuaded him not to press me for more. "How is Pinkhurst involved?"

"There was a proceeding. Adam was the scrivener."

Chaucer nodded. "I will send him a letter with instructions once I'm back in Greenwich. Pinkhurst will give you all you ask."

"Why not walk with me now to the Guildhall and speak with him together? The matter is urgent."

"He is with Exton's retinue above Oxford, scribing about fish, and won't be back for some days." The incoming mayor, a powerful fishmonger, was known to be fiercely protective of the city's fishing rights along the Thames, always a subject of dispute between London and Oxford. "Besides, John, your matter cannot be more urgent than my own. Though the two are closely related, I believe."

"Tell me."

"You are aware of my current office in Greenwich?"

"You are justice of the peace."

"For the most part I pursue minor delinquents and scofflaws," he said. "Trespassers, regraters, extorters — I help track them down, haul them into our various gaols, keep them safely in check until delivery to the eyre or the manor courts, depending on the level of the offense. Not the sort of work

I'm suited for."

"I should think not." I tried to imagine Chaucer arresting a hardened thief.

"I don't mind it, though," he mused. "After so many years in the customhouse, at the king's and the mayor's cough and call, I suppose I needed a calmer sort of criminality, and a more restful place to write. The country air uniquely cultivates a man's figures and rhymes. Though it's just as murderous a place as the city."

Poetry, murder: my friend always possessed the capacity to skim from light to dark, from salvation to sin and back again, and without a flicker of self-doubt. It was a trait I loathed and envied at the same time.

"At least twice a week I am forced to throw someone in one of the Kentish gaols," he continued. "We have perhaps two dozen of them. I have come to know nearly all of them quite intimately, even in these short months in office."

"How does this concern the Walbrook killings?"

We had reached the market barns, where Chaucer stabled his horse while in Westminster. He spoke to the boy, then turned back to me. "You must come to Greenwich, John, and see for yourself," he said, now in English. "Otherwise you won't credit it."

"What have you found out?"

He coughed and said in a low and regretful voice, "I know where they died, John."

I blinked.

"And I believe I am close to discovering who they were," he said.

"When shall I come down?"

"Tomorrow. I will make the arrangements myself."

"That is short notice, Geoffrey."

"Short notice, short ride."

"I will be there before noon," I said. Jack Norris was still missing, and given what I had just learned of Adam Pinkhurst's role in the discord between Gloucester and Brembre I was loath to leave the city. Yet the Walbrook murders had too sharp a hook in me already to ignore the fresh bait Chaucer was dangling at my mouth.

"Good, then," he said. "Ask for me at the Thistle across the green from St. Alfege. They'll know where I am when you arrive. You will stay the night." He hesitated. "And it is your turn, I believe."

It was. I had come prepared. From my hanging bag I removed a small quire of parchment, which I had stitched roughly before leaving the priory for the Scrope-Grosvenor hearing. Chaucer took the booklet from me and fanned the pages. "What is

John Gower feeding me today?"

"You will find it quite topical," I said. "Some lines on Wrath and Hate, two brothers who have been much in my thoughts."

"Very well," he said, stuffing my quire in a bag suspended from his saddle. "Until tomorrow, John," he said, and then Chaucer mounted and was gone, swallowed by the parliamentary rabble.

Chapter 23

The village of Greenwich lies roughly four miles from Southwark, a short enough distance that I was tempted to take the long ferry and go by water, though the day's crisp, dry air prompted me to make the journey on horseback instead. I departed St. Mary Overey that morning under high and blowing clouds that dappled the road in swift shadows as I rode along. Watling Street leaves Southwark at the far end of the high street to curve gently through the country parishes. The road was busy with herders, workers, and retailers hurrying themselves and their wares into the city. Flocks of sheep for the Southwark butchers and the autumn slaughter, loads of Kentish lumber, a parade of carts, wagons, and laden mules groaning for space on a crowded byway. It seemed that every commodity unable to reach London by water reached it by Watling Street, traveling up and into the bowels of the city through Southwark and the bridge. In the other direction flowed an equally varied chain of conveyances: carts returning to their rural origins laden with foodstuffs, a lady's wardrobe, a suit of plate armor bound in oiled cloth.

A mile after leaving behind the Southwark high street I fell in with a company of monks making for the priory of St. Martin, a long journey nearing its end. The monks themselves were a sullen lot, unwilling to make idle talk with a stranger, so I slowed my horse to edge alongside their lay servant, a young man who looked perhaps twenty years old and, I guessed, eager for worldly conversation.

"What news, young fellow?" I asked, slipping him a few groats. Travelers were always one of the richest sources of information, and though their accounts could very often be discounted as unreliable hearsay, they invariably afforded new perspectives on the wider world, ever welcome to a city dweller like me.

The company of Benedictines had left Dover in early July, he told me, their charge to deliver the news of their prior's death to as many houses in their order as practicable, and gather prayers and Masses in return. He reached back to pat one of his bags, a

359

cylindrical packet of boiled leather strapped firmly to the saddle. The heavy parchment roll had been inscribed by some thirty Benedictine abbots, abbesses, and priors from Plymouth to York, he said, and the monks were just now completing the brutal circle begun twelve weeks before. Prior to their arrival in London the company had been traveling along the coast road from Norwich, stopping by several houses at the sea edge of England.

"Talk's all of Burgundy and King Charles," said the young man. "Extra garrisons at the ports, looking out over the channel to Sluys, 'specially after rumors a those Genoese cogs captured down at Sandwich. King's men have hired whole flocks of men, women, even little boys and girls to watch up and down the coast, sound the alarm at first sight of the French fleet. They've bought up half the fishermen on the coast, pressed their old boats into service. And on land you got plowmen sharpening their scythes, herdsmen seeking new pasture inland, scared mothers stitchin' their daughters' queynts shut against all the rapin' to come."

He laughed gruffly, prompting a craned neck and a glare from one of the monks up ahead.

"Nothing remarkable, then?"

"Well now . . ." He thought about it. "There was one odd thing, little twig that's been nubbin' at my mind. Forgot about it once we left the coast, but now we're in Kent it comes to me again." He looked up and around at the landscape.

"And what's that?" I said.

He slowed his horse a step, keeping an eye on the monks. "My recollection's stuck, it seems."

I handed over another coin. He sat up in his saddle, took a long draft from his skin, wiped an arm across his mouth.

"Not a week ago, this was," he said. "We was in Chelmsford, two days up and out from London. Market day, all the usual crowds, and the sheriff's criers were on the corners, shouting the king's messages. One of them pricked up quite a few ears."

"Oh?"

"A prison escape, it was, with some killings involved. Would have been the regular sort of hue and cry, the sheriffs seeking out the usual highwaymen and so on, calling on the help and aid of the commons in bringin' them all to the bench. What plucked me, though, was that one of the fliers is a woman. Gentlewoman, in fact, of Dartford, escaped from Portbridge gaol. Killed a guard, or so it was cried."

"A gentlewoman? That *is* rather unusual." Though even as I said this I recalled the city crier outside Guildhall Yard, who had undoubtedly been spreading warnings about the same fugitives and asking for help from Londoners in their apprehension. Normally such shouted proclamations would go straight through my skull without stopping, and I had heard nothing in the shouted list of official business worthy of my attention that day.

Now the proclamation took on a darker resonance. I wondered what Chaucer, as local justice of the peace for the sprawling shire, might know of the fugitive pair — if pair they were. Dartford was just a few miles beyond Greenwich, well within his jurisdiction, and he would surely have been involved in the initial hunt after the killing at the Portbridge gaol.

"Do you recall their names?" I asked him.

"I do, strange enough," said the young man. "Heard the cry three times and can't get them out of my head."

His silence lengthened. More coins traded hands.

"Margery Peveril's hers. Robert Faulk's his," he said, and nothing else. The crier's words came back to me in fragments as he

362

rode ahead. *Know all present . . . poacher of His Highness the king's forests . . . gentlewoman of Dartford and murderess of her husband . . . do now flee, together or alone, through country and city . . . destination unknown . . .*

I parted company with the monks after the ford over the Ravensbourne, which was flowing low, and within less than an hour of closing my gate door at the priory I was riding up the hill to Greenwich with the steeple of St. Alfege a stub against the sky. Upon reaching the high street and the Thistle I dismounted, arranging for my horse's stabling with the inn boy, and looked out over the Thames. The village's situation gave a wide vista on the river, on which several ships at various stages of construction were docked by the building yards. Greenwich had recently become a major den of shipwrights, many of them swart crews from the south boasting the latest techniques from the ports of Italy and the Holy Land. From that spot in front of the Thistle I could make out the faint echoes of their shouts, oaths and curses traded in tongues as foreign to my ear as modesty to a baron.

"Why, our Southwark oyster has left his shell!" Chaucer, leaning on the inn door, greeted me with a curt wave. "Good to see you in a rural mode, John."

"Let's hope I survive the day." I joined him at the door, suddenly thirsty, looking over his shoulder for the innkeeper.

He steered me back toward the yard. "No quenching for us, not for several hours. Retrieve your horse, John. We must set off."

"For where?"

"You will see." His face looked troubled.

"Tell me, Geoffrey."

"Things are worse than I thought. Much worse, if what I have heard this morning is true. We must ride at once." He gave a curt signal to the yard boy, who went off to retrieve our animals.

I thought for a moment. "Is this about these fugitives, Geoffrey? A man and woman who fled a manor gaol in the Portbridge hundred?"

"In part," he said, looking mildly surprised at my information. "Peveril and Faulk are the talk of the shire, though their escape is the least horrific aspect of this matter. I can scarcely believe what I am about to show you. I will say no more at the moment, as I want your fresh judgment on what you see."

Our horses arrived, and we set off down toward the main road, where traffic had slowed somewhat following the mercantile rush of the earlier morning. We had several miles to ride, and as we passed by an empty gibbet at a crossing Chaucer said, "I have read your couplets, John."

"The quire I gave you yesterday?"

"You've figured Homicide as the tongue of Wrath. I like that very much. I can see it, flickering serpentlike at the imminent victims of murder, or snapping like a whip at the feet of the almost dead, tripping them up in the courses of their lives." He started reciting my verse back to me. A booklet passed to him late the day before, and he already had my lines by rote.

"Homicide, as old books sayeth
(And no man may gainst them prayeth),
Be the sharpest tongue of Wrath.
To meet Homicide in thy path,
To see his maw in church or hall,
Is to know man's course since our Fall.
Whose life endeth in Homicide
Shall vengeance seek on every side.
With touch of lathe and turn of screw,
The engine of foul murder true
Doth roll our conscience in black pitch,
And casteth man in Hate's own ditch."

He looked over at me with an admiring smile, a rarity in this poetical circumstance. "Now the lathe and screw are verdant images, aren't they," he mused. "And yet — and yet I don't see the precise point of the 'engine' or how it could be working in the way you describe . . ."

And so it went, so it always went with Chaucer and my verse, the well-meaning criticisms twisting like knives through my ribs. We rode another mile, as I listened to him prattle on about my sagging lines and stale images, ever with the best of intentions, of course, the most friendly disposition toward my making. Nothing could reduce me to a more childlike sullenness than Chaucer's blithe cruelties.

Chaucer, too, sank into a studied silence once he had dispensed with my verse. He seemed ill at ease, agitated in his saddle. We passed a large manor house at the edge of a half-cleared wood, then rode over a wide and swiftly flowing creek spanned by a stone bridge, well kept despite the heavy traffic on this byway from London. Upstream a train of late wheat wagons was lined up before a mill on the eastern bank, the tenants waiting their turn at the stone. Chaucer's position allowed us to cross without paying the toll to the guards, though at the far end our way was barred by the bridge's hermit. Robed in black with a closely cropped beard and a hood in the newest style, he cut a vivid contrast to the happily unkempt figure of Piers Goodman, a presence still heavy in my thoughts. I found the bridge hermit's fastidious attire infuriating.

"Fair welcome to you, Master Chaucer," he said with a bow to my companion.

"And a happy morning to you, Brother Roger."

The hermit beamed up at me. "Sixpence for your crossing, good gentle," he said with an entitled primness, his palm open by my left foot.

I heard myself scoff. "Here is a groat." I flicked it down at him.

He caught it in the air, looked at Chaucer.

"John," my friend murmured, turning from the affronted hermit. "You would never insult one of your own mouths. Please do not slight mine."

I hesitated, my anger ebbing. "Of course." I handed down eight pennies to make up for my rudeness, and after a satisfied nod from the hermit we were on our way.

When we had got beyond the man's hearing Chaucer half turned in his saddle. "Margery Peveril," he said at last, a certain reverence in his voice, as if the name were a minor sacrament.

"The woman," I said.

"The woman, the murderess, and now the

fugitive." Chaucer hocked his throat, spat off to the side. "An unlikely fugitive, but a fugitive nonetheless. And I am charged with finding her, apprehending her and this Faulk, the smith, and bringing them both to London in chains for a glorious hanging before the commons."

"What do you know about her?"

"Margery Peveril," he said again, this time with a harsher inflection. "Not a lady, but an esquire's wife, the respected mistress of a minor manor between Portbridge and Dartford, along the river Darent. I met her soon after my own arrival in Greenwich, the first week I was in office as justice of the peace. The only other time I saw her was just after her arrest."

"Tell me about her."

"An attractive woman," he said. "Perhaps twenty years of age, pert, lively, though never a flirt or gossip, and by all indications a faithful wife and true. Strong-willed, beloved in the parish, with a reputation for great and genuine piety, and always bounteous toward her husband's tenants — perhaps overly generous if anything. Her late husband's tenants," he corrected himself.

"The husband?"

"Twice her age, and Walter Peveril was a tyrant," Chaucer said. "From a minor gentry family, the *most* minor, you would have to call them, with a bitter disposition toward everyone around him. Beat his servants and his horses, had his tenants whipped on a whim. His wife suffered a great deal, it is said."

"Children?"

"None, though they have been married four years. My wife is barren, he'd say in his jars. One of the sources of his anger, perhaps."

"There is no doubt that she killed him?"

"None. The servants heard a struggle in the hall, a scream, some furniture knocked down. They went in and she was sitting by his corpse with a bloody hatchet in her hand as poor Walter's life left through his neck and chest. The sheriffs brought her in, and she'd been in the gaol at Portbridge until the — that is where we are heading now, before . . ."

He let out a frustrated breath. "I must apologize for my silence, John, and my clumsiness with you. There are things here I cannot fathom, that go so far beyond my experience that I don't know how to comprehend them."

"Will you simply tell me what has happened, Geoffrey?"

"I must see for myself first, and I want

you to have your green eyes on this, without bias from what I have to tell you."

I glanced over at him. "You do remember, don't you, that you called me out here not about this fleeing couple but about the ugly mess in the privy channel?"

He returned my gaze. "I do, John. I do indeed."

With that he turned from me, smacked his horse on the flank, and trotted ahead, closing our conversation. In another hour we had passed the river road to Dartford and arrived at the Portbridge manor, or Bykenors, as Chaucer called it, named for the family that had anciently controlled this part of the parish. The manor house was located at the far southeast of the Bexley heath, which we skirted along the southern edge. The soil out that way was dry, inclined to a gravelly loam that kicked up in ugly sprays from the hooves of Chaucer's horse.

We dismounted some distance from the manse itself, near a disused barn that fronted a two-story building of timber and Kentish stone. Heavy bars had been fixed across the windows on both floors, and the lower doors were secured with two knotted sliding beams at the top and bottom.

"The Portbridge gaol," said Chaucer, indicating that we should tether our horses on a nearby fence. "We won't be here long, though the lord and his lady have recently left for the autumn pilgrimage to Jerusalem, so we have the place largely to ourselves, aside from Tom Dallid there. The reeve." He raised an arm to wave at a man approaching us slowly from the manor stables, limping badly with each step. Chaucer made the introductions; then Dallid stood and waited for us to begin, looking uncomfortable. The reeve had troughed his head, judging from the dripping hair and beard. Bloodshot eyes, ale breath, and he was clothed in the distinctive Kentish jet, with a square-cut cotte over loosely fitted hose dyed a uniform black.

"Dallid manages the manor farms for Portbridge," Chaucer explained. "He also serves as keeper of this gaol, which we use for those accused awaiting delivery to the general eyre. Most of them stay locked up here for many weeks until the judge arrives."

"Or many months, aye," said Dallid. "This last lot? Most of them'd been within since June or thereabouts. Whole summer in m'lord's sweetest hole." He cackled.

"And how many prisoners were confined here as of four weeks ago?" Chaucer looked at me as he asked the question.

The reeve pursed his lips, raised his chin

to look at the sky. "Eighteen, it was."

"Who were they?" I asked Chaucer. "Horse thieves, highwaymen?"

"A potent stew of felons and general misdoers," he answered. "Five were apprehended poaching in the king's forests. Robert Faulk, one of the fugitives, was among their number, from all the way toward Canterbury, hauled up here awaiting delivery to King's Bench. Four were from a company of highwaymen who waylaid a shipment of silks from Dover. Then two horse thieves, two cattle rustlers . . . I'm forgetting now. Two of the men had raped a neighbor's daughter, and the rest were within for various felonies."

"Eighteen men, then, were being kept in this gaol," I said.

"Seventeen men and one woman."

I finally understood. I looked from Chaucer to Dallid. "The woman, then, was —"

"Margery Peveril," said Dallid. "And a wretched wretch she was after a few weeks in the cellar."

"You kept her in the *cellar*? Whyever would you do that, no matter her alleged crime?"

Dallid bit his lip. "It was stay down the cellar or go abed in a prisonhouse a' rough men, and all the foul dalliance and swyving

372

that would lead to. You ask me? It was a *gift* to the lady to stow her down there with the rats and such."

"A gift," I said, squatting to peer through the bars into the structure's cellar. The space beneath the stone building was frightfully low, barely high enough for a full-grown man to crawl about like a dog. Even from where I hunched it stank. In the faint light from the cellar window on the other side I could see a spread of clutter in the middle of the area: a thin straw pallet, a jumble of filthy-looking blankets, a bucket for her waste. All of it surrounded a thick post to which Margery Peveril had apparently been chained. My gut heaved.

"That Peveril, she liked to act the beneficent," said Dallid to my back. "But she was a murderer, she was, thick and through."

"And a sow, to judge by your treatment of her."

"Least you won't find my sows axing their masters, nor their hogs," said the reeve with a strong note of righteousness. "But Dame Margery Peveril? Chopped her own lord husband through to the neck bone. One, two, three strokes it was, and a gush of blood wide and deep as the Darent. I seen them take the rushes out off the floor after they put his body in the cart. Had to peel 'em off for the stick. Looked like a fellow was dragging a halved mutton across the manor yard to the drive, smearin' the master a Portbridge's very life on the grasses and stones. So — treat Dame Margery Peveril like a dog? Suppose I did, and it was a sight more than she deserved."

He looked about to stalk off until Chaucer placed a calming hand on his arm. "There, there, my good Dallid. My friend here is a Southwark man. He has little moral sense about such things. He intended no offense. Did you, John?" He widened his eyes at me.

"I did not," I said, catching myself and giving the reeve a slight nod. "And my apologies if such an offense was caused. The circumstances . . ."

"Course," he said curtly. "Now, Master Chaucer told me you'd have questions for me?"

"I do," I said, eager to get to it. "You said many of the prisoners were here since the summer, and that they were within until four weeks ago."

"Aye."

"They are no longer in this gaol?"

"They are not."

"Where are they now?"

"I've no knowing as to that."

"Where were they taken initially, then?"

"Sire?"

"Where were they taken after their removal from Portbridge? Were they sent to Dartford? Or to another manor gaol?"

He shrugged, his eyes shifting. "Don't know where they went then, don't know where they are now."

"Eighteen prisoners awaiting delivery and eyre under your watchful eye, and you have no sense where they went, where they are now?"

"No, sire."

"Whyever not?"

"Didn't ask."

"Why not?"

"Weren't the sort to take questions, not from a reeve, leastwise."

"Who moved them then?"

A slight hesitation. "Some men."

"How many?"

"Five — no, six."

"Six men, then, moved your eighteen prisoners out?"

"Aye," he said. His eyes shifted right. "Maybe eight."

"Did you know the men?"

"Not by sight nor name."

"Did they wear badges?"

"That they did."

"Of what livery?"

Silence.

"Whose men were they, Dallid?" The question we had been leading up to, the question I assumed Chaucer had brought me here to ask. "Whose men removed your eighteen prisoners?"

I handed him a few pennies. He looked down at the coins, then up at Chaucer, who gave him a sober nod.

"They were the duke's men."

A dull ache began to form at the base of my skull. "Which duke?"

He looked again at Chaucer. Another nod from my friend.

Dallid exhaled. "Gloucester," he said softly.

"Woodstock?" I said.

"Aye."

"Thomas of Woodstock empties a manor gaol in Kent? Under whose warrant?"

Dallid shrugged, almost sadly, I thought. I looked at Chaucer. "Geoffrey?"

"Gloucester holds great sway here and in the rest of Kent, John. Emptying a remote country gaol such as this one would have been an easy matter for the duke."

"But to what end?"

Chaucer's mouth was set in an unbent line. He turned to Dallid. "I thank you, Tom. You have been most helpful."

376

The reeve's nod this time was sullen, scowlish. As we retrieved our horses and mounted, I watched Dallid slink off toward the manor house, his back hunched over a secret he likely regretted sharing — and, I suspected, others he had yet to tell.

We made it quickly up to the main road, where Chaucer turned us west, toward Dartford.

"You think these missing prisoners answer to the privy corpses?"

"I do," he said.

"Eighteen prisoners in a Portbridge gaol, less our two fugitives, and sixteen bodies in the London ditches. You don't believe this is a coincidence?"

"I know it is not, John."

"You'll share your reasoning and proof with me?"

"I shall, within the hour."

"Yet why has Dallid cooperated with you, Geoffrey? Isn't he in fear of Woodstock, as much as anyone else in these hundreds?"

Chaucer leaned over in his saddle. "I have sliced a leaf from your quire, John," he said. "Our friend Tom Dallid is a debtor of the highest order, with well over ten pounds owed to taverners and tinkers and grocers throughout this part of Kent. And debtors, as we know, make the poorest and most incautious thieves. He has been stealing from his lord for years to pay his creditors, and though he fears the wrath of Gloucester more sharply, he fears the sword of his lord more frequently."

"Though his lord is on pilgrimage," I pointed out, concerned about Chaucer's looseness. "You trust his tongue?"

"I am a king's justice of the peace, John. I hardly fear the petty resentments of a country reeve."

His words struck me then as haughty and lax. To trade in sworn secrets, to barter with lies and threats, to buy and sell the best information while knowing its quality and heft: my business is a demanding craft, with little room for the inexperienced or naïve. It requires as much skill and discernment as the delicate embroidery on an archbishop's cope or the patient smithing of a great sword. To see Chaucer employing it with such lightness was worrying.

The middle of the afternoon, a lowering sun. We had ridden the half of an hour or so from Portbridge manor back roughly to the east, with turns at two crossings, and now reached the top of a narrow wooded valley, a shallow cleft between two rows of hills several miles south of Greenwich. We descended to the point where the road started to skirt the edge of the forest.

Chaucer reined in and dismounted. "The woods this way are thick. We'll leave these fellows here."

We tied our horses to some low-hanging branches and entered the woods. The trees around us were alive with the clicking whispers of jays, the impatient whirrings of warblers unhappy with intruders. There was no path leading us from the road, though I noticed some broken branches low along our way. Chaucer seemed to know where he was going, however. The growing dimness as the woods thickened made our progress slow, and we were reaching that time of day when my eyes were at their weakest, now further beset by obtrusive stands of saplings and shrubs, the deceptive play of shadow and light on flashing leaves.

Several minutes of walking brought us to the edge of a clearing, an oval perhaps forty feet by sixty and free of trees, whether by the hand of Lady Nature or man I could not tell. The angle of the sun against the highest limbs cast the area in a single broad shadow waffled in yellow and orange, like some fiery shield borne down from the sky. At the center of the glade were the remains of a large fire, which, judging by the number and spread of the charred logs, must have been quite something to see. The air was soft, only the slightest remaining tinge of ash carried on a gentle breeze that rustled the leaves overhead.

"There," said Chaucer, pointing across the clearing to the western edge.

I looked and saw nothing.

"Follow me," he said.

We walked over to the far trees. He reached for the branch of an oak, fingered an incision in the bark. "Just there."

I leaned forward, taking the wood in hand. "A cut branch?"

"Not cut," he said, walking farther along the edge of the clearing. "Here is another, and another. John, look at this trunk."

I joined him before another oak, a wide-trunked variety free of branches along its first ten feet. Two holes a forearm's length apart marred the grooved bark, the outer layer of which had splintered angrily along the edges of the impressions. Something about the holes looked familiar. I stuck my finger within up to the second knuckle. My fingertip touched what felt like metal. I had to be sure.

"Give me your knife," I said. Chaucer removed a long knife from his side, holding the blade and presenting the handle. The ivory butt was cool against my palm, the grip firm as I dug and hacked away at the lower hole in the tree. Eventually I had widened it sufficiently to insert the tip of the knife beneath the object lodged at the bottom. A push, a pull, and the object loosened, spilling out of the hole and into my palm.

Chaucer looked down at it. "A lead ball?"

"Iron shot," I said, confirming this gingerly with my teeth. The ball had retained its shape even in the hardness of the wood. It was identical in every respect — width, weight, and composition — to the balls Thomas Baker had removed from the corpses at St. Bartholomew's.

"There are more holes here and here." Chaucer had left my side to continue his inspection. Despite the gloom it was easy to make out the condition of the forest in that quadrant. The whole western edge of the clearing was savaged as if by some high-grazing herd of pigs, feeding on branches instead of roots. It looked like someone had attacked the trees with a dull axe.

"What's this?" he said, and stepped into the trees. I lost sight of him for a moment. There was a grunt, and he emerged with an arrow in his grasp. He inspected it, then handed it to me. Not a rustic hunter's shaft but a missile worthy of the royal armory, perfectly fletched, its length smoothed and polished to an impossible gleam. The arrow was tipped in a beveled triangle of iron. I brushed the blade edge along the pad of my thumb. The arrow could have peeled a grape.

"There's another on the next tree," said Chaucer, pointing beneath the limbs. "And a bolt run in alongside it, as if someone were targeting the trunk."

I looked at the opposite end of the clearing, to the east. The trees there were similarly ravaged, and I suspected we would find arrows, bolts, and balls lodged in their trunks and limbs if we cared to look. A glade in the woods, elms, ash, and oaks wounded to east and west — I looked down. In our initial inspection I had failed to notice the ghoulish signs that now shouted to me from the forest floor. This Kentish ground had been touched by little rain for some weeks. Perhaps it was the work of my imagination or a trick of my poor eyes, but on certain leaves there appeared faint traces of dried blood, congealed in the October chill, the marks of heels and heads where bodies had been dragged from the area.

I stepped to the edge of the clearing, my eyes now taking unaccustomed strength from the particular combination of sunlight and dark. At one of end of the clearing there was a stump, chest high and as wide around as a fry pan. The ash tree had been recently felled, I saw as I walked over to it, the wood still green and rough-hewn from the strikes of an axe. Most of the trunk lay on the forest floor, leaving only a stump in the ground. Its uneven top was scorched in a rough line dividing the middle. I rubbed my fingers along the blackened surface and brought them to my nose. Sulfur.

At the other side of the clearing Chaucer had moved to a similar stump, also newly created from the trunk of a felled elm. We each stood behind our respective length of fallen tree. Our eyes met in a heavy silence across the glade.

"There was a battle here," he said, walking slowly back toward my position. "A skirmish of some kind, with gunners, archers, crossbowmen —"

"Not a battle," I said, sure of it now. We met in the dead center of the glade. My limbs felt heavy, as if trying to pull me to the soil with the sixteen men who had died here. "A battle is two-sided, with both companies armed and opposed. This was a massacre."

"And this as well," said an unfamiliar voice.

My neck prickled. Chaucer froze, his hand halfway to his head.

We turned as one.

Three men, bunched together and emerging from the trees at the north side of the clearing. Not rough country men, of the sort one might expect to find in a remote Kentish wood. These were true soldiers, clad in the well-cut raiment of an elite company serving a high lord: linen tunics, woolen hoods, badged armbands wrapping their sleeves — though the livery was folded under and obscured, hiding any sign of their lord. Military men, battle-hardened and unflinching as they confronted two unarmed strangers in the woods.

The man on the left drew his sword. The one on the right did likewise. The middle soldier had already notched an arrow, its point gleaming in the fading sun. The string was taut and the shaft seated, aimed at my throat. My vision darkened and narrowed to the arrowhead's lethal point, and God's living earth stood still.

CHAPTER 24

An apprentice, having fallen from the smithy loft and broken his arm, now sat whimpering on a table edge at the corner of the foundry yard. Hawisia watched from the house door as Stephen helped the surgeon set and splint the limb. The boy leaned into him, his moist, reddened face crumpled in pain. Stephen gently grasped his shoulders and soon enough the work was completed.

"You're a strong one, Tom," said Stephen soothingly as the apprentice tried to fill his lungs.

"Not a splintering fracture, as I feel it, and no skin broke." The surgeon checked his knots before the final wrap. "Four, six weeks and you will be swinging your hammer again, my good fellow."

The apprentice grimaced at the babying and pushed himself from the table with his uninjured arm.

"Give thanks to our leech, Tom." Marsh

poked the boy in the chest. "Gratitude is ever a finger of God."

"Aye, Stephen," said the apprentice. He nodded at the surgeon. "I thank you, Master Dobbes."

The surgeon waved a hand before his face. "You will thank me by keeping yourself out of high places. God save those young bones for another day."

"Aye." The apprentice skipped off to join his fellows at the other end of the yard, bravely waving his splint.

Hawisia paid the surgeon, who went out the front through the shop room. "You are good to our boys, Stephen," she said when they were alone.

A rare kind word. It felt strange coming from her mouth, though it was merited. Stephen's face hadn't acknowledged the compliment. He finished gathering up the scraps from the surgeon's work, then glanced somewhere over Hawisia's shoulder.

"They miss their master," he said with a blank stare. "As do I."

"As do we all," she said, puzzled by his manner. He looked about to say more; then his mouth snapped shut. His eyes were tired and pouched.

"Stephen —"

"I must be off," he said, still avoiding her

gaze. "We're short copper. Bradley's've got a lot I can take for a good price."

"See to it, then," she said. He turned to walk away. His head was down. His feet dragged along the dirt. One of them caught on a clump of horse dung, and he stumbled forward, graceless and clumsy.

Since Robert's death and his sentence at the wardmoot Stephen Marsh had become a glummer young man, true. He could be sullen at times, trying to mask the understandable bitterness he felt at being chained to Stone's in the servile way he was. Yet Hawisia had never seen him go about as he had in recent days, so ragged and careless. Shirts and breeches soiled, face going swart and unwashed from one day to the next, as if he were suffering from some unnamed madness.

It had something to do with these snakes and tubes, of that she was certain. Over the last week she'd observed him several times at his dark work, the forge fired all through the night, tinking at the small serpents, forging iron and pouring bronze into these long rods, thinking he could hide it all from her. She was on the verge of confronting him about it, yet wanted first to understand the nature of his work — and, if she could, discover who was paying him for it.

Once Stephen had left on his errand she walked over to the smithy, where two apprentices were throwing dice. "Clear out of here, the both of you. And give me those dice. Now go shovel the stable." The apprentices obeyed, and soon she was alone. She hoisted herself on the stool, put her feet on the bench, and got her next look at the top shelf.

Two long rods of iron, with one of Stephen's snakes affixed to the middle of each. She lifted one gingerly and fingered the serpent. It was hinged. The snake moved at her touch, its gaping mouth reaching for a small pan hammered into the rod. The whole of the thing smelled vaguely of sulfur. She set it down and picked up the next rod. Nearly identical, though with subtle differences in its heft and balance.

She angled one of the rods away from herself and saw the hole at the end. She put her fingertip to it, then brought the finger to her nose. Sulfur again, and her finger was covered in soot. Another smell came back to her then. The scent of saltpetre and sulfur, the damp powder Robert and Stephen had made up in the clay pit to test the strength of their cannon. Her husband had made a jest of it, hadn't he, ordering the apprentices to line up and piss in the pit.

He'd pissed, too, as had Stephen Marsh. Robert even invited Hawisia to come and contribute to the cause.

The finished powder, though, had been no matter for laughter. As Robert warned, once mixed the powder would be as unstable as it was deadly, needing but a single spark to set a house aflame. He'd carried a measure of it out to the yard, poured it into the belly of a bombard, then touched the side of the thing with a coal. A flash, a great *crack,* then a new and acrid smell came floating across the yard with the smoke. Not the woodsy aroma of a slowly burning fire but a sharper scent.

It was a smell Hawisia remembered well, the very stench coming from the end of these rods. The stink of the devil.

Stephen Marsh was making guns.

"Mistress Stone!"

A man, calling from across the yard. Hawisia hastily replaced the rod and snake, climbed down from the bench, and left the smithy. Mathias Poppe, beadle of Bread Street Ward, stood at the back door to the shop.

"Mistress Stone," he hailed her as she approached.

"Fair welcome to you, Master Poppe." She hastily brushed her hands along her dress.

The ward official was the owner of a bake-shop in the next parish and a close friend of her late husband's.

"A few moments, if you please?"

"Of course, Master Poppe. We'll speak in the shop." He turned to follow her within.

"It's passing good to see Stone's sitting well, bells and pans and all," the beadle said as they entered the display room. He asked delicately after her health, the general state of the foundry. Poppe seemed friendly enough, solicitous as usual. He'd been a frequent presence around the shop, a tavern companion of Robert's, a strong talker about every subject you might name. Yet he was clearly avoiding something, dodging around a topic he seemed reluctant to broach. Hawisia was about to prompt him for his frankness when he got to the matter himself.

"Your Stephen Marsh," said the beadle, not looking at her. "Is he about?"

"Whatever could you want with Stephen?"

The beadle tongued a lip. "Have a few questions for the fellow, is all."

"What sort of questions, Master Poppe?"

"In honesty, mistress, I'd rather not say. We've had some inquiries from a sheriff from — looking into a — well, into an incident on a tenancy."

"What sort of an incident?"

"I am more than confident that this business has nothing to do with your Stephen, nor with Stone's. Yet thoroughness is a virtue in such matters, so I must speak with him, and soon. Is he about?"

"He is not."

"Might you know where he is?"

"He's after some copper. Over at Bradley's, he said."

"When do you expect him to return?"

"I couldn't say, Master Poppe."

"Then perhaps you might answer a question or two for me yourself."

"Happy to."

"Was Marsh about the foundry last Wednesday?"

"Last Wednesday," she said, trying to remember. She shook her head, seeing no reason to be elusive. "He was gone from the foundry that day, Master Poppe. Gone from the city indeed, as he had some business to transact for Stone's."

"Up by Ware?"

This surprised her. "Aye, halfway to Ware. Some ingots of tin, from a thrifty peddler he'd heard from. Had a large lot to sell cheap."

"Some quantity of tin, you say?"

"Aye."

"And the name of the peddler?"

"That I can't tell you. You'll have to ask Stephen."

"Oh, I'll ask him, Mistress Stone. Have no concerns on that score."

She found his manner prickling. "Pray tell me why Stephen Marsh's whereabouts that day are of interest to you, Master Poppe. What was this incident, and how does it concern him?"

The beadle traced the tips of his fingers across a sacring bell. "All I can say, mistress, is there's a bad situation on one of the hundreds up there. A death."

"A *death*?"

"Aye," he said. "Daughter of a tenant farmer by Tewson. Body was found in a small wood up that way, hidden away in the bushes, poor girl. And the way she was killed . . ." He shook his head.

"Surely you cannot think Stephen was involved?"

"What I can and cannot think is beside the matter, Mistress Stone. The fact is, your Stephen was —"

"He is not *my Stephen,* Master Poppe," she said, with a pointed formality.

"Excuse the figure, mistress." He held up a placating hand. "I am simply following my orders. A young woman met an untimely

392

end, a death other than her rightful. When such a thing happens we must cooperate with the sheriffs of the shire, wherever such cooperation may lead us." His voice softened. "And in this case, dear Hawisia, it has led us direct to Stephen."

"But how? Why has Stephen Marsh, of all people, been spotted for this?"

Poppe sighed. "That's the difficulty, you see. He was spied going out by Bishopsgate that morning, alone, by one of the guardsman who knows him by reputation. Then spied again coming back in by bell of four or thereabouts. And there was a merchant company saw a lone rider answering to his description leave the road just east of where the girl met her end. The tenant's daughter went missing that very afternoon, and hadn't been seen since. Not until some sheepman's dog found her two days later, on the Friday it was."

"The tin peddler, then," she said. "Find the tin peddler, ask him about Stephen, and this goes away with no one harmed, jailed, or hung."

Poppe gave an agreeable nod. "We find the fellow, confirm that Stephen was up there for tin, as he said to you he was, then we shouldn't have any more reason to trouble him over this. You see, mistress?"

"I do," said Hawisia, though despite his reassurance she felt no easier about the beadle's inquiry. She would send Marsh over to Poppe's bakeshop upon his return, she promised him, and the whole unpleasant business would be behind them.

When the beadle had gone Hawisia stood for a long while at the counter, struggling to make sense of what the man had told her. A lone rider, a woman killed — and Stephen Marsh in the area, supposedly riding toward Ware by himself. With his guns?

Throwing a heavy mantle over her shoulders to mask her condition, she left the shop to look for Stephen. Bradley's was a peddler of scrap metals in the next parish. Stephen would likely be making his way back to Bellyeter Lane along Fenchurch Street. She waited for him outside the cooper's shop at the crossing. The wait was not long. As the bell at All Hallows Staining stroked, she saw him dodging around a wagon, his head down, hands swinging slowly at his sides.

"Stephen," she said. He stopped when he saw her.

"What is it, mistress?"

"The beadle has come by, asking questions."

No surprise on his face, nor unease in his

voice. "What sorts of questions?"

She watched him closely, the resignation already rimming his eyes. "About a dead girl, up toward Ware."

He blinked.

"Another of your accidents, was it?"

His lips quavered. "Mistress —"

"Come along." She spun around and strode down Bellyeter Lane. He followed her meekly. When they reached the foundry she led him through the house door.

"Go into the chapel," she said without looking at him. "Remain there until I come for you. You understand?"

"Yes, mistress."

She went out to the yard, kept herself busy for the next several hours, her thoughts racing. The beadle returned at the end of the day, this time bringing along a constable. She lied them off, claiming Stephen had never come back from Bradley's. Hawisia could sense Poppe's skepticism, though thankfully he did not press her on the matter. Now she would have to wait.

Hours later Hawisia descended the inner stair in the dark and cold, palms whispering along the rough wall. She turned before the kitchen, walked along the screens passage toward the street door, then came to the

395

low entrance leading into the chapel.

She ducked beneath the beam and stepped down into the family chapel, a long and narrow chamber sunk several feet below the first story of the main house. It had been added only two years before, after Stone's best-ever string of sales, when Hawisia's vanity led her to declare that a chapel would be a fitting ornament for a wealthy founder's house. Robert had resisted, the frugal man, but she had won out in the end. The chapel was fully shuttered against the autumn chill, though with no fire going in the altar hearth the room was bitterly cold, and the first thing she saw was the icy breath of Stephen Marsh as he came to his feet at her entrance.

A servant had lit a candle from the kitchen coals, and in its wavering light Hawisia witnessed Stephen's present state. Skittish hands, trembling limbs, a fear burning in his eyes. If she didn't know better Hawisia would have guessed he was afflicted with a fever or pox.

"Mistress Stone." His head hung low.

She stepped forward and reached for his chin, opening his face to her own. "Look me in the eye, Stephen, and tell me true. You killed this little faun?"

His lips loosened. "I did."

"With one of these snake guns, was it?"

He gasped. "How — how did you —"

"Never you mind that. What happened?" She let go his chin.

"A misfiring is what it was. I heard something in the woods and I spun round and the snake came down —"

"Yet you hid her body beneath a bush. The act of a coward, that, and a fool."

"Aye, mistress. After the accident I was taken with fright's what it was, and didn't think it out, and now . . ."

"And now you face the sheriffs, Stephen, and the shire court by Ware. Had you found a shire justice, told him what happened, you might have begged a jury for mercy or gotten the ear of a barrister. But dragging a girl's bleeding flesh into the shrubs? You will hang for certain, Stephen Marsh."

"It seems so," he said softly. "Unless you help me, mistress."

She lowered her voice to match his. "First my husband, now you've killed this girl, both with your cursed metals and arts. And you have the shamelessness to ask me for succor and aid?"

Stephen, surprising her, knelt and took her hands. His were hot on her skin, despite the cold in the chapel. "Shame's too poor a word, mistress. Your husband was the finest of men, the greatest of teachers. Every day I

397

see him again before the cast. Ten times a day I see him there, trusting me with the pour as always, and I tip the smelt again, and I see his arm bathed with fire again, hear him scream again. You cannot know the weight of it."

Oh, but I can, Stephen, she thought.

He looked up at her, his face glistening with tears and phlegm. "All I can ask is your forgiveness, Hawisia, and your aid."

She gazed down at the man, feeling the grip of her own conscience, pushing against it with all her will. Why, if she hadn't learned the source of Stephen's recent distress she would have been *enjoying* the great change in him. It was as if all his pride and arrogance had whistled out of his soul, like a bladder slowly losing its air.

"You are a fool, Stephen Marsh," she said. "A weak and womanly fool." And what does this fool deserve?

Hawisia wanted nothing more than to swing open the street door to call for the watch. But open Stone's gates to the parish constable and the foundry itself might be lost. Harboring a fugitive criminal carried stiff penalties, and Hawisia wanted no truck with Guildhall fines. This was Stephen Marsh's affair, not hers. Stephen Marsh's guns, Stephen Marsh's snake, Stephen

Marsh's crime.

Yet Stephen Marsh *was* Stone's foundry, the source of its wealth and the only hope for its future. His hands, his mind, his skill. If he was caught and hanged there would be nothing for her. Worse, nothing for her coming child. What she needed — what they both needed — what all three of them needed — was time.

A beam of fired gold flashed from the altar. She turned her head, gazing up at the gilt cross, and at the sight of it found new confidence in the solution she had devised. Not a permanent answer, not by a long measure; yet it would protect the foolhardy man for the time being, keep the simpering rabbit free from the talons of the city laws, though only if she could get him there without harm or seizure. It was a risk: to herself, to Stone's and its livelihood. Hawisia Stone didn't like risk.

"We'll leave at once," she announced, rubbing her hands, thinking over the route.

"To where?" said Stephen.

"You shall see. I'll just fetch my coat." She went to the hall and came back through the screens passage to the chapel, bundled against the cold.

"Come," she said, beckoning for Stephen to follow. He took his own coat from a pew and came meekly along. She stepped up from the chapel and led him back through the passage to the street door. Hawisia peered out onto the street through a half-shuttered window. A thin moon overhead, the street cast in low light — low enough, she hoped, for what must be done. No sign of the parish watch, not yet at least.

She unbarred the door and pulled the hasp slowly toward her. The hinges were well oiled and made no sound as the door swung open. Stephen followed her down into the street.

Violators of curfew were not dealt with lightly by the city, and Hawisia risked a spell in the Tun should the two of them be caught. Yet she knew this parish, knew its turns and twists. They slipped along Belly-eter Lane silently until they came to the turn onto Fenchurch Street. Hawisia was about to move forward when she heard voices, approaching from the direction of the parish church.

She pressed her hand on Stephen's chest, flattened him against a wall. Two men. She listened to their idle chatter. The parish watch, trolling the streets. Soon they passed, their swung lanterns pushing puddles of light along the lane.

Hawisia grasped Stephen's wrist and

pulled him with her until they reached All Hallows Staining. The churchyard gates were closed against the night, though this was hardly a barrier. They skirted the wall to the small opening before the porch, and soon they were together within the parish grounds.

She led him silently around to the detached house that served as the parish rectory, a squat bump against the south wall. The chimney was still smoking. With no delay she knocked thrice at the door, repeated the poundings. Soon they heard a moaned protest from within. "A moment."

Eventually the rectory door opened to reveal the face of Father Martin, the parson of Staining. "Mistress Stone!" he said in surprise, then raised the candle to look at her companion. He frowned, the upper part of his body rearing back. "And Stephen Marsh. You are —" A short gasp as he understood the purpose of their visit, though he still had to ask. He cleared his throat. "What do you seek from your shepherd at this hour of the night?"

Hawisia looked at Stephen, back at the parson. Then she spoke the only word that might save the neck of this flawed and invaluable man.

"Sanctuary."

CHAPTER 25

The bow released. The gentle *twang* filled my ears as the missile streaked for my eye. Already in that moment before impact I felt the arrowhead slice through the tissues of my eyeball, destroying my vision even as it ravaged my skull and brain. Yet just as he sped forth, Death held himself at bay in some strange dilation as my vision filled with an illusion of sudden change. The arrow, as it hurtled toward its target, began to slow; then, with equal purpose, to shrink from one end to the other, collapsing and shortening on itself, gathering its full length into a compact roundness hovering before my eyes.

All that was left in the end was a dull metal ball, a sphere of iron, small at first, then growing until it assumed the mass of the world before my eye, as if the entire earth had been moved by the hand of God to stand in my way and fill my vision. I fumbled for my own quiver and bow and aimed an arrow at this giant, threatening sphere, the easiest of targets. Yet my fingers could not release the string, and I stood frozen, impotent against the great round weapon looming before my eyes, as if shooting vainly at the world.

I awoke washed in sweat. Chaucer, crushed next to me on the thin pallet, was snoring heavily. After talking far into the night we had both slept fitfully, our minds pressed with the peril of our situation. Only half a day before we had been roaming freely around the Kentish countryside. Now we were jailed in a nameless keep, with a single loaf between us and no coin to buy our way out and home. Our purses had been emptied, our horses and bags seized, our bodies handled carelessly as we were bound by the wrists and thrown over our saddles to be led along. The men had covered our heads with sacks, and by nightfall we'd had no sense of where we were or what would become of us. Hours later, as the day broke, I felt no less uneasy about our coming fate.

After several minutes in quiet thought, I stood and walked to one of the three narrow slits in the wall, squatting to take in the view. Day had broken not long before, the treetops and fields awash in a burned haze, the chill air mingled with smoke from a fire somewhere down below. We were being confined in the uppermost floor of a small towerhold, which was perched on a high promontory overlooking a gentle downward slope to the east. The Thames was not in sight, though to the north I could make out the glinting blur of a tributary snaking through fields and trees, flamed with the early sun. The river Cray, perhaps, or a branch of the Darent. We were somewhere southwest of Dartford, as I reckoned it, a few hours' ride to Southwark, though my home could not have seemed more remote as I hunched by the close aperture.

Chaucer stirred on the pallet. "John?" he said in a morning croak. I looked at his waking form in the rising light, his yellow, sun-washed hair plastered to his forehead and cheeks, his beard in need of a trim. He had slept in all his clothes, and his cotte was bunched uncomfortably at his midsection.

"Our blinders are off now, Geoffrey," I said. "We are prisoners, where I don't know. Do you have a guess?" To my weak eyes there was little to distinguish one hill or field from another.

He groaned loudly, stretched, then rose and came to my side. Kneeling on the wooden floor and wedging his forehead into the beveled slit, he glanced in both directions, then did the same at the other two openings. "We are in Bexley parish, I would say. Foots Cray is there, just beyond that second rise, and St. Paul's Cray beyond the next." I followed his pointing finger and saw or at least imagined a small manse on a low hill, perhaps a quarter mile distant. "I know the keeper of Bexley Woods," he said. "If I can manage it I will send him a message through one of the servants here, with promise of a good fee."

I looked at him, wondering where he got his confidence. Rather than questioning my friend I let hunger guide me to a basket near the trapdoor, which was locked against our possible descent. The castle guards had left us with some bread, cheese, and small ale, which we consumed quickly and with little talk between us.

After a final swallow, Chaucer leaned over and patted my knee. "Don't worry overmuch, John. We'll jaw our way out of this."

"How can you know that?"

"I am a member of Parliament, a justice of the peace for this shire. These soldiers may be ruffians, but they are hardly murderers."

"*Hardly* murderers? More than likely they

are the men who massacred those prisoners in the woods. What is to say they won't do the same with us?"

"Their lord, whoever he may be, would not allow it."

"We know nothing about these men, nor their lord. They wore no badges and no collars, bore no banners. I recognized none of them, and as you'll recall they made little talk on the way here from the gaol."

"There is a code of behavior when it comes to holding gentles as prisoners," Chaucer said with far more assurance than I could summon. "It remains in place even in the wars between the English and the French. No torture, no privation, no hanging. Those men wouldn't have left us food if they intended us to die. A code, John. They will not harm us."

"Is this the same code that massacred those men and threw them in the privy channel?"

He raised his chin, ignoring the question. Hours later, when we were starting to lose our patience with the close chamber and with each other, we heard footsteps on the stairs below. The trapdoor opened to show the head of one of our captors, the bowman from the previous afternoon. He clapped the board to and gestured for us to follow.

We were led from the low tower and down into the hall, a close-ceilinged chamber with a tired fire sending slow puffs of smoke to the vented roof. Drab hangings were spaced randomly along the walls, all of them tattered or scorched. A large pile of broken furniture had been stacked in a far corner. The kitchen door hung askew on a single hinge.

"Not a keep I visit often enough." We turned to see Thomas of Woodstock, Duke of Gloucester, standing below a recessed window, and I could not have been more surprised. We bowed deeply as he approached us, then watched him turn for one of the trestle tables to either side of the central hearth. He took a large oaken chair. We remained standing.

"Your accommodations have been comfortable and to your liking?" asked the duke.

Chaucer bowed. "Infinitely so, Your Grace."

"I hardly bother to have this heap of stone servanted prior to my arrivals. The hawking around this part of Kent can be quite rich, though, so I suppose it's worth maintaining in some minimal way."

"And in what great palace do we find ourselves, your lordship?" Chaucer asked.

"The Rokesle hunting lodge, if you must

know. It came to me through my dear sister, the Dowager Countess Joan."

"May her memory be cherished, your lordship."

"Oh, it shall be, Chaucer, it shall be."

We held a respectful silence in honor of Joan of Kent, mother of King Richard and the most beloved woman in the realm in the years prior to her death. The countess had fallen ill and died at Wallingford Castle just last August. Tongues were wagging that the king's loss of his mother was what had turned him so cold these last months, as his severity had increased toward those around him.

"Now to this matter of your trespass," said Woodstock, breaking the stillness. "You were in my forest, Chaucer. A poet abroad in the woods, snapping my ducal twigs, stamping my ducal leaves, disturbing my ducal dirt. By what right do you intrude on my properties?"

Chaucer inclined his head. "With respect, your lordship, we were merely out for a ride in the countryside around Greenwich."

"And what are you doing in Greenwich?"

"Your Grace, I have been retained by His Royal Highness since midsummer."

"In what office?"

"I am justice of the peace for the shire of Kent."

"I was not informed of this by Westminster, though I suppose you cannot be blamed for that." He lifted his jaw in my direction. "And who is your companion here?"

Chaucer looked at me with a glint in his eye. I bowed. "My name is John Gower, your lordship."

The duke reared back in his chair, his mouth agape, then quickly recovered himself. "We have never met."

"We have not, my lord."

"Though by your reputation I feel that I know you quite well. Like a smear of dung on my boot."

I stared at the duke's collar, lined with fur and cinched too tightly against his neck. This was the man who, by all indications, had ordered the slaughter of eighteen prisoners, the disposal of their corpses in a London sewer channel, and who knew what other atrocities. Now I too was but a smear of dung in his eyes.

"And I am aware that the presence of John Gower in a lord's castle cannot be good tidings for the lord," the duke went on. He looked at Chaucer. "You have come with a threat in your purse, have you? Some hope of extracting a kidney from our royal gut?"

The duke was trying for game, though his unease was apparent.

"Hardly, your lordship," said Chaucer. "Gower here is merely a friend I've invited out to Greenwich for a few days to escape the Southwark filth. He, like me, is a poet, a versifier of great prolixity."

"Though one of considerably lesser talents than your own, if all the talk is to be believed," said the duke, and I did not flinch beneath his cold and condescending gaze. Chaucer said nothing in my defense, nor did I expect him to.

"So now I have Geoffrey Chaucer and John Gower trespassing together in my forest, asking questions of my tenants at Bykenors, stirring up demons. And you claim you were abroad to catch the air, for a few hours' amusement, do you?"

"The mass murder of innocents is hardly an amusement, my lord," I said, hoping I would not regret my rashness. It was as if the Holy Spirit descended into the castle hall to inflame the crown of the duke's head. He rose as two of his attendants moved from their stations along the walls. He waved them off. He approached and stood before us, his chin forward, his strangely centerless eyes alight with fury.

"What impudence, and from such a dark-souled man. He speaks for you as well, Chaucer?"

"I —" Chaucer stammered, then glumly sighed. "He does, my lord. Though you are Duke of Gloucester and the king's uncle I must hear your lordship's account of the incident in the forest."

"The 'incident,' you say?"

"Yes, my lord. Eighteen prisoners unaccounted for at Bykenors gaol. We suspect they were — that they died in the forest where Gower and I were apprehended yesterday. By your men."

"That's what you suspect, is it?"

"Yes, Your Grace," said Chaucer.

"And you believe that because this incident occurred on my lands it was done at my behest?"

"We have no evidence to suggest so, Your Grace. I am simply helping the sheriffs investigate the matter as justice of the peace for the shire."

In fact there *had* been evidence. The strips from the duke's banner binding the victims' hands. Yet if I revealed my knowledge of Brembre's destruction of the silken remnants I would virtually ensure our deaths at Gloucester's hands.

"Eighteen dead, you say. Where are the

corpses, then?" This time the duke's question was directed at me.

"The churchyard at St. Bartholomew's, Your Grace," I said. "They were taken there after being dumped in the privy channel below Cornhill. And there were sixteen dead, not eighteen. Two, it seems, managed to escape."

"How horrible," said Woodstock, his voice flat. "You are confident they are the bodies of the prisoners?"

"I am now, my lord," I said. Seeing no reason to conceal what we had discovered in the clearing, I went on. "They were killed with small powder guns shooting iron balls. Handgonnes, Your Grace."

"I see." The duke looked anything but surprised, his bland expression masking whatever inner turmoil our presence was stirring. "You know, nothing would pleasure me more than to see you both dangling from those trees back there, or from the Dartford gibbet. Yet I suppose I can't very well hang a king's justice of the peace, can I? Not with all that's unfolding in Westminster this month." He put a finger to his lips. "You shall receive my account in good time. You have my word."

Chaucer bowed, looking relieved. "That is all we can ask, Your Grace." They both looked at me expectantly.

I thought of Piers Goodman, that line of bodies on the St. Bart's ground, and here was the man responsible for it all. "With respect, my lord, this matter is too grave for further dilatation."

Gloucester scoffed. "Don't bait me, Gower. I am not one of your fish to be speared in a barrel with a farthing and a secret."

"This atrocity is hardly a secret, Your Grace, despite the best efforts of its perpetrator."

"John," said Chaucer, a warning in his voice.

The duke shot him an angry look. "I know what you saw in those woods, Chaucer." Back to me. "Or rather what you think you saw. I saw it, too. But be forewarned that friendly appearances may soon prove cold illusions."

"Yes, Your Grace," I said.

"Yes, Your Grace," he mocked me, then stepped forward and leaned in, ignoring Chaucer for the moment. "Tyranny and desperation are frequent bedfellows. Our chronicles teach us as much." He had turned his head slightly so that his lips were mere inches from my left ear. In this intimate posture he whispered words that would stay with me in the weeks to come. "The truth wheels above you, Gower, yet you fix your eyes upon the ground. A king will do anything to stay a king. *Anything.* You would do well to remember that as you go about your foul work."

He backed away, and we bowed as he turned for the door through which he had come; we were dismissed. With a visible reluctance the duke's men returned our bags, knives, and purses (these last somewhat lightened), then led us out to the central courtyard, where our saddled horses were waiting. An hour's ride toward London brought us to the crossing where Chaucer would turn for Greenwich. There we sat on our horses for a short while, discussing the events of the last two days, both of us in foul tempers only darkened by the duke's dismissal of our inquiries.

"You are for Southwark, then?" he asked me.

"I am."

Chaucer tried to convince me to return to Greenwich with him, claiming a distracting night of parsing poetry would do our spirits some good. I declined, with more than a little regret. I would always envy Chaucer his too-easy ability to separate the various parts of his life one from the other, as if his moral soul were a dovecote, divided into dozens of chambers each designated for a distinct fraction of his attention and care. One for Parliament, one for poetry, one for murder; one for his wife, one for his mistresses, another, increasingly small, it seemed to me that year, for his friendship with John Gower. Chaucer's attention would flit happily from chamber to chamber, never allowing those darker places to impinge on his enjoyment of the lighter, while I always found myself consumed by the matters most before me at any given time. And in that moment, as we separated on the Kentish road, there were three: an emptied gaol, a clearing in the woods, the beguiling whispers of a duke.

CHAPTER 26

"You must recognize, Mistress Stone, that this affair puts the parish in a passingly awkward position."

"Yes, Father," Hawisia said piously, wanting very much to smack him.

"Requests for sanctuary are quite unusual, and must be dealt with delicately."

"Yes, Father."

"I shall require some immediate information from you, then, and from Stephen."

"Yes, Father."

Hawisia Stone and the parson of All Hallows Staining had just stepped onto the church's west porch, where they spoke below the loud bustle of Fenchurch Street. They had left Stephen within, huddled glumly in a side chapel at the end of the south aisle.

It was late morning on the day after their midnight arrival at All Hallows. The priest, though young and newly settled into his living at Staining, had not been pleased to be roused in the middle of the night by a pregnant widow of the parish and a criminal claiming sanctuary, and had taken Stephen in only after extracting her promise to return the following morning to give a fuller explanation. Hawisia had none of the old parish obligations to draw on with this fresh-faced sprite. Why, it was Master Stone who'd cast the very bell thirty feet above their heads, and as a worthy gift to the parish. A gift that should have purchased some forbearance on the parson's part, or at least some measure of kindness from a tender of the Staining flock.

"Of all the churches in London only St. Martin-le-Grand exercises the privilege of permanent sanctuary, Mistress Stone," he went on in his priestly tone. "Now that Stephen is here he cannot leave or he will be apprehended. There are already watchmen along Fenchurch Street, working in shifts to ensure he remains within our walls. He will be taken the moment he steps out."

Hawisia had seen them for herself now that the news had spread. Two men of the parish she knew by name, pacing importantly around the church and its small yard, rubbing their hands, eyes slitting through the gates, watching for Stephen Marsh to break the bounds. "Yet surely he is right to claim sanctuary here," she said.

The priest shifted on his feet. "At All Hallows we are bound by agreements in force between the church and the realm. They are as unshakable as Jerusalem and Athens. A night on the chapel floor is one matter. But there are steps that must be followed before I can officially admit him to sanctuary and allow him to stay."

"What are these steps?"

"First Stephen must confess his sin. What is the nature of his crime?"

She looked him straight on. "He has killed."

"Here in London?"

"Up below Ware. It was an accident, he says. I believe him."

"Your belief carries no weight. Stephen must confess this deed for himself, whatever way the worldly law takes him. Only then may I declare him truly in my protection as minister of this parish, and only with approval of the bishop of London."

"How long may he remain within these walls, Father?"

He raised his chin, looked down at hers. "The right of sanctuary is neither inviolable nor eternal. Once he confesses Stephen has forty days to surrender himself to a trial.

418

Otherwise he must abjure the realm, though that option will be at the discretion of the justices, not the church. The king's coroner will make a visitation soon to gather the facts as Stephen remembers them."

"I understand, Father."

He licked his reddened lips. "And then there is the subject of payment. Sanctuary does not come free." His voice lowered and sober, as if to signal the matter of most importance in this affair.

Hawisia dug a finger into her purse, masking her disgust. "I'll have one of our 'prentices bringing him his food, so no need there. What's it to sleep on a stone chapel floor? Twopence for the first week, shall we call it?"

"Well." He coughed. "He will hardly be sleeping on stone, mistress. We have a feather-and-straw pallet in there, newly stuffed. Some woolen blankets for warmth. He may want to keep a candle alight in the chapel if he likes. Tallow hardly bubbles from a spring, now, does it? There is also my meeting with the bishop to consider, and I shall be speaking with the alderman of the ward tomorrow. A parson's time is freely given, Mistress Stone, though not so freely compensated. Stephen Marsh's presence here has increased our burden tenfold.

So let us call it a shilling for the week, shall we?"

His tongue, lizardlike, flickered from his mouth again to moisten his thin lips.

"A shilling, for a cloth stuffed with straw?"

"And feathers and down, Mistress Stone. It is a reasonable sum, though perhaps I can be content with fifteen pennies."

"Very well," said Hawisia, handing over the appropriate number of coins. When this business was over she would have to see about getting the parson removed. A wealthy widow of the parish with a full tithe could bend ears aplenty among the wealthier guildsmen, and more than once she'd seen a parish priest get a shoe at his arse for angering the wardens. Content with fifteen pennies indeed.

"We should go inside," said the parson. "I will hear Stephen's confession, then move this forward. I cannot do more for him, Mistress Stone."

She smiled sweetly. "I understand, Father, and I am grateful for the assistance you have rendered."

They went back into the church and approached the side chapel, where Stephen sat against the north wall. Painted above him was a vivid scene of Mary visiting Elizabeth, each of them reaching out to touch the other's belly, neither as large as Hawisia's prominent mound.

She listened as the priest repeated to Stephen the terms of sanctuary as he had explained them to her. The two men went through the chancel screen toward the altar, where Stephen would give his confession, with the priest as witness. Contrite murmurs, the priest's questions, a careless death carelessly absolved. Stephen remained within as the priest returned to the bottom of the nave.

"May I speak to him before I depart, Father?" said Hawisia, craning to look through the door of the chancel screen.

The priest shook his head. "I have instructed him to pray. He is to remain in the chapel by the altar for the better part of an hour." He put a finger to his lip. "As you are here, we should speak about the baptism once your child comes forth. Have you purchased a chrisom cloth, or considered your churching offering to the parish?"

Hawisia, having had enough of the parson's worldly wants, turned for the doors. "Time for that after the birth, Father," she said wearily. "I shall return in the days ahead, and my 'prentice with Stephen's meals."

Hawisia stood on the west porch, gathering her breath and her wits, breath and wits she'd sorely need in the weeks to come. There were metals to purchase, bells to sell, a foundry to run, a child to birth. She closed her eyes and whispered a prayer. "Jesu, forsake me not. Bind me to thee with sweetest knot. Give me of thy sweet love. I ask thee high above." She looked out beyond the gate to the city teeming with life, and started the slow walk back to the foundry.

CHAPTER 27

On London Bridge, just past the midpoint between the Southwark side and the St. Magnus green at the city foot, there is a narrow gap between houses that affords an expansive vista down over the river toward Westminster. In years past, before the slow darkening of my sight, I would sit in that spot for hours on end, surveying from that high perch the spires and towers lined up across the sky like sentinels at a wall. All Hallows, St. Mary Somerset, St. Peter, St. Paul's, once sharply defined, now little more than remembered outlines in a hazy distance.

That day after my return from Greenwich I had come to this spit of stone in hopes that this broad view down upon the city might help me loosen the threads all tangled in my mind. Why bring the sixteen bodies to London, let alone cast them in the privy channel? Why not bury or burn them out in

Kent, where no one would ever find them? As Chaucer had warned me early on, someone seemed to want the victims to be found, perhaps even identified, and all fingers pointed to Gloucester. If the reeve was to be believed, the duke's men had taken the eighteen prisoners from the Portbridge gaol to meet their fate in the woods. It must have been his men as well who brought the sixteen dead to London to toss in a foul grave. Yet what was to be gained by such a violent and risky act? What did the king's youngest uncle hope it would achieve?

There was also the practicality of it, the daunting mechanics of such an endeavor. What would it require to bring so many bodies from a wood in Kent to a London privy channel — and to accomplish it all secretly, without word getting out and abroad? First a group of tight-lipped men, all implicated in the massacre and invested in its concealment. Two or three wagons in Kent to haul the corpses along the road from the forest to the river, the procession guarded and masked as official business, and likely ending up on the bank somewhere well west of Greenwich, given the distance and the tides. Next a wherry or barge up the Thames, with the water bailiffs paid off to look away — little difficulty there. Then, that same night, a crew to transport the corpses through the narrow city streets and up to the privy at Cornhill. Several armed men keeping watch in case of discovery. Also a good-sized cart — and thus a carter.

I heard once again the words of Piers Goodman. *And had a carter of Langbourn Ward up here — oh — last week? Weeping mess he was, too, with a sad sad sad sad story to tell about his cart and his cartloads.*

The murdered carter, a snag I hadn't yet tugged. My connections at the coroner's office, once deep and strong, were tenuous at the moment due to the death the year before of Nicholas Symkok, the subcoroner. While Symkok had sung in my choir for many years, I had nothing on the man newly installed in his position, so our transactions were straight purchases of fact and rumor. A quarter noble for an inquest report, a few pennies for a name.

I called at the coroner's chambers early that afternoon and told the subcoroner what I was after. He remembered the carter's case, and once my coins were in his hand he found me the entry in the coroner's roll for the date in question. *On Wednesday the even of St. Edwin's Day after Michaelmas, Jankyn Bray, a carter of Carter's Way in the parish of St. Nicholas Acon, lay dead of a death other than his rightful death in the channel of Walbrook below Cornhill, having been discovered there by Alan Pike, gong-farmer of the parish of St. Mary Aldermary.* The entry went on to recount the summoning of the jury and the determination of cause of death: to all appearances, a knife across the throat and multiple stabs to the chest and head. No witnesses, no suspects.

Upon reaching the edge of Langbourn ward I asked a few shopkeepers for directions to Carter's Way, a twig of an alley off St. Nicholas Street. At the open end of the alley four carters were gathered, waiting for any small job and the pennies it would bring. Stones, kegs, coals, corpses: a carter will haul anything for anyone if the right coin kisses his palm.

"Load for you, sire?"

"Faggots or coals for your hearth 'n' home, good master?"

"A carter a' courage, a carter a' care, a carter a' can-do, a carter a carter a carter for you, sire."

A more irreverent one was leaning beneath the archway. "Transport to Tyburn and the gallows tree, sire? When your time comes you call on your Robert Bray here, sire. He'll make your last ride comfortable as can be."

His companions shared a forced laugh. Grubby, brash, sour of breath, Bray was a wiry young man with a defiant air about him, and it was clear from the distance they kept that the others were uncomfortable in his presence.

"Robert Bray," I said. "You are Jankyn Bray's son?"

He showed me an arrogant jaw. "Was, more like. Suspect you know that already."

"I do," I said. "God give your father rest."

"In an eternal bed of dung," muttered one of the others.

Some rough laughs, and Bray turned on him. "Shut your maw, Thomas Daws, or I'll nail it shut to your coillons."

The offender rolled his eyes and said nothing as his fellows closed around him, all of them ignoring Bray. I showed him a coin and gestured for him to follow me into the alley. He hesitated for a moment, then shrugged gamely and came along. We stood just within the archway from Fenchurch Street. The tenements here were built out and nearly touching, with only a sliver of sky visible between the upper stories. Broken wheels, cracked axles, and unused sideboards lay stacked against the outer walls on either side, the whole area a busy testament to the meager trade of lading.

"Your father died last week," I said.

"Aye," said Bray.

"Thrown in the privy channel."

"Happy reminder, I thank you for't."

"A victim of murder."

"Why, you must be a master logicker up Oxford with that mind a' yours, sire."

"The coroner's inquest yielded no suspects."

"Not so I heard neither. My poor old father killed dead but not a man killed him, so the sheriffs tell us."

"Do you have any notion who might have wished him harm?"

"That's what the sheriffs' men asked, aye. No thoughts on the matter, myself."

"What about his work?"

"What about it?"

"Did he talk to you about a job along the wharf? Something recent, and under his cap?"

Bray shrugged. "Never talked to me 'bout any of his haulings."

"This would have been a night job."

He started to shrug again, but his shoulders froze halfway down. The corners of his eyes lifted just slightly. "Night cartin', you say."

"In the weeks before his murder. Did he say anything to you about a special commission, or a peculiar request?"

"Only carters out at night be the soilers, moving shit about and out the walls," he mused, avoiding my question. "But the gongfarmers hire that out, don't they?"

"So he spoke to you about this job?"

He looked at my hand. I palmed him a few pennies and he tossed his chin, indicating a narrow house halfway down the alley. "Didn't speak a whip to me. But I heard him talk about it with her."

"Who?"

"His smooth coney back in there. Lower floor."

"Your mother?"

He laughed roughly, raising his voice. "Not mine. Dead, like him. That one's just a piece a queynt. She'll be my own soon enough, you'll see."

"Soon enough, he says," joked one of the others at the loud boast.

"Oh, we'll all see that day right soon, Robert Bray," said a second. "Shapely gallant such as yourself, got the slit linin' up out to Mile End."

Bray shot them a snarl. I left him standing there, spitting at his fellows.

The house he had pointed out to me was indistinguishable from the others along the alley. They all seemed to hang there, dilapidated and frail, as if they might collapse at any moment and leave the passageway a pile of broken boards and rubble. A deep step down into a drainage ditch and I was at the door to Jankyn Bray's house. Outside it stood his horsecart, the two wheels positioned at the edge of a ramp to allow access to street level. Deep, long, well maintained, easily capable of carrying four or five men, whether living or dead. Three loads, then, perhaps four. His horse would be stabled somewhere nearby.

The door sat half open. I looked within. A woman, quite young and pretty, sat on a bench, nursing an infant at her breast. Her eyes were closed, her face wan and troubled even at rest. Her head was leaning against a wooden beam to her side. I ducked out and waited until I heard the child start to protest the end of its feeding, then stepped back to the doorway.

"Mistress?"

Her eyes remained closed despite the infant's mewl, her head still angled against the beam.

"Your pardon, mistress."

At last one eye fluttered open, then the second. She straightened herself and came to her feet. The baby slapped at her cheek.

"Yessire?" she said, looking stunned at the

appearance of a gentleman at the door of her squalid home.

"I have come to ask you about Jankyn Bray."

Her eyes darkened. "Won't find him abouts here, sire. Gone to his grave, my Jankyn. Left me with this joy." She heaved the infant to her shoulder, stroked its narrow back.

"I know, and I am very sorry, Mistress — what is your name?"

"Elizabeth Saddler."

"Mistress Saddler. Jankyn was a carter."

"Yes, sire."

"And well respected in the trade, from what I have gathered."

"He was that. Always the first asked for along Carter's Alley, by lord and tradesman alike."

"Was he known as a discreet man?"

"Sire?"

"Did he keep mum about his business, not given to gossip like the young fellows up at the end of the alley?"

"None a that for my Jankyn," she said. "The closest carter you could find in the ward, and that's sure. Pious, too, always visiting that hermit, spilling his sins and sads."

"Did he speak to you about any of his

more . . . unpleasant commissions?"

"Unpleasant, sire?"

"This would have been a job at the river. A night haul up to Cornhill, near the crossing at the Poultry."

She turned away, hiding her face, a palm going to the infant's head.

I looked around the humble dwelling. "You have little to lose, Mistress Saddler, and a new mouth to feed, now without Jankyn's income. Let me help you."

I jangled my purse. Her hand traveled down the infant's back, her strokes growing shorter, hurried.

"All I need is a name, or even a location," I said. "Did he tell you which quay he hauled from, or its rough location?" The Thames waterfront with its many docks resembled the gap-toothed mouths of a hundred old crones. A barge of bodies could have been unloaded anywhere.

"Two half nobles and a quarter as well, Mistress Saddler. You and your child may sup on this bounty for a month and more."

Her eyes widened at the sum. She considered it. "They'll come for me then, won't they," she said, bouncing her infant. "And this joy. Toss him in the dung like his father on account of I opened my mouth to th' likes of you."

432

"They may," I allowed. "Though I am as tight-lipped as your Jankyn. The only secrets I breathe are those that need breathing. This one does not. Your information will be well protected, Mistress Saddler."

She sighed. "Jankyn knew it was rotten, that job."

I waited, let her draw out the thought.

"Old friend of his slips up along Carter's Way, lipping about a job the next night. 'D'you want it, Bray? Yours for the having if y'do, Bray, and it's three shil for you, Bray.' Jankyn took it without a thought, though there was something in the matter of it that smelled overfoul, so he said."

"What was that?"

"The coin, s'what it was. A half noble, for one night's work? Fivepence be more like what Jankyn'd expect for such a job."

"Did this friend tell him what he would be hauling from the river?"

"No."

"Did Jankyn suspect what it might be, have any sense at all?"

She set the infant on a small table, the only flat surface in the room. With a rough and oversized blanket she bound its quivering limbs, like a cook bunning sausage. She looked up at me as she completed the task. "What was it he carried that night, good master? Do you know?"

I averted my eyes from the snug young life on the table. "Dead men," I said. "Cartloads of death."

She nodded, as if my ponderous response made perfect sense. I set several coins down next to the child.

"The loading was to be at Lyman's wharf," she said, picking up the money rather than the infant. "John Lyman's the friend of Jankyn's who set 'im up with the job. He'd boat the load from wherever it come from, and Jankyn was to haul it up Cornhill."

"Who is John Lyman?"

"Fisher, eeler. Has a dock under the bridge, down from the water gates. Those bad steps bankside of the fishwharf. You know the spot?"

"I do," I said, and there was good logic in it. The men who met the carter had chosen to put in along a particularly chaotic stretch of the wharfage, amidst a messy jumble of warehouses, misshapen docks, and random piers just before the bridge. The site also made sense for its distance from the Long Dropper. The men bearing the bodies would have received their cartloads right below Thames Street, which they could then have taken quickly west to the Dowgate channel, then north to the privy along Walbrook Street.

After leaving the young mother I made the short walk to the bankside. There were three separate fishing docks at this wharf leading out from the bank, where fishermen busily sorted their catches as the gulls hovered and cawed for scraps. Fishmongers picked through the catch as a crew of boys emptied nets onto the long cleaning tables set back from the river. There the work of scaling and gutting for bakers and lords' stewards was done, the offal raked and swept into the river.

I approached the nearest cleaner, a stout, bare-chested fellow, his bronzed skin and breeches slimed with the day's catch, hands on hips as he took a brief rest.

"Where might I find Lyman's wharf?" I asked him. He turned on me, his beard glistening and matted with sweat, the whole of him freshly pungent with his work.

"John Lyman?"

"Yes."

He pointed to a length of rough and splintered boards stubbing out five feet over the water, where a fishing boat bobbed gently. "That's his skiff there. Won't find him taking it out though, not today at all rates."

"Why is that?" I said, turning back.

His lips tightened. "Lyman ha'n't been adock these three days, nor's any soul laid good eyes on the man. Probably drowned, poor boar. Slipped off the quay, could be. We lose one a month to the Thames, sad to say. Water bailiff's like to find him, by and by. Lessen he's already floated out to Gravesend, which could be."

A coldness spread along my arms and rose to prickle the back of my neck. I turned from the fisherman and walked to the water's edge, then looked at Lyman's craft. Though in poor shape it was quite large for a fisherman's riverboat, long and with high gunwales, easily capable of carrying seven or eight dead men up from Greenwich, or wherever along the Kentish bank the victims' bodies had been handed in.

Two loads, possibly three.

That night, well after curfew had rung, I retraced the likely route of the sixteen corpses, coining my way across the bridge from Southwark and bribing a shore constable to trail me and keep the night watches in the parishes from troubling us. I began at the river, where I had learned that day of John Lyman's death. By night the lapping of the Thames against the wharfage and gunwales created a calm and watery patter, joining with the creak of rope and settling board in the river's nocturnal chorus. Moist stairs descended to the water.

I stood on the lowest step, looking out across the gently roiling surface, thinking of a drowned fisherman. It was John Lyman, then, who had been hired to float the dead men across the river, from somewhere east of Southwark. To bring them here, to his own quay along the wharf, then hand them up to the waiting carter above. He would have been helped by some of his patron's men, whoever he was. A man of sufficient rank for his name alone to keep the water bailiffs and shore patrol at bay. A man like Thomas of Woodstock, Duke of Gloucester.

I paced up the narrow steps, imagining each body bent between the hands of two men, to be tossed in Jankyn Bray's waiting cart. Four loads of four bodies each, creaking along up to Cornhill. I walked the full length of it through the nighttime stillness, the lamp-bearing constable ten steps behind me at my request. Along Thames Street we passed the darkened bulks of All Hallows the Less and All Hallows the Great, the gaping emptiness of the steelyard, then turned northward along the Dowgate up to Walbrook Street. On certain corners pendant lamps hung from posts, pale beacons to the night walkers and ward patrols, the occasional daring violator of curfew. Only once was I accosted, two men policing the parish of St. John the Baptist. The constable hailed them off, spoke to them quietly, slipping them a few of the smaller coins I'd given him for the purpose.

We stopped at the privy below the stocks conduit, across the street from the church of St. Stephen Walbrook. The trickle of the Walbrook sounded from below the Long Dropper, the earthy scent of waste and rot in the air. I walked up three steps and opened the privy door, which groaned unhappily on old leather hinges.

"Your lantern," I said to the constable. "Hold the door open for me, will you?"

He backed away, his free hand waving me off.

"What is the problem, constable?"

"I don't fancy holdin' a privy door for no one, good sire." The movement of his head was firm and fast, like that of a child refusing a chore.

Exasperated, I held the door myself, then beckoned for him to approach. "I didn't pay you to watch me piss. I simply need your light. Will another fivepence convince you?"

He hesitated, peering up and down the

street, then finally complied, taking the steps up to the privy door, which he held open as I entered the Long Dropper. The constable's lantern revealed three round holes along the seat box, all too small for a grown man's body, though the covering board lifted easily. I inspected its edges. Four iron nails had been removed, two bent stubs still protruding from the board, another from the box. Given the angle between the door and the seats, the constable was holding the lantern directly behind me as I peered into the dark pit, nearly overwhelmed by the stench. With the depth and my own shadow it was too dark to see the channel below.

"Closer in, if you will."

"Sire?"

"The lantern. Bring it over here so I can gauge the distance."

He gave a shallow and nervous laugh. "Not on St. Bride's toe. One bad puff and the whole place'll go up, and I don't fancy the choke. But it's fifteen feet down, more or less."

I shrugged, thinking nothing of his reluctance in the moment. Back on Walbrook Street I stood beside the central gutter, puzzling it out now that I had retraced the perpetrators' many steps. You would want at least two men waiting behind with Lyman and the skiff, I reckoned, another two accompanying Jankyn up to the privy, where they would unload the bodies, lift the covering board, and toss the dead men through the opening. A crew of six to eight to perform the operation in London, then. And, on the other end, a wagon or cart on the far bank somewhere well west of Greenwich, perhaps Redriffe given the distance and currents, with several men waiting for the skiff's return to take the second load.

A considerable enterprise, involving at least a dozen men, perhaps as many as twenty. Lots of potentially loose tongues to threaten with the knife. And, of course, you would need to pay off —

I slowly turned. From above the orb of his flickering lamp the shore constable stared at me, his eyes eerily aglow in the flame, something fearful and desperate in them. He was armed, a short sword and knife scabbarded along his belt.

I glanced back at the privy, then again at the constable as the words of the fisherman resounded in my head. *Lyman ha'n't been adock these three days, nor's any soul laid good eyes on the man. Probably drowned, poor boar.*

Then I knew.

"Murder!" I bellowed, backing away, mouth to the sky, the greatest sound my lungs could muster. "A murder! Summon the watch! The parish watch! A murder done here! The hue and cry, good London, the hue and cry!"

The constable twisted on his feet, looking about with a guilty man's desperation, his hand on the pommel. What I'd just done was a risk, as I would end up seeming the fool if I had guessed wrongly.

I stepped toward him, my hands spread open as a chorus of men's shouts and clapping windows echoed from nearby lanes. "You have nothing to fear from me," I said to him quietly. "When the watch and the beadle arrive we shall simply tell them we saw a body in the channel below the Long Dropper. You will be credited as first finder."

His eyes narrowed, seeing a way out. "You will not inform the sheriffs of my —"

"You were bought for silence, not murder."

He nodded like a child eager to please. "Aye, sire."

"But you must tell me who hired you. Whose men bought your silence, constable?"

Some shouts, rushing feet; the watch was almost upon us. "It was Gloucester's men," he whispered. "Badged with those twisted geese, wings out like this." He spread his arms in imitation of Gloucester's fluttering swans.

"You've little to fear, then," I lied. "And here we are." The first watchmen had arrived, and the next minutes passed in a loud and ugly confusion as clusters of men, official and not, came to enjoy the spectacle. Lanterns were brought into the Long Dropper, loud voices confirming the first sight of the body I had suspected would be found in the channel.

"A grown man it is, lyin' faceup. Splattered somewhat awful. And it — oh no."

"What then?"

"There's another. Smaller one. Looks to be a child."

"Ah, the stench."

Soon the parish constable arrived to join the throng and take control of the situation. Robert Griven, a respected master carpenter and a solid parishioner of St. Stephen, was too honest a man to sing for me, though not an enemy by any means. After getting a look at the bodies for himself, Griven started giving orders, sending someone for the ward beadle, three to gather lanterns from nearby corners, another riding for a crew of gongfarmers known to be working down in the Fleet channels by the Thames that night.

Three men from this crew arrived before long and went into the Walbrook ditch through a gap between houses, roping themselves down one by one, calling for light and lines. Eventually the first corpse was hauled to the bank by two of the gong-farmers, then dragged to the street by a rope under its arms. The victim's face and body were washed off with buckets of clean water from the stocks conduit, which also pro-vided the two gongfarmers with a cold shower as the crowd gathered around the corpse.

"Why, that's John Lyman, that is," some-one said, lowering a lantern to the victim's face.

"The fisher?"

"Aye. Wife's passed but has a fair daugh-ter. Elizabeth, her name is. House is in Cripplegate Ward just without. I'll go fetch her m'self."

Now the child was handed up. One of the gongfarmers, his face startlingly clean above the filth that matted his clothing, had the body in his arms. As he set it beside the first corpse I felt a gathering dread.

I had watched the whole procedure from the porch of St. Stephen across Walbrook

443

Street, this city's fumbling machinery of wrongful death. Now I forced myself to approach the middle of the scene, where a small crowd surrounded the two bodies, obstructing my view. I pushed my way through and looked down upon the dead boy. Water still trickled over his face, dripping through the child's hair and exposing a severed ear on his left side. A mat of hair, clear skin on a pale face, the cutpurse's cruel punishment visited on his head. Yet only the one ear was missing. This could not be Jack Norris. Pity and relief mingled in my conscience.

"He's just there," someone said. I looked up to see Griven murmuring with my friend the night constable, who pointed me out. Griven approached. Short, stocky, darkened eyes still bleary beneath his cap.

"First finder, are you, Master Gower?"

I turned from the bodies. "That honor would go to your constable, I believe."

His eyes narrowed. "You hired Shalton for a night walk, did you?"

"I did."

"And why's that?"

"Ask Ralph Strode."

"I am asking *you,* Gower. Why were you about at night in this ward?" When I said nothing he tilted his head up in an ugly

444

scowl. "Shalton's saying naught, but I know you're not as thick as that fellow. How'd you know, Gower, hmm?"

"You are parish constable, Griven, not the king's coroner, nor a justice. I will be happy to share my knowledge at the inquest. Not before. If you are suspicious of my motives here, I ask you, again, to talk to Strode."

He considered me for a moment longer, then blew out an annoyed sigh and turned away. The shore constable came to my side to walk me back down to the bridge, which I crossed in a dispirited state of mind. Another death, more bodies cast into the bowels of the city, a witness pursued by men willing to murder an earless child for his silence.

CHAPTER 28

Ralph Strode appeared at my house late the following morning, a day still and cold, with lowering clouds and a struggling sun. Despite the weather I sat out in the small garden beneath the last skeletal vines clinging to an arbor, listening to the opening of the noontime office from the priory oratorium. My eyes were closed against the leaden sky, the Latin hymn circling in my ears — *rector potens, verax Deus, qui temperas rerum vices* — when a graveled voice interrupted the silken flow of the canons' song.

"We pray most fervently at noon, St. Ambrose tells us, for that is when the divine light is at its highest and fullest."

I squinted up at Strode, who eased himself onto the wooden bench crosswise from my own. "And its most clouded," I said.

He allowed the silence to lengthen. "What were you doing out there last night, John?"

"What you asked me to do weeks ago," I said flatly. "Looking into these killings, pulling all the needful threads."

"John Gower, the sheriff of Southwark, panting after murderers and their traces."

"The tracks of wolves," I said. "It was you who set me onto them, Ralph. Why the rancorous air?"

"Seems an unlikely happenstance, doesn't it?" he said. "John Gower, sniffing around the privy where sixteen men bedded in shit. And lo! On the one night he chooses for his illegal outing, two more show up in all their foul plenitude even as their souls mount to the celestial sphere."

The ever philosophical Strode. I had been planning to visit him at the Guildhall that day to tell him what I had learned in Kent. Instead I told him all of it now. His shoulders fell at my description of the Portbridge gaol, the woods, the encounter with Gloucester. When I had finished, we gazed together toward the eastern span of the church, the soaring buttresses clinging to its sides like clawing hawks.

"Is all of England to end up in the Walbrook, then?" he said in a voice gruff with despair. "Are dukes and their factions to be given free license to murder and maim prisoners and carters and children, with no

447

accountability, no hope of arrest?"

"Did Griven send you?" I said, wanting to remain with more immediate events. The constable had been riled the previous night, and I assumed he had spoken with Strode early that morning.

"Griven?" He scoffed. "Not likely. I am here at Rysyng's request. The alderman got wind of your presence by the Walbrook from the sheriffs. He asked me to look in on you."

"What did you tell him?" I said, wondering if Rysyng had revealed any of what he had told me.

"Little that he didn't already know or guess. There is no burying these killings, not after all that has passed since our pleasant morning at St. Bart's. The sheriffs are riled to the point of revolt, and the aldermen whisper of impeachment. Murder will out, despite the mayor's efforts to keep it in."

"Will Brembre thwart this investigation as well, then?"

"I've spoken to the coroner. The inquest has been delayed a week, perhaps two."

"I'm hardly surprised," I said, thinking of Gloucester and the night in his keep. "Delay seems to be the only constancy in all of this. Has Brembre confided in you?"

Strode fanned a hand before his face. "He

grows more distrustful by the day, wild-eyed with suspicion, as if the very walls are closing in on him. First sixteen unknown bodies in the Walbrook, then the ravaged corpse of that carter, now a fisherman and a boy cutpurse. The privy channels are become a charnel house. It seems almost as if —" He stopped, his lips shutting tight, a deep frown lining his brow.

"As if someone is taunting Brembre," I completed the thought, testing him. "Taunting London herself." Strode, I suspected, still knew nothing about Brembre's entanglement with the swerver, nor about Gloucester's extortions. Perhaps Rysyng was not as careless a gossip as he seemed — or too frightened of Brembre to loosen his lips without a threat.

The bench moaned as Strode shifted his weight forward. "The crown is stepping in, John."

"Oh?"

"The chancellor has grown alarmed at the wantonness of it all, and these suggestions about Gloucester will only rile him further. He has sent several royal pursuivants to the Guildhall, to aid in the investigations, so they claim. In reality they will serve as his ears and eyes on the city, and Brembre knows it."

"I had thought the earl saw all of this as a London problem. What explains his sudden change?"

"That's the reason I have come, John." He was about to continue when several voices sounded from the house behind us. He looked over my shoulder, his face grim. "I believe your answer is arrived."

Through the higher branches on the arbor I saw Edmund Rune coming out of my house through the kitchen door, with Will Cooper leading him toward our benches in the priory garden. Our greetings were cordial, though I was confounded by the presence of the chancellor's secretary at St. Mary. He sat beside Strode, the two of them pressed together on the narrow bench. Rune began generally enough, discussing the state of Parliament and the current threat to the chancellor.

"The pressure is immense, and King Richard seems prepared to accede to the appellants' wishes," he said.

"The chancellor will step down, then?" I asked.

"Or be impeached, should the Commons approve the article."

"What will happen after that?"

"Will they come for the king?" asked Strode.

Rune shook his head. "I think not. The chancellor's impeachment should appease them, along with the lord treasurer's. Beyond that — who knows? Once a predator gets a first taste of meat, no creature of flesh is safe."

The canons began a psalm with antiphon.

"How will the lord chancellor respond?" I asked. "Is there a chance he might remain in office?"

Rune's eyes flashed with anger. "Not without King Richard's support, which doesn't seem to be forthcoming, his lordship's long and loyal service to the House of Plantagenet be damned."

"Long as the Thames itself," Strode put in. "The earl deserves better from His Highness."

"His Majesty, you mean to say," said Rune wryly. "Or so he insists on having himself addressed in recent months."

"Let's not plant the seeds of sedition in the priory's garden, if you please." I glanced toward the oratorium. Strode laughed gently.

"Perhaps you are correct, Gower," said Rune, then breathed out a long and florid sigh. "Some things are above mere *politique*. Indeed that is why I have come to see you this morning."

I watched his face, searching for purpose.

"The chancellor feels that the security of the realm is at stake. He believes this latest news I bear merits the careful attention of the crown even in the midst of this crisis at Westminster, and despite the efforts of Parliament to depose him."

The sentence sounded practiced, as if Rune had mouthed it several times on his way over the river. "Go on," I said.

"There has been another massacre. A market town called Desurennes, a day's ride from Calais."

A bird swooped down from the near buttress, bringing memories of my last and only visit to the Pale of Calais, that ugly tongue of French land won by old King Edward some forty years ago and held as English territory since the great siege. I had traveled there with Chaucer in the first year of Richard's reign, accompanying him on his mission to Paris for the marriage negotiations for the hand of Princess Marie of France. Despite their failure, we had spent several weeks in Paris, yet what stayed with me most were the haunted and hate-filled looks of the townspeople as we rode through the villages of the Pale, a region beaten down by its English occupiers yet still riven with dissension. Such massacres of the innocent were nothing new in the province, where dissidence and outright revolt among the native populace were constant threats. So it remained.

"Were the victims prisoners?"

"Townspeople, farmers," Rune said. "An attack on a market day, along the town walls, and by English troops. Women and children among the dead this time, in the dozens. Those who weren't granted the mercy to die were gruesomely wounded."

"Guns?" I guessed.

"Handgonnes. Many of them, and longbows as well. An English company in the bright of day advanced on the town, slaughtering all before them."

"Surely the captain of Calais will bring these men to justice. They must have been part of his garrison."

"That will not be so simple," Rune said. "There's great anger throughout the Pale, with all set on bloody vengeance rather than the king's justice. The Calais garrison already sucks up a quarter and more of the royal treasury. Even that may not be enough to hold back rebellion once it comes. Desurennes has a reputation for sedition. Well deserved, and it's no secret that new flames are sparking throughout the Pale. Stamping them out is one of the captain's sworn duties."

"Though not with such methods, I hope," said Strode.

"Perhaps not. Yet fire must be met with fire, some would avow," he said grimly. "The whole of the Pale is a cask of powder waiting for a spark. The people fear another attack — as do I."

The canons had moved on to the collect, intoned by a cantor whose lone voice sounded faintly across the priory yard.

"Why have you told me all this, Rune?" I asked him. "Do you suspect the two massacres are related? And supposing they are, what can you expect me to learn about this new incident in the Pale that you haven't already learned yourself?"

My visitors exchanged a look. Ralph nodded slightly. "There is something else, John," said Rune.

The use of my given name by the chancellor's secretary felt uncomfortable, too intimate. I scarcely knew the man, and he was in my own house uninvited.

"In addition to the massacre at Desurennes, there are disturbing reports out of the Pale. Reports of English ships along the coast of Flanders, between Calais and Sluys, selling saltpetre to the Flemings, allies of France and Burgundy. The company appears to be trading in arms to be used against England, and just as the French fleet prepares to sail against our shores."

"Treason," I said, and once again I saw this whole affair as an expanding circle, drawing more and more into its noose.

"The chancellor asks that you make your way to Calais. Your ostensible purpose will be to see what you can learn about the massacre and who was responsible. You will lodge at the house of Pierre Broussard, a wool broker. French, but one of our most trusted men in the Staple Company."

"Chaucer knows him?"

"He must, though we've not spoken about the affair. The chancellor requests that you say nothing to him should you see him before your departure. When Chaucer left the wool custom he bent some beaks across the sea, in Calais and Middleburgh alike, so his involvement would do more harm than good."

All of this was moving too quickly. "Why have you come to me, Rune? This is an absurdity. I have no men in Calais, no sources in the Pale. What role does the chancellor wish me to play here?"

He fixed Strode with another look. Before either could reply I spoke. "You said my *ostensible* purpose is to look into the massacre. What is the real purpose of this visit? Why are you here, Rune?"

Rune tightened his lips, then said, "Reports have come to us from an informer, a man slipping in and out of Calais in recent months, journeying overland between Flanders and the Pale, keeping an eye on the French fleet at Sluys. We've been paying him well for his information, which has been solid and reliable. Now he claims to have proof of the identity of these smugglers. That is your second task."

"Again, Rune, I fail to see —"

"He says he will give it only to you, John Gower, and to no one else."

Rune's words hit me like a slap to the cheek, drawing me to my feet. "I want nothing further to do with this."

Rune stood with me. "He will make contact after you arrive in Calais."

Strode struggled up as well. "John —" he began.

I held forth my hands, as if to shield myself from what he was about to tell me.

"We are here at the lord chancellor's command," said Rune. "He believes, as do I, that the answers are in Calais."

The canons' chanting had ceased with the close of the minor office. Edmund Rune spoke into the silence. "You must sail from

456

Gravesend at the earliest opportunity," he said. "You will travel through Calais to Desurennes, learn what you can about the massacre, then return to Calais. Our informant will contact you there."

"This is an impossibility, Rune," I said, my distress mounting. Strode was about to intervene when Rune cut us off.

"Enough." His face bristled with impatience. "There is no choice in the matter, Gower. This is out of your control and ours, and it transcends the politics of the moment. Would you put your comfort here at the priory before the security of the realm?"

My face had gone rigid, and I was about to object again when he held up an appeasing hand. "You must pardon my manner, Gower. It is wearing on a man, to work so closely with a lord so admirable and good when the king and the Parliament will do nothing to support him. May I go on?"

I nodded tightly, arms crossed over my chest. Rune was all sincerity and true concern in that moment, the embodiment of all that Michael de la Pole had meant to England and its kings in years past. As the voice of the chancellor he deserved attention, perhaps compliance. Yet there was a sickening weight on my heart as I waited for the revelation to come.

"Tread carefully over there," said Rune, now businesslike. "The captain of Calais, William Beauchamp, is Warwick's brother, a strong ally of Gloucester's against the king. He knows nothing about this gunpowder trade, or so we believe. When you speak with Beauchamp you must stay silent about our man and what he tells you, on peril of your life."

"And his," Strode added.

"Who is the informant?" The only question that mattered, though I already knew its answer.

Rune turned to Strode, who looked upon my agitation with sober and sympathetic eyes. Ralph stepped toward me and clutched my arm, fitting words of Scripture to this small calamity. " *'For this my son was dead, and is come to life again. He was lost, and now is found.'* "

I stared at him, deaf to the gospel's sweetening words. "Again," I whispered, still unwilling to believe.

"Yes, John," Strode gently said. "This man in Calais is Simon Gower."

My son.

■ ■ ■ ■

PART III

■ ■ ■ ■

CHAPTER 29

A lift to the sky, a smack in a trough, and for the third time in an hour I emptied my stomach between my feet. My eyes burned with sickness as I clung to a post below-decks with the barrels and bales, every surface slick with sea and pelting rain. Ropes and timbers groaning like whipped bulls, our feet pressed on the ends of bent clinker nails, the cog tossed on a river of hell, and dry land the remotest of memories though we had left hours before.

Perfect sailing weather, the crew kept insisting with a cruel kind of glee.

That crossing from Gravesend to Calais was only the third time in my life I had been aship. The first was at the insistence of my father, who brought me with him for a visit to his cousin's manor in Brittany, years before age would teach me discomfort. The second took me on a trip to Paris with Chaucer during the marriage negotiations for King Richard. That vessel, a royal galley accustomed to ferrying kings, dukes, and earls across to France, cut the waves like a short sword through a mound of suet. I remembered a calm sea, no hint of sickness, forty oarsmen pulling at the rhythmic call of their master.

Nothing as humble as this ship, which, I learned upon embarking, had set sail from the Holy Land that summer. In Portsmouth the vessel had been pressed into service by one of the king's admirals, and now the crew were girding themselves for war between powers, though it was hard to see where they might fit in, and on whose side. The merchant ship was a world worthy of Mandeville, fifteen swart and hearty men, heads wrapped in colorful scarves of impossible colors to match the variegated hues of their skin, which varied from sun-scorched red to nut brown to black as devil's pitch. Though they spoke in innumerable languages they seemed to share a patchwork tongue all their own, befitting the culture of a crew gathered from the far corners of the earth, and indifferent to the nature of their cargo, whether men of war, Flemish cloth, or spices from the east.

Only two of them were Englishmen. Northerners, one of them kind enough to comfort me through my several hours of misery. "Think nowt an it, squire. Earls, duchesses, queens — why, e'en the highest bloods lase it aff Dover, and no shame in it nathah."

Though shame, I reflected between bouts of sickness, comes in many forms.

Perhaps it should not have surprised me to learn that Simon had been spotted working in and around Calais on behalf of an unidentified patron. The year before, in one of the darkest episodes of my life, Simon Gower had returned from Italy to deceive me and, worse, betray his sovereign nearly to the point of disaster. A book of seditious prophecies, a jealous rivalry over a woman, a young king's life hanging by a silken braid. I vowed never to forgive him, even as the crisis seemed to pull us closer than we had been in many years. Afterwards I remained unsure whether Simon's betrayals had been solely the result of youthful carelessness or part of an elaborate game of subterfuge I still could not comprehend.

Such trickery, it seemed, would forever define our relations. Though I had originally sent him to Italy to join the company of Sir John Hawkwood, Simon had been working all along as an agent for the chancellor himself, and without my knowledge. From his childhood Simon showed unique abilities in the ways of deceit. Charming, swift of brain, too quick for his teachers and too slippery for his father, he possessed a natural inclination toward those covert worlds of counterfeit, espionage, and artifice he now inhabited, and a gift for languages and learning unrivaled by any other man I have known. In other words, Chaucer would wryly observe, he is your son.

Now this son had returned, and in an equally enigmatic guise. From playing with fire during last year's crisis, he had moved to playing with its most dangerous and explosive agent. *And so you will make thunder and lightning,* writes Roger Bacon of gunpowder, and when I thought of Simon in the harrowing days that followed I thought of him with fire in his hands, hurling missiles of flame at the world around him.

So it was that I found myself on this cursed ship, tossed wantonly from wave to wave as the hours and miles passed. There was one other passenger, a trader in cloth heading for the staple at Middleburgh. I spoke briefly to him on deck during a rare lull in my sickness.

"Dry land cures all ills," he said to me at the starboard bow. A mast bobbed in the fair distance. Though young he had a head with thinning hair over a pleasant face, tawny from the sun. His eyes too were brown, and they teared in the sea wind as we looked out over the swell.

I put a hand to my stomach. "On the next crossing I'll bring a hammer, I think, and simply put myself to sleep."

"Pennyroyal and wormwood," he said wisely. "Mash it together with vinegar and oil, apply it to your chest."

"I am out of fortune's favor, then. No herb garden on this vessel."

"Nor vinegar, I fear."

A meaningless exchange, and I never learned his name.

We pulled into the harbor at Calais under a hazed sun, the rowmen taking us through an elaborate system of sluices, dams, and dykes that kept the waterways flowing around the town. There was much admiring cant on the ship about the ingenuity of the master of the engines, whose job it was to oversee the maintenance of the system that kept the town defended and dry.

As we neared our berth a dinghy pulled alongside, allowing the ship's master to pay the toll to the representative of the *échevins*. Though Calais had yielded its status as the English staple to Middleburgh in recent years, money still flowed through the brokers' hands, and the gold mint alone spat out more coins than even the Tower in those years. The Pale remained the main conduit for innumerable commodities into and out of England. Cloth and tin, lead and wine, and especially wool: sacks and fells by the hundreds and thousands.

On the quay the cloth merchant bid me a brisk farewell and walked off to arrange transport to Middleburgh. The way up from the harbor to Calais Gate was a quick but sodden one, and with no pattens available, my shoes and the lower part of my breeches gathered weight and filth that clung coldly to my legs as I finally reached a patch of dry stone beneath the gate. The whole area bristled with spears, the garrison sharp, drilled, on alert for hostile movements by sea or land. The captain of Calais was known to be a fierce and demanding military leader, and it gave me some comfort to see our troops arrayed with precision and strength along the walls, the watchtowers well manned. In London, despite the formidable preparations there, it could often be too easy to forget the looming war, with the French navy massed just up the coast at Sluys, threatening to embark at any moment.

The watch passed me in and I asked the

way to the wool broker's shop, proceeding along a street that felt oddly similar to one of its counterparts in London. Old King Edward was known to have refashioned Calais in the English style, changing everything from the quality of paving stones to the appearance of shopfronts, though I had not realized the extent of the surface similarities. I could have been walking along Cheapside or Cornhill, ducking in for a pie or measurement for a pair of shoes.

Yet Calais was less a town than an ugly, hulking fortification, looming over the port and the surrounding lands and marshes it exploited like a gore-slicked raven at its meal, and the whole atmosphere of the place was one of unsettled gloom. Even the bustle of the market was subdued, and Staple Hall rose up in its unsightly height over the central square. The faces I saw on the streets were tight and drawn, all averted eyes and suspicion toward strangers like me. The town expected war, and soon.

From Pierre Broussard, too, I got nothing but open hostility. The wool broker was leaning against his door when I approached the shop, gazing blankly down the street. At my arrival he turned his head slowly, looked me foot to forehead, and drew a short sniff of air into his nose, as if I were a rotting fish left at his door.

"You must be this Gower," he said in English.

This Gower. Broussard acted aggrieved at the first sight of me, a Londoner come to trouble his home and his trade. Though he appeared young, he had a pinched and ugly face, eyes spaced too closely, a crooked nose that swooped up at the end, where it blossomed into a reddened ball peppered with black spots.

"Your room is in back," he said, now in French. "Three nights?" He held out his hand for payment.

"Perhaps four," I said.

"A quarter then. More for your meat at the suppers."

I gave him the quarter noble, though I nearly had to beg ale and a light meal out of him to ease the recovery from disembarkation. The inn's hall was closed for repairs to the ceiling, he claimed, so I ate in a back room off his baking kitchen, the heat from the ovens doing nothing to still my traveler's nerves.

I spent the remainder of that first day in Calais coining as much information as I could about the massacre at Desurennes from the many English residents of the town. The news had spread like a gust of

468

wind among the French villages of the Pale. The general feeling was that a rogue faction from the Calais garrison had been responsible for the atrocity, though no one wanted to speak of it with a stranger. The tavern chatter was subdued, with few willing to speculate on any less obvious motivations behind the attack. Discontent in the countryside, a shared anti-English sentiment among the towns, hints of rebellion and alliance with the French: nothing more specific, and I learned little that Edmund Rune had not already told me back in Southwark.

The following morning I was awakened from a fitful sleep by the Mistress Broussard, who rapped loudly on my door with no sympathy for my throbbing head. I had been summoned, she told me, by Sir William Beauchamp, the captain of Calais himself, who expected me at the castle within the hour. After a hurried meal I gathered some things and walked to the keep, a block of stone to the north of the city gates, announcing myself to the gate-keeper, who in turn summoned a page to lead me to the captain's chambers. Through the slitted walls in the west tower I got a glimpse of the town's outer perimeter defenses to the north. Trenches carpeted in sticks, bulwarks bristling with spikes, all prepared for a French army reportedly strengthening by the day.

The offices of the captain of Calais were situated in the castle's second-floor gallery. I was led through the adjoining rooms of clerks and secretaries, speaking in hushed tones, the bureaucratic hum of an office well run.

In addition to his duties as captain of Calais, Sir William Beauchamp, the Baron Bergavenny, served as the crown's envoy to Flanders, and was thus a powerful figure in the king's diplomacy. Beauchamp was also the younger brother of the Earl of Warwick, standing just outside that innermost circle of lords making trouble for King Richard and the chancellor in the Parliament that fall. He was a catlike man, small of face, his movements and his speech careful and calculated. I had met him several times, once in quite unpleasant circumstances, and he had impressed me with his ability to appear elusive and straightforward at the same time.

His chamber was modestly furnished, with a single window looking out on the fortifications below. On the opposite wall hung a shield emblazoned with his family's arms, a bold gold band differenced with a crescent sable. His greeting was cursory but not rude as he waved me in.

"You chose not to return to Westminster for Parliament, my lord?"

He moved a lean arm slowly across his desk. "I have an island to defend, Gower, and against a force the likes of which England hasn't seen since King William sailed from Normandy. Thousands of ships a few leagues north of here, massed along the fjords and in the sea, ready to fly like so many darts into the breast of the realm. Calais will be the primary agent of defense by sea. Its captain can hardly spare a fortnight for politics."

"Of course not, your lordship," I said. "Though in this season, politics seems to be eating more than its share of fortnights."

A slight smile. "So says my brother the earl. He wishes me to return to London before Exton's riding, which he will be accompanying along with Gloucester. He claims that London could use the additional livery." The king would often use such civic rituals to show a pretense of solidarity between the realm's various factions, now fighting like dogs and bears in a Southwark cage. A day of feigned peace, years of ferocious rivalry set aside for a few hours of shallow ceremony. Yet if the Duke of Gloucester and the Earl of Warwick were

471

among the lords leading the Riding, it was not difficult to foresee an ugly clash marking the new mayor's official assumption of office.

"I trust his lordship the earl will allow for your absence, my lord."

"He will have to," said Beauchamp. "And what will Suffolk do on that momentous day, do you suppose?"

"That is up to the earl, my lord."

"It is good to know that you have the trust of the lord chancellor, Gower," he purred. "Michael de la Pole's word is the very mint of Westminster."

This was dangerous ground. As belted earls Gloucester and Suffolk were equal in rank, though the chancellor's elevation was more recent, and he was regarded as something of a usurper by the king's opponents. To show too much enthusiasm for Michael de la Pole in Beauchamp's presence would not be helpful. Before I could shape a suitable reply he came to my aid.

"The chancellor must go, Gower. There is no other way. He is being impeached even as we sit here."

The observation had been made in an easy but uncompromising tone, and despite all I had been hearing back in London and Westminster it was only in that moment that I truly understood the inevitability of the earl's ouster.

"May the next chancellor fit the office with the same dignity he has shown, my lord," I said, risking a small and final show of loyalty.

Beauchamp allowed it, moving on gracefully to the apparent object of my visit. "This incident — this atrocity — has roused me, Gower. Here I am, doing what I can to keep the peace in this region, and a massacre takes place under my nose." He wriggled it, as if to sniff out the perpetrators. I could almost imagine whiskers. "The burgesses are in a heating roar, to say nothing of the Hainaults, lords of Le Quesnoy. We have powerful garrisons at the castles of Oye, Marcke, and Guisnes. I have paid spies in nearly every village in the Pale. Yet I got no wind of this until the deed was done. I have sent my sheriffs down there, along with the coroner of Calais, but there's no sense of who these men might have been, or where they went once they shot up the town. The gunners seem to have appeared as if by magic out of the woods, then dissolved back into the trees once they'd murdered half the market."

"They like the forest," I said, almost to myself.

473

"What's that?" he said sharply.

"They have done this before, my lord." I described the discovery in the Walbrook, though left the connection with Gloucester and the Tower unmentioned.

He in turn told me what he knew about the killings at Desurennes and the progress of his sheriffs' investigation. "You will want to begin with Pierre Longel, a witness. The old man was selling cheeses that morning up against the walls. He was not injured, though he saw several next to him killed and maimed — including his grown son. He was a soldier upon a time, and I'm told he has good information about the nature of these weapons and the tactics of the offending squad."

"Very well," I said, and thanked Beauchamp for his assistance. I had just turned at the door to his chamber when I was seized with a strange and sudden desire. "I have one last question, your lordship. Or rather a request."

"What is that?" said Beauchamp.

"I see that your defenses include large cannon. Bombards, culverins, and the like."

"What of them?"

"Do you keep handgonnes in your arsenal?"

He moved slightly, then pawed a cheek.

"Are you suggesting that the Calais garrison was responsible for this massacre?"

"Not at all, my lord."

"Then what do you want with our hand cannon?"

"With your permission, I would like to see one fired."

"A singular request."

I inclined my head. "It is that, my lord." I asked more out of curiosity than necessity, having developed a keen interest in the workings of the handgonnes. For weeks I had been tracking down the men who had employed the newfangled weapons against the victims found in the sewer channels, and now, it seemed, against the market crowd on this side of the sea. I had yet to hold one of these weapons myself, or witness one employed in firing.

"I see no virtue in these weapons," Beauchamp mused. "Clumsy, loud, the opposite of stealth. They take an eternity to reload, cannot be aimed with any reliability, and are as likely to explode in a man's face as kill his enemy. Their only use, as far as I can see it, is to awe our enemy into submission with their noise and fire."

"Surely they are being refined by His Highness's armorers."

"Not that I have witnessed, though there

are rumors."

"Rumors, your lordship?"

"There is talk of clever inventions, unforeseen developments at the Tower. One of my lieutenants has heard whispers of a new gun they have called 'the Snake.' A more lethal weapon than our rough tubes, and more efficient, or so it is claimed."

"The Snake," I said, intrigued by the designation. "What distinguishes them from the guns you have here?"

"That is unknown to me." He stood. "I see no reason not to honor your wish, given the distance you've come and the task you've set yourself. Let me see what we can prepare in short order."

"I thank you, my lord."

"It's less than nothing." He led me out into the gallery, where he summoned one of the guards waiting against the doors into the upper hall. "Smithson," he called, snapping his fingers.

"Yes, my lord?" said the guard, head high.

"Take Master Gower here down into the yard and have Usk ready one or two of the small guns for him."

"The handgonnes, sire?"

"Yes, from that store in the west keep."

"Aye, sire."

Beauchamp nodded a curt farewell and

spun on his heel, heading back to the captain's quarters. The guard led me down to the yard, where he spoke to a man named Usk, who looked me over with that soldier's tired disdain for the noncombatant. After ordering out a few of the small guns, he took me to a corner of the castle yard in which a large quantity of wood had been piled to nearly my height: splintered boards, broken beams, the remnants of a shack. I would be shooting into the pile, he told me, and the boards would prevent the shot from caroming off the stone walls. Nearby a cook and his boy had set a meal for the soldiers on a log-and-board table, a fire crackling and smoking behind them.

Another soldier arrived with the guns. He had four of them, simple-looking devices consisting of tubes of bronze bolted to wooden helves, each weapon no more than four feet in length. Along the barrels were fastened several metal rings, giving the guns a ridged appearance. We each took one in hand.

"First pour a quantity of powder down the barrel, just so." He demonstrated on his weapon, taking a pre-measured flask of grained powder and tipping it into the barrel. I followed his example on my own handgonne.

"Now the patch and pellets. We use these." He handed me a small wad of parchment that cupped a handful of pebbles mixed with metal shavings.

"Not a single ball?"

"Not in these guns." He shook his head grimly. "Tried it on the first of them, but the thing exploded in our man's hands and took two fingers clean off. Smaller shot means less pressure, the smiths tell us. So. Smaller shot."

He twisted the parchment over the pellets and placed the wad on the end of the barrel. Then, using the rounded end of a rod — a drivel, he called it — he rammed the wad home so that it was lodged between the powder and the mouth of the barrel. I copied his movements.

Once the gun was loaded I examined the barrel, which appeared to be fashioned of iron staves.

"Hammer-forged and welded, not cast," he said, tracing a finger along the barrel of his weapon. "The seams are beveled and welded, and the whole kept together with these rings along the barrel."

"I see."

"Firing pan is here, touchhole here." His finger brushed a round indentation near the stock. In the middle of it was a small hole drilled into the barrel. "That's where your powder sits when you ignite, and the spark passes through the touchhole. Wait a moment."

He walked over to the cook's hearth and took a coal from the fire, returning with a glowing stick. He handed it to me and prepared himself to fire at the pile.

"When I give you the nod, you lower this into the pan. Very simple, just a quick touch, then move your hand away, see?"

As I watched he raised the gun to his armpit, pointed the mouth of the barrel slightly upward, and nodded. I lowered the glowing stick into the pan, heard a brief fizzle, then —

Crack.

A stunningly loud report as the powder ignited and the gun fired, singeing the hairs near my knuckle.

Usk laughed as I shook out my hand in the air. "Your turn."

He helped me position the gun beneath my arm. "Now point the barrel toward the target, just . . . there."

I did as he told me.

"Keep the stock snug, as if you're couching a lance, though not too tight."

I had never held a couched lance, though I knew what he meant. I positioned the end of the helve between my arm and chest, applying as much pressure as I thought would keep the gun in place.

"One final instruction. You will want to close your eyes at the moment I touch the coal to the powder, or you may end up blinded. We have had men lose both eyes at once firing these guns."

How rich that would be, I thought, to be blinded by a handgonne rather than waiting for Lady Nature to take her course with my eyes. I briefly considered putting on my spectacles for protection, though I wanted to see the effects of the shot and the impact of the pellets.

"Are you ready?"

I nodded. Usk blew on the stick, creating an inch of orange, then brought the glowing coal toward the pan. I tensed, squeezed the stock beneath my arm, and readied for the touch.

Crack.

An ear-splitting report. The gun erupted in my arms, the acrid smell of burned powder rising to my nose. I had blinked, of course, and seen only a split moment of the flash, though the stock had remained steady beneath my arm. Before me a curl of smoke ascended from the woodpile. With my skull ringing like a belfry I handed the gun to

Usk and approached the pile.

In the middle of a large sawed beam I found the peppered holes created by the projectiles hurled from my weapon. The wood still smoldered along the edges, the handgonne having wrought considerable destruction for such a small weapon.

I asked to fire again. He handed me a slightly different weapon this time, with a longer barrel but no stock. This one I was told to put over my shoulder. It used more powder and fired a larger scatter of stones. After I loaded and tamped he fastened a rag about my head.

"To save your ears," he said wryly as he knotted it in back.

The concussive force of the second gun nearly knocked me to the ground, though I managed to stay on my feet while the smoke wafted and cleared. A board at the front of the pile had shattered with the impact, throwing splinters of wood in every direction. I thought of a shield, and what such a weapon would do to the unarmored body of a man.

Beauchamp was correct in part. These handgonnes were awkward and inelegant weapons. The assistance of another man was required to ignite the powder, and they seemed quite perilous to those firing them.

Attempts to hit a target from beyond forty or fifty feet would be futile, rendering the guns largely useless for precision combat from any great distance.

Yet what struck me most forcefully was how simple the weapons were relative to the terror and awe they inspired. No real skill, no dexterity, no sense of aim was necessary for their use, merely the correct sequence of powder, shot, and flame. I knew from youthful experience how difficult it could be to launch an arrow effectively from a bow, how many months were required to hone such skills before an archer could hope to shoot with any accuracy or speed. With these handgonnes, by contrast, a man needed only the small measure of strength necessary to lift the barrel or stock to the armpit or shoulder, and with it a soldier of no skill or brawn would become instantly capable of killing a man, woman, or child.

The garrison's guns had thrilled me with their terrible potency, their muscular allure. I was both smitten and repulsed, seduced by the simple power of the guns yet troubled by the new modes of violence they threatened. I thought of Prometheus, stealing the first flaming brand from the gods and bringing it triumphantly to man. The invention of fire gave us warmth, even as it cursed us with myriad new ways to suffer and die.

CHAPTER 30

The roads were crowded that afternoon with groups of merchants and many others making their way south from York, the last large town before the Palatinate of Durham. The pilgrims were still two leagues from Doncaster, where, they were told by a passing trio of riders, they would find lodgings scarce indeed for their large company. At the advice of a local carter they decided to push several miles on to Aldwick le Street, a market town where the carter's brother worked for a keeper. Upon arrival in the village they found a commodious inn with a comfortable barn, a wide hall, even private rooms for the gentles.

Ten days had passed since the joining of the two companies. They had merged comfortably, though Margery still worried about the widow and what she might gossip on her way south. Robert was worried, too, she could tell, though he said little about the

matter. It was late on market day in Aldwick, a welcome relief from the drudgery of
the road, and several stalls were still open
as dusk approached. They ate pies of seasoned fish before the church and were now
strolling along the short length of the high
street, imagining themselves safe and content. She found it more than pleasant to
mingle in a larger crowd and take in the
noises, smells, and tastes of a northern
town. The bread up here was darker, the ale
sweeter on the tongue, the smoke sharper in
the nose, the children merrier and freer than
the straitened youths of Kent.

The market noise also allowed them to
speak quietly without fear of an eavesdrop-
per.

"You treat me as if I be the sire of some
great manor," he was saying. "Yet I'm a
poacher and a common laborer, Elizabeth.
A cook by trade, as the good mistress Mariota told you. My father was a cook before
me, his father before him, and every other
father back to the time of King Cnut, and
I've the smoke of the kitchen in my blood
and the stink of the pot in my seed —" He
stopped himself, shook his head. "Forgive
my common talk."

"There is naught to forgive, Antony." She
edged closer to him. "Nor is your talk rough

by any measure I can hear. You have learned to speak like a Sussex gentleman. A born esquire, a man of means and position."

"Not born, but *feigned.*" She heard the exasperation in his lowered voice. "For you this be all according to kind, on pilgrimage as a gentlewoman. But for me the feigning is weary work, Elizabeth. Makes a week at the ovens feel like a swim in a pond," he muttered.

"Psst," she said, dismissing his needless doubts. "There are wealthy merchants in Durham and York with no more high blood than the shoes you are wearing or the horse you've ridden for the last week. Yet you think you are unworthy of a gentleman's life? Why, the lord mayor of London himself — *Sir* Nicholas Brembre, mind — comes from common stock, yet he rules the city as its very king, his wife as queen."

"Faulks're hardly suited to the office of mayor, nor even beadle. And we are quit of London forever, I am afraid. I sh'll never be a wealthy lord of the Strand, despite your great work upon me." He smiled kindly at her.

" *'When Adam delf and Eve span, who then was the gentleman?'* " she whispered, the treacherous rhyme trilling from her tongue.

His eyes flashed a warning. "You'd turn

486

me to one of Wat Tyler's rebels, would you? Defying my station, crying for the heads of chancellors and archbishops."

"Better their heads than ours." She turned slightly, stared boldly into his eyes, reading his fiery thoughts. You say I have changed, Margery. That I have grown from a common cook into this convincing semblance of a gentleman, like a rough length of iron beaten into a charger's shoe. Yet you are the one upon whom this flight and this journey have wrought the deeper change. You were a meek mistress in your former life, of gentle birth and tender disposition, worn down by a cruel husband who sought to beat you into a submissive pulp of fear and passivity. Now you have been reforged in the flames of hardship and need, fired by the bellows of death gusting at our heels. And I, Robert Faulk, I have cooked you.

Well — she shook her head, smiled at her overly colorful thoughts. Perhaps they were hers after all. Yet in his burning gaze upon her form and her face she could feel a new assurance, something like a lesson in how to love. How to begin again, and to endure.

"Where are we going, Margery?"

They had reached the downwind edge of the market, where pungent crates of fresh river fish and dried cod were spaced around the fishmongers' stools. It was the first time he had asked her this so directly, despite their weeks together. She had hinted around at the subject, keeping vague with him. *We are going to the north country,* was all she had said, and the Durham pilgrimage had seemed a blessing. Now she felt she owed him the truth.

"I have relations in Scotland," she said, her voice low and careful. "My father's niece on his mother's side. I last had news of them two years ago, when affairs between England and Scotland were more at peace."

"Marcher family, are they?" he asked.

"Far from it. They live to the north, along the coast. Her husband is steward for the bishop at Kilrymont. She had a letter sent after her second child's birth. She will surely take us in, if we can just reach her."

"Still there then, she and her husband?"

They have to be, she thought. And what if they are not? "Yes. Of course they are still there."

"How are we to get there from Durham? Neville and Clifford are the fellest of north-guards, it is said." Sir Thomas Neville and Sir Lewis Clifford, the lords of the east and west marches, the hardened protectors of England from invasion by the Scots — and soon enough, if the rumors held, the

French. "Border's carefully watched, and we've no passes or patents to get us through."

His worries annoyed her. "We have information. About these new hand cannon, how they use them, what they intend to do with them, and how their armies and towns might prepare." The men who had taken the prisoners from the Portbridge gaol had been overly free with their talk, thinking their captives as good as dead. "This is information we can sell to the Scots, and with it buy our way beyond the border."

"Now you'd render me *worse* than Wat Tyler." A low growl. "The Scots are allied with the French. You'd make us traitors, Elizabeth." His face had reddened, and she feared pushing him too hard.

"The men who shot the prisoners in those woods, they were the true traitors to the king, and to justice," she pressed on, willing him to see. "It was wanton slaughter. I wish no part of a king whose associates would commit such villainy. You do, Robert?"

He shook his head. "We cannot know those were the king's men, and even so, to sell the secrets of the realm to the cursed enemy? That be not right, Elizabeth — not for me, not for you."

She tossed her head. "If that sharp cook's

mind of yours has a more sensible plan, please share it with me, my dear husband and spouse."

He turned away angrily. She closed her eyes, disgusted with herself, terrified he would break with her. They completed the circle of the market with her gentle apologies and soothings bouncing off his broad back. He said little the balance of that day. His pride was wounded, she could see, and that would not do. She needed him strong, capable, resolute, and confident in his role.

That night she came to him on the floor. Their quarrel, still unresolved, shot through the quiet urgency of their first coupling. His hands seemed to know her as her husband's never had, teased at her most secret of places and most private of wants. He took his time with her, playing her body as a harpist plucks his strings of flesh, and only then did he enter her, and she marveled at the strength and girth of him, at her own wanton pleasure in this utter, shameless sin.

Afterwards, as she coiled against his nakedness, she spoke softly of their plight. "I am an Englishwoman, Robert, but I am also a Scot."

He was silent, pushing a finger between the knobs of her spine, moving upward to her neck.

"There are sound reasons for this flight. Stay with me, Robert. Protect me. If we can run or buy our way past the English border guard we will be safely abroad, and then . . ."

"And then?" he whispered in her ear. Her hair was loose. He toothed it, lipped it.

That was the question, though to her a less pressing one than the journey itself and the peril they still faced.

They came together again in the morning, and spent the first part of that day aglow on their saddles, horses drifting together, then apart, lost in the dangerous wonder of it, their rancor forgotten.

At the first crossing north of Aldwick two Yorkshire sheriffs waited upon the travelers. The sheriffs had dismounted, tied their horses to nearby trees, and now stood in the middle of the junction, their palms toward the company.

"Where do you hail from, good gentles?"

"We are of Essex, London, and Kent," said their leader, "and are now bound for Durham and St. Cuthbert's shrine." He related the joining of the two groups, their progress along the road, the stop in Aldwick the night before.

"We are devoted pilgrims, good sire," said

Constance, jangling her coat, which was festooned with saintly trappings of every color, shape, and substance.

"Truly we are," Catherine added as she touched a relic pinned to her girdle.

"Show your badges, if you please." The sheriffs started mingling with the company, inspecting wares, asking soft questions, looking carefully at faces.

The pilgrims busied themselves with their various badges from journeys past, some leather or cloth patches sewn onto their garments, others medallions or brooches of pewter, lead, and even silver bought at sacred sites.

Margery had none, nor did Robert. Constance, she noted, was proudly showing four badges of Becket, all of hammered tin, each purchased for a penny or two in Canterbury in years past. Eventually a sheriff reached them.

"It is our first pilgrimage," Margery said, trying to sound bashful.

"At my insistence, and our parson's." Robert put a hand on her arm.

"We are not seasoned travelers like the others." She glanced aside at Constance, who was watching the exchange intently.

"Yet you chose Durham for your first voyage?" The sheriff's eyes were on his face, not hers.

"It was thought —," she began.

"Sir?" the sheriff cut her off, still focused on him. "A long journey for a first, and with such a young wife to saddle along the way."

His companion laughed. The pilgrims had gone silent, watching the exchange.

"Why Durham, if you please?"

Robert stared down at the sheriff. Her heart sped. She willed him to answer.

"It was the dun cow," he finally said, looking off at a distant hill.

"The dun cow, you say?" said the sheriff.

Titters from the pilgrims. He seemed to be losing all his sense.

"The dun cow," he repeated. "It was always my favorite story of St. Cuthbert, that dun cow, and my parson's as well. Upon a time, you see, a group of monks went looking for a final resting place for the body of the saint. The abbot had a vision, and in that vision the blessed Cuthbert demanded that his body be taken to a place called Dunholme. No one had ever heard of this Dunholme, nor knew where it might be, and the monks were in a kind of despair. Eventually the company came upon a milkmaid searching out a cow. And what sort of cow? A dun cow, she said. As they stood in the road another milkmaid came by, and the first asked the second if she'd seen a dun cow go by. 'Why yes,' said the second maid. 'It went up that path just there, toward Dunholme.' The monks took the body of St. Cuthbert along up that path, following the milkmaid all the way, and there, at the end of the path, they found the dun cow chewing at the grass in her favorite spot. Dunholme, now Durham, of course, and there Cuthbert's shrine was built and his body laid, and soon enough the church and the town were built around it. And so as we pilgrims walk the road to Durham, we follow in the steps of that humble dun cow, as I have wished to follow its steps since I was a child. At the end of that path we shall graze in the lord's mercy and grace, God willing — and sheriffs willing."

It thrilled her to hear the laughter and admiring murmurs prompted by his story, from both the pilgrims and the sheriffs, whose small suspicions were quickly allayed. Soon their talk turned to the purpose of their vigilance.

"A French ship has been found shored up above Bridlington," said one of them. "Out from Sluys, most like, and set to keep a mustard eye on our preparations in the northern shires." He went on to describe some of the crown's efforts against the

French in the area, the merciless hunt for agents of their allies the Scots.

"You'll see two cursed Scots dangling from the gibbet as you ride into York, you will," said a sheriff with a satisfied nod. He looked around at them. "Any of you met or heard of such vagrants and spies, consorting with Scotsmen in these parts?"

Headshakes and sober denials all around. Soon the company was on its way with the sheriffs' blessings.

They rode in silence for the rest of that day, as words could do little to convey what they felt within. He looked over at her several times, and when she met his gaze she smiled grimly at him, as they shared their newfound lust and the certain knowledge of their peril. They sensed a world closing in around them.

CHAPTER 31

Entering Desurennes that week was like visiting a desolate church during pestilence time. The people's faces were either twisted in sorrow or emptied of all passion, yet against my expectation I sensed little anger at the renewed appearance of English soldiers in this broken village. There was rather a shared sense of resignation apparent in the town, as the residents endured the lingering effects of the massacre.

Le jour de canons, they had taken to calling it. The day of guns.

The village lay some nine leagues from Calais along a well-maintained road. Beauchamp had sent along eight strong riders, all of us leaving at dawn and arriving before dusk, taking lodging at an inn that also served as the central gathering place for the market village. In the morning the soldiers brought in the old man mentioned by Beauchamp to speak with me in the hall.

He was perhaps ten years my elder, his parchment skin taut against protruding bones. He sat before me stiffly. Despite his age his back was board-straight against the table behind him.

We spoke in French. He told me how the strange men had first appeared. They came not from along the road but from within the forest, then calmly prepared their weapons, lit a fire on the gentle rise above the market, acting friendly and unconcerned with the townspeoples' curiosity. Everyone saw the start of their approach with the guns, yet no one knew what the weapons were, and thus no one believed the market was in danger. Only two of the strangers were archers, he said, hiding their bows until the last moment. They stepped forward first.

"The guards went down, and that was when I knew," he said. "I was standing at the edge of the market, where the horse line forms, when I saw the first arrows fly. Two capable archers were all they needed, and the guards of the gate were slain. Then they advanced on the market."

He gave me a few more details: the number of troops, the formation. Each of the assailants had fired four guns already loaded, while a second man was required to light the powder, as I had experienced in the castle yard at Calais. It was relentless, he said, like a forest of limbs cracking all at once, bodies falling right and left, bits of blood and flesh flying through the market. His own son had fallen near the end of the assault, before the company turned for the woods and disappeared.

The old man's face was a waxen slate empty of passion. I considered him, this bereaved father, and wanted him to tell me more. "You are a former soldier, are you not?"

"*Oui, monsieur.* I fought for King Philip at Crécy." Beneath the man's sorrow I heard a touch of pride in his voice. The Battle of Crécy had been fought some forty years before, near the beginning of this seemingly endless conflict between England and France. It represented the first use of gunpowder cannon by the English — bulky, inefficient ribalds, though they did good work, according to every account of the battle I had ever heard.

"And you are well familiar with the tactics of companies and brigades."

"I am."

"Then perhaps you might give me your thoughts on the guns."

"Monsieur?"

"I have fired several of these — these *canons de la main* myself," I said. "They are remarkably inefficient. Had all of those men been armed with longbows they would have slain twice the number of villagers." Then I posed a question that I realized had been nagging me since visiting the woods with Chaucer. "Why would they attack with handgonnes, do you suppose?"

His eyes brightened with the challenge to his mind. He looked at the floor, thought for a long while, then gave a slow nod. "It was a trial," he said.

"What's that?"

"An assay is what it was," said the old man, his gaze still on the floor but his nod strengthening. "They were testing their guns, weren't they. Wanted to see how we would react, how we would dance in the fire of these new cannon." Finally he looked up. "Whether we would fight back."

An assay. What would a crowd of innocents do if a company of handgonners were to fire on them en masse, pin them against a wall? Had the assault in the Kentish wood also been a trial of sorts, a test of new weapons on the flesh and fear of eighteen prisoners? And — the more urgent question — were the assailants planning a third attack?

During our exchange I had noticed a young girl flitting around the yard, looking shyly through the two outer doors to the hall. Her eyes were shadowed, her face drawn. She seemed to want to enter the hall, though some hesitation or fear held her back.

"Who is the girl?" I asked one of the town guards after the old man had left.

He looked at me sadly. "An orphan now. Her parents went down in the shooting, there before the gate. She was up on the walls, along the parapet, when it all broke out, and saw two city guards taken down with arrows during the final approach. She says she was sent there by the leader of the squad just before the guns."

"In sympathy?"

He raised a shoulder. "Perhaps, though several other children were slain in the firing."

"I would like to speak with her if I may."

He regarded me coldly. One of the Calais garrison, also in the hall, rebuked him. "Bring her in, or I will seize the little wench myself."

The Desurennes man made no reply as he left to get the girl. She sat where the old man had sat. Her eyes, deep-set, darkened, puffed with weeping and lack of sleep, rolled aimlessly about as I observed her.

"You were there, demoiselle," I began. "The day of guns."

"Yes, sire," she said. Her voice was tinny, high and sweet like a sacring bell.

"And what are you called, my young lady?"

"I am Iseult."

"A meaningful name," I said gently. "It may help you find your Tristram when the day comes."

"I have already found him, sire. He died at the market, like a dog," she said, her voice going flat as a pond. "I saw him give the ghost there, bleeding on the ground."

"Will you tell me about it, Iseult? Tell me what you saw?"

She twisted her lips into a sad pout, her eyes darkening, though her voice stayed eerily calm while she spoke. "Mostly his neck, when the thing went in. A ball, they said it was, afterwards. But when I saw it I thought it was a garland. Was like a blooming rose round about his neck, spread out in this deep, bright red, like a ruby necklace circling his collar. Did you make that necklace for me, my king? For it is a beautiful necklace, sire."

Her mouth widened as she grasped what she had said. She brought her palms to her face, then started to beat and tear violently at her eyes. I reached forward and took her wrists, thin as sticks, and pulled her arms away from her face. She shook her head in a rage, and I held her until she was be-calmed and still. Her shoulders heaved; weak chokes escaped from a small and delicate mouth.

A woman appeared in the doorway. I gestured her away.

"Do not cast out your eyes, Iseult," I said to the girl. "Our eyes are our windows to God, and to the world He has made. They are one of our greatest gifts. Go gentle on your eyes, Iseult." I let that calm her for a little while, then, when her breathing had slowed, I spoke again. "Please, Iseult, for the sake of your Tristram, and of your poor mother and father. Tell me what you saw."

She told me, sparing no details. The cracks of the guns, the whizzing of the balls through the air, the puffs of sound as they struck flesh and stone, the stink of powder and death. A dark magic in her child's mind.

"Now I need the testimony of your ears," I said when she had finished. "Iseult, listen to me. I know from the monsieur there that you approached the men on the hill. That you spoke to one of them, and that he spoke to you. Was there anything he said to you, any words you could comprehend?"

She shook her little head. "He seemed a nice man. He showed me his birds."

"His birds?"

"*Oui,* sire," she said, and her eyes recovered a gleam. "There was one thing he said to me, and in my own tongue. I had forgotten but now I recall it. He said, 'Do you like swans, little mother?' And he showed me the swans on his arm." She looked up at me, and I felt the pulse quicken in her tiny wrists. "Two great white swans they were. Like this."

She thrust out her elbows, feigning the busy flapping of a bird's wings. Then she encircled her neck with her hands. "Those swans, they were choked with gold, sire."

The Bohun swan, doubled and gorged. The household badge of Thomas of Woodstock, Duke of Gloucester, a mark of his affinity and *familia.*

"And was there anything else?"

"Swans again," she murmured. "The last thing the man said to me before I went to the wall."

"What was it, Iseult?" I leaned in toward her, not wanting the guards by the door to hear her reply.

Her eyes lost their focus as her mouth curled into the saddest of smiles. *"Rappelez-*

503

vous les cygnes, petite mère," she said.
Remember the swans, little mother.

Chapter 32

"Marsh. Stephen Marsh."

He heard his name again, then the clap of hands.

"Marsh, you must come awake."

The priest, back to trouble him for coins. Stephen rolled onto his side and dug his knuckles into his eyes. The straw pallet had lost all its softness over the days of his confinement, the chapel's stone floor any trace of warmth with the coming of the autumn chill. A thin blanket was all he had for covering, so he'd kept everything on for bed, even his tunic. Not only his joints but also his clothing fought against him when he sat up to stretch away the sleep. Two dogs traded muffled barks somewhere outside, and a thin ray of morning light caught dust before the faded paintings on the chapel's western wall.

"Coming, Father," Stephen called to the priest.

He struggled to his feet and went to the curtain, drawn across the narrow entryway to the disused chapel to shield the ugly bedding from parishioners. The chamber functioned as makeshift lodging for the occasional undistinguished visitor: a family member of a rectory servant, a seeker of sanctuary like him, a vagrant on a cold night with a few coins to spare the parson. Stephen was the parish's only boarder at the moment, and the parson let him have his peace for the most part in this period of forced confinement. Stephen had spent the first of these days idling about the church, then started to help the priest with some minor fabric repairs in exchange for his keep, a broken hinge on the screen gate, a few bent nails in the benches, his tools having been sent over by an apprentice from Stone's.

He had also tried to speak with several parishioners in and out of the church that week, though news gets out quickly in such matters, and already the entire ward was abuzz with Stephen's new status as a man wanted for a girl's death. Though he had known many of these men and women all his life, some since before the deaths of his parents, few would spare him so much as a friendly glance or nod. Even his brother could not bring himself to look Stephen in the eye — and all for an accident of circumstance and timing.

"Yes, Father Martin?" he said when the curtain was pulled aside.

The priest's look mingled distaste with warning, both explained by the presence of the man behind him.

"Fair morning to you, Marsh," said William Snell, stepping around the priest. "You are looking poorly."

"What do you want, Snell?" Stephen backed into the chapel. The priest turned away, skulking up the north aisle toward the altar.

"I want you, Stephen." The armorer stepped in after him.

"What can you want with me now? I have killed a woman, with a weapon fashioned for the Tower. Surely the king's wardrobe can want nothing to do with Stephen Marsh after such an incident, and all the talk it's spawning."

"*Sed contra,* Marsh," said Snell, looking amused by Stephen's distress. "I am really quite impressed at your facility with these guns of yours. From what I understand you spun on your heel and shot the girl in her delicate neck from fifty paces."

Marsh felt his fury rising. "How can you

know that? I revealed those details only to Father Martin, within the privity of confession."

Snell's eyes crinkled at their edges. "Confession." He turned to look out on the nave, visible through the chapel's interior window. The priest was murmuring in low tones with one of his lay deacons on the near side of the chancel screen. "A sacrament to buy and sell, if you know the right price."

"And the right priest," said Stephen bitterly. He thought about the armorer's knowledge, and the consequences of the priest's indiscretion. If confession was not to be kept sacrosanct, how could he expect sanctuary to protect him? Was he safe any longer within the walls of All Hallows Staining? Would he be turned over to the city sheriffs or the watchmen outside, to be carted through the streets to Newgate and then the gibbet? Why, there was nothing now between his neck and a hanging but the word of a false priest! He began to doubt the wisdom of Hawisia Stone's bringing him here, and to wonder where he might find a true measure of protection against the law's probing finger.

"The Tower, Stephen," said Snell, as if a confessor himself, discerning his inmost thoughts, teasing out his fears. "Come with me. You have no real choice."

"I will abjure the realm," said Stephen grandly. "Father Martin says I may do so in lieu of a trial. All it requires is a writ from the king's coroner, and I shall be free to leave England of my own will and under my own power."

"What power?" Snell rejoined, almost jovially. "A naïve young fellow like you cannot survive abjuring the realm. As soon as you set foot outside the walls you would be attacked and dragged to your death by the family of that girl you shot. And where would you go, Marsh? Wales? Dublin? *France,* where you would be interrogated and tortured before meeting your end? Better to die now, on the rope of a skilled hangman."

Stephen, jellied in his legs, shuffled to the far corner of the chapel and leaned on the splintered altar, a width of scorched oak. He looked back at Snell. "And the Tower can offer protection?"

"Of a fashion," he said. "At least your natural talents would be employed to the benefit of the realm, even as the disposition of your case is sorted."

"Yet I will be considered a fugitive, to be hung on sight."

"As you are now," he countered. "Con-

509

sider your situation, Marsh. Here at Staining you are in constant jeopardy, and I cannot see this parish harboring for long a man who has done what you've done. But in the liberties of the Tower you would be safe. Protected. The justices and serjeants won't dare pursue you there. Why, there are men within the compound who haven't stepped outside those walls in twenty, thirty years. Criminals, slaves, deserters. Not that you would be counted among their number," he added hastily. "But it will give a space of time to let this affair work itself out. Once you are installed in our foundries, before our own forges and anvils, doing what you do so well, why, all this will come to seem like a night terror."

"The Tower, then," Stephen said, wishing he could discern a ray of hope in the armorer's words. "I shall send word to Mistress Stone, then there will be the —"

"No need for that. The less she knows about your whereabouts the better, hmm? Wouldn't want to put the widow in jeopardy."

He wouldn't, though the thought of leaving Staining without informing Hawisia was difficult to stomach. He felt a fresh and unfamiliar loyalty to his mistress, alone in the world yet willing to risk so much to save

Stephen at his most miserable and endangered. In the moment, though, there seemed little he could do.

"Time is short, Marsh," said Snell briskly. "Move along."

They left the church together, Stephen carrying only a bundle of clothes tucked beneath his right arm. Snell led him down along the walls through the eastern edge of London, a walk that Stephen took in some fear, looking out all the while for the sheriff's men. They reached the barbican without incident, however, and Stephen took a last glimpse of the river to his right. As he paced across the span over the moat Stephen felt as if he were walking through a gate of purgatory itself, down into an infernal machine of war, and such sensations of doom were only heightened once he found himself in the yard and the armorer's precincts, where at least a dozen masons were being directed in the construction of several new kilns and furnaces along the north wall. The air was choked with ash and burning lime, grimy smiths at the forges hammering tangs, drawing out blades, folding steel upon steel, the din of metal ringing from every surface.

Snell placed a hand between his shoulders. "Your serpent guns are just the thing,

Marsh. My own master is quite pleased with them, you know."

"Is he?" said Stephen, his head spinning with the sudden flattery.

"Those two you left here last time? They have done good work already, and now we need more. One hundred of your snakes, Marsh. Make them strong in barrel and true in aim, whether forged or founded I don't much care, but with this firing device of your invention affixed to each one. I have already conscripted four of the cleverer smiths to work under you and hasten the process along, and you'll have the near foundry to yourself. Consider yourself master here, Stephen. Recover your pride, straighten your spine, and act accordingly. You may test the guns just there, against the wall." He pointed to the place where the noble beast had died. "If you do my bidding and accomplish this task, your crime may well be forgotten, or at the least forgiven."

"I thank you, Master Snell," said Stephen, bowing to the armorer, a small spark of hope in his breast.

Here Snell paused, stepping in, his eyes going cold with a suddenness that nearly took Stephen's breath. "Though make no mistake, Marsh. Should you fail me in this you will suffer, and your death will be slow. A lion makes an adequate and entertaining target. But a man? There is no comparison." He laughed, the false warmth returning to his face. "Now get you to work."

The armorer left him, and Stephen was left to gaze at this small world of iron and fire — this world that for the present was his. At Snell's orders a number of metalers broke off their work and came to meet their new master. Two founders Stephen knew from the city guild stood off to one side, awaiting his command, and before him stood four smiths, strong men of the forge, their faces blackened with smoke, and all to do his bidding.

Stephen allowed it to surge within him once more, the allure and power of the gun. He blinked, pushing away the doubts, then issued his first command.

"You," he said to the first. "We need iron, four of the arm bars to start. Bring them here, and I will show you what we are about. And you," he said to the founders. "Copper and tin, eight parts and two."

"Eight and two, Marsh? Are you —"

"Yes, eight and two, and you will soon know why. Get it bubbling now, will you?"

They obeyed. Next an apprentice approached him hesitantly, offering an apron of boiled leather, thick and long. Stephen donned it, then took up a hammer from the main smithy table and started giving the men their orders. Soon enough he felt himself slipping into his familiar role from Stone's, as he moved among the forges and foundry, correcting a young hand here, providing an older one new direction there.

He took his own turns at the anvil and cauldron, making folds upon folds of iron, new foundings of bronze, sizzling blooms of metal in the flames, and when he came to the forges he found new strength in the shaping, the bending, the welding, the plunging and hiss. These weapons would be the greatest and most fearsome works of his life, he vowed, and soon he stood as some young demon amidst the fires and the men, commanding these monstrous births of snake and gun.

It was late the following day when Stephen finally called for a pause in their work, a rest well deserved by the metalmen under him. He had labored through much of that day and night before, pushing his workers to forge along with him, and now he wanted to reward them with strong beer or cider rather than the piss-weak ale served out by the Tower seneschals. Only the armorer himself could authorize that, he'd been told, so at the bell of five Stephen set down his hammer, took off his apron, and walked toward the structure housing Snell's chambers. Though it was the first time he had visited the building since his initial visit to the Tower, he felt no fear as he climbed the narrow stairs, confident his request would be met with approval, even pleasure. For Stephen was, after all, the pride of the royal armory — and not only that, but the artist responsible for bringing a new breed of handgonnes into this coming age of war.

Why yes, he thought with a shivering pride as he climbed up the stairs, his soles a whisper on the rock. Despite the humble start at Stone's, the confounding sentence at the wardmoot, and the unfortunate accident in the woods, look at me now, will you! I am Stephen Marsh, master gunsmith to His Royal Highness King Richard! I have ascended to this office with the speed of a hunting wolf, and who is to say I cannot climb ever higher? Even an appointment as chief armorer of the Tower wardrobe isn't out of the question, albeit William Snell holds that position currently. Yet how long can he last given the vagaries of royal favor — especially once it's known that a superior craftsman, a higher quality of mind, is making his guns for him, already leading the men of the armory in their needful work for the crown?

He had reached the darkened landing before Snell's chamber. The door, he realized, was already slightly open. *Must have that repaired,* Snell had said during Stephen's first visit to the Tower. The bad latch allowed a sliver of light to escape, along with the low murmurs of two conversing men. Snell had another visitor before him. Stephen would abide in the antechamber, he decided, as his matter was hardly urgent. The men of the armory could wait for their refreshment, even as they waited on their new captain. Soon enough, however, Stephen's curiosity got the better of his judgment, and he stole softly forward, putting an ear to the crack.

"In any case I hope it all meets with your approval," Snell was saying.

"My approval is the least of our worries," said the other quietly. "It is the duke whose wants we must satisfy."

Though Stephen could not see the visitor's face it was apparent he was talking down to the armorer. The man's voice was clipped and distinctive, with the confidence of a lord's, and at first this deafened him to the content of their talk — though not for long.

"And you are familiar with his wants?"

"His Grace will no doubt be pleased," the visitor said. "These devices are an ingenious bit of work, and he will enjoy this small adornment to his arsenal."

"We can only hope so," said Snell, sounding doubtful. "Burgundy's artillery is the wonder of Christendom. One minor innovation will hardly buy us favor if it comes to war. Or so it seems to me."

"Think of our gift as a token of fealty, then," said the other man. "Yes, a few hundred of these feeble handgonnes crafted by your farrier will wilt in the glare of a thousand longbows. You have said so yourself, Snell. Yet it is the gesture that matters in such affairs."

"I hope you are right, or all our efforts will vanish in our own smoke."

"We are doing everything we can to guard against such an outcome."

"Yes. Though I worry His Grace will prove changeable, not a man of his word."

"You should read the chronicles. With the invasion Valois may well swallow Plantagenet like a hawk swallows a mouse. Yet King Charles is hardly William the Conqueror. He will not be tempted to flood our wild and primitive island with his dukes and counts. England will be ruled from abroad, of that we may be confident. And its domestic overseers will be men who have already proved themselves loyal to the winning side." A heavy pause. "Men like us, my good William."

Stephen heard the clap of palms on knees and the shuffle of feet, though in his fury at the insults he failed at first to register what these sounds signified. His handgonnes *feeble*? His serpentine device a *minor innovation*? His craft no better than that of a *farrier*, a mere maker of horseshoes? How *dare* these two slander his talents and craft in such a way?

Then he realized his peril. The men had risen too quickly. They were about to leave the room. Stephen was trapped in the antechamber, giving him no chance of making it down the stairs without detection. He had no choice but to squeeze himself into a niche in the walls not three feet from where they would pass on their way out. He made himself as small as possible.

"Very well, then," said Snell as he came out the door to his chambers.

The visitor's head was turned away, his hood already drawn up against the cold. No livery on his cloak or coat, though there was considerable wealth in his fine raiment.

"Exton rides in one week," said the man

518

in a low murmur. "Seven days, twenty men, one hundred serpents. Your gunsmith is up to the task?"

"I have no reason to doubt him. He is a proud fellow, but the Tower has a way of beating pride out of even the hardest men. And Marsh? He's of the softer sort, I'm afraid."

The men shared rough laughter as they descended the stairs. Then they were gone.

CHAPTER 33

As Beauchamp had requested, I reported to the keep immediately upon the return from Desurennes. He asked me not into his chambers but into the keep's upper hall, a narrow though high-ceilinged room looking out distantly on a dimming sea at dusk. A servant brought me wine and a light meal, which I ate quickly by candlelight as I told him a portion of what I had learned at Desurennes — all but the most important detail.

"You are quite sure, Gower?" he said.

"I am, your lordship."

"No other signs? No evidence of responsibility, nothing to suggest who might have done this to those poor villagers?"

"I am afraid not, my lord. The attackers came and went without leaving the barest of traces, it seems."

He gave me a long, catlike stare. I wondered what he knew, and whether my colloquy with Iseult had been overheard.

"Perhaps your renowned skills have left you, Gower."

"Perhaps," I said, sitting back. "Though I am certain there is nothing more to be learned, at least not in Desurennes."

"You will return to London, then," he purred.

"At first light, your lordship, or as close to it as I can manage." Though I was on English soil I felt suddenly vulnerable and alone. Simon was supposed to have made contact himself, yet I did not think it wise to remain in Calais any longer, regardless of the chancellor's wishes. Edmund Rune's pursuit of his treasonous smuggler would have to do without me.

"Very well," he said, seeming eager for my absence. We parted cordially, though I felt his eyes on my back as I walked out of the hall. One coin slipped to a sailor and he could have me tossed off a boat half a league from shore, to sink like a stone in the sea.

Curfew was ringing by the time I left the keep. Calais took its evening bell less seriously than London did, it seemed, despite the town's militant posture, regarding it more as a warning than a sentence. There were several evening gathering places within the walls, one of them between the church

521

of St. Nicholas and Stapler's Hall, where at least a hundred townsmen milled about. On my way back to Broussard's I passed through the large square and left by way of Rigging Street, which cut off at an angle from the main thoroughfare in from the gate.

As the noise from the square faded I heard footsteps approaching from behind me. At first I thought nothing of their hurried patter. At the next corner I cast a glance over my shoulder. A lone figure was approaching. His face was hidden behind a cloak, only his eyes visible beneath the dark hood.

He saw me looking back. His pace quickened. I rounded the bend at a faster pace. I was on an oblong section of the street sided by two high walls providing no means of escape, nor any place to hide. Starting to run, I slipped on a slick spot and fell forward, jamming my arm. The pain spread from my elbow to my hand. As I struggled to my feet I heard the slap of my pursuer's shoes on the pavers.

I glanced back as I staggered up. He was thirty feet away now. Twenty. His hand went to his belt. There was the flash of a blade. I half turned, making for the next street, cowering beneath my uninjured arm as I ran, expecting a thrust between the shoulder blades at any moment.

Another sound, from off to my left. A grunt, hurrying feet, an impact.

"Ohf!"

Sounds of a struggle, then silence.

I looked back. In the middle of the widened part of the street a man bent over my hooded pursuer, now prostrate on the ground. Still, perhaps dead. The other man was patting his sides and front, searching him.

I did not stay to see the result. I rounded the next corner, but now the second man was chasing me. In my state I had no strength to resist him. A hand clutched my injured arm. He had me. Yet I turned into him, hand balled into a fist, prepared to defend myself with my good arm.

"Father!"

He threw me against the wall, and I felt the blood drain from my face.

Even in the near darkness Simon's countenance was as familiar a sight as my own hand, though it had changed for the worse. A new and whitened scar ran down from his forehead through his left cheek, ending in an ugly star-shaped mark just above the line of his chin. A bark of French from the square, more running.

"The watch," Simon whispered fiercely.

"We cannot talk here. Come." Still grasping my arm, he ducked beneath a slanted beam and took me down a narrow alley and through a series of linked passages winding snakelike through the buildings around us. It was a part of the sea town left untouched by King Edward's renovations, a labyrinth of hidden courts, odd corners, and sudden staircases that quickly took us out of reach of the watchmen.

Soon we arrived at a tall, narrow house to one side of a small courtyard. We climbed three flights of stairs to a low door that had been left open to the night. Simon closed it behind us, then with some effort flinted up a flame.

My son, still short of his twenty-fourth year, looked well above his thirtieth. Simon had aged in the mere fifteen months since I saw him last, leaning over me at night, staggering across the priory yard with the fate of a kingdom clutched in his hands. His face was gaunt, with a greyish cast to his skin, which sat too taut over the visible bones of his face. He had lost much of the physical grace that once distinguished him. Even in his worst moments Simon would always be at ease with himself and those around him. Now he was shaky and restless, as if his limbs were animated by some maddening ague.

Attending to my throbbing arm appeared to calm him somewhat. I sat silently as he bandaged the limb. He seemed practiced at it, as if used to repairing the minor injuries of his companions in stealth, and I let him do what he would without complaint.

"Not broken, certainly," he said. "A minor sprain of the wrist. Keep it bound for several days."

I could not look at him and instead gazed around the chamber. No hearth and thus no fire in these upper rooms, only a thin clutch of greased rushlights, the weak flame casting our distorted forms against the close walls and low ceiling. When he had finished with my arm he sat across from me. His leg worried the seat of his chair. He reached up constantly to wipe a palm over his brow, which was not moist, though in his agitated state he seemed if anything feverish and ill. His eyes shifted right and left.

"Who was that man?" I finally asked. My first words to Simon since that night at the priory house.

"You don't know?" His voice was hollow, with no resonance or depth, as if coming from behind a muslin cloth.

I shook my head.

"He was your traveling companion. He sailed with you from London."

I thought for a moment. "The cloth merchant?"

Simon stared at the rushlight. "He is no cloth merchant, Father."

"You know him?"

"We have met," he said darkly. "He was a killer for coin, with twenty knifings to his credit. His target tonight was you."

"Apparently."

"I am more than glad that he failed."

"I should hope so," I said, and he looked away, his leg bouncing anew. Simon had just saved my life. Yet why did I suspect he had also had a hand in jeopardizing it?

"I have been following you since your arrival from London," he said, almost shyly.

"How did you know I was coming to Calais?"

"I didn't know, not in advance," he said. "But I have men at the docks and generally receive word upon the arrival of passengers, particularly newcomers to the Pale. I was as surprised to hear of your disembarkation as you were to see me tonight. I didn't think you would come."

"You learned where I have been?"

"From one of the servants of Broussard. You went looking into the killings at

Desurennes."

"Yes."

"What have you learned?"

I scoffed. "What reason would I have to tell you anything I've learned?"

"None," he admitted. He tapped a finger. "Though surely you suspect some connection to this business with Gloucester and Snell."

A name I had heard any number of times in recent weeks. "The king's armorer," I said.

"He is a longtime ally of Gloucester's," said Simon, his tone subtly changing. "That is why I contacted the chancellor, Father, and asked to speak with you, and only you. Snell is not simply laying in powder and weapons for the Tower and the crown. He has become a notorious trader in arms against the interests of England. I've learned that he is selling saltpetre to Burgundy and France by the barrel."

"With Gloucester's approval?"

"More than his approval. It is Woodstock's men who have been bringing it across and selling it here."

"And you believe the king's uncle conspires so openly against England's interests?" I asked, hearing the skepticism in my own voice.

"What I believe is not of relevance. It is what I have seen that convinces me, and what my paid men up and down the coast have seen. With my own eyes I have witnessed Gloucester's men unshipping kegs of saltpetre from a cog off Dunkirk, then rowing them into Burgundy's maw."

"How do you know they were Gloucester's men?"

"They wore his bends, flew his colors off the ship."

"What proof do you have?"

"Nothing written," he conceded. "There is only my word, and this."

He pulled a piece of cloth from somewhere in his coat. It was a heraldic bend, a band meant to be worn around the forearm, with a badge of embroidered kidskin sewn into the cloth. The badge itself was lozenge shaped, displaying two white swans, their wings spread wide, their linked necks collared in gold with a chain descending to entwine the birds' webbed feet. The same bend described by poor Iseult.

"Where did you get this?"

He looked down at the badge. "In Dunkirk. I was watching one of the docks as an English ship unloaded. A cog, bearing a large shipment of saltpetre. Two of the men were arguing on the high quay. They were drunk, I believe, and the dispute involved a maudlyn they had hired to come aboard. It soon came to blows. Nothing murderous, just two sauced sailors swinging their arms, a bit of wrestling. But in the struggle one of them had his band ripped off his sleeve, and it fell to the ground. I waited until they'd left the quay, then went and retrieved it."

I fingered the badge, the embroidered feathers and chain. I had seen dozens like it on the streets of London, and more recently in Gloucester's castle in Kent, where the duke's men had imprisoned Chaucer and me in the tower. The duke seemed to have an endless reserve of men. Hauling bodies on the Thames and through the streets of London, gunning down a market in the Pale, and now this.

"Did you ever speak to any of the company?" I asked.

"No," he allowed. "I spoke to one of their buyers from Sluys, and learned that the arrangement has been going on for months. Since before Pentecost, he told me."

"I can hardly bring myself to believe it, Simon. The Duke of Gloucester —"

"You must believe it, Father. I have seen it, and it can't be denied that his men and

Snell's are involved in the highest treachery."

"And killing all in their way," I murmured, newly awake to my peril.

"Saltpetre and gunpowder are a mere portion of it, Father," he said. "They are also trading in guns." Simon stood and walked to a high pair of shelves by his door. He reached up, lifted a long object off the lower shelf, and brought it to me. It was a handgonne, of a similar length and heft to those I had fired at the Calais keep. A tube-like length of metal bolted to a carved wooden stock, a priming pan hammered into the barrel, a small hole bored through to the chamber.

There the similarities ended, I saw as I slipped on my spectacles. For unlike the Calais gun, a rough if lethal contrivance, this weapon had been crafted by a master artisan. The barrel was of bronze in an octagonal shape, widening slightly from bottom to top, the stock expertly fashioned to join the metal with a smooth seam. I suspected the barrel had been poured at a foundry rather than beaten and welded at a smithy, though I could not be sure.

The gun's most distinctive feature was its firing mechanism. I rotated the weapon in the rushlight. Several inches from the butt end of the stock was a curved length of metal fashioned to resemble the spiraled tail of a snake. The twist of iron ended in a cleverly wrought snakehead, with a piece of cord held clenched between its fangs.

"The Snake," said Simon, reaching forward to finger the serpentine mechanism.

The Snake. The same name Beauchamp had given to the gun rumored to be in development at the Tower. As Simon showed me the weapon's parts I marveled at the ingenuity of this new gun in my hands. The center of the snake's body had been attached to the gun with a hinged lever, the fulcrum sitting at the point where barrel met stock. By lifting the snake's tail at the stock end, the user of the weapon would be lowering the serpent's mouth — and thus the glowing cord — into the firing pan.

The gun could be both aimed and fired, then, by one man alone, without the need for a partner to light the priming powder with a coal, indeed without the use of a coal at all. Instead the powder would be set alight with a cord anchored between the snake's teeth, and the gunner could run from place to place on the field of battle without relying on a stationary fire to light a coal or stick.

The Snake was a small revolution, a

marvel of efficiency, a fierce and fell weapon. I wondered what other innovations were being imagined and engineered in the royal armory.

"How did you get this, Simon?"

"It was lifted from the same cog by one of my men at Dunkirk several days ago. He hooked over the side by night and found it wrapped in sailcloth belowdecks. I have two of them. This one is mine, to do with as I wish. The other is for you, to take back to the chancellor. I have already shortened it for ease of transport, though the snake is intact."

He went to the shelf and brought over a stubby version of the same handgonne, with most of the barrel sawed roughly away. The wooden stock had been shortened as well, leaving the device no longer than my forearm. Simon took the gun from me and laid it carefully on the table between us.

"And now I have a question for you." He leaned forward, his leg stilling beneath the table. "Who knows you are in Calais?"

"The chancellor, certainly, and his man Edmund Rune. Ralph Strode knew I was coming over as well, and of course Beauchamp."

"Could Gloucester have been informed?"

"Not by the chancellor," I said. "Yet

Beauchamp is the duke's close ally against the earl. He might have got word back across while I've been here, though the timing would be rather strait."

"Perhaps," he said.

I felt compelled to ask him, "Who is paying you, Simon? Who is your lord and master this year?" My voice sounded bitter, even to me.

"Hawkwood," he answered instantly. "He pays me well to keep my fingers in the pies, and like him I am happy to sell what I know. In this case, however, I am offering it freely to you, and through you to the crown. To see this plot unfolding against my country and my king does not sit well, even to a man like me."

Sir John Hawkwood, the great English mercenary who had made half of Italy his domain in recent decades, hiring his services to popes, cities, dukes. It was three years now since Simon had left London to join Hawkwood's company. That he was still in the ruthless mercenary's good graces after what transpired last year came as a rude surprise. I regarded him closely, wishing for a look at the workings in his head, as opaque to me as the mysterious gears in a clock tower.

"No man may serve two masters, Simon,"

533

I said quietly, preachily.

He lowered his head to place his chin on his folded hands. He looked into the burning rushes as he spoke. "You have quoted only part of Matthew's verse, Father. Allow me to turn the leaf for you. *'No man can serve two masters. For either he will hate the one, and love the other, or he will love the one, and despise the other. You cannot serve both God and mammon.'* " His eyes tilted up, hooded but clear, and he gave me a sad smile. "We have made our choice of master, Father. We are servants of mammon, you and I, our only difference lying in the source of our servitude. What men and their private affairs are to you, nations and their secrets are to me. Things to slip from purses and sell to strangers, with little regard for law or convention."

Beneath the dark cast of his words there was a strange but welcome clarity in Simon's comparison, a sense that he had freshened the air between us with such a forthright admission.

"You will remain in the Pale?" I asked him.

"For now," he said. "Though given what has just occurred I suggest you leave as soon as you can, and as discreetly."

"Yes, though . . ." I hesitated. "I will need your help, as I know no one in town, nor along the harbor."

"I will arrange for your departure in the morning. A man will come here at first light. He will get you safely through the walls, take you down to the harbor, and put you on a ship to London. You cannot go back to Broussard's, nor to the keep."

"No, I see that," I said, thinking of the few things I had left in my travel bag at the wool merchant's house: some clothes, a favorite writing tablet, a Latin book of myths and their glosses. The book would be a great loss, though perhaps I might send for it once back in Southwark. My own skin, I reasoned, was more precious than the parchment leaves making up a manuscript.

With the details of my departure settled we sat in silence. Simon had calmed somewhat, as had I, and it came to me how great a risk he had taken to acquire the information passed on to me. What I perceived as weakness in him might be instead a hidden strength, a reserve of bravery and fortitude beneath the foolish and puerile exterior I knew. Simon served the worst of men, though perhaps was on his way to becoming a better man himself.

Even as I had these sentiments I spurned them. Simon had lied to me so often and so casually that I needed to remain distrustful of every word from his mouth. Yet I longed to ask him to gloss for me the book of his experience, to untangle the braids of hardship, deception, and compromise twining through his adult life. Surprising myself, I reached to cover his clasped fingers with a palm. He moved his chin atop my hand, and in that position we remained until the rushes had reduced themselves to a single glowing coal.

At long last he moved against my hand, the smallest spark aflame in his eyes. "Tell me a story, Father."

"I —" My voice caught in my throat, and at once he was a young boy, and my eyes were strong again, and his hand was clasped in mine as I spoke to him of these myriad other worlds, of faery and dragon, of Arthur and Gawain, of gods of the godless and the myths of times past. It was a small thing we had shared before I turned from him, before my other children died and my heart hardened, losses piling on my shoulders into an unmoving burden. The rushes had gone dark, though an October moon waxed bright through the opened street window, which carried in the sea air from the west.

"Once, in Asia," I began, "there was a king named Cambuscan." As I continued he turned his head to the side, giving me a view from above of the scar blemishing his forehead and face. My weak gaze wandered its jagged course, as if to discern the unknown itinerary that had brought him here, to this humble room, from wherever he had been. I told him a long, wandering tale, and we conversed quietly into the night.

CHAPTER 34

Simon was gone when I awoke, having slipped out some time in the still hours, though the pallet we had shared still bore his impression and something of his scent. His man appeared, as Simon had promised he would, promptly at the ringing of Prime, slipping into the garret wordlessly, nearly silent. I gathered the few things Simon had left me, including the shortened handgonne, into a leather bag open on the table. The man slung it over his shoulder, and without a word he took me down the outer stairs to the street. Avoiding the gate, we took a meandering route to a postern door on the north side of the town, where Simon's man nodded for me to pay off the guard.

It was more than a relief to step outside those walls, though Calais was small and my mind would not be eased until I was safely aship. Soon we were at the docks, among the fishing craft at the north end, where my guide handed me off to a row-man who would take me out into the harbor. Our destination was a neat-looking balinger standing out in the water, twenty oars to a side and outfitted for war, its lone mast pointing skyward and topped with the flag of the Merchant Staplers.

As we pulled off from shore I looked back at the town and the castle, thinking of my son, and the miseries he seemed always to inflict. Somewhere in that heap of stone and fear Simon continued his machinations, spawning betrayals slight and great. Would I see him again? Would I wish to in another year, or another five?

The balinger's crew were all English, the master a weathered wool tradesman I had met through Chaucer years before. He took the purse I offered him without a glance at its contents.

A smooth crossing on fair winds brought me no sickness on the return to Gravesend, and before midday we pulled up the river past Tilbury on the north bank, standing out from the many vessels clustered about the quays. Here trawlers headed out to deeper waters, flat-bottomed boats plumbed the shallower ways along the coast, gulls dove for guts cast out by fishmongers. Along the shore builders worked at full tilt, shipwrights clinging to the new vessels like bees to a hive. On the high street in town I went to an inn I knew and asked the keeper for a look at the bounty bill from Westminster. Issued from the royal courts in dozens of copies, such bills were circulated and cried regularly along the realm's main roads and sea routes, listing the names of suspected traitors, pirates, and fugitives from justice, and, in time of war, asking for the aid of the commons in watching out for spies. Large bounties were promised to those who aided in apprehending such evildoers, though as anyone who sought to collect would quickly learn, such sums were larger in the promising than in the delivery. Yet the traveling documents had their uses. More than once I had found a piece of information in a bounty bill, a missing shard of knowledge that had helped me puzzle together a matter for extraction or purchase.

The keeper slipped me the bill along with my second ale. The list filled one side of a parchment roll. I quickly found the names I was looking for.

Robert Faulk, cook, for poaching	£20
Margery Peveril, gentlewoman, for	
murder	£20

This foul common man and this cursed woman, albeit she of gentil bloode, having broken from gaol togidere, do now sojourn in suspected compaignie of eche the othere, and do seke to flee the realm by any possible menes.

Twenty pounds. An enormous sum for such a bounty, and a certain sign that someone in the upper aristocracy was desperate to find the two fugitives and complete the work begun in the massacre in Kent.

For good reason, as Faulk and Peveril were not simply fugitives. They were witnesses to the crime that had started all of this. Where the two fugitives named in the bill were now, though, was anyone's guess. Concealed at a Kentish farmhouse, hiding out in London, making their way abroad, already captured and hung: the possibilities were as limitless as the world itself, and I had little hope of adding their testimony to my purse.

I joined a crowd on the long ferry from Gravesend, leaving at the turn of the tide and gathering all the news I could about affairs in the realm since my departure. I had been gone from London for less than a week, yet it seemed everything had changed in my absence. I listened to the chatter on the ferry.

No great war levy, then, 'spite King Richard's fondest plea to fight the French, though you have to bleed your heart a bucket for the Earl of Suffolk.

Impeached by the very Commons, he was, then ranted out by the Lords.

And a new lord chancellor for all to love. We give you Arundel, come to save King Richard's young hide.

A most wise and wonderful Parliament, everyone's shoutin' it. A new council to rule the realm, a dozen new helmsmen to steer our ship aright with good governance —

And land the lighter levies on our poor shoulders. Much better to have a council than a king taxin' our souls, though a penny's a penny in my purse at all rates.

Irreverent, slightly scandalous, though not touching treason; the sort of patter one often hears in the taverns and markets as a mark of casual discontent with the crown and Parliament.

Yet the news of the chancellor's impeachment, however expected, filled me with melancholy and a great worry for the realm. For years Michael de la Pole had stood as a fount of wisdom, prudence, and counsel, and while he had perhaps gone too far in supporting King Richard's steeper war levy, his had been a calm and durable voice of reason at Westminster, without the rabid factionalism infecting relations among the upper gentry of late, from Robert de Vere on one side to Lancaster on the other. The new chancellor, Thomas Arundel, was a man utterly unworthy of the office, in my view, a flatterer and a conniver of the worst sort. It was more than distressing to learn of the Parliament's successful ousting of a chancellor whom I had long counted my highest supporter in the king's affinity.

Once the ferry passed the Tower and pulled in by the customhouse I hired a wherry to take me to the Southwark bankside. Rather than shoring below the bridge or shooting through to dock at Winchester's Wharf, the craft at my request let me off a good way short of the bridge, along the eastern butchers' wharfs, nearly empty at that hour, though heavy with stench from the flows of offal and dung let loose in the Thames. Dodging around several piles of waste on the quays I took Butchers Lane above the wharf up to the high street, which I crossed while keeping a careful eye on the roaming crowds. Another two turns and I was at my own door, nestled at one side of a small courtyard against the priory wall.

Unlocked, though not for long. Once inside I pushed it to, turned the lock, and set the rising bar tightly in place.

Will Cooper took my cloak and coat, holding them over his arm as he greeted me with his usual efficiency. "Your bag, Master Gower?"

"In Calais. I will send for it next week."

"Very well," he said, then saw the distress on my face.

"Are you quite well, master?"

I nodded, calming myself. "I am, Will. Shaken from the travel."

"We have a guest in the house," he said.

"Is it Simon?" My heart leapt. Could it be —

His eyes widened; then he shook his head. "No, Master Gower. Not Simon."

"Ah," I said, recovering from the absurd hope. "One of your family then?" The Coopers, with my permission, had more than once invited relations to lodge at the priory.

"Warm yourself in the hall, if you will. I'll summon him from the kitchens, where my wife has busied him peeling roots."

"A guest at St. Mary's, peeling *roots*?"

He smiled and left me to my hearth. A few minutes passed, and I had almost dozed off from my weariness when Will returned, leading a reluctant boy into my presence. It took me a moment to recognize young Jack Norris. I could not have been more astonished if King Richard himself had appeared in my hall.

The boy stood straight at the sight of me, then gave a low and exaggerated bow. "The Earl of Earless at your service, sire."

"Tell me what you saw."

Another child, another witness to atrocity, things the young should never have to behold. We had gone to the hall and taken chairs at one end of the table. Jack Norris spoke, and in remarkable detail he related everything he had heard and seen on the night it all began.

He had settled down for sleep that evening in the church of St. Stephen Walbrook, where the parson was known to house and feed vagrants on occasion. Needing to relieve himself, he slipped out of the nave and up toward the crossing at Cornhill.

"Needed a squat, didn't I, and the parson doesn't take friendly to dunging up the nave or yard. So I sneaked me out for a visit to the Long Dropper. Don't have to pay at night. I was just stepping down a gutter 'cross the way when I hear the creaks."

"The cart?"

"Aye, a cart and horse, comin' right up the mids of the street, all dark, with no lamp to light the way. Couldn't cross now, could I, not if I hoped to stay out of the Counter or the Tun. So I made small and thought I'd wait for it to pass. But it stopped, didn't it, right spot in front of the Long Dropper. There's one fellow leading the horse, and him and two others with him start takin' somethings out a the cart, up the steps, and in. I could hear the splashings all the way across."

"Could you see their faces?" I asked.

"Not whiles they unloaded. Didn't get a look at any of those three, nor what they were throwin' in the Walbrook," he said.

I blew out a breath, unable to mask my disappointment.

Then Jack said, "Saw their master, though."

"In the dark?"

"Was a night constable came by," he said. "Had a lamp in his hand half-covered. Doesn't give a yell like the night watch always does. Instead he comes up to the master who's been standin' by the cart, like they're expecting to meet. The master holds out a purse, and the constable lifts his lantern to look at the coin. That's when I saw the fellow, plain as the moon."

"Describe him."

"Brown hair, brown beard, nice jet about him." He shrugged. "Looked like a fair lot a' higher men I seen in the walls."

"A lord?"

"Could be. Or a knight or a prince, all I know."

"Was it the mayor, or any of the aldermen you saw at the Guildhall that day of your father's trial?"

He shook his head. "Not one of them, I'm sure a that at least."

"Was the man wearing livery? Heraldry of any sort? A badge, a bend, a collar?"

He looked up, considering it. "Not as I saw it. His coat were plain, nor'd he wear a hat."

"You would recognize him, though, be able to choose him out of a crowd?"

"Oh, as to that, sire, aye, I surely would," said Jack with a fierce series of nods. "Know that face anywhere, I would, and the way he stands and such."

"Did the cart return a second time?"

"Aye it did, and it was a close thing, as my breeches was about my ankles when I heard it comin' back up."

All sixteen bodies must have been Thames-side, then, before their hauling up to the Long Dropper.

"Got out in time, though. Closed the door soft as you like, flew across th' way and back to St. Stephen's. Didn't think naught of the whole thing till I told my father of it the next day."

Once the news of the bodies had spread through the city, Peter Norris would have grasped immediately the significance of what his son had seen. No wonder that he twice tried to barter for his freedom and then his life with the information — which the mayor refused to entertain or even hear given his intimidation by the duke. Now the earless boy was being pursued through the streets by Gloucester's men, who had already murdered another cutpurse loosely resembling Jack.

"You have done well to stay alive, boy," I said. "You may remain here for the present. You will sleep in the kitchen and assist the Coopers with household tasks as they require."

"Yes, Master Gower," said Jack, eyes showing his surprise.

I looked over the boy's gaunt but able frame, trying not to think about his future. "You seem a bright one, Jack. Too bright to be cutting purses."

He shrugged. "I'll hie me out to Oxford then, guzzle up all that logic and Ars-totle.

Would that suit, Mas' Gower?" He met my
gaze, unblinking.

CHAPTER 35

Between Micklegate and the church of St. Martin a large crowd had gathered in the butter market, where a pilloried forestaller was getting some minor ridicule from the legitimate sellers in the booths. Margery purchased a disc of butter to go with the loaf bought on Bread Street. Robert drank cool cream from a passed farthing-jug. As they reached the edge of the crowd he watched her rip a piece of bread from the loaf and spread the thick butter on top. She passed the piece to him, then took the jug, washed it down. Yorkshire cream was a different thing than its Kentish cousin. Sharper, thicker, with a sour bite that reminded her of a green apple.

The company had reached York the previous day, with several of the pilgrims coming newly alive at the prospect of a great city and its many temptations. It had been agreed that they would remain an additional night to restore themselves before the final push north to Durham.

York was the only true city Margery had ever visited aside from London, and while it was quite small by comparison, its streets afforded a welcome bustle after so many days of travel through the countryside and its villages. The citizens here were well used to outsiders, too, and she enjoyed her interactions with shopkeepers and hucksters, negotiating their differences of tongue and word with none of London's often cruel contempt for strangers.

Along the shambles they walked past rows of capons and fat geese, carcasses and cuts of veal, mutton, and lamb, with Robert pointing out the flaws in the lesser meats, the rich marbling in the better. Cheese, fish, greens, and roots: he had a cook's eye for the fresh and the well colored, and Margery found herself hungering for some stew or sauced roast prepared by his hand. Such were the new intimacies of their relations, the transactions of taste, touch, and smell they shared as they rode and walked, coupled and slept, whispered and looked together at the world around them, as if this swiftly cooling autumn were become a florid spring.

They were standing in the yard before the

common hall when a city herald blew for their ears. As the noise lowered a crier ascended one of the horseless wagons before St. Martin. The crowd circled in and tightened, giving Margery the opportunity to press against Robert behind her, and him the chance to circle her lower waist with his hands. She felt the strength of them, wished he would lift her right there before these loud folk of Yorkshire.

The herald blew a last note, then gestured for his companion to begin. The crier looked down at a bill in his left hand. He cupped his right to his mouth, raised his head, and shouted over the crowd.

"Good gentles! Good commons, lords, and ladies alike! Gather round! Gather round, if you will, and hear these words I sing! By order of the high and honorable lord mayor of our city, John de Howden, I bear grim tidings, my good people of York! And what tidings are these? They are tidings of murder! And theft! And yet more murder! We are all enjoined, every man of us, to look abroad and close for one Robert Faulk, cook of Bladen Manor in Kent, and poacher of King Richard's own royal forests. He travels northward with Margery Peveril, gentlewoman of the same shire — and, goodmen of York, the murderess of her very husband!"

Margery's skin prickled as the venomous shouts of the townspeople swelled around them.

Whore!

Murderess!

The gallows for them both!

The gallows be too gentle!

She glanced right and left, to see if any of their company were among the crowd. None that she saw, though the crier would surely repeat the proclamation in the coming hours. She stood frozen before the wagon, with Robert clutching her tightly.

"Both are escaped from a king's gaol in the shire of Kent, and do now flee in adulterous lust together through the realm. There is great bounty promised from His well-beloved Highness King Richard to any man who would aid in their apprehension and seizure, singly or together. And you are warned, fair people of Yorkshire, you are warned to keep your doors shut against the foul intrusion of Robert Faulk and Margery Peveril into your homes and halls! For to knowingly harbor or succor such felonious folk is a seditious crime against the very crown, punishable by the same death to be meted out to them. So sayeth this dire proclamation, and so sayeth your lord mayor, and so sayeth your lord king."

The crier stepped off the wagon. As the

press loosened she grasped Robert's hand at her waist and pushed with him toward the edge of the square. Soon they found themselves on a narrow street winding toward the Ouse.

"We are as well as dead," said Margery, feeling her deepest fright since that night in the Kentish wood.

"They've no evidence we're not who we say we are," said Robert calmly.

She stamped her foot. "You are a fool. We must flee from York this hour. We'll not return to the inn. I have a stuffed purse at my waist, you have the coin I gave you, and we shall go —"

"Margery." He grasped her wrist, spun her to face him. "Think of it. Leaving the city alone would only draw attention to ourselves. We must abide here until tomorrow, then leave with our fellowship, just as we would if that cursed crier hadn't named us true."

He was right, of course, though as she fell against him she came as close as she had in weeks to giving in to her despair. A swelling part of her wanted simply to end this reckless journey north, to return to Kent and accept whatever fate the sheriffs and justices and God Himself wished them to face. Instead she took his hand and they returned together to the square. The crier was gone, the crowd thinned. Their meal at the inn that night was taken in the familiar company of the pilgrims, with nothing said about Margery Peveril and Robert Faulk, this fugitive pair from the south.

Would their fortune hold? In the days that followed no one in their company confronted them with the crier's warnings. Yet Margery was surely not imagining the dark looks and furtive whispers spreading through the fellowship as it crawled through the northern reaches of Yorkshire. Had any in their company heard Mariota speak Robert Faulk's name? Had the widow whispered her suspicions in those days before Margery threatened her? Even so there would be a hesitancy to speak against the couple, for Robert had slowly become the unspoken leader of this pilgrimage, giving small kindnesses and warm words to all. Everyone adored him, man and woman alike, his stories, his manner, his good humor and goodwill. Perhaps they were safe after all.

Perhaps. On the second day out from York she felt a burning in her back, a spreading unease. As Robert rode ahead she glanced behind her to see Constance and Catherine leaning toward each other like trees over a gulch, stealing looks ahead at her as they rode. When they saw her glance back they ceased their talk and straightened themselves, showing her the flattened lines of their lips. She said nothing to Robert about her suspicions, but for the rest of that day and the next, whenever Margery tried to slow her mount and ride at the rear, the sisters slowed with her, silently refusing to give way. They were like sheepdogs, or wardens guarding against a flight. Constance and Catherine, two sisters riding side by side, scowling, murmuring, trading whispers over the road.

CHAPTER 36

Would they come for me at night or by day? Was I safer in my home or on the streets? How closely were they watching me, if at all? The attack in Calais and the threat of a knife in the back stayed at the front of my mind as I settled in uneasily at the priory those first days following my return to Southwark. I found myself glancing out the windows, checking the bars on the doors, reacting to every stray noise with a swiveled head, a frightened glare. On the third morning I sent Will Cooper out through the priory gate to circle the outer grounds. When he returned with nothing to report I decided to risk a first outing since my return, giving Jack Norris strict instructions to remain within the house. I dressed down in some of Will's plain clothes, which fit me well and would make me less conspicuous on the streets of London, as would the hood pulled over my brow.

No one seemed to be following me as I left Southwark over the bridge and made my way into Aldgate Ward, a ward of metal and arms where smiths and founders busily crafted everything from plate and chain to grilles and bells. While the Tower employed many of its own workers in metal, the crown was jealous of the city's talents in the arms-related trades, going so far as to forbid their guildsmen to cross the seas in the retinues of magnates. It was also illegal by statute to export iron goods from England, let alone arms and armor such as the handgonnes lifted by Simon at Dunkirk.

Yet this serpentine gun, or so Simon had told me, was the invention of a smith working for one of London's many houses. An intricate and clever work of the hands, displaying a fine combination of delicacy, dexterity, and strength that only a master smith could be capable of forging. While metalworkers of all trades were required to stamp their mark on their productions, neither the gun nor the serpent bore the signs of their craftsmen — though forged marks were so common that such a sign would have meant little in any case.

Or so I thought. My intention had been to show the serpentine device to as many smiths, farriers, and founders in the precinct as necessary until someone recognized the work of the gunmaker. It was a considerable surprise when the first guildsman I consulted identified the maker immediately. He held the snake, turned it and felt it with the hands of an expert, then took a long squint at the patterned back of the serpent. A grudging smile. "That's Marsh's work, sure as I stand here."

"Who is Marsh?"

"Stephen Marsh, over at Stone's foundry."

"How can you know?"

"Recognize his work with my smith's eyes shut tight. But no need for that. See just there?" He pointed to a spot along the snake's back. I took out my spectacles and examined the area in question. There, within the waffled pattern along the snake's spine, the minute letters *SM* appeared between four of the cross hatchings.

"What is Marsh's reputation among those of your craft?"

He shrugged. "When it comes to London metaling, Stephen Marsh is the best. Everyone knows it." A corner of his mouth turned up. He snickered. " 'Specially Stephen Marsh."

"Where is his place of work?"

"Bellyeter Lane, off Fenchurch Street in

Staining parish. But you won't find Stephen Marsh there."

"Oh?"

"Poor carl's been in sanctuary at All Hallows Staining. Gossip is" — he leaned in, licked his lips — "he killed him a young lass up by Ware. The sheriffs and beadles been asking around for him, but he churched himself before an arrest, won't answer their questions. I worry for the widow." At my questioning look he said, "Hawisia Stone, the mistress at that house, and Stephen Marsh's mistress as well. The master passed this winter last." He shook his head. "Without Marsh's hammer it's passing hard to see Stone's staying afloat."

I considered the news about Marsh as I took the short walk down through the parish of All Hallows Staining. Another life taken, another thread pulled. How many more could there be to unravel?

The parson of Staining, young and new to the parish, stood on the western porch, haggling with a trio of carpenters over an internal repair. When they had trudged off he looked at me disdainfully. "Yes?" he said, taking in my poor raiment.

"You give sanctuary, Father?"

He sniffed. "Only to members of this parish. You are a stranger here. I have never

560

seen your face, now, have I?"

"Not likely," I said. He wore a gilded belt about his waist, his pointed and stylish shoes cut of the softest leather. A parson who favored finery. I cupped my purse in my hand, absently squeezed the gold and silver. His gaze went to my waist.

"What do you want?"

"Stephen Marsh. He is taking sanctuary here?"

The priest hesitated. "Stephen has committed a grievous and mortal sin. His crime is between himself and God, with no call for meddlers."

"Truly?" I said.

His head cocked to the side as he listened to the soft clink of mingled coins.

"Only a word with him, Father."

He parted his lips, eyes still on my purse. "He has left sanctuary."

"Where did he go? Back to Stone's?"

His eyebrows lifted expectantly as his hand came out. I dug for a coin.

"Not Stone's," the priest said once the gold was in his palm. "He's gone to the Tower. They came for him days ago."

"Who?"

"The king's armorer himself. William Snell."

■ ■ ■ ■

It took little time to locate Stone's foundry midway down Bellyeter Lane, a quiet byway off Fenchurch Street. A colorful awning, a sign displaying the foundry's lozenge-shaped stamp, a low bench set back from the side gutter. Though the display room was open to the street no one was there. I walked through to the yard. The space was well kept, with neat piles of wood and coals stacked along the north spans of the barn and smithy. Several square chimneys rose from two of the three roofs, though only one was smoking at that hour. Like the street in front the yard was relatively quiet, the only sounds coming from the direction of the foundry. As I crossed the yard I heard a woman's voice from within.

"More water on that side, Walter. And Hob, not so flat on the curve or you'll be through to the bricks. Now then, both of you. Step back and look at the shape you've made. Time for the striping, do you suppose?"

The woman I took to be Hawisia Stone, large with child, stood near a wide pile of brown clay, directing two apprentices in the shaping of a bell mold. Though dressed in widow's black she was hardly still with grief. Unconfined, animated, alive with the work, strands of loose hair swishing this way and that as her head went back and forth and her mouth barked commands. Even so her face looked pale and drained of blood, her eyes hooded and smudged.

"Mistress Stone," I said during one of the rare pauses in her discourse.

Her head swung in my direction. She reached up to wipe a patch of sweat from her brow. When her arm came down I could see that half her sleeve was covered in a dark patch of moisture. "Yes? What?" she said.

"May I have a word?"

"You've a commission for Stone's?" she replied dubiously, with a glance at my clothing.

"I don't, I am afraid."

She glared at me. "I have but a moment for you then. We've bells to pour." Her voice was weary and low yet sharp. She led me out to the yard. One of the foundry's cats approached to sniff around my feet. She nudged the animal away with her shoe.

"What is it then?" She folded her arms over her womb.

"I am here about Stephen Marsh," I said.

She raised her eyebrows in mock surprise.

"Well, now there's a rare thing. What about him?"

"Have you spoken with him in the last several days?"

"And what if I have?" She took a step back, looked me up and down. "You're not a beadle's man, not of this ward at all rates. You're with the new sheriffs, are you?"

"My name is John Gower," I said, sorting my thoughts. Here was Hawisia Stone, mistress of a shop that had recently lost its master and risked losing its most talented guildsman. A woman of significant means, heavy with her affliction yet resisting confinement prior to the birth. Instead she was out in the foundry with the boys and men, working them and herself to keep the shop alive despite her weakened condition. She needed help.

"I work alone, Mistress Stone," I said. "Yet I may well be able to help Stephen out of his predicament. Perhaps restore him to your shop. Not a promise, you understand, but a possibility, however faint."

"You'll need to restore him to the streets first," she said with a huff. "He sits in sanctuary presently, over at Staining."

"He is no longer there, mistress."

Her brow went up again, the surprise genuine this time.

"Marsh has left sanctuary," I told her. "He has been taken into the Tower."

Her exhalation was long and slow, her eyes losing something of their fierce glint.

I brought out the serpentine device. "Mistress, is this familiar to you?"

She stared at it. "Where did you come across that?"

"It was given to me in Calais. You know what it is?"

"It's a bit of a gun, isn't it? Stephen made it, and several like it, here in the smithy." She nodded toward a far corner of the yard. "Just there."

"With your knowledge?"

She scoffed. "Smithed it at night, and under my very nose. Wouldn't have had such a thing at Stone's if the master were alive."

"And Stephen used one of these snake guns to commit a crime. A murder."

"So the beadle says."

"You don't believe it?"

Suddenly her attitude changed, and her face shone with sincerity. "Not a murder, I'll be bound. He was out north of the walls, testing his guns. She came upon him and he killed her with the thing. An accident's what it was, so he says." Another test. She straightened her back. "I believe him. Spite of his night games and his slinking I do believe him, not that the Guildhall will."

"Yet he took sanctuary at Staining."

"Aye he did. My notion, and I put him there myself. Had no choice. He'd killed a girl, hid her body in his fright. Who'd believe his account of the thing after that, I ask you?"

"You saved him, then, didn't you? From the law. From a probable hanging."

"For now, at the least," she said with a firm nod. "Stephen Marsh is no murderer, whatever the constables might claim. He's not a warm soul, always distant from those around him, but there is a God's measure of good in him. I sense it, have seen it. It was an accident, that girl's death."

"I believe this entire affair is an accident of sorts, Mistress Stone." Her eyes narrowed. "Stephen has become involved in a series of events beyond his ken and well above his head. He is a pawn in an ugly war between factions, with his craft sacrificed to the cause of men who wish him no good."

"And you wish him well, do you, sire?"

"I wish him nothing. Yet I may be able to help him. And thus help you." A plan was forming quickly in my mind. For weeks I had been ruefully aware that I possessed no avenue into the Tower of London, no leverage of any sort with the royal armory at the foul center of this murderous business. Now, in this widow's palpable trust in the goodness of her captive guildsman, this peculiar mix of devotion and dependence she felt toward Stephen Marsh, I saw a way.

"Help me?" she said with a skeptical look. "Why on Noah's slaving back would you want to help a widow such as myself?"

I looked around the foundry, then back at its owner. "Mistress Stone," I said slowly, "I believe I have a commission for you after all."

"What's it to be, then?" She had raised her chin, and as she did the sun glimpsed out from behind the low cloud that had obscured it for the duration of our exchange in the yard. In its full light Hawisia Stone's beauty glistened like a cut gem. "A bell, a set of braziers?" she asked.

I smiled at her. "No, mistress. I have a different sort of job in mind."

CHAPTER 37

"You are alive, then." Chaucer placed a hand on my shoulder.

"Barely." I led him to the set of chairs by the hearth. "You were able to escape Westminster?"

"By a nail's width," he said. The Parliament was in a tense recess the remainder of that week to mark the new mayor's swearing-in and inauguration. Chaucer would be journeying back to Greenwich for several days, he told me, missing the Riding, and he was stopping over on his way east.

We sat together in the hall, where Will Cooper served us with spiced wine. Chaucer asked about Calais. I told him most of it, including the accounts of the Desurennes massacre and my own narrow escape, though I kept the information about Gloucester's trade in saltpetre to myself.

"Simon saved my life." It still felt strange

to put it that way, even to my oldest friend. "Yet he remains as elusive and mysterious to me as ever. Spying along the coast on behalf of Hawkwood, yet somehow finding a way to get needful information to the chancellor. The former chancellor," I corrected myself.

Chaucer looked glum. "I spoke to the earl this morning, visited him as part of a delegation from the Commons to speak about transfer of seals and accounts. To see a lord such as Michael de la Pole defeated in this way wounds the heart. Yet the Commons are riled against him nearly to a man, so there was no hope for his retention. Now he's lurking about Lintner, his house on the Strand, with soldiers from the Tower posted on the street and at the quay. Whether they are keeping him confined or guarding him from harm no one can quite say. He won't ride with Exton, despite King Richard's imploring him to do so."

"Why would the king make such a request?" The London hierarchy guarded its ceremonial prerogatives fiercely, frowning on any interference from the crown and the higher lords.

"A number of peers are riding with Exton and Brembre as a show of fealty to the king. King Edward asked the same at Adam de

Bury's Riding, and several others."

I remembered. Like Bury's some years ago, Exton's Riding would serve as an occasion to unite city and crown, the civic bureaucracy and the upper aristocracy, though given the difficulties in the current Parliament I saw little hope of peace between the factions any time soon.

"The king's *familia* is taking it hard," Chaucer went on. "No neck is safe, it seems. There is even talk of moving against Robert de Vere."

"What of Edmund Rune?"

"He remains loyally with the earl, counseling him that his return to power can still be effected, despite the impeachment."

"Can that be true, given what you've seen in Parliament?"

"Hardly," he scoffed. "Outside the earl's hearing Rune seems as resigned to Arundel's chancellorship as anyone else. We spoke on the street as the delegation was leaving Lintner. Rune tells me that the earl has found it hard to accept his deposition. He has been pouring sweet stories into the earl's ear to comfort the old man."

I thought of the deposed chancellor, the sacrifice of years of royal service to the political vagaries of the moment. The expedient cruelty of it. Rune's loyalty to the end was admirable, if futile.

"And these massacres?" Chaucer said.

"Everything points to Gloucester, in both cases," I said. "His livery, his men, his guns, procured through Snell at the Tower."

"A strange reversal, no? Westminster now belongs to the lords, London to the king. And Southwark —"

"Belongs to no one. I feel as if I should establish a private garrison in my own house, laying permanent guards at the corners of the priory yard."

"Well, you can afford it, John, and if it gives you safety . . ."

"What is it Tacitus tells us? *'The desire for safety stands against every great and noble enterprise.'* "

He smiled. "The chronicler is talking there about statecraft, John, not your more intimate trade. I do hope you will keep yourself safe."

"Safe and idle," I sighed, thinking of my lover's confession, a poetic work I had begun many months ago and wished keenly to complete.

"Perhaps this might provide some consolation, or at least some happier tedium." He removed a thick quire from his bag. The parchment folds were sewn roughly together along the spine, the writing unblocked into verse. I felt a stab of envy at the quantity of Chaucer's making, and a prick of irritation at its timing.

"A tale of Melibee and his Dame Prudence," he said. "It's a little thing in prose, a translation from a certain Renaud. A mirror for princes about the virtue of good counsel. I started translating it a few weeks ago and could not stop myself from finishing. It fits this season of corruption in Westminster particularly well, I think. False soothsayers, advisers who keep mum when they should speak the truth, young men who cry 'War!' the loudest, yet know the least about it."

"True enough," I said, taking the booklet from him and noting the unique look of the scribe's hand. "Is this Pinkhurst's work?"

"It is," Chaucer said. "He is back in town, you know. He's promised me he will help you in any way he can. He is awaiting your visit at the Guildhall with warmth and fair welcome."

"I thank you, Geoffrey."

"It's nothing."

"And who will narrate this little thing?" I said, paging through, though it was hardly brief. The tale of Melibee covered the entire quire, leaving off only at the end of the sixteenth leaf.

"The tale will be told by . . . well, by *me,* in fact."

"By you?" I glanced up from the booklet. "You are to be a character, then, in your own pilgrimage tale?"

He looked offended. "There are precedents, and much grander ones. Dante Alighieri casts himself as a visitor to heaven and hell. Surely Geoffrey Chaucer can imagine himself on a short journey to Canterbury. And who is this?"

His head turned. Jack Norris had slipped into the hall. The boy stopped when he saw Chaucer. His head was uncapped, his stubs clearly visible beneath his messy shock of blond hair.

"This is an honored guest of the priory. Jack is his name."

Jack bowed to Chaucer, who nodded back, looking both troubled and amused.

"A story for another occasion," I said as Jack dodged out.

Chaucer rose from his chair. "You are a man of peculiar alliances and loyalties, John. I hope you will find space to return to your own making in due time."

"As do I, Geoffrey," I said, silently forgiving him his small blindness.

"You cannot simply stay here in the priory, burrowed in like a hibernating bear," he urged me. "Yet you need protection. I don't want you to end up one of these factional men knifed in the street."

"You warned me that first day, didn't you?" I stood to walk him to the door. "Yet I meddled in this mess, and now I'm paying the price for my curiosity."

"Not quite the right word for your craft, John," Chaucer said with his elvish smile.

He left for Greenwich and I remained in the hall, puzzling it all out. A splinter company of English soldiers, armed with these new handgonnes, commits two atrocities and now surely plots a third. The first, a massacre in a Kentish wood, is a controlled slaughter with prisoners as its victims, the bodies hauled secretly to London for disposal in the privy channels. The second massacre takes place along the walls of Desurennes, a village in the Pale, a daytime assault on the unknowing population of a market town, the survivors left to fend for the dead and wounded themselves.

What next? With Lancaster abroad, Gloucester was the most powerful of the lords opposing the king, and the hungriest for war. Despite the extent and depth of his conspiracy, the duke himself remained free, untouched by the hand of justice. Gloucester carried both houses of Parliament in his palm, and I could see no way to avoid the reckoning that was surely coming.

Blindness, Christ tells us in Scripture, comes in many forms. "For judgment I came into this world, that those who do not see may see, and those who see may become blind." A paradox, one to which I had clung like a vine to a wall since first experiencing my own earliest failures of vision. Where shall my soul find solace when my flesh falters and quits? What inner sight shall I be granted once my outer sight fully abandons me?

A man going slowly blind builds up too much confidence in his other senses. Touch, taste, smell, hearing: all grow more acute up to a certain point, and yet one's thoughts inevitably dull somewhat, as the power of intellection wanes with the diminution of sight, the first and most primal of our worldly senses. As the eyes go, so goes the mind.

My wife, perhaps a month before her death, told me about the strange pleasure she first took in my eyes. We had been married already for over a year, with our first child four months from birth. Nothing like love had been felt or spoken between us, not yet. Ours was a marriage of families in pursuit of an heir, with love and lust no matter to all concerned. Yet in those middle months of her first affliction our attraction grew suddenly keen. Ignoring the stern injunctions against meddling with a pregnant wife, I sought out her flesh at every opportunity.

One morning we found ourselves coupling in the glare of a summer sun, which flooded our bedchamber with an almost heavenly fullness. I would like to think I remember that morning myself, though I cannot honestly say this is true. Yet what her memory took most clearly from that day, she told me all those years later, was the verdant intensity of my eyes, an unworldly green blazing down as I moved above her.

"You always had the keenest eyes, John," she said to me with one of her infrequent smiles in those final weeks. "The eyes of a hawk, able to sort wheat and chaff from a mountaintop."

Now I have the eyes of a mole, I thought, tunneling along, mouthing in all before me without sifting the soil for the worm. The blind, it is said, eat many a fly.

CHAPTER 38

A widow with a great babe in her greater belly: not an everyday sight at the Tower of London, and Hawisia was relying on the strangeness of it, and the silver in her purse, to get her an ear at the barbican. She left the foundry along Bellyeter Lane, walked down through the ward to Tower Street, and now stood by the entrance to the outer gatehouse, on the city side of this sprawling network of keeps, walkways, and bristling arms. The warden, summoned from his room above, regarded her as she stood within the King's Lip, the covered court before the barbican door. A thickset man, with a massive black beard spread across his doublet, sleeves of beaten iron clasped at his forearms.

"Want to speak with one of our wardrobe men, do you?" he said gruffly.

"Aye, that's it," Hawisia replied. "Name's Stephen Marsh."

"His office?"

"Makes guns."

The warden looked at one of the guards. "Snell's crew, then."

"I'll send the page?" the guard said.

"Do that," said the warden. The guard went in.

"Come along." The warden gestured her forward, and she stepped along the path to the barbican, the first time she had ever set foot within the great royal compound. Once they were in the tower the warden pointed to a half-moon wooden bench stretching along the wall from the causeway door to another opening that gave onto a staircase. She took the portion of the bench nearest the descending stairs, feeling the movements of her coming child within her. A kick. A squirm. Another kick.

The ceiling sat low over the windowless chamber, which was heavy with smoke and the sharp scent of dung and straw from the many boots treaded across the uncovered floor. Though only slits lined the walls, letting in little light, she could hear a general racket from out and over the moat channel, the music of coming war. The neighing of horses, the shouts of troops, the pounding of hammers on metal. From beneath and above her in the same tower she heard

578

other, stranger noises, the screeches and trumpets of foreign beasts in the king's menagerie. Hawisia had no interest in such creatures, though their rare clamor chilled her skin.

Soon enough there came a tired shuffle from the outer walk. She looked toward the causeway door. Stephen Marsh, accompanied by a Tower page seeming none too pleased at the haul up to the outer gates. Stephen walked like a beaten dog. Neck matted with whiskers, clothes sodden with sweat and ash, new burns streaking the backs of his hands. At the guard's direction he came and sat at her side. She could smell the smoke on him, the hard stink of unceasing work.

She took a breath and blew it sideways. "Sanctuary not high enough for you?"

She felt his shrug. "Had no choice, mistress. In here I'm safe from the rope for as long as they'll have me."

"So you believe. Yet what's to keep them from roping you up once they have what they need from you?" She watched him.

He leaned forward, elbows on his knees, and glanced back at her. "Little, in truth, not that I don't deserve it." His eyes were leaden blanks. "I killed my master your husband with a cauldron of molten ore," he said softly. "Killed that poor maid in the woods with a gun. Even shot a lion."

"A *lion?* What are you prattling about, Stephen?"

"And many more killings to come. Seems these hands be made for smithing death." He looked down at them.

"That is mad talk, Stephen Marsh."

His head swung from side to side like an old cow's udder. "Was I who killed your Robert, mistress, with that last pour, my haste. The mold was ready, the thickness was perfect, but he wouldn't give the go for the pour. He was about to say it, least I thought he was, move his hands away, but he never said it, and the mold man must always give the go before the pour, but Master Stone didn't give it and I poured anyway. I was impatient. I killed him."

"Stephen," she said.

He turned his head away.

"Stephen," she said again.

He looked at her grimly.

"I killed him, too."

"No, Hawisia."

She shook her head, brushed at her womb. "You'll remember. It was a large and impossible job, too much for our house. Twenty bells of every size, and two weeks to complete them all. Twenty molds, twenty cauldrons, twenty pours."

"Yet still —"

"Robert wanted no part of it," she said quickly before he could stop her. " 'Let us make five bells only,' he said, 'and my fellows in the guild will split the balance of them,' he said. Yet I insisted. 'Why, we can make them all ourselves,' I told him, 'and keep the coin for Stone's!' He pushed me, I pushed him back, and Stone's took the entire commission. Two weeks, and every morning and eve you and Robert were in the foundry, smelting, pouring, boring, sounding. And on the last day there were still three bells to complete. Robert felt that he'd done what he could, and it would be understood that we'd finish in a week, ten days perhaps. But I pushed him to finish *now*, told him Stone's would never rise to the top if he failed to complete its greatest commission."

Speaking the bleak truth lodged a new pain somewhere in her, even as it loosened another. "So he tried to finish, as I wished. On the day he died he was to pour the last bell but one. You were helping him, Stephen. You will remember his state."

"He could scarce keep an eye open," Stephen murmured.

"He was doing my bidding, and following

his fair wife's fondest wish at his death. To be mistress of the greatest foundry in London. I wanted to hear the music of Stone's foundry ringing from half the belfries within the walls. More bells, Robert! Bigger bells, Robert! Brighter bells, Robert! Had I not pushed him to climb he would be on this earth."

"Yet it was I who —"

She showed him a palm. "Your vanity, my ambition. We took his life together, Stephen." She felt a sharp movement in her belly. "Now it's yours we must save."

His fingers ran along the edge of the bench. "How, Hawisia?"

It was a hopeful question, despite the flatness in his voice. "There is a man came to Stone's yesterday," she whispered, keeping an eye on the soldiers.

"A sheriff?"

"Not a Guildhall man. His name's not important. But what he tells me is, things in the armory aren't what they seem."

Stephen gave a low murmur. "Aye to that."

"There is talk of an attack, Stephen. A massacre, and with your guns."

His eyes widened, and he nodded slightly. The warning, she sensed, was not entirely a surprise.

"This man, he seeks information on the

582

armory's doings, and will pay for it with great price. If you can learn anything of this attack, Stephen, the where, the when, you will gain the crown's favor. Even a royal pardon may not be out of the question. The kiss of the king."

"Truly?" Stephen said, his brow pushing up. "He believes the royal ear could still be bent in my direction, despite the killing up there?"

"Perhaps. But you'll have to tell what you know, or discover what you don't. This man, he —"

A harsh cough from the nearer guard. "That's time enough, Marsh. Mistress, you must leave him now."

Hawisia nodded up at the guard, then on an impulse leaned into Stephen's side, shielding her mouth with his neck.

"What is it you know, Stephen?" she hissed at his ear. *"Tell me."*

"Snell is a viper, mistress," he whispered fiercely. "If I say anything they'd kill me sure as we're sitting here. You as well, and that child in your womb."

"You must become hardened to these men and what they are," she said. "For you are not a man of death, Stephen. Think on your iron and your steel and your bronze, and you will find your strength, aye?"

"Aye," he said.

They parted, the guard now looming over them. As they stood, Stephen glanced out toward the customhouse wharf and the clutches of men walking and idling along the broad way. "They won't let me walk free, Mistress Stone, even for Exton's Riding," he said.

Hawisia followed his gaze, seeing it through his eyes. Any one of those men could be an informer for the Guildhall, waiting for Marsh to set a foot outside the Tower liberties and make himself vulnerable to quick arrest.

He put a hand on her shoulder and spun her to face him. The guard clutched his other arm. Stephen's eyes were strangely fierce as he said, "Not even for the Riding, mistress."

She shivered, discerning a message behind his words. Was that a flicker of resolve in his eyes? She wondered what it might spark and flame. Yet when Hawisia took Stephen's hand his touch was cold, as if his very soul had departed his flesh.

CHAPTER 39

It was into a clear, chill morning that I stole out of the priory and made for the Thames, with Will Cooper leading the way to look out for watchers. We left the walls of St. Mary Overey not by my own door but through the postern on the river side, our destination not the foot of the bridge but the wharfage, first along the walls of the bishop of Winchester's great palace, then past the mill and down Rose Alley. When we reached the river's edge I remained behind one of the old scalding sheds while Will coined me a float. He went to the waterfront and whistled for a wherry standing out forty feet. It approached, the waterman boarding his sculls as the craft bumped against the dock post. Still hooded, I slipped out and clambered over the low bow. The craft shoved off as Will backed away into the cluster of buildings along the shore.

The rower was a man I knew from many

crossings over the years. "Just up from the Fleet, if you will, Sanders," I said, pushing back the hood.

"Aye, Master Gower. The fosses there?"

"That will do."

"Ever tell you of my brother Edward lived over that way?"

"No, you never did, Sanders."

"A wheelwright, and never a rounder wheel did a man make." He went on about his brother the wheelwright, and in great detail, as we crossed the river: the carving, the tooling and lathing, the sanding and painting. One of those watermen who likes to jaw his way from bank to bank. We made small gossip as I feigned interest in everything the fellow had to say. It was an oddly welcome relief from the growing peril around me.

When we bumped up below the Fleet spill I paid the boatman, then walked along the ditch and up toward Smithfield. I took a winding route through the upper end of the market and skirted the ditch all the way to Bishopsgate, at this time of day the busiest portal into the city. Once through the walls I dodged west, avoiding Cornhill and the Mercery to approach the Guildhall from the north. From the yard I made for one of the detached buildings spaced along the western side of the hall.

The structure had been shuttered against the cold, though the central room was well lit, with numerous lamps and candles clustered to illuminate the work of the men within. The Guildhall scriveners were a quiet and industrious bunch, hived like bees in their cells at triangular writing desks positioned along the chamber's spine. There were nine scribes working at any one time, with three to a desk, each given particular tasks identifiable in several cases from the documents stacked or set to their side: court rolls, summonses, account books, writs of various kinds. At the middle desk, his back to the doorway, sat the man I needed.

"Pinkhurst," I said.

The scrivener looked up and half turned. When he saw me his pied face arranged itself into an arch and lofty regard. He had been expecting me.

"What is it, Gower?" he said. The others paid us little mind.

"May I speak to you, just out here?"

He looked down at his work, loudly sighed, then stood and shuffled out the door.

"What is it you want?" said Pinkhurst when we had reached the corner of the building. "As Master Chaucer knows, I've enormous amounts of work to do. Commissions from poets must be the lowest of my priorities for the time being."

One poet excepted, he didn't need to say. From everything Chaucer had told me, Pinkhurst's copying for him in recent years had been prompt and reliable, with little delay caused by the press of work for the city, crown, and guilds. Rather young, yet with a steady hand at the quill, the scrivener had already established himself as an invaluable scribal asset for numerous parties, keeping accounts for the mercers' guild and the wool custom while working doggedly for the Guildhall. Though written on parchment, however, what I hoped to ply from the scrivener that morning had nothing to do with poetry.

"I am here not for your services, Pinkhurst, but for your safety."

"As I told you, I am quite busy," he said, ignoring my darker implication. "Exton's swearing-in is tomorrow. We have numerous writs of appointment to complete, notarizations to effect, and the courts will begin again in two days' time."

"This matter concerns our lesser king." I tilted my head toward the Guildhall, knowing he would gather my meaning. According to Chaucer, Pinkhurst secretly despised

Brembre, a hatred I hoped to exploit.

He sucked in a cheek. "What is it, then?"

"I think you know."

He looked genuinely puzzled. "Do I?"

"A record of interrogation," I said. "A swerver was questioned here at the Guildhall. You were the scribe."

The lighter patches in his face paled further. "That record is not here, whatever Chaucer may have told you."

"Chaucer knows nothing about this, nor shall he."

"Nor do I. The record was seized."

I gave him a long and deliberate stare. "I hadn't believed it of you, Pinkhurst. That you would jeopardize Lady Idonia in such a callous way."

He frowned, his lower lip jutting from his mouth. "What does this have to do with *her*?"

I told him what I knew about the record's fate once it had left his hands. The mayor's chest, Idonia's letter, its interception by an agent of the duke. He looked at me, disbelieving. "So Lady Idonia used —"

"Yes," I said. I watched his young eyes crinkle in indignation. "Your admiration for the mayor's wife is well known, Adam."

Pinkhurst squirmed.

"I hope you will reconsider what you have

told me. The record has come into Gloucester's hands since the killings. How I don't know, but the fact is, the duke now possesses immensely damaging information on the mayor, and has been using it to twist him in the wind. If he makes it public, Brembre will suffer a great fall, and even greater embarrassment." I waited, then, "As will Lady Idonia."

Pinkhurst's eyes were now directed at the pavers between the two buildings. "I have heard whisperings of Idonia's discontent these last weeks," he said. "You can see it on her fair face, in her manner when she walks to and from her house. I cannot imagine what she is enduring. The blame, the fury, the humiliation . . ."

"And they will only increase should Gloucester use what he has, Adam."

"Yes," said Pinkhurst absently.

I let him think about it, then spoke to him gently. "You made a copy, didn't you?" A guess, but a sound one based on what I knew of the man's habits.

He closed his eyes.

"You still have it?" I said, confident in the answer. When he shook his head my heart dropped like a stone; then he blurted out, "I kept the original."

"What's that?"

"After the interrogation of Rykener I made a copy of the confession," he said, now in a low and urgent whisper. "The sheriffs were terrified of what Sir Nick would do if he got wind of it, so they asked me to make an additional copy for safekeeping, while giving the original to the keeper of the rolls for inscription. Instead I switched them. The original has her — his — the swerver's mark on it, as well as the seal of the mayor's own recorder. I made a rough copy of the confession, without the documentary trappings of signs and seals. *That* copy is the one the mayor seized when he stormed into the recorder's office and took it from my hand."

"So that copy is the record that Gloucester has used to force Brembre's hand."

He nodded tightly, a somewhat proud smile above his ugly. "The copy was good enough to deceive the duke, it seems. Yet nothing would be easier to forge. The original was in my own hand, after all."

"You must surrender it to me, Adam."

He shook his head. "If it gets out that I gave the mayor a falsified copy rather than the sealed original —"

"Why then you will be the mayor's savior." His eyes widened in bewilderment. "Think of it. Who had the foresight to make a feigned copy and preserve the damning original safe from harm? Why, Adam Pinkhurst. And all along the mayor has been terrified that Gloucester would use the original record to question his natural manhood before the eyes of London."

His lips tightened.

"I will pay you any price you name, Pinkhurst. For the record and your discretion."

"My *discretion* cannot be bought, Gower." He looked offended. "It comes with the service I provide, as much a part of my copying as the gall scratched from my pen. What I copy I keep close, and always have."

"Then consider this a payment for a very fine piece of parchment in your possession."

Pinkhurst looked at the heavy purse dangling from my fingers. He took it, weighed it in his hand, then turned silently for the scriveners' building. Before long he came out, a document in his hand. He put it in mine. I put on my spectacles and examined the interrogation. The recorder's seal, the swerver's mark, the names and stations of other magnates identified by Eleanor Rykener as her jakes. I flipped it. The overleaf was blank. No letter from Idonia.

Meanwhile Pinkhurst had fingered open the purse. He spilled the silver and gold out on his palm, mouthing the count.

"Is the mayor within?"

"Exton?" he said, not looking up.

"Brembre."

"Cleaning out, I believe. Reluctantly."

"Very well."

Without a glance at me he turned and disappeared back inside. I stood in the shade and looked down at the document in my hand, still weighing its fate. A threat or a gift? It would serve well as either one, and given the names it contained I could harvest sweet-smelling buds for years from its florid branches. Yet in this case, I decided in the end, prudence must win out over ambition. Though Brembre would no longer be mayor two days from now, he would remain a man of immense power, and as I have learned through long experience, the fruit of favors owed will often taste sweeter than the ripest threats.

Court was off at the Guildhall and had been for two weeks, with all the attention of official London on the doings of Parliament up the river. It took whispers, coins, and several guards to get from the yard into the northwest corner of the building, where the mayor held private audiences behind two movable partitions that would be stacked along the walls on court days.

He was standing when I stepped within the chamber, looking down at a mess of documents spread before him on a trestle table. A fire crackled in the hearth behind him. From midway up the opposite wall rose a high window, once clear and clean, looking out on the yard, yet which Brembre had replaced with an unglazed substitute to ensure privacy but maintain light. Now the opaque surface created a dappled sheen along the floor, and a gleam of suspicion in the mayor's eyes when he glanced briefly at me before returning to his work.

"Gower," he said.

"Lord Mayor."

"It's a busy day at the Guildhall. Exton's swearing-in is tomorrow, his Riding the day following. What brings you here?"

Watching him closely, I said, "The confession of a swerver."

His hands froze. His face remained undisturbed. "What confession is that?"

"This one." I held out the document.

His head turned slowly toward me. "But — but I took —"

"You seized a copy, Lord Mayor, made by Adam Pinkhurst. This is the original, affixed with your recorder's seal. Your wife's letter does not appear on the back."

He stood and walked around the table,

594

approaching me with an attitude stiff and almost submissive. The mayor took the document, set it on the table, and pulled a candle near. He murmured his way through the opening clauses, then scanned down the document and fingered the seal. I heard the brush of his fingertip over the swerver's mark at the base of the parchment. He turned to the overleaf and stood staring at the blank surface.

"Gloucester," he said softly.

"Possesses a good forgery, with Idonia's letter on the overleaf," I said. "And perhaps knows it, but also knows *you* believe he has the original." A pause. "You are free of the duke's web, Lord Mayor."

As I watched Brembre absorb this change I saw his shoulders relax, though cautiously, as if the most crushing part of a great weight had been lifted from his back yet might return at any moment. He looked askance at me. "Surely you didn't come here to peddle this sheepskin, Gower. I have a dozen armed men just outside this chamber. You haven't even a sword at your side."

"It is a gift, Lord Mayor."

Brembre barked a laugh. "A gift? John Gower doesn't give gifts. That would ruin his reputation! Why, in addition to me this confession names two lords, a bishop, and a prior among this swerver's arse-swyving jakes. Why are you not using it against them, and against me?"

"You cannot use it either, Sir Nicholas, for obvious reasons."

A weak, grudging smile.

"The confession is not given freely," I said. "It comes with a request."

"What do you want?"

"Several things. First, protection."

"Protection. From what?"

"From Gloucester and his men," I said. "One of the duke's agents in Calais attempted to murder me days ago."

"Protection, then," Brembre said, taking this in. "Guards at the priory?"

"Two for now, until this is resolved," I said. "And the same to accompany me around the city. Not as grand as your entourage, though enough to keep me alive for another fortnight."

"Very well." He flicked a hand. "I will have it done this hour."

"And you will now move on Gloucester?"

"A mayor doesn't simply move on a duke, Gower," Brembre mused, a hand rubbing at his chin. "Gloucester is a powerful force. His allies have played this Parliament like a chessboard, and even freed from this . . . encumbrance, I can see no easy means to bag the man for these killings."

"There may be a way," I said.

"Oh?"

"The duke has committed treason, Lord Mayor. He is selling gunpowder to the Duke of Burgundy."

His hand ceased its motion. "Quite a serious accusation, Gower. What proof do you have?"

I pulled out the heraldic bend that Simon had given me in Calais and placed it on the table. "This fell from the arm of one of Gloucester's men on the quay at Dunkirk. It appears the duke has been selling saltpetre to the French along the Flemish coast, with the aid of William Snell, king's armorer. I believe as well that Snell has commissioned a new sort of handgonne with the same purpose in mind. The duke's men are responsible for another massacre in the Pale. Desurennes, a market town. They used small guns." I told him what I had learned from Simon about the gunpowder smuggling, and what the girl Iseult had said to me in Desurennes. *Remember the swans.*

"Why are you bringing this to me?" Brembre said. The mayor examined the bend, fingering the duke's embroidered badge.

A question I had expected. "I intended to bring it to Edmund Rune and the chancellor, though with the recent impeachment the earl is no longer in power — and I don't imagine the new chancellor would look kindly on an accusation of this sort against his chief supporter among the lords. But you are now one of the king's most powerful allies in the realm, Lord Mayor. You alone have the means of bringing this before the king and forcing his hand against Gloucester."

"Perhaps," said Brembre, sounding dubious. "Yet Gloucester and his allies want war, and soon. The duke knows my counsel and the chancellor's has been against his own. And he's punishing me for it, the wily hare. My men beaten and harassed, my merchant ships and warehouses torched to the ground" — here he gestured to Rykener's confession — "my letters and muniments intercepted and stolen. And the greatest insult of all: a pile of bodies in my privy channels, shot up with these handgonnes or hacked to death. Gloucester has been acting with impunity in London, and believes I will do nothing to stop him, not with this whore's interrogation in his hands. So he lords it about the city as if he, Thomas of Woodstock, were the mayor rather than Nicholas Brembre."

Or Nicholas Exton, I silently reminded

him — though everyone believed Exton's mayoralty would be a continuation of Brembre's, with a transition in name only.

"The Duke of Gloucester, leaving his spoor everywhere he goes," I said.

Brembre looked up, his eyes darkened. "I will have Gloucester's men rounded up, then, as many as we can find within the walls."

"There may be a better way, Lord Mayor," I said.

He waited.

"I have found Peter Norris's witness."

He sniffed.

"The witness whose identity you refused to learn before putting Norris to death," I said. "It is Norris's son, Lord Mayor."

"The cutpurse?"

"The boy is at my house. He saw a man I believe to be Woodstock overseeing the dumping of the corpses in the Walbrook."

"A duke, about the London streets at night, tossing bodies in the privy? Difficult to credit, Gower."

I shook my head, my confidence rising. "You are wrong, Sir Nicholas. Gloucester would have trusted no one else with the task. He is known as a controlling lord in his domain, one who would never trust an underling with an operation of this sort. It was his men who emptied the Portbridge gaol, his men who slaughtered the prisoners in the woods, his men who brought them to London and threw them in the ditch. For you to find, Lord Mayor."

"And who would believe the word of a boy over that of a duke?"

"Young Jack's testimony is only one part of the proof against the duke. There is the bend given me in Calais, the word of the Portbridge reeve. And there is Gloucester's banner, bound around the wrists of the victims."

Brembre looked at me for a long moment, then rose and went to a low cabinet, returning with several sheets of frayed silk. The strips were in foul tatters and still smelled of the privy, though even with just two of them side by side we could make out the shape of Woodstock's swans. Brembre had not destroyed the damning evidence he'd seized, despite what Strode had believed.

We stood there, the duke's guilt shouting up at us from the mayor's table.

"Gloucester will fight, you know," Brembre said. "He'll deny involvement as far as the moon if he has to. Is it worth the risk of civil war to bring a criminal to justice, however horrendous the crime?"

"I share your hesitation," I said. "Yet this

goes beyond murder. The duke has betrayed the safety of the realm, with powder and guns both, and no thought to the consequences."

His gaze remained on the table.

"You are a London man, Sir Nicholas," I wheedled. "I am of Southwark. Our lives and our towns are gravely threatened by the French force at Sluys. Thousands of ships, and the burning of London on a close horizon. The duke's actions are threatening the realm, and the very life of this city."

"Yes," he said.

"I may be a conniver and an extractor, Lord Mayor," I went on. "You may be a ruffian, with a taste for violence and corruption." His lips pursed. "But we cannot allow such a betrayal to weaken the hand of the realm."

"Then I move on him," Brembre said, with a gathering strength in his voice. "And risk civil war."

"It may not come to that," I said. "Gloucester is not Lancaster. He is powerful but not invincible. To raise a standing army to defeat the king would require the combined might of the other lords. Mowbray, Warwick, Arundel. If you can expose Woodstock as a traitor in their presence and the king's, you would have a chance of isolating Gloucester and bringing him to justice."

"And breaking this appellant faction from within," said the mayor, his eyes coming to life. "Thus strengthening the hand of King Richard." He turned to me. "It must happen soon."

"A suggestion, Lord Mayor."

"Go on."

"Beauchamp told me in Calais that the king has expressed a desire for the lords to process with Exton to Westminster, as a sign of fealty and solidarity."

"Yes," said Brembre, with a scornful smile. "Another empty pageant, painting a rotten wall with loyalty where there is treason within. Though by rights Exton must formally invite them to ride before they are permitted to mount with the procession."

"He should invite them today, then, as a show of goodwill, a gesture to appease the king at a difficult moment for his relations with Parliament," I said. "After the Riding all of them will naturally be in audience at Westminster before King Richard. Exton will process through the great hall and kneel at His Highness's feet. You will be at Exton's side as the king takes his hand and blesses his election as mayor. As you know, it is customary for the king to ask the new

602

mayor if he wishes any shows of royal favor to mark his inauguration. At that moment, Exton will ask King Richard to consider a pressing matter of war. Exton will then turn to you, the king's truest friend, the man who stood with him at Mile End against the rebels and did as much as anyone to save his head. You will present the case against Gloucester in the hearing of the peers of the realm, calling on their duty to expel a rotten apple from their fair barrel."

Brembre, warming to it, said, "It pains me to make such an accusation, Your Highness."

"And I would presume to do so only under the direst of circumstances, my liege lord," I said.

"And only with indisputable evidence of the highest of treasons, sire," said Brembre.

"Then you bring forth the banners, the bend, the boy," I said. "And if Gloucester counters your accusation by raising the swerver interrogation, you simply laugh and demand that he show proof."

"Which he may well produce."

"If he has thought to bring the confession with him. Unlikely, and even if he has, so much the better. It is an obvious forgery. Even your wife knew it was a mere nothing, a jest. That is why she wrote a letter on its overleaf, you will say. Showing it before the king will only weaken the duke's hand."

We exchanged looks, thinking it through. It was a perilous plan, and much could go wrong, yet it had the appeal of surprise. At last Brembre said, "You should be a captain or an admiral, Gower, rather than a — whatever it is you are."

"You are overly kind, Lord Mayor," I replied, with the doubts wheeling through my mind. The lords were already disposed strongly against the king. It would take a convincing performance by Nicholas Brembre to achieve the desired effects. A weak plan, and a desperate one.

My concerns must have been visible on my face. "I am not a fool, Gower," the mayor said. "I know what is at stake here, as well as the risks." He looked around as a burst of shouting from the yard drifted through the silence of his chambers. Brembre had spent many years as lord mayor of London, and now, at the end of what would prove his final term and at the very height of his power, he projected a melancholy awareness of things coming to an end. "Leave me, Gower. And, Bernes?" he barked to a waiting attendant. The man had slipped in unnoticed and stood by the edge of the partition.

"Yes, Lord Mayor?"

"See to Master Gower's guard, will you? Four men for Southwark and the priory starting this moment, rotated out for the next two weeks. Exton will approve on my word after tomorrow."

"Yes, Lord Mayor." Bernes spun on his heel and left the chamber.

Brembre regarded me. "I thank you for this, Gower. You have prevented a great deal of anguish with the recovery of this record. Perhaps even helped to save the city, and certainly my relations with Lady Idonia." He allowed me a mayoral smile. I returned it, thinking of the new and heavy coin in my purse of favors owed by this powerful victualler. He dismissed me with a promise to speak on the morning of the Riding. Before returning to Southwark I stopped in on Hawisia Stone. She was in the foundry's display room, thankfully seated this time, though even at rest she appeared greatly afflicted, her breathing labored, her skin flushed.

Our exchange was brief. She had spoken with Stephen Marsh at the Tower, she told me, though could get nothing out of him about the guns, nor discern a glimmer of Snell's plans.

"Wouldn't say much of a word but mum,"

605

she said between breaths. "Wanted to shake the fellow but he just stood there like a sapling."

"Did Marsh give any indication that he understood the peril his guns are causing the realm?"

She shrugged heavily. "Was his own peril seemed to be more on his mind."

"How so?"

"Kept looking over his shoulder, like the guards're listening to his every breath," she said.

"What about the pardon? Did you hold it out to him?"

"Aye, that I did. Didn't seem to move him, not that I could see."

Her news was not as bad as it would have been an hour earlier. If all went according to plan, Snell would be exposed at Westminster along with Gloucester, so penetrating the Tower was no longer as crucial to subverting their treachery. Yet Snell's wanton violence and trade in arms remained a distinct threat.

She moved a hand up to rub at her chin. "Was only one bit he said that seemed peculiar."

"What was that?"

"Told me the Tower wouldn't let him out even for the Riding."

"Surely not a surprise, given his circumstances."

She shrugged. "That's why I thought it strange, Master Gower. He said it again, right before he was taken back down. Said it heavy, like he wanted me to hear him well, as if it were a message. 'Not even for the Riding,' he said."

"He said this in the hearing of the guards?"

"Aye."

"And how did he seem when you left him, mistress?"

She said one word. "Afraid."

CHAPTER 40

Stephen could scarcely bring himself to lift his mallet, nor bend a sheet of steel, nor even stir the coals at the foundry forge, so weary were his arms. He looked out at the Tower yard, the ordered chaos of coming war. The serpentine guns had been completed at Snell's orders, and now the armory's attention had turned back to the necessities of the coming battle. Twenty London armorers had been ordered within for the week, their wares spread out on the ground. The business of the day was jack-of-plate, more of the rough outfits than he could have imagined possible. Small iron squares cut from hammered sheets, each awl-punched with a single hole, then laced together between two layers of cloth to form a sleeveless hauberk, using undyed wool brought in by the bolt from the clothiers' shops along Broad Street and Cornhill. No refinement in this craft, no art, no clever joints to lessen the weight, as on the armor of knights and lords who could afford such contrivances. No plates for the shins, the feet, the neck, the arms; no couters for the elbows, no poleyns for the knees.

This was infantry armor, scalloped in unsubtle layers up the front with nothing in back, and rough-hammered helms to go on top. *Naught fancy or newish,* London's armorers had been warned by Snell. *Efficiency and numbers. Those are your orders.* They obeyed, the pieces fastened together with old leather thongs cut from worn harnesses and even their own discarded aprons. The goal was quantity, armor to suit five thousand men, perhaps ten, depending on how much time remained before the French invasion from Sluys.

The worst part was outfitting the horses — not the knights' shining war mounts, but the laboring beasts charged with hauling the wheeled engines and gun carriages into the front ranks. Again, nothing subtle or polished or painted, just raw plates of sufficient thickness to stop an arrow or bolt whistling from above, a few rivets where back met neck. Hundreds of them, each to be encased in dull sheets of hammered iron, huge swaths of it, bent over neck, back, and rump, all to save the hide of a mute and fear-shitting beast.

Never had Stephen seen such a mass of men toiling over the same sorry tasks, never had he witnessed such a waste of talent and industry in the service of slaughter. He knew many of the armorers and their apprentices, had seen the cleverly wrought suits of plate and chain they were capable of crafting for knights and higher lords. And he knew and admired the work of Stone's rivals in the founding trade, the melodious bells poured, bored, and sounded to every house's version of perfection.

No longer. Now that the serpentine guns had been completed Stephen was merely one of two dozen metalworkers muling for the Tower armory, hammering steel and iron as a scullery maid peels carrots and roots. Half of London's smiths pulled from the clever art of gates and grilles, their precision work sacrificed to the cause of war and its blunt instruments. Now all these crafts had been intermingled, with none of the beauty and subtle art that distinguish the mysteries of metal each from the other. In the Tower of London, it seemed, England's metalworkers had become no better than slaves.

As for Stephen? *The softer sort,* as Snell had branded him. He wondered if that was how the world saw him, as a weak and pliable man. Yet not everyone thought him soft, he assured himself. Not Hawisia Stone. *Think on your iron and your steel and your bronze, and you will find your strength,* she'd told him. It was those words that had inspired him to risk those final hints to his mistress. Had she comprehended their meaning? And even if she had, would there be time to use them to any effect? The new mayor's Riding was now two days away, and as he watched the teeming work in the armory he felt a new despair. He wanted to believe the clouds would clear and all of this go away with them, that he would escape the dark vision of these last weeks to find himself pardoned, relishing his freedom, even working contentedly for Hawisia Stone and serving out his sentence with proper contrition for what he had done. Yet what could a pregnant widow hope to accomplish against the malignant force of the king's armory?

The cooks' shouts rang across the yard, signaling the midday meal for the Tower's companies of laboring men. They poured out from every corner of the compound, carpenters and masons, armorers and smiths, farriers along with the stableboys and numberless others, lining up at the kettles to receive their food and ale. The men sprawled wearily along the wall with their meals, hollow trenchers of water-thinned cream mixed with oats and barely warmed.

As Stephen choked down another bite of the tasteless gruel William Snell appeared among the forges.

"Marsh," he called out, beckoning him over. Stephen trudged to his master's side.

Snell led him beneath the awning of the gun shed, where the hundred barrels and stocks Stephen had made stood by the tens.

"Your little snakes will be put to use soon, Marsh, and quite memorably," the armorer said, looking out over his arsenal. "Be sure all is prepared. By tomorrow night I want you to check every one of these handgonnes. Every barrel, every stock, all the pans and chambers, inspected by your hand alone. The serpentines especially. The guns must be in firing order. Cleaned, scraped, greased, tightened — whatever you must do to make them ready. Is that understood?"

Stephen looked out past the cooks' tables and over to the wall, where the king's lion had collapsed. He saw the other deaths he had made, the flesh ravaged by his craft. The flaming arm of Robert Stone, the ruined neck of a country maiden. And in that instant, as Snell waited for his under-ling's reply, Stephen knew his greatest work still lay before him.

"I shall check them, Master Snell," he said, his voice ringing as clear as Stone's finest bell. His work-bent spine straightened with the challenge. "I shall check every last one of them. You may depend upon it."

CHAPTER 41

The presence of Brembre's guards, rough and rude city soldiers stationed in the yard and patrolling along the walls and adjoining alleys, had created a minor stir at the priory. St. Mary Overey was not accustomed to the presence of armed men on its grounds, and the prior himself had dropped by my house to air his tentative but sincere concern. The Order of St. Augustine is an order of peace, Master Gower. Our canons are men of the quill, not of the sword. A promise of generous compensation calmed his clerical nerves. The men's habitation at the priory would be temporary, I assured him, their presence the result of a misunderstanding soon to be resolved.

It was the twenty-eighth day of October, the Feast of the Apostles Simon and Jude. Across the river Nicholas Exton would be swearing the oath and kissing the book at the Guildhall, with the morrow set aside for the new mayor's Riding to Westminster. My own sad palace felt like a prison, though there was little I could do but wait until the following morning, as I did not want to risk another venture through the streets. In the hall, suffering through a bout of nervous tedium and unable to concentrate on my own verse, I found my eyes wandering to Chaucer's bulging quire. I had placed it on a side table after he left. He had described the work as a mirror for princes, a discourse on good counsel and the mitigation of violence: needful subjects at the moment.

Looking for distraction I reached for the booklet. The prose was written in the elegant hand of Adam Pinkhurst, which by this point was nearly as familiar as my own.

Heere beginneth Chauceres Tale of Melibee. A yong man called Melibeus, myghty and riche, bigat upon his wyf, that called was Prudence, a doghter which that called was Sophie. Upon a day bifel that he for his desport is went into the feeldes hym to pleye. His wyf and eek his doghter hath he left inwith his hous, of which the dores weren faste yshette.

At the opening of the tale Melibee goes out to the field, leaving his wife and daughter at home. While he is gone his house is invaded by a group of his enemies, his wife assaulted, his daughter wounded grievously and left for dead. Upon his return Melibee finds his daughter at death's door and vows to take vengeance upon the perpetrators of this violent crime against his family and home. Yet Prudence, his wife, intervenes, counseling forbearance even in the face of such a horrific crime. Following an involved debate between those counselors advising restraint and those arguing for war, Prudence offers a series of learned opinions on the wisdom of good counsel, all of them drawn from the writings of learned authorities: Cicero, Seneca, Plato, as well as the books of Scripture. At the conclusion Melibee decides to stay his hand, even forgiving his family's attackers at Prudence's urging.

It took me the large part of two hours to get through the tale, which Chaucer had written in a flat prose rather than in the fair forms of his typical verse: rhymes, couplets, stanzas. Here the style was almost bleak in its plainness, the tale hardly as accomplished as one of his obscene fabliaux. The tale of Melibee was in my judgment a poetical failure, little more than a straightforward translation from his source, and I wondered what possessed him to plan its inclusion among his Canterbury tales.

Yet it could not be denied that the tale was a topical and timely meditation on the nature and perils of counsel — perhaps too timely, as it seemed to capture the raging dispute among the realm's governing bodies in our own moment with a dangerous precision. The appellant lords lusting for war, the king and his deposed chancellor pushing back, every counselor murmuring one thing in his lord's right ear, another in his left. Though I had my doubts about Chaucer's plan to assign himself such a peculiarly artless tale, its inclusion in the pilgrimage collection would constitute a form of counsel in its own right, aimed at instilling the virtues of prudence and discretion in its readers both lordly and common.

As I went to my bed that night, with Brembre's men still patrolling the house and the priory walls, Prudence's words remained with me, her proverbial wisdom worming through my thoughts as my eyes shut against the long day. Know your friends from your enemies, shouted truths from whispered lies. Always distinguish good counsel from bad, and ethical counselors from evil ones . . .

In the stillest hours of the night, before I would normally wake from first sleep, I sat rigidly upright, the words of Chaucer's tale ringing in my ear. *In the examining then of your counselor be not blind . . .*

Throwing on a heavy cloak, I padded down to the kitchen hearth, where the Coopers kept coals alive through the night, and lit a candle. In the hall I fired two more and positioned them around the quires containing Chaucer's tale. Spectacles balanced on my nose, I found the portion of the tale that most clearly addressed the quality of counselors. *"For trust well that commonly these counselors are flatterers, namely the counselors of great lords,"* Prudence was warning her husband. *"For they try always rather to speak pleasant words, inclining to the lord's desire, than words that are true or profitable. And therefore men say that the rich man seldom has good counsel, unless he has it from himself."*

I read on, my heart rushing furiously as my mind gathered suspicions like a demon gathers souls.

"In the examining then of your counselor be not blind. You should also mistrust the counsel of such people as counsel you one thing privately, and counsel you the contrary openly, or whisper the counsel they have given you secretly into other ears. For Cassiodorus says that 'It is a sleight of hand to hinder you, when he shows to do one thing openly and does the contrary privately.' Upon that thing you wish to have counsel, absolute truth should be said and observed; this is to say, tell truly your tale. For he that speaks falsely may not well be counseled in the case of which he lies. You should also hold in suspicion the counsel of such people as reveal their counsel to others without your consent."

When I had finished I stared down at Chaucer's quires, the shards of deception assembling themselves in my mind.

With tremulous hands I folded my spectacles and returned them to their pouch. The texture and substance of the fine leather on my fingertips was somewhat calming, even as I felt myself begin to question the unquestionable. A pile of nameless prisoners slain with guns. A village massacred. A brash mayor too cowed to confront the magnate responsible for the atrocities. Bands of badged men, flaunting the livery of their master as they commit wanton murder upon the helpless and the innocent.

There was the nut of the thing. Livery and heraldry, the language of lords. I thought of

Scrope and Grosvenor. Two lords, each of them enlisting the peers of the realm in claiming the arms he believes are rightfully his. For a man's livery is inseparable from his name, his honor and belonging, his very soul. A man's arms are his truth and his troth.

Or are they?

The beginning of wisdom lies in doubt, so Peter Abelard writes. *By doubting we come to the question, and by seeking we may come upon the truth.* All along I had been seeking, questioning, searching for the truth. Yet had I genuinely opened myself to doubt, to the afflictions and setbacks brought on by a rigorous questioning of the known? Or had I allowed an arrogant confidence in my own dark skills to guide me down a road of false conclusions?

Be not blind. Since that morning in the St. Bart's churchyard, I had followed an oiled chain of logic, one thing leading to another in a seemingly unbroken series of links and connections. A murder, a mayor, a duke; a maudlyn and a scribe. Corpses, guns, banners, the witnessing of children. A serpent with a burning cord in its fangs, a flashing knife in a dark square. The word of my son. And behind them all two gorged swans before a tree, their shapely necks entwined in a twist of unmistakable culpability. How precious. How neat.

Yet now, as I returned to my bed, a different vision flashed before me, a sad spectacle of ineptitude and error. I saw John Gower, hobbled over a stick, walking blindly along a trail of polished stones, his weakening eyes discerning only what had been arranged for them to see. *A king will do anything to stay a king,* Gloucester had murmured in my ear at that Kentish keep, an attempt at deflection and intimidation, as I heard it then. I could not be wrong. *I could not.* Even as I whispered such assurances to myself I sensed their weakness, my will to harvest strong connections from the barren soil of coincidence.

Be not blind. The coming day would tell. In the morning, in the hours before Exton's Riding, I would either confirm or put to rest this rising suspicion. Then I would know. I closed my eyes that night awash in doubt, aware that the morrow might well bring disaster, and that the blame would forever be my own.

CHAPTER 42

That morning the company reached the southern border of the County Palatinate of Durham and the liberty of St. Cuthbert's land. Winds gusted down from the north in great rushes of cold, moaning through the scattered trees, gathering the brittled leaves into dry spirals that shot skyward before lowering to the road to swirl among heads and hooves. The land around them had changed over the last several days, as the company snaked through the northern moors, the endless heaths spreading out in all directions, large stones littering the barren hills on either side of their route.

As they rounded one of these low hills Margery saw an obstacle on the road ahead. A bar lay across the way, a log resting atop two pillars to each side of the way. On the eastern hand there was a small tollkeeper's encampment, with a stone hearth, two rough huts, and an open pavilion, where a pair of soldiers lounged by the road on an enormous rock the size and shape of a lord's table. At the approach of the company one of them pushed himself off and ambled slowly toward the bar, gnawing on a leg or flank bone as he looked them over.

She shivered, willing the man to hurry it along. They had ridden that morning in the middle of the company, staying largely silent, the anticipation and dread only mounting as they neared their final destination.

"Fourpence a head before the town," said the guard between bites, head sweeping left and right, mouth still working the meat. *Farpence a head afore the toon.* A northman's tongue, the words barbed and bristling in her ears. "And a word of advisement for visitors to the lands of St. Cuthbert's between Tyne and Tees. Though you're yet a full seven leagues out from Durham, here the bishop is as good as your king, see?"

He waited for their nods and yeses.

"Vary good. Now f'yar coin." He hailed his companion and the two of them proceeded to lower the bar, first one end, then the other, taking their time. Once the log lay flat on the ground the pilgrims crossed into the Palatinate, the horses stepping delicately over as their riders' coins clinked into a shallow clay pot the first soldier held up for the purpose.

Robert paid their toll along with the others and they passed over the bar, into the bishop's liberty of Durham, one large and meaningful step closer to the Scottish marches. She glanced over her shoulder as the remainder of the company made their payments. The sisters Constance and Catherine, riding near the back again that morning, had paused by the bar — to negotiate a smaller toll, she assumed, and why would they not, given their undisputed sanctity?

Yet as she watched she saw Constance point up the road — toward her. She turned away. Her heart thrummed in her ears, the day darkening before her.

She considered saying something to Robert, weighed the chances, but what would she say, what could he do? Flee across the countryside and they would be hunted down like harts. Stand and fight and they would surely be downed on the spot. He had no sword, no bow, no arrows to nock in his skillful and killing way. Instead she said a prayer, watched the road before her, and braced herself tightly in her saddle.

And soon felt somewhat reassured. She heard no hooves of pursuing mounts, no shouts from behind. When she next turned

Catherine was speaking urgently to her scowling sister. Their imprecations to the tollkeepers seemed to have fallen on deaf ears. Another respite, for how long she could not know.

In Derlinton they found lodgings in a private house, the company dispersing for the night around the village. Robert slept soundly. Margery was fitful, unable to keep her eyes closed, much less sleep. Finally an uneasy slumber came, and with it a dream of a new home, and the lowland hills.

She was just waking from her first sleep when she heard it. The soft moan of a door, a shoe crackling the rushes in the next room. Their host? She thought so, but saw no light beneath their door.

Then she heard the whispers. Two men, perhaps three. They were outside, beyond the shutters. She clutched Robert's arm, shook him awake. "Someone is here," she whispered in his ear.

His eyes came open and he leapt up, immediately alive to the danger. There were no weapons in the room, nothing to use to defend themselves. He grasped her arms and moved her against the wall farthest from the door and window, pushing her head down until she was huddled on the floor. Then he reached up and pulled himself into the rafters above.

The silence lingered. A dog barked faintly. The door burst open. The shutters cracked. The first intruder came through the door, his short sword a vicious gleam in the night. He went straight for the pallet, assaulting it with four strokes before realizing it was empty.

From the rafters Robert came swinging down to kick the man against the wall. The sword clattered to the ground and he grasped it just as the shutters splintered with another crack. He still had the surprise on them, and took the first man through the window with a thrust to the gut. The second, sensing the danger, shouted for his fellows, but Robert was already on the inside man. There was slicing, hacking, grunts of pain, then Robert grabbed their attacker and twisted his neck to a snap. Two dead inside, one outside and warned.

He spun toward her. "Take whatever you can." He struggled into his coat as she gathered some of her clothing, the purse of coin that had gotten them here. Bearing what she could she followed him into the main room and outside toward the stable.

"Who's there?" came a shout from the house behind them.

As they ran they looked wildly left and

right for the third assailant. Nothing. They reached the stable, open to the night. Four horses. They chose the two they knew, but no time for saddles. They led the horses out of the barn.

"Mount," he said, cupping his hands. She stepped up and he threw her over the beast's bare back. As she spun on the animal she heard the thud of footsteps behind him, saw a silver slash in the moonlight. He grunted in pain and fell to the dirt. The attacker raised his sword.

Margery heeled her horse. It jumped toward the attacker, startling him, giving Robert just enough time to kick the man's legs from beneath him. There was a brief struggle on the ground, then it was over.

As more shouts came from the house and street he rose and pulled himself onto the other horse. She kicked her own in the flanks. They were off, skirting along the stable and out to the street, the shouts of the townsfolk ringing out behind them. They rode north along the central way. As they neared the upper edge of the town a door opened to the left. A candle flared in the darkness. Two faces over the flame. Constance and Catherine, their eyes wide with wonder and fright.

Margery and Robert rode through the

night in silence, the fear clawing at their backs. He was hurt, badly, though he never moaned nor spoke a word of complaint. Their mounts took the road at a steady pace, not too swiftly to tire, nor too slowly to risk apprehension from behind.

Dawn came on without incident. They must have been less than a league from Durham, she reckoned it, and still they had not encountered another group of riders, though that fortune would surely not last. As they forded a wide and slow-moving creek he spoke for the first time in hours.

"Margery," he said. "Margery, I must stop now." His voice was weak, sickly. She felt her only real terror since that night in the woods.

On the shallow far bank he slid from the wide back of his horse and staggered toward the water. She dismounted and tied their reins together. He had collapsed at the creek's edge.

It was a grievous wound, she saw, a gash on his upper right thigh that sent spirals of blood through the water, dark coils in the rising light. With his knife she cut away the surrounding portions of his breeches and saw the extent of it. The opening was deep and wide, beyond her powers to heal. She wished for a surgeon but settled for a poultice, crafted from chickweed leaves, which she mashed up with mud from the bank. She smeared it into his wound, making him groan in agony.

He clutched at his leg. She pushed his hands away and had to sit on them to keep him from worsening the wound. She held him behind his neck with one hand, cooled his face with the other. His eyes fluttered open. More blood, leaking out around the poultice. His grip weakened. He fixed her with a stare, gave her a slight smile, raised his hand, then lowered it. At last he was still. She looked up at the sky, at circles of birds whorling in the chill morning air.

CHAPTER 43

From the wharf bankside of the Temple
Church a narrow stone stair climbed up
through the wide yard toward the level of
the Strand, the broad road leading from the
walls out past Charing Cross nearly to Westminster. Along the south side of this avenue
marched a colorful series of great palaces
and houses, all facing the Thames and
showing the arms of their inhabitants:
bishops, lords, some wealthier knights, a few
successful tradesmen. Over the years many
smaller structures had been built up against
the back walls of these houses. Let to hostel-
ers and shopkeepers and facing the smaller
residences across the Strand, these randomly spaced buildings and fronts lent the
avenue its flavor as simultaneously a busy
commercial district and a fashionable place
of residence for the monied. In the middle
of it all sat the charred ruins of Lancaster's
Savoy, still uncleared since the Rising five

years earlier. The land around it had been partially reclaimed since then, though the palace itself remained an unsightly hulk on the waterfront, overgrown with weeds, shrubs, and even young trees.

At nine on the morning of Exton's Riding I had summoned the mayor's guards and made for the Thames with Jack Norris at my side. We floated over the river to the Temple wharf, this time aboard a small craft let and rowed by one of the mayor's guards. I had explained the plan to Jack as we crossed. He was bedazzled at the prospect of an audience with the king, an unthinkable thing for an earless cutpurse and the son of a hanged thief. Though I told him honestly of the risk in witnessing against a duke, he seemed determined to reveal what he had seen, whatever the consequences. He would remain with me for the balance of the morning, with both of us to be allowed into Westminster Hall on the word of Nicholas Brembre.

Our first destination was Lintner, the Earl of Suffolk's large house less than a quarter mile up the Strand from Lancaster's ruined palace. I decided to avoid the house's wharf and enter discreetly from the street side, as the servants did, and pay a guard or attendant to announce my visit to the earl himself. We neared the house's street wall, currently the site of a traveler's inn alongside a furrier's shop. I asked one of the guards to wait there with Jack for my return from within. With the other guard behind me I entered the narrow passage between the inn and the furrier's shop, and soon was at the rear postern. Two men wearing the livery of the Tower stood guard. They leaned on pikes and were otherwise armed with long knives and longer swords. One of them recognized the mayor's man.

"Well now," he said to the other. "A Guildhall boy. What say you for yourself, Tilden?"

My guard said nothing, keeping his chin up and his eyes averted.

The Tower man lifted his pike, tapped it on the stones at his feet. "What say you for yourself, Tilden?" He took a step toward us. Tilden's hand went to his short sword.

"None of this, my good men," I said, stepping between them. "There is enough hatred between the Tower and the Guildhall to feed everyone without your help." I looked at the Tower guard, held up a quarter noble. "I seek an audience with the chancellor."

"The chancellor?" he scoffed. "There's no chancellor within these walls that I know of. Merely an earl."

"The earl, then," I said.

"Ah, the earl."

"Aye the earl, you sodden jake," muttered my guard. The second Tower man now stepped up.

The postern door swung open. "Enough!" The speaker was John Staines, the steward of Lintner, a level-headed man. He regarded me closely. "Gower," he said.

"Staines. I'd like to speak with him, if it's possible." I nodded toward the house. "And soon."

The Tower man still had not taken my coin. Staines did. "Come along," he said, stepping aside and letting us into the earl's garden. "You are his lordship's only caller today." The door closed behind us, and I asked the city guard to remain there until I returned.

Staines, surprising me, put a hand on my arm as we stood within the gate. "I am glad you are here, Gower. His lordship finds himself suddenly unwelcome within his customary circles. He feels himself disgraced."

"Only in his own eyes," I said to the steward. "His reputation will surely outweigh these immediate troubles."

"Surely." He sounded skeptical.

"Is Edmund Rune about?" I asked, testing him.

Staines shook his head. "He left some time ago. He is the only one those Tower men will let in or out of Lintner, and now he is about on business for his lordship. We would like to get the earl out of London, today if we can. Rune is hoping the Riding will provide some distraction. He is making arrangements now."

In his distress Staines had said too much, and his mouth clapped shut. I felt a rush of unease, a sour taste in my throat. The steward led me through the garden and into the grand house, a series of wide and elegant rooms that had been furnished and decorated over many years of the earl's service to the crown. Lavish tapestries hanging from every third wall, others painted in scenes of civic and religious splendor, with particolored molding framing the doorways, and carved figures entwined among the foliated lintels. The chapel, which we passed on our way to the hall, shone like a box of jewels, chill air breathing from the depths, a haze of mingled hues glowing out from the windows on the east end.

Michael de la Pole, Earl of Suffolk, sat on an oaken chair above a balustrade off the house's summer hall. When Staines announced me he remained still in his seat, giving the slightest nod to acknowledge my arrival.

"My lord," I said softly to his back. He moved just slightly, sniffed. "I am truly sorry for your plight, my lord."

"Yes." He spoke without emotion. "Exiled from Westminster, mere weeks after my very voice opened Parliament. Now I am prisoner in my own home, nor will I be permitted to ride along for Exton's procession this morning. Rune has enjoined me not to attend, nor to dignify the opposing lords with my presence, though I suspect Gloucester and his men have prohibited it in any case. A hanging will be next."

"Not so, your lordship," I said, reassuring him even as my alarm increased. "Men will see reason in time, and after all the king is your staunch ally."

"What a warm comfort, that thought." He shifted his body so that his side was to me, and I could see his smirking lips. The earl's face, haggard and sagging, had greyed in the weeks since I saw him last. "Old King Edward, now *there* was an ally. Reigned for fifty years, and never once did his support for his counselor waver. His grandson has proven more . . . variable, shall we say. I try to advise him wisely, help him act in the realm's best interests over his own. Yet my words run like melted wax out of his royal ear."

"Though surely His Highness values your safety and wisdom," I said, trying to mask my rising impatience. "Has he summoned you to an audience since the bill of impeachment was raised?"

He shook his head sadly. "He was at Eltham to receive Gloucester and the others, all demanding my head. Then Richard rode up here to Westminster at Gloucester's bidding to dismiss me and the treasurer. He remains there now, awaiting Exton, though without his most loyal counselor."

"And your own counselor?" I ventured.

He sighed. "A good man."

"Where has Rune gone, your lordship?"

The earl gave a melancholy shrug. "He makes plans for my removal from Lintner. Edmund assures me this deposition is temporary, that we will reassume our high position in a matter of days. When the smoke clears, he says."

We, I noted with a chill, and almost smelled the smoke. "Has he said how soon?"

"More or less."

"Tell me his exact words to you, my lord. They are urgently important."

Finally the earl turned his head to regard

me full-on. He frowned. "He said to me, 'If you are not restored to the chancellorship by the close of Hallowtide, your lordship, I will cast myself from the highest parapet in Westminster.' Now there's an ardent counselor, eh, Gower? He'd give his life just to make his lord believe in himself again. And perhaps Edmund's staunch hope will win the day after all." As he laughed his eyes flashed with their old hale gleam, and for a moment I too wanted to credit Rune's reckless prediction, which he had surely uttered to his lord with all the confidence of a cornered snake.

"Yes, your lordship," I said instead. "Perhaps it will."

The earl turned from me. *By the close of Hallowtide,* Edmund Rune had proclaimed. All Hallows' was now three days away, with the completion of All Hallowtide in four. What would it take, I thought with a cold dread, to reinstate a deposed chancellor in the space of merely four days?

A distant king, one able to wash his hands of the matter.

A decapitated Parliament, frightened enough to remove the new chancellor and restore Michael de la Pole to his position.

Above all it would require a pile of dead nobles. Gloucester, Arundel, Warwick, perhaps Mowbray: the magnates arrayed against Michael de la Pole and King Richard at Westminster. Four assassinations, all in the coming days.

Or one massacre.

I left the summer hall briskly, making my way to the house's back garden and exiting with Jack and the mayor's guards onto the Strand. As the alley door closed behind us I saw a familiar figure approaching from the direction of Fleet Street. It was Edmund Rune.

His head was down, his brow furrowed in thought. Grabbing Jack roughly by his arm, I turned away and pretended to examine some pelts displayed by the furrier's door.

Jack, however, was frozen in place, staring at Rune as the earl's counselor approached us.

"Jack," I whispered, gesturing for the guards to obstruct his view up the street. They started to move. "Not now, Jack."

He would not listen. The boy's face had gone white, and as Rune neared the gate Jack's arm rose slowly, his finger pointing unmistakably at Rune's face.

"Master Gower, that's —"

I moved forward and clapped a hand over the boy's mouth. I forced his arm down to his side, spinning him away just as Rune

638

reached the gate.

Rune saw me. His mouth gaped.

"Gower," he said, recovering with a feigned smile. The guards stepped aside as Rune paused with the gate door open. "What brings you to the earl's —"

Then he saw Jack, peeking out from beneath my arm. Rune's eyes widened, then slowly rose to meet my own. His lips quivered before curling up into the slightest of smiles.

TataTOOM-taTOOM-taTOOM. The clarion trumpets of the city heralds echoed distantly from the walls, enlivening the air around us. I looked down Fleet Street, then back at Rune. His eyes, a cold and metal grey, flickered with pride. He blinked.

"You are too late, Gower."

The door closed behind him, and he was gone.

CHAPTER 44

The pain starts as a dream. Blood, a great puddle of it, spreads across a tiled floor. An unseen woman bends over the flowing mass. She holds a heavy rag in her hands. She goes to her knees. The rag moves across the crimson pool, sucking the puddle up in places, broadening it in others. Each time the rag is soaked through, the woman's hands lift and squeeze the saturated cloth. The blood leaves the rag in short, rhythmic bursts at first, then there is one long gush that thickens and spreads the puddle and the floor becomes a pond, slick and messed with wet. Now the blood is water, a blooming gush between her legs. And the rag, Hawisia realized on waking, was her own flesh.

Her middle seized up for a moment, then released her. The next thing she felt was the wetness, a sensation of spreading and flux. Then another wrack of pain as her insides twisted first one way, then the other. It seemed as if everything within her was tugging at everything else. The pain spread to her back, flared there, girdled her middle, tightened, and finally released.

She staggered to her feet, bent over, sucking breath, shocked at how quickly it was all happening. "Bella!" She called for her servant. "Bella!" It was dawn. The girl should have been awake.

She shook her head, furious at her thickness. No, not dawn, not dawn. She'd already been awake for an hour at the least before going up for a small nap in the midmorning —

Another seizing. She grunted through the pain, writhed against the wall, sank to the floor. When her cheek touched the rough rushes she knew she was still alive.

The seizing passed. She half stood and threw open the shutter onto the yard. She wanted a guildsman, an apprentice, a yard boy, someone to run for Rose Lipton.

Empty. Where was everyone? Of all the times to —

She remembered. Nicholas Exton, the new lord mayor, the Riding to Westminster and the throne of King Richard. All of London would be lined up around the Guildhall Yard and along Cheapside.

And all of London meant all of Stone's foundry. Four apprentices, two guildsmen, two house servants, two yard workers, ten in all, not counting Stephen Marsh and herself, not a one of them about but Hawisia. She listened.

The neighing of an old goat, a crow's random caw. Hardly a sound in all the parish. Only a distant human clamor from the direction of St. Paul's and the Guildhall. But not up here, in the far corner of the ward. Here all was silence. And silence, on that day, meant death.

She endured the next seizure with Rose Lipton's child-proud face at the front of her mind, the focus of her pain and hate. The hurt ripped her middle and left her gasping for breath.

There was no stool for the birthing. Merely a straw pallet, and herself. Hawisia gritted her teeth, pushed herself up, and sprawled on the bed just as the next seizing shook her from within.

CHAPTER 45

His guns and his snakes, all of them, were now being doled out among this band of thirty men in the Tower yard. Stephen watched from afar as each of the infantry-men received three of his creations, bundled in cloth and slung over a shoulder for the march to their destination, wherever that might be. He did not recognize this company from his time within the walls. They were not Tower men, nor did they show any lord's livery on their arms or chests, neither bends nor badges. The men were ranked in no particular order he could see, though what they lacked in discipline they made up in brashness and spit. Hard, seasoned men, with little patience for lordly niceties or royal pomp.

Another man had joined Snell at the foot of the Wardrobe Tower, where they stood before the assembly of soldiers. He was tall, brown-haired and bearded, with an air of command. The two seemed to be arguing about something; the subject could not be heard, though this must have been the same man he had overheard speaking with Snell the week before. After giving an order to the leader of the company, Snell and his companion walked toward the Lion Tower and the city gate. The company remained in the yard until the next bell sounded from the king's chapel, then began walking toward the south part of the complex.

Curious, Stephen followed the company around the ward wall and toward the water gates. Rather than leaving through the barbican up above, he saw, the thirty men would be passing out through the river doors beneath Becket's Tower, presumably to board a waiting barge. Two Tower guards stood at the river gate, one on each side, pulling the door chains to allow the company to exit. The doors came slowly open, their inward swing forcing the members of the infantry company to move back until they were nearly abreast of Stephen himself.

With a sudden thrill he realized that no one was watching him, and for good reason. The other armorers and smiths had been relieved that day in order to attend Exton's Riding to Westminster, and the few of Snell's regular men who might recognize

Stephen were gone with them. Seeing an opportunity, he stepped briskly forward, his heart racing with the risk, and joined them as the doors came fully open, then shuffled with the men toward the river. Not a one of them paid him any mind, assuming he was leaving on Tower business. The guards, not watching for anyone to escape, failed to spot him among their number.

No waiting barge on the water. Instead the company took a sharp right turn and processed along the narrow passage above the moat fosses. This walkway, a span of board and brace, would be cut or burned in the event of an attack from the river, and it made for a somewhat perilous route above the waters. Stephen remained with the men until they reached the quay east of the customhouse. He stopped there, looking back at the massive hulk of the Tower, scarcely believing the sight. The company of soldiers continued along the wharfage, nearly empty for the great civic occasion.

Stephen watched them go. Then, in an almost dreamlike state, he walked toward the customhouse, then up to Thames Street. He paused at the corner to look about and behind. No one had followed him from the Tower, it seemed, and no watchmen had been looking for him to appear. He went north along Mark Lane and past All Hallows Staining, walking freely through the streets of London for what might surely be the last time given what he had done.

The streets and lanes were empty, wondrously so. It happened just a few times a year, for processions by the mayor or the king, and on that day it suited his purpose well. At first the vacant parishes seemed a sinister thing, as if swept by pestilence, the high houses leaning together in malicious allegiance to choke off the sky. Then, as the length of Fenchurch Street opened up before him, he began to see the city in its full majesty, a great cathedral cleared of its sinners and their sins.

Soon Stephen reached the lane before the foundry. The gate was latched from within but he knew its tricks. Now he was standing in the yard, looking about at his home. Yes, *home.* Stone's was where he belonged, practicing the simplicity of his craft. He looked at the smithing shed, saw his favorite hammer hanging there, felt his palm and fingers curl around it.

Tra-DOOM.

A clap of thunder sounded from the west, followed by another. Strange, Stephen thought, for the sky is as glowingly clear as the sweetest water. A cloud of birds rose as if carried on the distant roar of the crowd, though it might have been a moaning wind, and soon enough quiet settled over the foundry yard once more.

Stephen breathed deeply, closed his eyes. The face of his master came to him then, the sight of a dead girl on the forest floor.

Crack.

Crack.

Crack.

The guns, at a distance of a mile. He opened his eyes. His litter of snakes, their faint explosions of fire and steel echoing along the canyons of London, bowled from Aldersgate along Cheap, past the Guildhall and Cornhill, and into the ears of the man who birthed them. His greatest invention, destroyed in a glorious waste of powder and flame. They will quiet soon, he thought, and we shall see what comes of it all.

Then he heard a scream.

CHAPTER 46

An ale wagon had capsized outside Ludgate, throwing full casks to burst open on the pavers, making of the forecourt a slippery mess, with a dozen men arguing loudly over cause and culpability. We went up to Newgate with no happier result, as the Riding would be coming through shortly and no admittances were permitted until after the procession. Finally, as I started to give up hope, the guards at Aldersgate allowed us entry. We quickly made our way past the Goldsmiths Hall, then around St. Lawrence Jewry, ending up on Cat Street, thick with Londoners waiting upon the new mayor. Exton had taken his oath outside the hall the day before, with Brembre handing over the sword and doing his part to reinforce the illusion of a transfer of power.

The Riding procession had just started to move out from Guildhall Yard. Nicholas Exton was mounted on a tall charger, the sword of the city borne proudly before him as Brembre, the aldermen, and other civic officials fell in behind. Ralph Strode was there, heavy in his saddle, as were the sheriffs, the beadles, and the masters of London's numerous livery companies, all sporting the colors of their guilds.

Everything was as it should be — with one terrible difference. At the front of the procession rode the higher nobles, all there at the invitation of the mayor to precede him to Westminster. I counted ten lords, among them Thomas de Beauchamp, Earl of Warwick; Richard FitzAlan, the new chancellor and Earl of Arundel and Surrey; and Thomas of Woodstock, Duke of Gloucester: the three lords at the head of the appellant faction, their banners borne by heralds arrayed before them. In a rising panic, I thought through the next quarter hour, wondering where the massacre would take place, casting about for any means of stopping it. From the Guildhall the procession would ride down to Cheap, bound for Newgate to avoid St. Paul's. Once beyond the walls the riders would descend to Fleet Street, and from thence to Westminster along the Strand.

The procession pushed past St. Lawrence Jewry to the clatter of the crowd, the singing and playing of the minstrels, the re-sounding trumpets, the thudding drums, cheers both wild and constrained as the city greeted its new overlord. The press was too thick to penetrate. There was no way to reach Brembre, who was already on the far side of the yard from my position. The lords had disappeared beyond the church.

I hurried along Cheapside on foot, with Jack at my heels and the mayor's guards on either side, the four of us mingling un-noticed among the throng, allowing me to assess the likelihood of an assault on the magnates. The entire entourage was well armed, the lords heavily guarded in front and back. An attack from the sides would be ineffective, as there was too little distance between the procession and the streetside buildings to allow for anything but a minor disruption.

We had reached the wide space before Newgate. I moved to one side, flattening myself against a wall to allow the procession to pass. A few knights, then the earls with the Duke of Gloucester, soon to be safely out of the city. Any attack would have to come outside the walls. Unless —

I looked up.

Tra-DOOM.

An enormous explosion, from just within

650

the gate. Splinters of wood flew in every direction. A horse reared and shrieked, its rider hurled from its back to crash down upon the stones.

As the ringing in my ears started to fade I heard screams of fright and pain, shouted orders, the clash of bared swords. Lords and knights sliding from their mounts, leading the animals along as shields against an unknown foe.

Then the handgonnes.

Crack.

Crack.

Crack.

Crack.

Crack.

Crack.

A multitude of shots, too many to count. I threw myself beneath the wooden awning of a baker's shop, clutching at my knees, making myself as small as possible while waiting for a ball to strike my chest or neck.

Crack.

Crack.

I had lost sight of Jack. Then I saw him, darting between the wheels of two carts on Cheap. The mayor's guards had fled in the opposite direction. I was alone.

Crack.

Crack.

Now the screams. As hundreds of Londoners fell to the ground Iseult's story of the massacre at Desurennes flashed through my mind. Ripped chests, shattered skulls, torn necks.

Crack.

I had a vision of the men in the St. Bartholomew's grave, children bleeding and ravaged on the ground. Around me others were scattering or ducking behind and beneath whatever they could find. Even Woodstock himself cowered between the wheels of a water wagon, his shoulders hunched against the violence from above.

Crack.

Crack.

More screams, a panic of men and women fleeing from the center of the square.

Crack.

"Aieee!!!"

A howl of pain, distant not near. I risked a look out toward the gate. All was turmoil, the mayor's Riding dissolved into a chaotic melee of humans and horses, hands and feet. Yet despite the shots and screams I saw no dead in the gateyard, no spills of blood and brains as I had expected.

Crack.

"My eyes! Douse my eyes!" someone shouted high above.

"Leave off! Leave off!" ordered another.

"Down the guns! Down the guns!"

Crack.

"Jesu's blood. Put it out!"

"M'shirt's aflame!"

"Down the guns!"

Crack.

"Douse my eyes, for Christ's mercy!"

I looked up cautiously, still half cowering beneath the baker's awning. A group of men, yelling back and forth along the walls. Yet these particular screams, I soon realized, had come not from the scattered crowd of lords and citizens in the gateyard. The screams of anguish were sounding from overhead.

Crack.

"AAARRR!"

A flash of powder over the gate parapet.

Crack.

Another, and a gun exploded in a soldier's hands. The flame leapt at his face. He slapped at his singed brow.

Crack.

This one to the left of him, the tower parapet above. Another misfire. The soldier threw the gun away from himself, shaking his burned hands and clapping them against his hauberk. The weapon spun in the air, hit the awning, then clattered to the street not ten feet from where I crouched. Looking left and right, I crawled out through the fleeing crowd, seized the gun, and returned to my position.

A barrel, a stock, a snake. The gun, I saw, was identical in all respects to the one Simon had given me in Calais.

The shots ceased. By this time a number of the lords' guards had recovered their wits. Arrows were flying up to the ramparts, shot by a cluster of archers, several of whom held shields overhead to guard their fellow bowmen. I heard shouts from the direction of St. Paul's. Soon the archers were joined by the mayor's own swordsmen, a large company from the city guard. Blades were drawn, and other guards were now sprinting for the gate stairs to ascend the walls.

Brembre's men had arrived too late. If the guns had fired successfully, the cream of English chivalry would have lain slaughtered in the yard. Yet the weapons had misfired — all of them. Could it be —

"Drop it, on your life."

A sword at my neck. I swallowed slowly.

In the examining then of your counselor be not blind. Slowly I looked up into the cruel glare of Edmund Rune.

Chapter 47

"Rise."

I looked down at the familiar gun in my hands, no help against the sharp sword in Rune's. I dropped the useless weapon on the stones as I stood.

"Through there." He pointed to a passage between the baker's and a vintner's shop next door. The gateyard was still a melee. The clatter and whistle of arrows and bolts, shouts and threats flying up and down from the walls. One man holding a blade to the chest of another would hardly be noticed in the chaos.

"Now!" Rune commanded.

I obeyed, backing down the passage with his sword still at my chest. With my final glimpse of Cheap I saw a pale face and earless head against the scattering crowd. Jack Norris, staring after me. Then he was gone.

Rune backed me through the alley to a darkened and empty seld, roughly roofed and open at four sides. Through the narrow gap at the opposite end I could see the rush of citizens along Thames Street, hear their distant shouts as news spread of the incident at the gate.

Rune dropped his sword to his side, though I had no doubt it would pierce my heart should I seek to escape or scream for help. My feeling as I stood there was something like the sensation I had experienced in the surgeon's chair, donning spectacles for the first time, the blurred made clear, the dulled edges of things newly sharp and precise, as everything I had seen in those weeks assembled itself with a startling clarity.

"Why, Rune?" I asked him as I waited bleakly to die. "All of this, merely to incriminate Woodstock?" Still a guess, but one that had been creeping up on me over the last two days. The one answer that made sense of it all.

"It was the only way," said Rune, his jaw tensed in fury. "Gloucester is the leader of the appellant lords, and they do his bidding in all things. They must be turned against him."

"The gunpowder," I said. Ships unloading at Dunkirk, a bend conveniently lost in a fight on the quay. "Convince the Lords and

Commons that Gloucester is dealing arms to Burgundy and France. That he is a traitor, and therefore unfit to lead an appeal against the king."

"Treason comes in many forms," said Rune. "Gloucester is a traitor of the worst kind, disguising his betrayals under a cloak of devotion to the realm. Think of how he must appear to King Richard and his fellow lords about now! Murdering the king's prisoners, without the process of law, and casting the bodies in the mayor's own sewers. Massacring townspeople in the Pale, without leave of the captain of Calais. Worst of all, peddling guns and gunpowder to our enemy. A duke acting rashly on his own, without consulting the lords or his sovereign, risking the safety of the realm."

Rune's plan had a sickening brilliance.

"You sought to isolate Gloucester," I said. "Leave the duke weakened and alone, a cowering traitor exposed even as he preens over his parliamentary move against His Royal Highness — and your lord the earl."

He beamed. "And secure a useful alliance in the event of a French conquest of our fair isle. A likely conquest, the admirals are telling us."

"You forged the duke's badge."

"Many times over. A few embroideresses,

a few baubles as reward, a few dozen badges to sew into bends. The simplest part of the entire enterprise."

Simple, perhaps, yet audacious in its violation of the mores of heraldry. Dozens of false bends and badges, circling the arms of Rune's men as they did their foul work in Kent, in London, in the Pale.

I asked him, "How did you connive Snell into your plan? He is the king's own armorer, appointed from Gloucester's own household."

"Snell is a craftsman in body, and a visionary in soul. His ambitions defeat his loyalty, and he bears none toward Gloucester. We both needed a particularly malleable assortment of men and material to do what needed to be done. I provided prisoners to him, he provided guns to me."

"What about the soldiers?"

"Snell hired men willing to be employed in the ways we both required."

"They were not Tower men?"

"Mercenaries," said Rune. "Englishmen all, but hired from a foreign source." His head tilted to the side as he regarded me in my new bewilderment.

I spoke the name. "Hawkwood."

"With Simon Gower as his willing agent."

I turned away from him, my eyes closed

against the truth.

"Sir John's most bloody-minded men," Rune went on in a smooth voice, taking a sharp pleasure in what he was telling me. "Twenty of them, English men all, shipped up months ago for special missions on behalf of the Tower. In matters such as these it's best to have native men operating on native soil, able to mask themselves according to the needs of the day. Men without faction or favorites. Men like yourself, Gower. And your cooperative son, who arranged for the hire of Hawkwood's men."

My eyes came open, cast to the ground. A shudder ran from my heart to the extremities of my limbs. Rune, then, had known of Simon's involvement in hiring the mercenary company when he sent me over to Calais and the Pale — perhaps even earlier.

I looked up at the treacherous man, my vision cloudy and faint, and only then did I comprehend the depth of it.

He had already read my darkest thoughts. "That was *my* notion, you know, to bring you into this from the start," he said. "Ralph Strode is a cooperative fellow, with a bushel of wisdom, and equal faith in the goodness of the crown. He took my suggestion, didn't he? And you have been quite useful, Gower, snouting up all the dungpiles I've left for you along the way. Swans, powder, badges, banners, guns — even a feigned attempt on your life in Calais to convince you of the urgency of the matter. How fitting, to have the father of my intermediary with these mercenaries, looking into the very deaths they brought about!"

His laughter rang thinly through the seld as I swallowed these bitter truths. I thought of Strode's sober words in the St. Bart's churchyard all those weeks ago, the sixteen bodies in a morbid line — and John Gower summoned there to perform a role already scripted by the man responsible.

There was a clamor from Cheap. We would not be alone for long. Rune stepped toward me, ready to plunge his sword into my chest. But I had to know. I struggled over a bench, flattening myself against the back wall of a closed shop. "Did Simon know the attempt on me was a ruse?" Did he think he was saving my life?

Rune smiled. "Some secrets are best left unrevealed, Gower. As you know very well."

Whatever the truth, Simon, once again, had played both sides, following Rune's orders while just as blind as his father to their full motivation — or so I had to hope. My son's endless capacity to deceive roused me to wonder.

"The shootings in the woods," I said, stepping to the side, playing for more time, following Rune's chain of revelations. "It was a test, an assay. Snell was testing guns."

"Not only guns," said Rune. "People."

"People? Yet how —"

"These handgonnes are new to our world, Gower. They require new strategies, new tactics of war." He waved his sword through the air, distracted for a saving moment by his pride. "We know how longbowmen will react in the heat of battle. How speedily a great archer can nock an arrow, how many bowmen to send along an enemy's flank. Yet we know very little about small guns, how they'll fare in the bloody milieu of battle and siege. The element of terror and noise they might provoke in a village or city. Their degree of accuracy on a target relative to distance and quality of powder. Even how quickly they can be loaded and fired by one man. Or one woman."

"So you tested them." I felt sickened.

"Lions, prisoners, a pile of scrap lumber," said Rune. "A target is a target as far as Snell is concerned. Now, as for your role in —"

A flash of metal from the north side of the seld. "Drop your sword, Rune."

I looked left. Nicholas Brembre, blade

661

drawn, four archers at his side. Behind them cowered Jack Norris. His eyes were wide as ale-jars, his face red beneath his uncapped head, his stubs ugly and aflame with exertion, yet I had never beheld a more welcome sight.

Now a movement to my right. Thomas of Woodstock, his sword drawn, and two of his own men armed with long knives. They had entered the seld from the south, the direction of Warwick Street. The two great men stood opposed, Rune and I the third point in a triangle.

"And yours, Sir Nick," said the duke, though it was all bluster on his part. Brembre had four nocked arrows in his corner of the seld. Two were pointed at Rune, two at the duke and his men.

"You are mayor for but another hour, Nicholas," said Rune, a pleading note in his voice. "We are king's men both. Take the duke's life, not mine, and this whole affair will be behind us."

I watched Rune's eyes, their frantic shifts from side to side. The earl's counselor was attempting to get Brembre on his side against Gloucester, the king's chief opponent. If the duke were killed in the day's civic melee, the mayor's principal enemy in the realm would be eliminated, with no one the wiser. Brembre hesitated, the calculation visible in his narrowed eyes.

Then Brembre made his decision. He shook his head just slightly. Rune saw the refusal in his gesture as the four archers all took aim. He leapt, his sword tracing an arc from my chest to Brembre's. Two arrows took Rune in the throat, another in the left eye. The fourth clattered harmlessly on the wall behind me. Rune fell, his sword dropping from his hand as he clutched at his face and neck, his life leaking out around the shafts.

Brembre squatted over the man's body. He looked up at Gloucester, who gestured for his men to lower their weapons.

"Dead, or soon to be," Brembre said.

"I am surprised, Lord Mayor," said the duke as the standoff ended, weapons sheathed and quivered. "Your man had me at the end of his arrow, helpless as a doe. Why would you spare me?"

Brembre considered his response. "You are guilty of many things, Your Grace. Treason is not one of them."

The duke's face showed surprise. He inclined his head.

"And I trust you will recall my forbearance in the coming months," said Brembre. "His Highness the king requires our loyalty and commands our restraint. I for one intend to grant him mine." And he returned Gloucester's nod.

I looked at the duke, saw Rykener's confession and the evidence of Brembre's vice swirling in his calculating eyes.

It was a remarkable moment. Nicholas Brembre's third term as mayor was to expire officially later that morning, when Exton presented himself at Westminster. Yet in that final hour he had committed the most selfless act of his rule: sparing the life of the magnate who most fervently wished him dead, and thereby preventing heightened strife between the lords and the king, a civil war, perhaps even a royal deposition. Years later, in thinking back on the events of that autumn, I would marvel at how differently King Richard's reign might have turned out had Brembre's arrows flown.

"You have shown yourself worthy of your title, Lord Mayor," said the duke.

"Staying my hand was hardly an act of nobility, Woodstock." Brembre's nose rang out a final mayoral sniff. "Civil war is always bad for trade."

CHAPTER 48

Footsteps, on the inner stairs. She was not alone in the house after all. Was it Rose Lipton, or one of the servants?

"Who's there?" she called out weakly. Floorboards moaned, a shadow fell across the doorway, and Stephen Marsh appeared at the end of the gallery. His mouth gaped. He stared at her. Hawisia was too gone with pain in that moment to think about what his presence at Stone's might mean. She could scarcely speak.

"Do not come within, Stephen," she said, shaking her head and showing him a palm. "Birthing time. You must leave me." He wouldn't dare violate her privity, would he? He looked more frightened than she was as he stood there dumbly, the mute sheepdog. He needed a task.

"Stephen," she said between heavy breaths. "Stephen, you must run to Coleman Way and fetch Rose Lipton."

"The midwife," he said, shocked from his daze.

"Aye. Fetch her if you will." She huddled herself into another seizing, though not too soon to see his face brighten with the assignment. He was gone, and absent for three more of the clutching pains before he returned. Alone.

She lay on her side and glared up at him. He gaped down at her writhing form. He stayed near the bedchamber door, half in, half out. "Mistress Lipton wasn't at home," he said timidly. "Gone to the Riding, I suspect, with all the rest."

"Very well," she said, girding herself for the shame of it. "You will have to — *ohh!*" The sharpest seizing yet. It spun her thoughts around, shot through from toes to skull.

"Are you — can I —" He looked on, his face a mask of confusion and boyish fear.

"Stephen," she gasped. "Stephen, you must help me. You must — you must birth this babe."

He backed into the gallery, his hands up, his eyes round as shields. "Oh I could not do *that*, mistress. Not — not *that*."

Not *that*? Her fury rose above the pain. *Not that.* As if lifting her sodden dress and eyeing up her parts would put him in any worse state than he already was. She looked into his shifting eyes, thought of his strange mind, how it worked, how it tested things. Not the devil's mind, as Robert would jest. Yet not fully human either, was Stephen Marsh. He saw everything in the world as part of his craft. Hawisia, in a moment of clarity in the midst of her pain, saw herself as she needed Stephen Marsh to see her.

A machine.

She seized up, yet even through the agony she forced the needful words together.

"Stephen," she gasped when the worst of it had passed. "Stephen, this is a matter of mechanics, this body you see. Think of it as one of your devices, your snakes or your guns or your hinges. Bone, muscle, flesh, grease. Moving parts, all of them. Some fit, some not. Some work as they should, some not." She suffered through another seizing, her eyes blurring with the sweat.

"Yet the machine — the contrivance is meant to work, Stephen. God — God Himself *means* it to work, and God means a child to slip through. *Now make it work, by God's damned bones!*" She cursed through the first moments of the next seizing, and she swam in a deep and throttling pain, the longest yet. Something shifted inside her with this one; she felt an opening in her inmost parts, a need to push the damned thing out, and yet it could be too early, the babe could be twisted or choked or broken and then what would she do?

When the spasm passed, Stephen Marsh was at the foot of the bed. He had moved her onto her back somehow. His hands were on her knees, and his face had changed. The apprehension and boyish fear were gone, replaced by the confidence of the artisan. A smith at his forge, a founder at his mold. A craftsman, curious, quick, up for a new challenge. He told her to move to her hands and knees, then to her elbows and knees, and she did, exposing her nether world to him, queynt and arse and all, without a mind to modesty.

What Hawisia would remember most clearly from the hour that followed was the reassuring steadiness of Stephen's voice, the calm questions and observations as he manipulated her inner and outer flesh with the practiced adeptness of a born surgeon.

You'll be wanting to push. But not yet, mind. Circle's opening up but needs a mite 'nother inch.

Digging in your back, you say? Aye, makes sense, as the thing's turned about, isn't it.

Oil's what we need, just there, and there.

Ah, the feet. All ten toes, Hawisia, not to

fear. The thing needs a twist about now.

So it went, for over an hour more; he told her when it was done. At the hazy end of it she was on her back, clutching a slimed, screaming thing at her breast. A daughter. Robert Stone's living daughter, and her own. There were a few voices from the yard now, the youthful calls of the apprentices returned from the Riding.

Hawisia looked at Stephen, who sat at a chair by her bed. He had been with her for nearly half that day, his voice in her ears, his hands within her privity, pulling life from her womb.

"You did well, Stephen Marsh."

His eyes moistened. Hawisia handed him the sleeping babe. Stephen held the girl, smelled her swaddled head.

Stephen sat with the babe all that day as the servants and apprentices and guildsmen drifted back to the foundry, murmuring among themselves down in the yard and the shop, worrying over the presence of Stephen Marsh back at Stone's, wondering when the beadle or constable would come for him.

At the stroke of four Rose Lipton appeared in the gallery. Stephen had gone out to the barn, his presence known only to the workers of the foundry. To Hawisia the midwife looked angry that the babe was alive. Rose's hands were at her hips, her lips tightly pursed as she took in the sight of this widow lying abed, a new mother without her aid.

Rose inspected the infant, then turned to Hawisia's nether parts. "Quite a tear down there," she said, sounding pleased as she fingered it roughly. "Don't expect it to heal, and you'll want to watch for fever, poor dear."

"I shall."

"She was swift out of your womb as well," said Rose with a cluck. "And as we midwives will say, quick to life, quick to death. My own birthings were slow affairs, even the seventh!"

"She came legs first. Like a mallet with a big head," said Hawisia, smelling her sweet child, and silently thanking God a smith was there to take the handle.

CHAPTER 49

The ward was lit up with the talk in those first days after the Riding, every mouth a lantern burning with news and slander. Hawisia half listened as she went about her work in the foundry, knowing the truth was more wondrous than all the lies being whispered about the foiled massacre at the city gate. Stephen had told her what he'd done, and through the week of Hallowtide she kept him hidden in the 'prentice barn, the whole of Stone's sworn to a secrecy all warily embraced. Stephen himself seemed as calm and content as a fugitive killer could be, warming touchingly to her new daughter, whose visits to the barn fast became part of the infant's daily routine.

Over a week passed before Hawisia learned what was to become of Stephen, and thus herself and the foundry. The first sign came from Mathias Poppe, the beadle who had sought out Stephen for questioning about the girl's death in the woods. He arrived at Stone's on the Thursday, asking after Stephen.

"Haven't seen his face in over a fortnight, Master Poppe," she said, smoothing her hand over the small back of her child. "Not since he left sanctuary at St. Mary's."

He could tell she was lying, Hawisia suspected, though he let it pass, acting satisfied with her denial. She promised to let him know the moment Stephen Marsh appeared at the foundry.

The next visitors, less benevolent, were liveried men of the Tower wardrobe. She found the two of them slinking about the shop on the Friday when she returned from the smithy. Long knives at their sides, scowls on their hardened faces.

"Where is he?" the first one asked her, without so much as a word of greeting.

"Who?" she said, widening her eyes.

"You know well enough," said the second. He spat on the rushes.

Her eyes went to the ugly spurt, back to him. "You'll be leaving my shop now, the both of you."

"That's what you think, is it, my pretty mother?"

"And we as well," said a voice. Hawisia turned to see three burly workers at the yard

672

door, each of them trained up in the craft by Robert Stone and Stephen Marsh, and all bearing lengths of iron in their hands. Two apprentices stood behind them, looking young, frightened, but passing brave.

With the swords it wouldn't be an even fight, nor a long one, but it could be messy. The Tower men knew it. They left the foundry spitting oaths. "We'll be back for him, widow. You can wager on it. We'll be back."

The next visitor arrived the following morning. He appeared not at the foundry but at the house, knocking on the street door and asking for Hawisia by name. A servant came to her in the shop. She went through to the hall, where the man had been asked to wait for the mistress.

She saw John Gower standing by the glazed window in front, the Stone hours in his hand, opened to a thumb-rubbed painting of the Virgin and Child. She had not noted his height at his last visit. He was taller than her husband had been and a sight older, and though his hair had greyed he was not frail in any way. On his head he wore a plain and unfashionable cap of banded wool, something you might see on a middling mercer, and when he turned to her the tassels bounced on either side of his eyes.

There was something missing in those eyes. Not kindness, as his look was clear and open. Unfocused and vague, his eyes wandered left and right before settling on her, then crinkling at the sides, lifted by a good-hearted smile.

"Mistress Stone," he said. "I am here about Stephen Marsh."

"You and half of London alike, it seems," she said, leaning her broad hips against the central table, trying to sound hard. "What is it you want with me?"

"Merely to give you this." He held out a parchment. She took it from him, not daring to hope, though she was unable to read the clerical hand when she unfurled the thing. From it dangled a wax seal pendant on a strip of parchment tied to the main body of the document.

"It is a pardon, Mistress Heath," he said.

She stared at it.

"It pardons your man Stephen Marsh in the death of Eleanor Baxter of Ware. King Richard declares the matter an unfortunate accident, and proclaims the inestimable value of Marsh's service to the realm as adequate recompense for the death. I can translate the wording for you if you like."

674

"Please," she said, because she could find nothing else to say. She gave it back to him.

He took out an odd instrument of glass and lead, unfolded it, and set it on his nose. "It begins, *'Know all present and to come that I, Richard, king by the grace of God, in the tenth year of my reign, do grant unto Stephen Marsh, founder and smith of Aldgate Ward in the parish of St. Mary's, full and complete pardon . . .'* "

He went on, and though she lost the trail of his words she understood where they led. When Gower had finished she said, "Stephen hasn't been taken in yet, nor is there an indictment for murder."

"Nor will there be," said Gower. "The royal pardon may come before arrest, after conviction, at the gallows — anywhere His Royal Highness wishes it to come. King Richard seals many dozens of them every month. This one required little persuasion."

Hawisia shook her head, staring at the magic writing on the parchment. "A great power for a man to wield, even a king," she mused.

"I believe the king's power should best be used according to law," he said stiffly, "and to speak truthfully, I have difficulty with the royal prerogative if exercised too freely. Yet there are certain circumstances in which the law must yield to the pardon and pity of the king. This is one of them."

"You are King Richard's agent, then?"

He smiled. "Hardly, Mistress Stone."

"Then how is it that you speak with his voice?"

He considered his response. "The royal court is a diverse hive. Not all who labor there are unthinking drones. There are good men within those high walls, men who can be made or paid to listen to intercessors."

"You were the intercessor? For our Stephen?"

"A friend of mine was happy to intercede, on my word."

"But why?"

"I learned of Marsh's work at firsthand. Once in Calais, then again during Exton's Riding."

"You were there."

"I was."

"At the gate?"

"Yes, mistress." He hesitated. "I have fired similar handgonnes myself. I know what Stephen must have done, and believe I know how he did it. He saved innumerable lives, Mistress Stone. Important lives. Now he must work to preserve his own."

"He is in danger?"

"I don't know," Gower confessed. "A royal

pardon promises that Stephen will not die at the hands of the king, hung on a common gibbet. As for William Snell and the Tower guard . . . that I cannot say. With the death of Edmund Rune the king's armorer has escaped penalty. There is no good evidence against him, only rumor, and the crown is content with laying all of this on the chancellor's deceased counselor. Things will be cleaner that way, I suppose," he mused. "But Stephen Marsh will end this affair with a new and powerful enemy."

"At all rates," said Hawisia. To her the names and offices meant nothing, and she wished to hear no more about them. She reached out to press her hands to his. "God be thanked for this, and for you, Master Gower."

He left Stone's without laying those peculiar eyes on Stephen Marsh, the man whose pardon he had somehow conjured from the king's chancery. When he had gone Hawisia went out to the 'prentice barn and hollered for him. He looked fearful when he emerged, as if expecting arrest, and squinted in the unfamiliar light.

She handed him the pardon. He looked at it and handled it as delicately as he did her daughter. He fingered the king's seals, his fingertips whispering along the parchment.

He could read the thing no better than she could, though she could tell he knew what it promised.

"But how — ?"

"A mystery," she said. "One we should accept as a sign of God's grace, and a seal of his charity. Now we must live and work for the new moment we've been given."

"Aye, Mistress Stone."

"And in this moment, we have four bells to fashion. Two for the Charterhouse, one for All Hallows-on-the-Wall, and another for the east belfry at St. Alfege. You are ready for a return to your work, Stephen?"

"I am," he said, his voice gaining in confidence. "And to earn your trust."

"Oh, you have it, Stephen Marsh," she said, walking within to get her daughter. "You have it in full."

Later she watched him oversee the first pour. Two cautious apprentices, aproned and gloved, tipped out the bronze ore, a cauldron of fire flowing into the clay molds, hissing through the wax. *Like pouring out the sun,* and the sun brings death but life as well, as Hawisia Stone saw it. Someday, perhaps, Stephen Marsh might see it, too.

CHAPTER 50

For a moment, at least, it seemed I had Chaucer's unalloyed attention. I read. He listened.

"For Love is blind and may not see;
Therefore may we no certainty
Set upon his foul judgment,
But as the wheel about doth wend
He gives his small grace undeserved;
And from that man who has him served
Full oft he taketh all his fold,
As cutpurse stealeth groat and gold.
Yet nonetheless there is no man
In all this world who may withstand
His wrath. Now may we hope full fair
To witness peace and end of war,
And seek for remedy of Love
Where saints doth tread, our souls to
    move."

I stopped there. The lines came from a

long lover's confession I had been writing for some months, inspired by a royal encounter on the river the year before. During my short ride out to Greenwich that morning I had recited the lines to myself with a modest pride in my making, though now that I sat with Chaucer in his hearth-warmed hall my couplets sounded plain and empty to my ear. A cold night, bleak verse, weak ale: I found myself wishing I had remained in Southwark.

Chaucer liked to listen with his eyes closed, his forehead on a palm. At the close of the final couplet he turned and looked at me. "Quite a beautiful passage, John. The woe of witnessing is a powerful theme, one too often neglected in our versifying. Yet so many of our earthly crafts rely on witnesses and their testimony. Lawyers, chroniclers, clerks —"

"Justices of the peace."

His lips formed a smile that quickly faded. He looked away. "There was a witness in the woods."

"Oh?" I had known there was something Chaucer wanted to tell me about the massacre, though I hardly thought to hope for a firsthand account. We had spoken already about the attack at the city gate, my encounter with Rune, the crown's discreet dealings with Snell, the pardon for Stephen Marsh, arranged through one of Chaucer's old associates now in the office of the privy seal. Yet Chaucer, I could tell, had been keeping something back, waiting for the right moment. Now it had come.

"You met him, in fact," he said.

I thought about our trying days in Kent, the hollow eyes of a gaunt country reeve. "Tom Dallid?"

"The very one."

"Did Rune's men ask him along? Order him?"

"No, nor did they discover his presence. After they emptied the gaol he started to feel wretched about it, said he knew it was a foul business. He followed the prisoners and soldiers at a distance, to the edge of the woods, then left his horse, went after them, and concealed himself near the clearing. He saw it all unfold."

I remembered Dallid's face, the impression of sullen fear the man had left. "Rune said it was a test, of both men and guns."

"It was."

"How did it work?" Rune died before he had a chance to tell me. Despite myself I felt a lingering curiosity about the details of the mass killing that had started all of this.

"A simple game," Chaucer said. "Two

men facing one another across the middle of the clearing, the distance between those two stumps we saw. They're given instructions in how to load a handgonne, prop it on a stump, and fire. Then one is placed on the ground in front of each of the two men. Each prisoner is then ordered to load and fire at his opponent, and keep going until one of them dies."

"And if they refuse?"

"They are shot by one of Rune's archers — as indeed the first man was for refusing to play the game."

At least one was killed with an arrow, that one there. Half the shaft's still in his neck. Baker's observation, in the St. Bart's churchyard.

"All they had to hand was a pouch of powder, a pile of shot, a fire for the coals. Whoever triumphed in each round would remain in the game to meet the next man up. The last to survive would be granted his freedom."

"Or hers."

"Margery Peveril was to go last," said Chaucer. "Robert Faulk was the man opposing her. He had just killed five of his fellow prisoners, one of them apparently his cousin. Shot them without a moment's hesitation. Then it was his turn to face Peveril."

I imagined myself in his situation. "He could not bring himself to kill a woman."

"Not so," said Chaucer, shaking his head. "He was immersed in the game, fully prepared to slaughter her along with everyone else he'd shot. But when he went to raise his gun to the stump he saw that she had him beat. She'd watched carefully, you see, and by the time her turn came she had practiced in her mind the quickest means of loading the weapon. Half of Snell's men were jeering at him, the other half urging her to put the coal to the hole and kill Faulk. She raised the coal, and then —"

"She turned on them."

"And shot Snell's ablest archer in the face from ten feet. Across the clearing, Faulk did the same to the bowman guarding him. Even so it should have ended there, with Snell's men drawing and making quick work of them. But Faulk is a renowned poacher. The sheriffs in Kent call him the quickest quiver in the shire. Once he had dispensed with the archer he snatched up the man's bow, knelt by his corpse, and went for the others. He killed five of Snell's men, fully half the company that had taken the prisoners out there, then escaped with the Peveril woman through the woods. At the tree line they took two horses and lamed the others with a hunting knife. Then they escaped."

"Where did they go?"

"Northwards," he said. "They joined a pilgrimage to Durham, traveled with them to the borders of the Palatinate."

Cuthbert and his bones. "But they were coming from prison. How did they survive? Did they steal coin?"

"Peveril returned to the manor house after her escape, according to the loyal servants I questioned last week. Retrieved several large purses of coin she'd hidden away from her husband."

"And where are they now?"

"Dead, I would guess. He was injured badly in a struggle at an inn near Derlinton, the sheriffs report. They escaped on horseback, in what direction isn't known. I've had no news from the ports, which are carefully watched these days. As justice for Kent I would be one of the first to hear, but so far there has been only silence from the northern shires and the border. Her father's family is Scottish, and I've wondered if she might have relations there."

I considered it, though didn't see how they could survive unmolested. "The marches are well guarded. A man and a woman, traveling alone?"

"Alone, yes, though they are clearly a resourceful pair."

"Remarkable." I thought of my elusive, resourceful son, who had endured much worse than a perilous border crossing. "Their tale should be romanced."

" 'The Poacher and His Lady,' perhaps?"

"These handgonnes certainly deserve their own verses, whatever their flaws." I recalled Edmund Rune's dark homage to the weapons in the Cheapside seld. My hands still felt the guns, still wanted them. The warm length of the barrel, the smooth joining of iron and wood, the dangerous thrill of the shot. I wondered that something so lethal could possess such allure to a bookish man like me.

" *As swift as pellet out of gun, when fire is in the powder run,'* " Chaucer rhymed, and I realized I had heard the lines before. One of his dream poems: a temple of glass, an eagle, a vision of the Milky Way. As always, Chaucer's verse had got there first.

"They are devilish inventions, to be sure," he went on in his dreamy voice. "And William Snell the very devil incarnate, slipping from the hands of Lady Justice despite what he's done. This Stephen Marsh must be some new demon or demigod, but instead

685

of carrying divine brands from Olympus, he sires up guns from the bowels of hell."

We sat in silence as the brands in front of us crackled and hissed, our thoughts on the tools of war and crime, these instruments of violence running like dark currents through the long history of mankind. Abraham with his knife, King David with his sling and stone, Pontius Pilate with his cruelest cross, Arthur with his sword — and, now, William Snell with his guns, promising a future, by God's grace, we would none of us live to see. We remained in the circle of warmth as the flames sank to coals, and the fire slowly died.

CHAPTER 51

Some miles north of the river Tweed, where the moors and fells of Northumberland begin their slow sweep up into the Scottish lowlands, there rises a range of mountains, broad and hulking mounds. Since our first maker pushed them up from the earth, the Cheviot Hills have filled the horizon with a somber dignity, strong sentinels against the northern sky, separated by gentle cols of heather and peat. Wyndy Gyle, Bloodybush Edge, Cairn Hill, the great mount of Cheviot itself: along these desolate and disputed hills wends a border separating two lands, two peoples, two kings. From south and north alike the area is under the watch and protection of the wardens of the East March, English and Scottish lords who expend the lives of their men in the preservation of ancient rights, timeless claims of clan and kin.

Yet no border is impenetrable, no borderland fixed and rigid in the lived experience of its inhabitants and visitors. The region separating England from Scotland is an ever-changing land of mixed allegiances and divided loyalties among the marcher lords and the lesser families who inhabit this frontier. Like their own tangled relations, their lands traverse the wandering course of the Picts' Wall, that ancient barrier of half-buried stone that snakes across the border, to be met by innumerable roads and byways wending through empty heaths, along hidden valleys, over hills too many to name.

On the first Sunday of Advent, in the fifteenth year of King Robert's reign and the tenth year of King Richard's, a woman could be seen leading a horse down along the northern face of one such nameless hill. There was a fierce wind sluicing through the crags on that day, making an already steep and stony descent still more difficult. Yet she kept her footing well, her legs strengthened by long travel and wise experience. Her face had thinned over the last months, gone to gaunt yet still a thing of beauty to anyone looking at her, though there had been few enough of these in recent weeks. She pressed onward and downward, making her slow way north.

She walked alone.

Her horse, led by a thin and fraying rope, stepped along with equal confidence. A slight limp has come on in recent days, worrying her mistress. The mare's journey from Essex and the south had been long and trying, and like her mistress she had thinned; though like her, too, she was strong, agile, willing to struggle through the minor sufferings of travel with the promise of rest to come. Both knew their journey was nearing its end.

On the mare's broad back sat a man. He was asleep at the moment, and had been for the better part of two hours, though it was a healing sleep. For weeks, since their flight from Derlinton and the Palatinate, he had been ravaged by fever, closer to death than any man should come and hope to live. His leg had largely healed itself and remained whole, though like the mare he would walk henceforth with a distinctive limp. He was gaining strength by the day, walking slowly for stretches of the path, spelled by the mare when he grew weary.

Within another week they would join her relations on the coast, there to take up residence in a modest house on a bishop's estate, where they would serve the diocese and manor well. They would live as husband and wife, never taking the sacrament yet fully and properly wedded in the eyes of God. There would be children, four or five in number. They would be content and safe in their adopted home. They would live long, their years blessed with small fortune and great love.

This, at least, is how Chaucer might have ended the story of Robert Faulk and Margery Peveril, these intended victims of an unthinkable violence they together escaped, at least for a time. In my youth I made a pilgrimage to St. Cuthbert's shrine in Durham, traveling the same overland route traversed by Robert and Margery in their long flight from the Kentish wood and the horror they encountered there. Our company never made it as far as Edinburgh, nor even to the marches, though once in the Palatinate we could taste something of the northern air, imagine ourselves among the green and endless hills of a wild borderlands we knew then only through the minstrels' songs. Would such songs find Margery and Robert in the end, I wondered, or would their tale fade into the same long and tuneless oblivion that entombs so many bygone lives?

Chaucer is a lusty maker, a sharp-eyed poet of strong endings and firm moral lessons. Tales of learned roosters and cuckolded reeves, jests of broken wind, romances of pricking knights, the brief lives of martyred children and virgin saints. Even his tragedies make for a happy close, and if Geoffrey were to sit down and ink out a quire on the adventures of Robert Faulk and Margery Peveril, you can wager it would find resolution in a wedding feast with all the gilding, or some test of devotion and fidelity affirming the rightness and richness of their love. Upon reading the final lines you would doubtless set down the little book with some reluctance, give their story your tearful eyes and your sad smile, shake your head at the sobering beauty of it all. Oh, how bitter! Ah, how sweet!

I sip from the goblet of a darker muse. The stories I favor most are painted in the hues of choler, spleen, and bile, and they rarely end well. Tyrants drowning in a river of molten blood. Death's trumpet, blowing at the gates of the hypocrites. King Albinus, inducing his ignorant wife to drink wine from her father's burnished skull. Our atrocities require us to honor the strangest twists of our imagination, and without regard for the comforts of fitting issue or joyful resolution. A poet should not be some sweet-singing bird in a trap, feasting on the meat while blind to the net. The net *is* the meat, all those entanglements and snares and iron claws that hobble us and prevent our escape from the limits of our weak and fallen flesh. Perhaps in my own translation of their legend Margery and Robert will starve to death on a barren heath, or drown at sea in sight of Zeeland. For survival is a curse as much as a blessing. Think of fire, an invention that taught us to cook the flesh of beasts, to light our way at night, to cast a tuneful bell — to die by powder, flame, and ball. After his betrayal but before his rescue Prometheus could only watch as an eagle hooked and pulled at his liver. I would have ended the story there.

Back in Southwark, as I took the final turn past St. Margaret's Hill, Jack Norris went running ahead, eager for a return to the comforts of the priory. He, like Simon, had come to my aid at a dire moment, and I would never forget the wild in his eyes as he saw me backing toward the seld with Edmund Rune's blade at my neck. At one point along the high street he returned to my side, and together we followed a merchant striding up the middle as if he were lord of the town.

I bought a meat bun from a walking huckster. Jack ate it greedily, taking random bites from around the edges as he worked his way to the rich middle, shoving the strips of crust between his lips. His new cap had edged up over his ravaged left ear, exposing the dry stub to the wind. As he nibbled the last of the bun I pushed the cap down, awkwardly patted his head. He looked up at me.

"Am I to hie back over the bridge, Mas' Gower, now it's all done?"

The question was posed so innocently, with such openness and acceptance of whatever my response would be, that I had to look away. "You will remain at my house for the present, Jack. If it suits you, that is."

"What's that, Mas' Gower?" He moved his cap aside, put a cupping hand to the near stub. I repeated myself.

It took him a few moments to respond. "For a little piece a time it does. Though I have my work, so not overlong a stay." He patted the hasp of his knife, taking the same pride in the tool of his trade as a cordwainer might in his awl. As if common thievery were a sanctioned craft, the cutpurses a civic guild, with livery and station.

Ahead of us the merchant's gilt purse bulged almost obscenely at his waist. Jack was staring at it. Even I was tempted to reach for a knife.

"There are other ways, Jack," I said, putting a hand between his shoulders.

"Aye, Master Gower," the boy sighed. He drew closer. "Though none of them as quick."

I could not disagree.

Epilogue

Stephen Marsh came in from the foundry yard, stamping the cold from his feet and peeling off his gloves. He walked through to the display room, where Hawisia was speaking with a grey friar. They paid Stephen no mind as he edged along the side of the room toward the hearth.

"How long must the brethren wait, Mistress Stone?" the Franciscan was asking.

"Third week of Advent, could be," Hawisia said in a low voice, so as not to wake the babe. "We are backed up near to Mile End with all the orders, and down a metalman or two. Even Greyfriars can't expect a quicker bell, I fear."

At her foot, near the hearth, sat the low cradle Stephen had crafted some weeks ago. It was designed with a small nook for Hawisia's shoe, allowing her to rock it easily while standing or sitting nearby. At the moment her right toes were wedged beneath one of the rockers, and as she spoke to the friar she pushed up gently to move the cradle forth and back, forth and back in a soothing motion. Stephen felt a nip of annoyance that Hawisia was failing to take advantage of the nook, though the infant seemed calm. He would bring it up later, perhaps.

"A long wait, Mistress Stone," said the friar.

To Stephen the cradle looked a bit close to the fire. Hawisia moved her foot away as he approached. He inched the crib back a few nudges, then squatted and peered down into the wooden box.

"Aye, but can't be helped, not if you want a Stone's bell."

The infant was swaddled tight, perfectly still.

The friar sighed. "The doctors of the *studium* are indifferent to the music of bells, though the warden is quite particular. We shall wait patiently on you, Mistress Stone."

Stephen reached for the babe's nose, the finest pearl.

"You will not regret it," Hawisia said. She concluded her business with the friar, who left the shop on a rush of cold and clatter. Hawisia went out front to take in the foundry sign. Once back inside she barred the door, closing the shop snugly on the ending day. Stephen sensed her looking at him, that new fondness in her gaze. He felt it, too, and the warmth of her trust.

"I will watch her for a time, mistress."

"Very well," said Hawisia. "I'll see about the coals."

When Hawisia was gone he loosened the swaddling around the infant's body, allowing her hands and arms to escape. They no longer performed those strange jerking motions they'd made in his early weeks when she was loose like this. Her movements had become more deliberate, still excitable but also artful in that curious way her hands swam through the air, grasped for the world and its shapes.

Her name was Mary, after the Blessed Virgin. Mary Stone, quite a name to live with, though Stephen had quickly come to cherish it in the babe's first moon. He ran a finger along one of Mary's forearms, no longer than the head of a smithing hammer, or the rod of a short awl. The babe's fingers grasped the smallest finger of Stephen's left hand. A powerful grip for such a tiny creature, a soft coil of muscle, bone, and fat. He stroked the closed fingers. An infant is a perfect machine, like a woman's birthing parts, he thought, remembering Hawisia's labor. Knuckles. Joints. Skin. Ears impossibly, horrendously small. Lips and a mouth and ways to make the strangest of noises.

Stephen settled into Robert Stone's old chair by the hearth and lifted little Mary out of her crib, his finger still in the babe's fist. She would not let Stephen go, though he tickled her under the arm, stroked her skin. She burbled, gripped harder. Stephen tried to pull his finger from the babe's hand and still she would not release him. Stephen laughed, trying again, yet Mary was fiercely strong, wasn't she, a human pincer. She raised Stephen's finger to her mouth and gummed contentedly, her small eyes fixed on his own.

Remarkable, Stephen thought with an almost painful burst of love and pride, and the strong tug of Mary Stone's grip aroused his imagination to a sudden and un-prompted vision. A new device, fitted for these wee hands. His eyes widened at the absurdity of it. Ludicrous, unthinkable. Yet he had thought it, after all, and as it worked on his mind he saw no reason such a thing could not be done, and in this very shop. He had made a hundred guns by his own hands and orders, after all, only to destroy them all in the end with a small plug of lead in the chamber. Who was he to deny further such inventions to the frail and defenseless? Why, the king's armorer himself had said it, by God's body and bread. *The handgonne is the ultimate weapon of the weak.*

Stephen Marsh brought his nose to the top of Mary's little head, taking in her pure scent. His eyes closed, and he saw a child, a girl of eleven or twelve years. She was somewhere along the bounds of a city or a keep. She stood on a wall or peered through a slit. All her mind was on defending what she had, the people she loved, the place she lived, her virtue and the very sanctity of her flesh, and in her silken arms she cradled the smallest gun the world would ever know.

HISTORICAL NOTE AND ACKNOWLEDGMENTS

This book has its origins in a few surprising sentences from T. F. Tout's classic work *Chapters in the Administrative History of Mediaeval England* concerning the existence of "handguns" in the Tower of London armory. Since coming across Tout's account of the royal armorers and their *handgonnes* some years ago I have been curious about the earliest emergence of handheld gunpowder weapons before 1400, as well as the technological culture that, for better or worse, first developed them through a long process of trial and error. This was a culture evoked by Geoffrey Chaucer in his *The House of Fame,* which describes a blast speeding out of a trumpet "As swift as pelet out of gonne, / Whan fyr is in the poudre ronne." The simultaneous allure and horror provoked by the new guns is apparent in the writings of contemporary chroniclers, who have given us sporadic accounts of their use among both military and civilian forces, including a group of rebels who assaulted the manor of Huntercombe in 1375 with an array of weapons that included portable "gonnes."

Research for this novel has immersed me in the depthless fields of military history and the history of technology, particularly the metal industries and the crafts of smithing and founding, which were quite often located in the same shops in the fourteenth century. The works that I have found particularly indispensable for the details of trade, manufacture, and innovation include Kelly DeVries, *Medieval Military Technology*; Robert Douglas Smith and Kelly DeVries, *The Artillery of the Dukes of Burgundy*; and Howard L. Blackmore's indispensable guide, *Gunmakers of London 1350–1850*. I am particularly indebted to Lois Schwoerer, who shared with me the manuscript of her forthcoming book *Gun Culture in Early Modern England*; and to Sean McLachlan, author of *Medieval Handgonnes* and one of the world's leading authorities on early gunpowder weapons, for his last-minute help.

Many thanks are owed also to the community of artisans, gunsmiths, and re-enactors who have revolutionized our understanding of the early development of gunpowder weapons in recent years through their use of original materials and medieval technology. Their work continues to correct the erroneous but durable assumption that medieval *handgonnes* were primarily instruments of "shock and awe," used to sow terror rather than gain military advantage. Working from the very few early descriptions and illustrations of these weapons, they have challenged historians' understanding of the velocity and lethality of projectiles, the potential swiftness of load speeds between firings, the comparative strengths of smithing and founding, the accuracy of targeting, and other technological dimensions that the scant historical documentation alone cannot reveal. The Swiss craftsman Ulrich Bletscher, for example, has shown that it is possible to penetrate steel plate thicker than most surviving medieval armor with a ball shot from a forged iron gun using homemade powder. Multiple experiments with replicas of the Tannenberg *handgonne* (which is cast of bronze and likely shot iron or lead balls) have similarly confirmed the relative power of such gunpowder weapons. I have seen the hands-on work of several of these artisans and spoken, Skyped, or e-mailed with a number of others (including a craftsman known to me only as "Teleoceras"), and I am deeply grateful for their time and care in answering my many questions despite their suspicion of my motives.

The tenth year of King Richard II's reign began in June 1386, and the autumn that followed marked the first great crisis of his kingship. Before and during the Wonderful Parliament of 1386, Richard and his closest advisers confronted fierce opposition from the appellant lords over war levies, the ethical conduct of the crown, and the king's blatant favoritism toward certain of his cronies. The most exhaustive treatment of this specific moment in the history of royal Parliamentary relations is John S. Roskell's *The Impeachment of Michael de la Pole,* which I have relied upon (along with the Rolls of Parliament) for a number of details in fleshing out the political moment. King Richard's emerging tyranny in these years was evident in any number of ways, including his self-regard; during this part of his reign Richard began insisting on being addressed as "Your Majesty," as the historian Nigel Saul has shown (thus correcting those who still insist that this form of royal address originated in the Tudor period). Meanwhile the country was facing the threat of a massive invasion from Sluys involving thousands of French and Burgundian ships, a threat ably documented in the third volume of Jonathan Sumption's definitive history of the Hundred Years War. If the medieval chroniclers are to be believed, Londoners reacted to the threat of invasion with widespread horror and hard work, clearing out the areas immediately inside and outside the walls and visiting untold destruction on the built perimeter of the city in an effort to prepare it for defense.

The Hundred Years War was characterized on all sides by numerous incidents of wanton and large-scale violence against civilian populations. The account of the massacre at Desurennes imagined in *The Invention of Fire,* though fictional, has been influenced in part by a 1382 incident at the Bridge at Comines recounted by the chronicler Froissart. David Green's revisionist account *The Hundred Years War: A People's History* emphasizes the brutality of the era's military cultures, suggesting that there would have been nothing unusual in this period about a massacre of dissident civilians for military purposes, whether strategic or technological. Sir John Hawkwood, the expatriate English mercenary, had recently led the butchery of nearly the entire population of the town of Cesena in the Romagna, an incident in which thousands of women and children met their deaths by sword over a three-day period.

Readers are enouraged to consult the historical note at the end of *A Burnable Book* to learn of the other kinds of resources I have drawn upon for the details of daily life, language, and so on. For *The Invention of Fire* I have turned to a variety of additional primary and secondary sources, such as Marcellus Laroon's engravings and drawings of London's criers and hawkers, which provided several of the street cries imagined in the city markets in London and York (one irresistible example of which I also anachronistically lifted from a play by Ben Jonson); Sheila Sweetinburgh's volume *Later Medieval Kent, 1220–1540,* which helped me plot the incidents and locations in that shire; Geoffrey Parnell's extensive work on the Tower of London, including its menagerie, armory, stables, and medieval fabric and geography; and recent work on the office of the medieval coroner, especially Sara M. Butler's extraordinary new book *Forensic Medicine and Death Investigation in Medieval England,* which is likely to inspire a new generation of historical crime novelists in the years ahead. As R. F. Hunnisett once put it, in medieval England "coroners almost invariably refused to hold inquests on dead bodies until they had been bribed to do so" — hyperbole, perhaps, but welcome hyperbole for the novelist. On a lighter note, I am indebted to Richard Newhauser for an insightful chat over lunch in Charlottesville about John Gower's "sweet tooth" — a phrase Gower invented, it turns out, and that gave me a reflective sentence in chapter one. The character of Hawisia Stone was inspired by Johanna Hill, inheritor and operator of a foundry in the parish of St. Botolph following her husband's death. The known details of her biography, as recovered by Caroline Barron in a chapter of *Medieval London Widows,* are remarkable testimony to the variety of economic and social experiences characterizing women's lives in the late medieval city.

The story told here has also led me to explore the official role of Geoffrey Chaucer in the system of shire justice in Kent. This stretch of the poet's life has often been imagined as a period of rural semi-retirement, as Chaucer left London to take up residence in Greenwich. Yet the office of justice of the peace, which Chaucer had recently assumed, entailed any number of duties relating to the administration of law:

settling disputes, taking indictments, even assisting in the apprehension of violent criminals and their conveyance to gaol. With all due respect to his skeptical friend Gower, the notion of Geoffrey Chaucer's aiding in a murder investigation and pursuing escaped fugitives during these years is more plausible than fanciful.

In addition to those named above, numerous friends and colleagues have given aid and advice in various forms. Many thanks are owed to a number of fellow writers I have had the pleasure of getting to know (or know better) over the last several years, especially Jane Alison, Nancy Bilyeau, Geraldine Brooks, John Casey, Jenny Davidson, Sarah J. Henry, Katherine Howe, Hugh Howey, Mary Beth Keane, David Liss, Jennifer McMahon, Jenny Milchman, Caroline Preston, Virginia Pye, David Robbins, Leslie Silbert, Art Taylor, Rupert Thomson, Christopher Tilghman, and Simon Toyne. I have benefited greatly from their generous willingness to share their time, wisdom, and experience. Others have provided support with invitations for readings, panels, and various events that have allowed me to introduce my work to new and diverse audiences. Here thanks are owed to E. A. Aymer, Katie Brokaw, Scott Bruce, Holly Crocker,

Barbara Ferrara, Andrea Grossman, Jonathan Hsy, Matthew Irvin, Eric Jager, Wan-Chuan Kao, Michael Kindness, Ann Kingman, Lana Krumwiede, Rosemarie McGerr, Michael McKeon, Ingrid Nelson, Myra Seaman, Wayne Terwilliger, and Bob Yeager.

My students at the University of Virginia teach me time and again the power of historical fiction in shaping our comprehension of and empathy with the past and its human actors. I learned an enormous amount in this regard from the thousands of students around the world enrolled in "Plagues, Witches, and War: The Worlds of Historical Fiction," a massive open online course I taught in the autumn of 2013; I thank them deeply for their attention and enthusiasm. Once again I am grateful to the editorial staffs at William Morrow (New York) and HarperCollins (London). Rachel Kahan and Julia Wisdom are brilliant and tireless editors who have championed my writing while helping me understand the craft and profession of commercial fiction. Many thanks as well to Trish Daly, Jaime Frost, Tavia Kowalchuk, Ashley Marudas, Rachel Meyers, Anne O'Brien, Aja Pollock, Kelly Rudolph, and Kate Stephenson. Only my extraordinary agent, Helen Heller, knows the depth and extent of her contributions to this novel.

As always, my family has provided all the support, love, and humor a writer could want. Anna Brickhouse remains my best reader and critic; my mother and mother-in-law both read the manuscript with their typical precision and care; and my father has always been a source of unconditional kindness and inspiring capability. *The Invention of Fire* is dedicated to Elizabeth and Robert Brickhouse, loving parents-in-law (and, to others, loving parents, siblings, grandparents, friends) whose values, warmth, wisdom, and courage I have come to treasure over many years.

ABOUT THE AUTHOR

Bruce Holsinger is a fiction writer and literary scholar who teaches in the Department of English at the University of Virginia in Charlottesville. His debut novel, *A Burnable Book,* is set in the alleys and halls of medieval London, where the poets Geoffrey Chaucer and John Gower spent much of their lives.

He is also the author or editor of six nonfiction books on medieval literature and culture. His work has garnered major awards from the Modern Language Association, the American Musicological Society, and the Medieval Academy of America. His research has been recognized with a Guggenheim Fellowship, and he is the recipient of research fellowships from the National Endowment for the Arts and the American Council of Learned Societies. Holsinger's scholarly books have been pub-

711

lished by the university presses of Chicago, Columbia, and Stanford.

He lives in Charlottesville, Virginia with his family.

The employees of Thorndike Press hope you have enjoyed this Large Print book. All our Thorndike, Wheeler, and Kennebec Large Print titles are designed for easy reading, and all our books are made to last. Other Thorndike Press Large Print books are available at your library, through selected bookstores, or directly from us.

For information about titles, please call:
  (800) 223-1244

or visit our Web site at:
  http://gale.cengage.com/thorndike

To share your comments, please write:
  Publisher
  Thorndike Press
  10 Water St., Suite 310
  Waterville, ME 04901